BLIND
PROPHET

BLIND
PROPHET

BLIND PROPHET

Bart Davis

DOUBLEDAY & COMPANY, INC.
GARDEN CITY, NEW YORK
1983

Library of Congress Cataloging in Publication Data
Davis, Bart, 1950–
Blind prophet.
I. Title.
PS3554.A9319B4   1983   813'.54
ISBN: 0-385-17980-4
Library of Congress Catalog Card Number 82–45241

This book is dedicated to
SHARON DAVIS,
who is everything to me.

ACKNOWLEDGMENTS

My special thanks to Robert Gottlieb of The William Morris Agency for his constant support; and to Hugh O'Neill of Doubleday.

Also, I gratefully acknowledge the unselfish and invaluable assistance of the following people who gave so freely and with unflagging warmth:

James B. Schultz, U.S. Air Force Space Division; Los Angeles

Dr. John Lawrence, NASA, LBJ Space Center; Houston

Anthony S. Makris, American Security Council; Washington, D.C.

Andy Myers and Tony Griggs, Bell Laboratories; Murray Hill, New Jersey

Hubert Griggs and Leslie Vock, Kennedy Space Center; Cape Canaveral, Florida

Marsha L. Kracht, LBJ Space Center; Houston

Roy McCarter, National Meteorological Center; Silkman, Maryland

Miriam Reid, Grumman Aerospace; Bethpage, New York

The Staff of the American Meteorological Society; Boston

Major Sherwood "Woody" Spring, Astronaut, LBJ Space Center; Houston

Bill Brobst, COMSAT; Washington, D.C.

Dick Martin, Lockheed; Marietta, Georgia

Lt. Cmdr. D. J. Schmidt, U.S. Naval Station; Brooklyn, New York

and to:

Lorraine Kutzing, who never fails me; Brandon Davis, Steve Weiss, the officers and crew of the U.S.C.C.C. *Dallas* and, as always, to Daniel J. Comerford III, for his friendship.

Teiresias, you are first in everything,
Things teachable and things not to be spoken,
Things of the heavens and earth-creeping things.
                         —*Oedipus to the blind prophet*

How should the birds give any other than ill-omened voices,
Gorged with the dregs of blood that man has shed?
                         —*Teiresias, the blind prophet*

PROLOGUE

Paris, 1965

The cocaine roared into his nostril and almost at once, the familiar, curiously detached feeling of euphoria washed over him. Handing the gold straw back to the vacant-eyed brothel attendant, he turned to stare at the bodies straining on the bed.

Sitting on the bed, he preferred, for now, just to watch the beautiful brunette woman thrash between the two men who impaled her simultaneously from front and behind. One of the men sensed his gaze and twisted around to grin and beckon. He smiled back but shook his head.

The drug was taking deeper effect now, and he felt his jaw clench in reaction to it. A slow, feral smile spread over his face as he thought of what their controls at CIA Station Paris would do if the security checks ever uncovered their visits here. He watched and shared his friend's pleasure and found humor in the obvious answer, "We would be screwed."

With his blood pounding from the rapid heartbeat, he reached over to caress the flesh in front of him. Gone were all thoughts of the CIA and its burdens. Gone were thoughts of his own ambition. His gaze wandered; his hands moved without conscious direction. Sensation attracted him; different feelings; different textures.

The group had changed position, the men now locked together, inverted and thrusting, leaving a hurt, petulant expression on the woman's face. Seeing him, she opened her legs wider and her fingers traced slow circles on her breasts . . .

Valentin Kasimov was not enjoying the performance of his two adversaries. The one-way mirror showed a complete view of the sexual gymnastics in the next room, but Kasimov's KGB training and personal predilections held him aloof. His lips twisted into a thin, straight line.

"It is demeaning to have such as these for enemies," Kasimov said to his sergeant, who stood near, operating the movie camera.

"I agree, Lieutenant. Most demeaning, sir," said the sergeant sternly, turning away to conceal a delighted wink to the corporal recording the sound.

"But I suppose we must search under rocks if we are going to hunt snakes," ventured Kasimov philosophically, watching the two CIA agents change position with the prostitutes again.

"Or in bed to find bedbugs," chuckled the sergeant.

Kasimov's angular features only hardened so the sergeant shot a quick warning glance to the corporal, who he sensed was about to offer some witticism of his own.

"When will you make your first contact, Lieutenant?" asked a deep, well-educated voice from the back of the room.

Kasimov had almost forgotten about the colonel who was observing and rating this, his first "solo" operation. The elementary nature of the question irritated him. It was a textbook query, and Kasimov put a school-lecture tone in his voice to answer it.

"First contact with the agent-to-be-turned is made when the operation officer has sufficient power to engender total emotional response in said agent."

"Very good, Lieutenant Kasimov," conceded the colonel. "Define 'total emotional response,' if you please."

Kasimov hesitated for a moment, knowing that this response would be quoted word-for-word in the report to Moscow.

"In my mind, sir," he said evenly, "it is the agent-to-be-turned's complete and unquestioned understanding of my ability to destroy him."

The colonel made no response to this so Kasimov turned back to the mirror. The foursome was in still another configuration.

"Sergeant, I feel we have sufficient stimulus. Develop the films and bring them upstairs within the hour."

The sergeant and corporal turned off their machines and left quickly. Only the colonel remained behind, and he left his chair to stand beside Kasimov in the now silent room.

"You will turn them today," said the colonel.

"Yes, sir," replied Kasimov. "I anticipate no problem with such as these. Where there is one vice, there will be others. Greed, ambition, lechery; it is all the same."

"Valentin," the colonel sighed, "even when you were a student, I counseled you against this arrogance of yours. Soon I will file my report to Moscow, which, like all the others on you, will be outstanding. Then you will be given a command of your own. But you will have no one to protect you or to explain away your arrogance, Valentin. I fear your superiors will resent your attitude and use it against you."

The colonel put his hand on Kasimov's shoulder in a gesture of affection but let it fall away when there was no response.

"I will survive to serve the State," said Kasimov simply, and the colonel noticed that his eyes never left his prey. "Like a cobra," thought the colonel as he left the room.

Alone, Kasimov allowed the first smile to cross his face. In his mind he reviewed what was to come, how the targets would react when he sprang his trap. He enjoyed imagining their fear, their shock, and ultimately, their total surrender.

"I will call them Castor and Pollux," he suddenly decided; and leaving the room, he walked unhurriedly upstairs.

PART ONE

1

Vandenburg Air Force Base, California, 1984
Monday

". . . and the excited crowds awaiting the landing have been growing steadily since early this morning. The astrophiles, as we've come to call these thousands of space enthusiasts and well-wishers, grow more numerous each time the Space Shuttle flies. And this flight has the historic significance of being not only the first to launch and land at the same point, but the first to carry an operational payload in the Shuttle's cargo bay. For a more complete explanation of these issues, we're going to go to Jane Sloane of our CBS network affiliate in Houston. Jane? . . ."

"Thank you, Ted Currin. This is Jane Sloane at Mission Control in the Johnson Space Center. As Ted mentioned just a moment ago, this flight of the Shuttle, *Constitution,* differs significantly from the previous flights.

"As you can see behind me, the Mission Control Center is not the usual scene of feverish activity. Right now it's being used only as a backup system to the main Control Center at Vandenburg itself. Some have called Vandenburg Air Force Base the first U.S. spaceport and technically, that's true.

"To accommodate the numerous Shuttle launches slated for the future, the main runway has been lengthened from eight thousand to fifteen thousand feet, the space launch complex has been renovated, payload preparation rooms have been added, and storage facilities for the solid rocket boosters and external fuel tanks—the apparatus on which the Shuttle lifts off—have been constructed.

"Further, the Shuttle is carrying its first payload, a two-ton Nimbus weather satellite which will be used to study the behavior of the atmosphere and will allow us to predict more accurately whether or not to carry umbrellas or picnic baskets when we go outside.

"At the much-toned-down Mission Control Center in Houston, this is Jane Sloane reporting. Back to you, Ted . . ."

"Thank you, Jane. As you mentioned, the changes here at Vandenburg Air Force Base have been legion. Truly, we are in the Space Age.

"The weather track is perfect today. The sky is clear and almost cloudless. The temperature is high, over ninety degrees here; but compared to the more than twenty-five hundred degrees the *Constitution* will experience on re-entry, that seems somehow minor. At that temperature, the Sierra Madre range, thirty miles behind us, would melt into a pile of sludge and flow into the sea.

"But the spacecraft, *Constitution,* is only half the story. Perhaps even the minor half. The real story of human achievement comes from the men who are flying it. Let's go to our special report: The Men."

"Lieutenant Colonel Christopher Leyland is the youngest astronaut ever to command a Shuttle. A graduate of the University of Ohio, he is the youngest son of retired Admiral John Leyland and the younger brother of Senator Arthur Leyland.

"Leyland earned his commission at the naval officers' pilot school at Pensacola, Florida, and spent three years as a Navy fighter pilot in Viet Nam. There he flew a record number of combat missions successfully and was awarded numerous decorations, including the Distinguished Flying Cross, and earned the nickname of 'Stick' for his almost legendary flying skill.

"Leyland joined NASA in 1979 and was immediately selected for Shuttle training. He is unmarried, thirty-six years of age, six feet one inch tall and has brown hair and brown eyes.

"Major William Cooke has had wide experience in both the military and civilian worlds. A top Air Force transport pilot until 1979, he left the Air Force to become Chief Test Pilot for Grumman Aerospace in Bethpage, New York.

"Cooke is known as a quiet man, more reserved and businesslike than most in his trade, but the respect for his steel-like nerves and his commitment to professionalism is universal in the flying community.

"He joined NASA in 1981, immediately after the first Shuttle mission, to be, as he put it, at the front.

"Cooke is married to the former Susan Moore, has three children, and lives in Houston. He is forty-one years old, five feet ten inches tall, and has sandy-blond hair and blue eyes."

"This is Ted Currin at Vandenburg Air Force Base in California and this word just in. That roar you can hear in the background comes from the crowd's reaction to a confirmed report from Vandenburg Control that the re-entry burn was completed right on schedule at 8:46 A.M. California time. That means, if all goes as it should, touchdown is under an hour away!

"And I have here sitting beside me a man who has some special reasons to be proud today.

"Senator Arthur Leyland has ably represented the people of Ohio for the past four years. A longtime supporter of the use of space for military uses, Senator Leyland has a double victory today: the next step in what some call the conquest of space and that this step should be taken by his younger brother, Christopher. Let me welcome you here today, Senator, and congratulate you personally."

"Thank you, Ted. It's a great day for the entire country. The space program has revitalized all of us and restored our faith in national ideals. In America, the sky is no longer the limit."

"A great deal of attention has been focused upon your family over the past few weeks, Senator. What do the Leylands think of Christopher's achievements?"

"As you know, Ted, Christopher is the baby of the family. Maybe for that reason he's always been special to all of us. I just spoke to my father, who's home right now watching the landing on television, and he and I share the same feeling. We are very proud . . . very proud, indeed."

"A number of writers have compared your family, Senator, with the Kennedys of Massachusetts. The Leyland family has been an important name in Ohio for over a hundred years. Most of the men have been in government or military service, and, unfortunately, you've had your share of tragedies, too. Your father, Admiral John Leyland, was severely wounded when his ship was attacked during

World War II, and your younger brother, Timothy, was killed in action in the very last days of the Korean War. How do you feel about the risks your brother Christopher is still taking?"

"One of the things that my father always taught us, Ted, was that there was no such thing as a free lunch. The cost for freedom, or progress for that matter, is always high. The family hasn't paid that cost gladly; we've paid it because that's the cost."

"Has the success of the Shuttle program had an impact on your political goals, Senator?"

"I believe, Ted, that the American people are finally realizing the vast potential that space offers us. As you indicated, I am especially interested in the military aspects of that potential. Throughout history, there has never been a nation that has achieved superiority in any significant strategic category that has not tried to translate that superiority into some foreign-policy benefit.

"My colleagues and I want that benefit to fall to the United States and not to the Soviet Union. I am happy to say that this notion is steadily gaining ground in Congress, and we will begin introducing legislation during the next session backed by a bipartisan coalition."

"Thank you, Senator Leyland. I see some of your people want you to get along to Launch Control to hear the re-entry dialogue. Thank you again, Senator."

"A pleasure, Ted. Thank you."

"That, ladies and gentlemen, was Senator Arthur Leyland, sometimes called the 'Scholar Hawk' by those who say . . ."

Arthur Leyland rose from the canvas-back chair, paused to loosen his tie and remove his tweed jacket, and followed his closest friend and adviser away from the cameras.

Tom Crowley had been a part of the senator's political life since, as a college student, Crowley had successfully managed Leyland's campaign for student-body president. White-haired and immaculately dressed in banker's gray pinstripe, Crowley was often mistaken for the senator and Leyland, in his tweeds, for some lesser staff member.

"Nicely done," Crowley said as they walked through the heat-shimmering air toward Launch Control.

"Someday I swear I'm going to tell them the honest truth. That I'm scared to hell when Christopher is up there," responded the senator darkly.

"Not till we get the legislation through, if you please. Till then, you're a paragon of pride."

The senator thought of his father at home, confined for much of the last twenty years to a wheelchair. He knew what the Admiral would be feeling today, watching Chris do the things that he himself could no longer do and that Arthur had never done. In some ways, the two were very similar, Chris and their father, both stubborn and as strong as Ohio oak.

"They also serve who only stand and wait," he muttered to no one in particular, and Crowley suppressed a smile.

The dust-free, cold air inside the Launch Control Center was a welcome relief as the double doors shut smoothly behind them. The launch team was seated at computer consoles and a steady stream of data was pouring in and out of their computers to the launch director. A large screen in the front of the room held the information on the *Constitution*'s position, and red and green lines across the screen outlined the trajectory of the Shuttle's return track.

Off to one side a technician was seated at a separate computer facility. His job was to monitor the data from Vandenburg Control and compare it to the data from the backup Control Center in Houston. Any discrepancy would be immediately noted and, if necessary, control would be shifted to the facility at the Johnson Space Center.

The senator listened for a while to the strings of numbers and coordinates and tried to make some sense of them. Failing that, he tried to establish the *Constitution*'s presence on the big board. With great relief, he caught the eye of Barney Swanson, launch director, who, sensing his concern, flashed him the thumbs-up.

Swanson, a thin, lanky ex-pilot who had been with NASA since the early Mercury flights, ambled over smiling warmly. Some congressmen meant trouble; this one meant plaudits and increased appropriations. That, and his relationship to Chris, guaranteed Senator Arthur Leyland the red-carpet treatment at any NASA facility.

"In answer to all of your unspoken questions," said Swanson easily, "the kid's doing just fine."

Leyland pointed toward the course tracing on the screen and Swanson answered his silent inquiries immediately.

"Exactly ten minutes ago, *Constitution* sliced into the upper atmosphere," said Swanson, "at a height of a hundred and fifty kilometers—ninety miles. Their angle of attack was a perfect forty degrees—that is, the upward slant of the Shuttle's lifting surfaces in relation to its direction of flight was perfect. Right where we want it. We always lose contact for a few seconds because of heavy ionization caused by the heat, but telemetry's got 'em right on course."

"That's good to hear, Barney," said the senator gratefully. "Just get them down in one piece."

"Step into my parlor, Senator, and we'll show you how it's done."

The senator followed Swanson back to the launch director's console in the center of the room and slid into an empty chair between the L.D. and the CapCom. By unwritten NASA law, the CapCom, or Capsule Communicator, was always a former astronaut. In this case, the CapCom was Dick Holter, of the Apollo 8 mission, and most transmissions to *Constitution* went from the L.D. through him to the Shuttle. In an emergency, a man experienced with space flight could save valuable time where every second might count. For the next few minutes, Swanson was engrossed in his multi-screen data display, but when he looked up, the smile was still on his face.

"Fifty-eight miles up, fuel zero, and your brother's riding the heaviest glider in history, eighty-odd tons. The air is thick enough so that the aerodynamic controls take over. Right on course. Look at the beautiful blue dot; that's the *Constitution*."

On the screen, the red and green trajectory lines had fused into one track terminating at Vandenburg. A blue dot glowed brightly about ten inches from the end of the line.

Abruptly, the speaker above Holter's console burst into life and even the static could not disguise the exhilaration in Chris Leyland's voice.

"Vandenburg . . . This is *Constitution* . . ." A string of numbers followed.

"We copy that, *Constitution*," responded Holter. "You're looking real fine."

"Roger, Vandenburg. But Cooke and I like this so much we thought we'd go around again . . . See the pyramids one more time . . ."

"Negative, *Constitution* . . . Daddy says playtime's over . . . Let's bring it into the barn . . ."

"Roger, Vandenburg . . . We copy . . . Altitude eleven miles; speed seven six seven miles per hour . . . beginning final approach . . ."

"Roger, *Constitution* . . ." acknowledged Holter.

The senator smiled at the banter, somewhat relieved by its gleeful tones. The blue dot was closer now to the end of the line. He heard Crowley breathe more deeply behind him.

"About sixty miles out," said Swanson. "Like to say hello?"

The senator nodded, not quite trusting his voice to be as buoyant as either Holter's or his brother's.

"*Constitution* . . . This is Vandenburg . . . Have a man here who says he knows you . . . Can you take the call?" queried Swanson through his own console.

"Roger, Vandenburg . . . Put him on . . . We got nothing but time here . . ."

"Okay, *Constitution* . . . Here it comes . . ."

"Ah . . . This is Arthur . . . Nice to have you back, Christopher . . . Is everything okay?"

"Roger, Vandenburg . . . Artie? How the devil are you? . . . Be right down, son . . . Wait, will you?"

"Roger, *Constitution* . . . disrespectful clown . . . Couldn't drag me away . . . Over."

Swanson nodded and keyed communications back to Holter.

"They're almost right over us now, Senator," explained Holter, "and diving. Chris is passing by to put the craft through a series of giant S swings to lose more speed. Then they'll make a great U-turn back around and land at a speed of over two hundred miles per hour. Be about ten minutes."

The senator began to make appreciative sounds for this running commentary, but suddenly the radio burst into life again, and the sudden urgency in Chris Leyland's voice tore through the control room.

"Vandenburg . . . Vandenburg . . . This is *Constitution* . . . Emergency . . . Emergency . . . Cabin skin burn-through . . . Just picked it up . . . Must have occurred during re-entry, possible tile loss . . . Computer malfunction . . . Wind increasing to force six . . . Like we got kicked in the tail . . . Emergency . . . Computer malfunction . . . Speed increased to five hundred MPH . . . Way off glide path . . . Emergency . . . Do you copy?"

"Roger, *Constitution* . . . We copy . . . Roger, off glide path . . . How do you read your position?"

"Vandenburg . . . I'm looking straight into the Sierra Madres . . . Cooke's checking our computers . . . I'm going manual . . ."

"Roger, *Constitution* . . . Stand by . . . Keep her up, Chris . . . Keep her up."

The senator looked past the sudden feverish activity to the big board. The blue dot that symbolized his brother's life had spun off the trajectory line like a child shooting off a slide. Thirty miles beyond them were the Sierra Madres, and the increased speed that had resulted from the tremendous pressure of the wind was driving the Shuttle straight into them.

Swanson's hands played over his computer console like a crazed pianist's. All over the room numbers and course projections were shouted out loud.

The senator barely felt Crowley's hand squeeze his shoulder. Six inches, he estimated, still staring at the big board. Six more inches and that bright blue light would impact with the mountains. Now it was five . . . Transfixed, he could not look away.

"Vandenburg . . . This is *Constitution* . . . She's banking . . . banking . . . Need more space . . . More space . . . ten miles . . . nine . . ."

Swanson stared at his board, horror contorting his features. There was nothing they could do, nothing on earth anyone could do. Someone in the back began to pray.

"Vandenburg . . . five miles . . . This bird's gonna turn . . . This flying brick is gonna turn . . . More space . . . Banking . . . Tighter, baby, you can do it, *tighter* . . . Come on . . . *come on* . . ."

The senator prayed for the blue dot, and Swanson for space which he knew did not exist. Throughout the room technicians stood and yelled and pounded their fists in frustrated rage, eyes glued to the big board.

"One mile, Vandenburg . . . turning . . . Maybe . . . maybe . . . Gonna be close . . . Gonna be close . . . *C'mon turn, you mother-fucker . . . turn . . .*"

The senator pictured the mountains closer and closer. The ship screaming toward the jagged peaks; closer. Two inches, no more space. The senator closed his eyes . . .

"Vandenburg . . . *turn completed* . . . We're all right now . . . See you soon . . . Coming on in . . . Over."

The computer printouts hit the air like confetti. People grinned and cried and hung on to each other in mad embraces. With face-bursting smiles, one by one they resumed their work to bring *Constitution* home.

Holter spoke breathlessly into his mike and relayed Swanson's data.

"Roger, *Constitution* . . . You're a little high and fast . . . Flatten your glide to one point five degrees . . . Air speed three-thirty . . . Gonna be a little bumpy . . . Landing gear down . . . three hundred feet . . . two hundred . . . one hundred . . . fifty . . . Touchdown . . . Well done, Stick . . . Really well done . . ."

Senator Arthur Leyland stood up and walked slowly out of the room.

Word of the near fatal malfunction had spread quickly. Just as quickly, tales of Chris Leyland's performance had spread, already growing to heroic proportions in the media's retelling.

It was over an hour before the senator could see his brother and then only because of his position. Inside the debriefing facility, dressed in NASA coveralls, Chris Leyland leaped up from his seat and with an unselfconscious yelp threw his arms around his brother.

"Artie!"

"Please, Christopher, you know I hate to be called that," said the senator, disentangling himself.

"Anybody tell you lately that you're a stuffed shirt?" asked Chris affectionately.

"No one else has the temerity," said the senator, holding his brother with both hands on his shoulders.

"I'm awfully glad to see you, Christopher." And this time the senator could not, nor would not, prevent the hug that engulfed him.

"Those last few minutes must have been hard for you, Arthur," said Chris when they broke apart.

"I would have preferred major surgery," said the senator dryly.

"It's part of it, though. Always will be, I suppose," said Chris more seriously. "I'm not even sure any of us would change it. You should've seen Cooke, Artie. The goddamn Sierra Madres coming straight at us, and he never even took his eyes off the instruments. Just kept calling out our position and trying to cut our speed. A real pro. You know what he did when we finally made the turn? He

looked at me with that real straight face of his and asked me if I
wanted to try that again now that we had the hang of it."

Both men laughed, and the last of the senator's tension subsided.

"By the way, Chris, I think I can get the FCC to drop formal
charges in the light of the moment's enthusiasm."

Chris looked at him blankly.

"The FCC and the several million people who were listening to
your last radio transmissions sometimes take offense at such polite
phraseology as 'turn, you motherfucker.' Though I can't see why,
can you?"

"It just slipped out," said Chris ruefully.

"The only thing that bothers me is that your eloquence will probably outlive mine. Well, enjoy the day and all that's waiting for you.
I'm flying to Rome on Senate business, those NATO arms talks, for
a few days, but I'll be back in Ohio on Saturday. See you there?"

The two men got up and clasped hands.

"Wild horses, Artie."

"Wild horses, Chris."

Washington, D.C.

". . . *the success of the Shuttle program had an impact on your
political goals, Senator?*"

"*I believe, Ted, that the American people are finally realizing the
vast potential that space offers us. As you know, I am . . .*"

"Turn the sound off, Jim," said President Brendan Connors,
frowning at the picture of Senator Leyland.

"Would that we could shut him up that easily," White House
Chief of Staff James Parienne quipped, rising from the linen-covered
mahogany table and crossing to the bookcase on which the TV sat.

Monday's lunch had become one of the traditions established
early on in Connor's tenure in the White House. Every second Monday, Connors gathered in the gold-carpeted Roosevelt Room for
lunch with his closest political and economic advisers, some of
whom had been with him since his early days in Oregon. Parienne
had joined Connors in that gubernatorial race, as had presidential
adviser Terrence Clancy.

The other regulars were Barbara Reynolds, National Security Adviser, a more recent entry to the inner circle who had been selected
by Connors after a distinguished career in the intelligence services,

and Secretary of State Harold Powell, who had served in two other administrations and was considered by many the top international strategist in the country.

"I'm not sure how I feel about the man personally," said Connors, intently watching the silent TV screen. "I think old money still makes me uncomfortable."

"He's pleasant enough," Powell observed over his coffee. "Just a bit obsessed with space."

"His clout is growing, though, and days like today turn his ideology into a cause célèbre," added Clancy. "I wouldn't treat him casually."

Barbara Reynolds studied the men at the table—Connors, whose thinning gray hair curled over his weather-lined face with its penetrating blue eyes; Parienne, a short, portly man with an ever-worried expression; Clancy, a big-boned giant who looked more like a bodyguard than a former Rhodes scholar; and Powell, older, white-haired and immaculately attired, veteran of a thousand political crises.

"I think," she said slowly for more emphasis, pushing back her still vibrant brown hair "that the whole idea of space for military purposes is ridiculous from a national security standpoint. The ultimate purpose of any war is to secure territorial advantage. Why in God's name would anyone fight over space? And to think we could contain a nuclear war to that theater is as absurd as thinking we could choose one person from each side and let them fight it out. Once it's started, it won't stop, *can't* stop till a side is annihilated. That's the reality of the nuclear age, not a polite war over a vacuum."

"There's another factor, Mr. President," said Clancy, "and that's cost. The economic situation in the Soviet Union is steadily worsening. You've seen the satellite photos from Prophet; bread lines in Moscow, famine in parts of Czechoslovakia and Hungary, revolution in Poland. The Soviets can't *afford* to duplicate our Shuttle program and don't even have the technology to do so if they could. There is no race for space anymore; we've got it all to ourselves."

Parienne balanced his knife on the tip of a finger and frowned. He began to tap the knife against his hand to underscore his points.

"We depend so much on hardware in the sky that I worry about our vulnerability up there. Comsat and Intelsat networks for communications, Navsat for navigational purposes, Meteosat for weather, Marisat for maritime communications; AT&T has their Intelpost electronic mail system functioning now; IBM has their Satellite Business System; Comsat has their television satellites, and that's just some of the civilian projects in space. Then think of all of our military hardware in the sky; the NSA communications satellites, the Nuclear Force Communications System, even Prophet, on which the Company and NSA rely. We've got over two thousand satellites in orbit and not one damn way in hell to protect any of them."

The president listened closely to each point in the argument. He had cultivated an atmosphere of openness at the lunches.

"There's no question of vulnerability," shot back Reynolds hotly. "There is no technology presently available to the Soviets that could endanger more than a fraction of our satellites. You'd get no argument from me about CIA and NSA overreliance on Prophet. But ICBM's just aren't going to be able to hurt the network. In the time it would take for an ICBM to get to any of our military hardware, NORAD would know about it, the National Reconnaissance Office and the Air Force Satellite Command would be instantly notified, and the Prophets would be in a totally different orbit when those ICBM's arrived. Do you really envision a skeet shoot in space with nuclear weapons?

"The Prophet reconnaissance satellites allow us to monitor visually the entire Soviet military posture, including their defense framework, anywhere in the world, twenty-four hours a day, every day of the year. No other country in the history of the world has had the tactical advantage that gives us. We can see, actually *see* if troops are massing on the Polish border, *see* if their ships enter the Persian Gulf, *see* the size of their harvests at home. No more guesswork, no more conjecture by hosts of CIA analysts. We can read the Russians like an open book. My God, that has devastated their foreign policy. How can they try to bluff us when they know we can tell them the name of the general that is commanding their front-line battalion and, using Prophet's sighting ability and NAVSAT's guidance system, deliver an ICBM into the back seat of his staff car? Wars are born in secret. They can't roll out a single tank without our knowing about it."

"I don't think that's the point here," broke in Powell. "Technology is going to become more sophisticated; history proves that over and over. We may not even foresee the kinds of weaponry possible in the next century." He pointed to the south wall and its painting by Huggins depicting the first naval action of the War of 1812. "Could that navy have predicted sonar and torpedoes?"

"The situation's not analogous, Harold. In the current geopolitical situation, any new research is going to come from us. No one else has the economy to finance it. Prophet has shown no evidence of any kind of building for weapons research in any corner of the world, and its lenses can tell whether or not a man dyes his hair from three hundred miles up. Conjecture's fine, but it's just not happening," argued Clancy.

"But it could," said Powell evenly, refusing to budge. "Don't count the Soviets out of the race just yet. I'm well aware of their food and energy disasters, of Poland's revolution, of their problems in north Afghanistan. But I tell you this, pushed to the wall they will react. They'll have to."

"But they will not be able to," said Reynolds, tossing her napkin onto the table. "SALT V is going to stop ICBM production and SALT VI will eliminate them. Look at it this way, would we permit the total visual reconnaissance of the USA if we could prevent it? The answer is no. It is clear to NSA that the Russians permit it because they are, and always will be, powerless to do anything about it."

"As always," said Connors to the group, rising, "I am enlightened by all your thoughts. However, I must ultimately agree with the notion that, at least for the foreseeable future, space is our fiefdom. For the time being, I will oppose Leyland's legislation for increased appropriations and a new weapons-research timetable. The federal budget is not unlimited. Thank you all for your spirited discussion. Same time in two weeks. I look forward to it."

Moscow

2 Dzerzhinsky Square (8 P.M.)

". . . and not to the Soviet Union. I am happy to say that this notion is steadily gaining ground in Congress, and we will begin introducing legislation during the next session backed by a bipartisan coalition."

"Thank you, Senator Leyland. I see some of your people want you to get along to Launch Control to hear the re-entry dialogue. Thank you again, Senator."

"It is rare we have such visible proof of our intelligence reports," commented KGB Chief Vassily Komarovsky, thrusting his chin at the television screen in his private office.

"These flights are front-page news all over the world. I only wish we had some news of our own to counter with," responded Dimitri Torgenev, Marshal of the Red Army.

"Grain or guns," sighed Komarovsky, "the age-old dilemma. When I sit at the Politburo, I sometimes think we have become nothing but bankers. Then I look across at you and know that I'm not totally alone in my idle thoughts."

"No, my old friend. You're not alone. We must feed the people, and we must protect the people. It seems the time has come when we cannot do both. And now this." He pointed at the television and thrust his finger at the off button angrily, cutting off the restricted-access satellite transmission.

"A good Communist has faith in the Party," needled Komarovsky lightly.

"A good party needs vodka," snorted Torgenev, supplying the last line to the old joke. Reminded of his empty glass, he crossed the spartan office to the liquor cabinet under the pictures of Lenin and Brezhnev. Bringing the bottle back to Komarovsky, he poured generous amounts.

"In what do you have faith, Vassily?" he asked softly.

Komarovsky lifted his glass as if toasting. "In three things, Dimitri. The KGB, the Red Army . . . and Nightsight." He downed the vodka in one swallow.

"Consider this, though," said Torgenev, pausing only to drink and pour again, "that if Operation Nightsight fails, the effect will be to signal a breakdown of our control from which we will never recover. It is the ultimate risk."

Komarovsky stared into his vodka for a long moment before standing and replying.

"Twenty years ago, I would have agreed that the risk outweighed the benefit. Even ten years ago I would have agreed. But the pressures from our client states have become unendurable, and the Americans have leaped ahead so quickly and decisively with their spies-in-the-sky and their Shuttle program that we cannot outpropagandize them as we did in the sixties, or outbluff them as we did in the seventies. It is the middle of the eighties, and we are drowning, Dimitri. And drowning men will, must, grab on to any lifeline.

"When the KGB created Caracal and later Nightsight, I had no idea of its ultimate worth to us. Now, there is no more convincing argument than need, no greater issue than expedience. We do what we must to survive."

Torgenev replaced the near empty vodka bottle and thought over his friend's words.

The KGB was organized into four main Chief Directorates, along with other lesser directorates with more minor functions. The First Chief Directorate was the foreign intelligence service; the Second Chief Directorate, the domestic security apparatus. The Fifth Chief Directorate was also domestic but concerned itself with dissidents and special groups; the Chief Directorate of Border Guards sealed off the borders from illegal entry or exit.

Within the First Chief Directorate was one of the most critical and influential subdirectorates in the KGB, the Scientific and Technical Directorate. Torgenev had seen firsthand their thousands of specialists who sat at data banks, each a specialist on some sector of the West's modern military-industrial complex, constantly monitoring Western technological advances. From this directorate emerged the priorities for all the other arms of the KGB. And from this directorate in 1969, the year of the American lunar landing, Caracal, which took its name from a small Persian Gulf animal, had been born.

Torgenev remembered the planning that had gone into Caracal's formation. Simply put, Caracal's function was to operationalize the findings of the Scientific and Technical Directorate; to prevent the West, with its vastly greater resources and economic base, from advancing technologically beyond the limits of Soviet research and development or, failing that, to confound, re-create, or steal that technology. Over the years, Caracal's area of concern had become increasingly military. Ultimately, it had generated Operation Nightsight.

His thoughts coming full circle, Torgenev looked up into his friend's face.

"You must know that if I saw any alternative, I would jump at it.

Any at all. But I do not. You have my support and the support of
the army. Nightsight can proceed."

"I hoped you would see it that way," said Komarovsky, his features unreadable to his friend. "Caracal is assembled; I think we had
best inform them."

Seated at a long gray table, Caracal's members were already in a
heated discussion which ended only when Komarovsky and the marshal came in. Taking his seat at the head of the table, with the marshal on his right, Komarovsky welcomed the other members. Stern
featured Nikolai Mikoyan, head of the First Chief Directorate;
white-bearded Vyacheslav Trapeznikov, president of the Academy
of Science; and Andrei Kosreiva, bespectacled and florid-faced, head
of the Scientific and Technical Directorate. Only one chair remained
empty.

"Comrades," said Komarovsky in the most businesslike tones.
"We are going to make Operation Nightsight a reality. This meeting
is now open for discussion."

"If the plan is to succeed, very little discussion is necessary, I
think," said Kosreiva, looking carefully at the others to see if any
took offense. "We need two elements we don't have: time and technology. Can you deliver these?"

Very slowly, the beginnings of a smile crossed Komarovsky's features.

"I believe we can, Comrade Kosreiva, one at a time."

For the next several hours, methods and proposals were accepted
or rejected. It was shortly after dawn when Komarovsky, squinting
at the pale light that leaked in through grimy windowpanes, pressed
the intercom button to speak to a waiting signals officer.

"Summon Kasimov," he said.

2

Had anyone cared to examine the books of the Postelli Marble Export Company at 23 Via Renaldi, they would have found a small but prosperous firm which ran steadily in the black; its major business the export of high-quality marble for interior design purposes. Every day, some fifty employees arrived, bought and sold, stockpiled and exported, sent cables and made phone calls, went out to lunch and left for home in the evening.

The CIA was proud of the fact that the company under which it had built the Rome station showed a profit every year and that employee turnover was low. Proud, too, was Postelli's president, who had worked with the OSS during World War II and had profited greatly by the association. Unlimited credit made business easier.

Underground, the four floors of the CIA station, fed by separate, secure electrical power from its own generators, functioned twenty-four hours a day. Most of the CIA people entered and exited through one of the private townhouses that served as a buffer zone around Postelli's or, for those of most senior rank, one of the private garages which held their chauffeur-driven limousines.

The Roman sun was blood red in the late afternoon sky when one such limousine left the garage and, turning right, passed slowly by the public park on the other side of the street. Though its tinted windows were opaque to curious pedestrians, from inside the man in the rear seat watched the park closely, counting the number of benches they passed and looking closely at the people who occupied them.

On the fifth bench, a shabbily dressed city worker fed plump pigeons. On the ninth bench, a pretty young woman ate a late lunch, a bottle of wine unopened beside her.

With the park behind them, the man did a rapid set of mental conversions. Then he abruptly ordered the chauffeur to take him to an exclusive men's shop near Embassy Row.

The bells that jingled when he closed the door to the shop behind him fit well with the antique furnishings. Bolts of fine cloth were flung over old oak writing desks and flowed out of French armoires in a profusion of grays and blues. A silver espresso service stood on one side of the large room, tended, at the moment, by a diminutive man in shirt-sleeves whose wristlet pincushion and tape measure indicated his profession as surely as a policeman's badge marks his.

"Signor Martelli!" cried the tailor in lightly accented English. "How good to see you so soon. I was delighted to receive your office's call this morning, and I am most happy to announce that your garments are ready."

"*Gracie,* Arturo. I believe I'll pass on the espresso today. I'm in a bit of a rush, thank you."

The fact that the man's name was not Martelli and that he had placed no order that day bothered him not at all. He followed the tailor to the dressing rooms. The shop held his measurements, and they had received calls like this morning's many times over the years he had been in Rome.

The suits he had "ordered" were already hanging in the triple-mirrored dressing room, a gray worsted wool and a rich blue silk. As always, an array of shirts, ties, and shoes had also been arranged for his selection.

"That is fine, Arturo. I will call you should I need anything," said the man, closing the door on the already departing tailor, who knew his customer's preference for solitude.

Waiting the prescribed five minutes, Martelli examined the cut of the suits, the feel of the cloth. He made preliminary decisions on shirts and ties. Then he rapped sharply three times on the center mirror, which opened as smoothly as warm butter spreads, revealing an ancient catacomb behind.

"Good day, Pollux," said Kasimov. "We have a project."

His return to CIA station was no cause for comment among the night shift for he often returned to work late. It was thought of as an example of the dedication which, along with a series of outstanding successes while on the Russian Desk, had led to his rapid rise in the Company.

He nodded politely to those he encountered on the way to his office, for his reputation as an easy man to work with had served him well by excluding him from the never-ending office gossip. Further, he was known as a man with no glaring vices and as a superior who always remembered his subordinates' birthdays.

The computer in his office was a restricted-access terminal and was keyed electronically to the palm prints of those of executive rank. Seated at the terminal, he withdrew a celluloid sheet and a single surgical rubber glove from his breast pocket. The celluloid sheet that he placed carefully on the read-plate of the terminal held two things—a palm print and the name *George Williams*.

Donning the surgical glove, he placed his hand over the palm print on the screen. At once, the heat from his hand activated the terminal which read the palm print which opened access to the data banks of the CIA.

Reaching into his pocket again, he withdrew a small notepad which contained Williams' access and authority codes. He entered them into the computer.

Then he typed the name ARTHUR LEYLAND on the keyboard and cross-referenced it to ROME VISIT and SECURITY and punched the operation button.

The whole of Leyland's route to and from the airport, his hotel, and his entire Roman itinerary were printed out on the screen. Working for ten minutes more, Martelli had established vulnerability points and potential sites. Ten minutes after that, he pressed the printout button, reduced the several pages to the size of a cigarette package on his Xerox copier, and shredded the originals. Turning off the computer, he waited until the chassis had cooled down, then put on his coat and walked calmly back to his car.

He ordered his driver to the Café Continental, where he had an excellent dinner of pasta, veal, and white wine. As the signals were correct, after dinner he retired to the men's room, left the reduced documents behind the toilet stall, and returned to his table to leave a generous tip for the waiter. Then he telephoned George Williams.

The apartment in the slum section of Rome was unfurnished, save for an old Formica table and chairs, and unoccupied, save for the black water beetles which scurried across the floor.

Nevertheless, when Kasimov arrived he made a thorough inspection and a complete electronic sweep of the rooms and of the vacant apartments on either side. Satisfied the place was "clean," he stood silently in the room's center, arms folded, and waited for a pattern of knocks on the door.

The first man to open the door did so cautiously, making eye contact with Kasimov before entering. This advance guard held his gun unselfconsciously and performed a series of hand gestures which Kasimov returned. Nodding, the guard disappeared from the doorway.

Some minutes later, two young men strode into the room; they wore leather jackets, tee shirts, and faded blue jeans. The first guard took up position inside the doorway.

"I am Renard, and this is Fredo," said the taller of the two. His hair was dark as was his face, brooding and insolent.

"I am Eris," said Kasimov, senses alert for any sign of betrayal. "Where is Paolo? It was with him that I have always done business."

"Paolo is dead," Renard said disgustedly. "The Red Brigade has a new leader and from now on you will work with me. Even the legendary Eris will deal on my terms. We are not Moscow's lackeys any longer, and your gold and guns are not enough."

"I see," said Kasimov, moving a step closer. "That is good, for Moscow has no need of lackeys."

The gleam of triumph showed in the boy's eyes. Eris had not even tried to challenge his authority. Renard moved closer. "That is only the first of the changes that will . . ."

Kasimov's stiff fingers caught him in the solar plexus in mid-sentence. Kasimov spun and kicked Fredo in the groin, his gun seeming to leap into his hand, catching the guard at the door in mid-draw.

Motioning the guard toward him, Kasimov removed his gun and

then, reversing it, clubbed him violently on the back of the head. The guard sprawled unconscious on the dirty floor.

Renard and Fredo were still moaning, clutching themselves where Kasimov had struck. Keeping an eye on Fredo, Kasimov grabbed Renard by the hair and shoved the barrel of his gun into Renard's mouth.

"You are about to die," he hissed into Renard's ear, "and no one will know of it except in bad jokes when we tell of the infant who spoke so badly to Eris. Consider your death, for it is coming soon."

The boy's face was transformed into a mask of fear. He could barely breathe. He smelled his own urine and couldn't stop his tears.

"Please . . ." he managed.

Eris put his face close to the boy's without removing his gun.

"I am Eris. I am discord and death. For you I will come in the night and shrivel your testicles and rip out your eyes. Ask of me. Ask those you know."

Fredo's pain was subsiding. Kasimov lazily kicked him again and returned his attention to Renard.

"Swear allegiance to me," he hissed again. "Swear it and live."

"I swear . . . I . . . swear it," groaned Renard. "I'm sorry . . . sorry . . ." he cried.

"That is good then," said Kasimov, hauling him to his feet. The boy was broken, his shoulders slumped, the look in his eyes one of defeat.

"They will not know of our little chat," Kasimov said, pointing to the bodies on the floor, supporting the boy's weight. "Only you and I. Now go and wash yourself, and we will talk of important matters. Go . . ." he ordered.

Fredo and the guard were just stirring when Renard came out of the bathroom. He looked to Kasimov for instructions, but Kasimov was content to let him handle his own people. He knew the boy must recover something of his courage if he was to be of any use.

Renard, seeming to sense this, grabbed Fredo and lifted him to his feet. He did the same to the dazed guard. Then he slapped both smartly across the face.

"Fools," he barked. "You have been tested by Eris and been found wanting. To be taken so easily is a mark of incompetence. Now resume your positions while we talk of important matters. Be grateful you are not dead." The guard slunk away, shamefaced.

Kasimov nodded approvingly, sitting at the table. From a pocket he produced the CIA computer printout. The boy sat opposite him like a schoolchild eager to please.

Kasimov pushed over the printout, along with a photograph.

"This is the target," he said.

3

Wednesday

Sitting on the couch in the plush apartment, he held his head in his hands and tried to look like a man trapped. George Williams was still calling him crazy.

". . . Do you have any idea what will happen to you when the Chief finds out that you're screwing his wife? You'll be licking envelopes in Tanzania. What possessed you? You, of all people? I just can't believe it."

"I know, George. Don't you think I've been through this? I've run out of choices. I hated to drag you into this, but there was no one else I could turn to. When I called last night from the café, I had been just sitting and drinking for hours. My efficiency's down; my people are getting edgy. I just don't know what to do."

"I appreciate your confidence, buddy. I really do. And I want you to know how very badly I feel about getting that promotion over you. I guess I've been standoffish lately because I thought you resented it. I'm sorry."

"Don't even think about it, George. The better man got the job. That's all. That's proved by my being here tonight."

George's flabby face wore an eager expression. Screwing the Chief's old lady; God, he thought, this guy's really gotten into it. He's putting his fucking life in my hands. A part of him was already figuring out how to use that to his advantage. "How can I help you?" he asked.

"The problem's this, George. The old man is going out of town tomorrow night and she wants me to come over. She's got some films or something, and the bitch is hot. She likes to play with herself while the film's on, and I'm supposed to . . . well, she's crazy."

"So where's the problem?" George grinned, savoring the vicarious thrill. "Put it to her before the old boy comes home."

"That's not possible. Tomorrow night, George, I have to meet the Vicar."

The words seared into George's brain like a spike. The Vicar! A Russian code clerk who was their most promising mole in years. Already he had delivered a ton of stuff on the Russian codes. And until this, the Vicar had been the sole property of the man who now sat crying before him.

"Postpone the lady," he said flatly.

"I can't. I tried. She threatened to tell her husband."

"Postpone the Vicar, then."

"Can't do that either. George, the meeting's been in the works for weeks. He's got the whole Level Five codings from their embassy. If I'm not there, even to signal a pass-by, we might lose the whole package. And I can't contact him before the meet."

George saw it all. In one stroke of luck he was being handed the Vicar, the L5 codes, and probably a posting in Langley and a house in Georgetown. If he were clever enough to take it. It was unfair, he thought, to take advantage of a friend by stealing his Russian. But, he consoled himself, that's what you get for fucking up so royally.

"What can I do?" he asked solicitously.

"I hate to ask, George."

"Buddy, isn't that what friends are for?"

"I sure hope so. George, could you make the meet for me, deliver the money, and take Vicar's case back to the shop? I'll get it in the morning like nothing went any different. Whadaya say, George?"

"You'll sure owe me one," smiled Williams benignly, "but I'll do it. Anything for the old esprit de corps."

"Thanks, George. I'll have the briefcase in my office at six P.M. You can pick it up there and get to the meet at seven. Okay?" He retrieved his topcoat and walked toward the door, but Williams stopped him.

"Where is the meet to take place?" he asked quickly.

"I'll tell you tomorrow. Maybe there's still a way I can do it. I'd rather not ask this of you unless I absolutely have to."

"Tomorrow at six then."

"Goodbye, George. And thanks. You've saved my life."

Arthur Leyland passed through the umbilicus to the arrivals terminal, grateful to be back on the ground. Embarrassed by the thought, after having watched Chris's performance barely forty-eight hours before, he kept it to himself. Crowley, who had been with him long enough to know the senator's fear of flying, contented himself with a knowing smile.

Inside the terminal, the expected group of media reporters surged around them, equipment buzzing, humming, and flashing. The senator answered questions freely, fully aware that Chris's flight would overshadow most of the political inquiries.

Crowley was the first to spot the approach of General Ezio Colanetti and his staff and began to urge the senator forward, away from the reporters. The general's reception was polite and congenial, and they were whisked past customs to a fleet of waiting limousines, Crowley finally separating from his charge.

"It is good to have you back in Rome," said the general when they had pulled away from the curb.

"It's always good to be back," responded the senator. "But why so many cars?"

"It is for the terrorists that we take so many precautions." The general shrugged expansively. "Security demands we move several cars at once, some filled with dummies, some with bodyguards, to confuse any attack."

"I'm flattered they think I'm such a priority target," said the senator brightly.

"They don't," said the general a bit uncomfortably. "I am the target. In your country's terminology, I am a right-wing reactionary. Consequently, I am a target for the communists, the socialists, the anarchists, the Red Brigade, and anyone else who has a cause to promote."

"I understand, General. But in the future I would like to have Mr. Crowley travel with me. He's indispensable."

"Allow us our gestures, Senator," the general said. "In this case, we should err on the side of caution."

"Very well, then. I won't make a fuss."

"Excellent. Now place yourself in my hands and all will be well. First, to your hotel where you can rest after your flight. We can begin our talks tomorrow after lunch. Agreed?"

"That will be fine. I'm looking forward to tomorrow."

4

At five minutes to six, George Williams came into his office. Williams' tension was apparent. The sweat on his neck, the way he folded and refolded his topcoat, his too-loud laugh, all betrayed a man with ulterior motives.

"Well," Williams asked almost at once, "are we on or off for tonight?"

"On, I'm afraid, George. There's no way out for me tonight."

He placed a locked leather attaché case on his desk. It was an expensive case, of fine brown leather, with a combination lock of the three-number type.

"Here's the procedure, George. His case is identical. The switch will be made at the second plateau of the Spanish Steps at seven o'clock exactly. This contingency was planned for, so the signal you must use to show I sent you is to be carrying the case in your left hand and a bottle of Chianti in your right . . . When you see him, switch the case and wine to the other hands. Then he'll approach, and you can make the transfer. Explain that I'm sick or something and that the next scheduled meet is still on. Okay?"

"No sweat, buddy," Williams said happily, picking up the case. "I hope to hell tonight is worth it."

"So do I, George. But I'm sure it will be."

The Vicar had been a code clerk for over ten years. Rome was only the latest of his postings. Watching the people in the street, affluent Westerners, had been at first an amusement in Amsterdam, became a preoccupation in Paris, and grew to an obsession in Rome. Now, every sports car that passed by his small window caused a hitch in his breath; every fur-clad, long-legged woman, an acute pain.

Vladimir Golenko's hand stole out unconsciously to caress the leather of his attaché case. Like the cars, it represented the wealth, no, the *quality,* that he would have so very soon. Just a few more "deliveries" and he would be rich and free to defect. The leather grew warm under his caress, and he looked again at the plain embassy clock.

At six o'clock the day shift ended and the offices began to empty out. The case resting comfortably in his hand, Golenko selected a knot of people moving toward the elevator and merged with them to descend three stories to the main lobby.

The elevator was crowded. At each floor, more people crowded in. Golenko hoped that fear had no smell.

At the main lobby the doors slid apart and the crowded elevator burst open like an overripe fruit. Golenko moved forward, clutching his case, but suddenly, tripping over some unseen obstacle, he sprawled headlong into the crowd, the case flung from his hand.

Immediately, people paused to give him room to stand, others helping him up. Golenko was frantic to locate the case, searching the floor, trying to keep his movements calm.

"I believe you dropped this, Comrade." Golenko wanted to embrace the kindly tusseled-hair janitor who handed him back his case.

"Thank you, Comrade. The elevator . . . too crowded," he managed.

"I usually wait till after the rush," the janitor confided.

"I will in the future," mumbled Golenko, and then he was at the checkpoint, through the checkpoint, and outside on his coveted streets. Without turning back, he made directly for the Spanish Steps.

The senator sat wearily in the back of the limousine, tired from the long day of meetings and still uncomfortable without Crowley's presence.

Relaxing somewhat, he thought about Christopher, more like a son to him than a younger brother. He hoped that someone might come along to settle Chris down. After all, hopping around in orbit was fine. But there were bigger stakes right here on the ground. And Chris could be so useful.

He had spoken of it to Crowley on the flight over. Perhaps some small, local office to begin with. Then, later, a Washington posting. If Chris could manage to keep his honesty in check and be more politically aware, he could do anything at all.

The softness of the cushions lolling him to drift, he resolved to speak to Chris in Ohio. He would be there. Wild horses couldn't keep him away. Wild horses, he thought dreamily.

On the street, Renard watched the caravan of limousines approach. He felt relaxed, almost euphoric. The first car was passing by. Not yet, he counseled himself. It will be the fourth one, Eris had said. Wait for the fourth.

The palms of his hands wet with anticipation, he waited.

The general's voice woke him sharply from his sleep. But the general, too, was dozing, talking in his sleep. The senator smiled to himself. "Old men," he thought; "we have grown so old." He smiled again contentedly and drifted back to a sleep filled with wild horses and Ohio.

He never heard the explosion that killed him nor felt the force of the blast that rocked the manhole cover through the car, exploding the gas tank into a paroxysm of violent fury.

Pedestrians on the sidewalk were showered with flying glass as shop windows burst from the shock wave. Bleeding, they screamed for help.

The other passengers in the limos, CIA bodyguards, Roman police, Italian military, ran from the cars, circling the scene in a protective ring. Some even tried to get into the burning car. Others pulled them away. A crowd began to grow, and sirens shrieked in the distance.

Tom Crowley, white-faced and trembling, stumbled from his car. Screaming incoherent curses, he tried to get to his friend. It took four policemen to stop him. Then, amid the acrid smell of gunpowder and death, he sat in the gutter and cried.

George Williams heard the sirens as he started up the Spanish Steps but ignored them. Some dumb guinea smoking in bed, was his exact thought. Carrying the case and wine bottle exactly as directed, he spotted the Russian descending the stairs and couldn't help the feeling of anticipation that swept over him. Langley was just one step closer, each step the Russian took.

When he was sure the Russian had spotted him, he switched the attaché case and the wine. For a moment, the Russian looked confused and stopped, but then his face cleared and he started forward again.

At the second plateau, where the steps flattened out to a wider area, Williams stopped and put down his case, gazing out over the city as any tourist might.

Hesitantly, the Russian walked over, clearly unsettled by the stranger.

"Don't worry, Vicar," said Williams evenly. "There's been a switch. Your man is sick, and I was sent to replace him."

Golenko heard the words and saw the case. It was sufficient to calm him.

"By the way," the American was saying. "There are going to be some other changes, too. From now on . . ."

"Do not move. Make your hands clearly visible. You are under arrest. Do not move," the stridently amplified voice blared over them. Agents, men Williams recognized, were coming at them from above and below, guns drawn. The voice never halted.

"You are under arrest. Make your hands clearly visible."

Williams saw the panic in the Russian's eyes at the same moment he knew he had been set up. Knee-weakening fear filled his mind, and he fought for control. There was a way out, had to be a way out —surrender, explain, he thought desperately.

But the Russian had dropped his case and reached into his coat. A small, shiny gun appeared in his hand.

Williams leaped for the Russian, but it was too late. Crazed with fear, he ran at the agents, gun firing, yelling madly in Russian that he was loyal. The volley of shots that followed tore his head into shreds. He careened over backward and fell down the steps.

Williams' anger at himself, at his "friend," at his betrayal, all merged and suddenly his gun was in his hand, for there was no escape and his anger overrode his training. They cut him down before he fired a single round, his spine severed by the automatic weapons. The bottle of wine fell to the steps, the wine spilling amidst the blood.

The Chief of the Rome station, Henry Talon, left his car and walked up the steps to the bodies. Retrieving the two cases, he opened them by breaking the locks.

Inside Williams' case were NATO memorandums, NSA documents, and CIA dossiers. Inside the Vicar's, neatly piled stacks of Swiss francs. The conclusion was inescapable. They had just shot an American traitor and his Russian control. He turned to the man who only the day before had brought him the startling evidence against George Williams.

"You were correct, as usual," he said. "Get a team to collect this garbage. I'll notify Langley. You did fine work. I'd expect a commendation."

"No, sir," said Pollux with appropriate humility. "No matter what he is, he was once a friend, and I'll not step on his grave. I'm truly sorry it turned out this way."

Even the Chief was impressed.

In an apartment overlooking the Steps, Kasimov watched the denouement of his activities. He had already disposed of the janitor's uniform and arranged payment to the Red Brigade for Leyland's death. Watching the corpses laid onto stretchers, he was satisfied that this phase of his machinations had been successful as well. The months of disinformation that "the Vicar" had sent, and Pollux had validated, were an added bonus.

He flexed his lean, hard physique, cramped from sitting at the window for so long, and reflected on the fact that he had gained no weight since that day in the brothel almost twenty years ago.

Then he thought of the Soviet leadership with their dachas and caviar, and a momentary stab of disgust ran through him. He turned from the window and left the room.

In the street, the CIA men had finished clearing off the Steps, and the sated crowd began to disperse in the Roman dusk.

5

Friday

Christopher Leyland held the crumpled telegram in his fist throughout the flight from California to Ohio. Franklin, the family's ancient chauffeur, had been red-eyed when he picked him up at the airport and had not protested when Chris put an arm around him in greeting.

Now, approaching the place of his earliest memories, the pain of Arthur's death became sharper. He had been too young to be fully aware when Tim had died. But the memory of the coffin rolling out of the Naval jet and the subsequent military funeral had stayed in his dreams for years.

Tim's funeral was also one of the last remembrances he had of his mother, her face thin, pale, and drawn, standing beside her husband, ramrod stiff even on his crutches. That was in the days before his father had accepted a wheelchair.

In the ensuing months, his mother's beloved horses had been ridden less and less, the clubs and societies she belonged to came to accept her frequent absences, and young Chris's question, "Why is Mom so tired all the time?" was greeted by hesitant answers and downcast eyes.

She died a year after Tim. Scenes of her funeral blended in his mind's eye with those he remembered of Tim's. Someone had told him the vice-president would be attending. The family would refuse the offer of Arlington. Their cemetery near the lake would be disturbed once again.

The electric gate that guarded the forest-lined driveway to the house opened at the chauffeur's signal. It was an old Tudor mansion with white plaster and exposed dark beams. The weather-stained brickwork of the chimneys and the leaded glass of the church-type windows all swam into focus for Chris. As the big car pulled to a stop, he felt his chest tighten with anger. His eyes burned with tears.

Katherine Thomas, who had served as his father's nurse and, later, took over so many of the things Chris's mother had done, came rushing up to him. Her beefy arms pulled him into her big, soft bosom.

"I'm so sorry, Christopher," she cried softly.

"I know, Katie," Chris said, pressing her dry, white hair.

"We were all so proud of you," she sniffled, "and looking forward to when you came home. Your father, too. But then, we didn't know . . . weren't sure . . ."

"You were correct not to make a fuss, my old darling. Just let me wash up and then I want to see my father. Where is he?"

"In his apartment. There are some others, too, in the library."

"You take care of them for a while, all right? Tell everyone I'll be down later."

"Yes, dear. I'll see to it." And she bustled off.

Later, Chris stood at his father's door. The apartment was self-contained, and all the conveniences necessary for the invalid Admiral's comfort had been installed. Chris hesitated before entering, searching for a tone for this first, most painful meeting.

John Leyland sat staring out a window, his frail and crippled body sunk into his wheelchair. Chris could sense his father's despair.

"It's good to have you home, son," the Admiral said, turning to him, his voice barely audible.

"Hello, Dad. It's good to be home," Chris said gently. "How are you feeling?"

"I don't know," the Admiral sighed deeply. "I keep trying to be angry and to hate the bastards that killed him. But I can't seem to find the strength even for that. I'm too damn old, Chris. Just too damn old . . ."

"You're not too old. You just need to rest. First Tim, then Mom, and now Arthur . . . it's too much in one lifetime, Dad. You have a right to feel numb. Can't you see that?"

"Maybe. But you have no idea what a terrible thing it is to outlive your children. It's like . . . like someone cut away my roots and my future both at the same time. There's no one left but you and I, Chris. Will you stay for a while?"

"For a while, I suppose. In a way, I'm just as unsure as you are. I had a lot of time to think on the plane ride here after . . . after I heard about Arthur. I'm going to leave NASA. I've got to be more involved in this world on the ground. Maybe I've finally grown up. Or maybe I just need to understand what killed my brothers. I truly don't know."

"I see," said his father quietly. For a moment there was no sound but his reedy breathing.

"Words like war or terrorism, they don't mean much, do they?" the Admiral said, the specter of his former self emerging ghostlike from his ruined body. "Then there's death, dispassionate and final.

"Timothy died because the Communists wanted Korea, Arthur because the Red Brigade wanted a general. I don't know what the hell any of it means anymore," he said, despairing again.

"It means what it always has," Chris insisted evenly. "You pick a side and do what has to be done. Isn't that what you taught us?"

"Words," muttered the Admiral. "Just words."

"More than words," Chris argued. "Arthur and I were as close as two brothers can be. And I can sit here and tell you that he had fifty good years, great years maybe. And he wouldn't have traded one second of them for a hundred mediocre ones. He made a real difference, Dad. His existence made a difference. You can't hope for more than that from any man's life."

"You know he loved you deeply, Christopher . . ."

"I know that," Chris said softly. "And you should know that, too. Hold on to it, because nothing else matters. And if it has any meaning to you right now, I want you to know that I have always loved you, too."

Tears crept down the Admiral's craggy cheeks as he stared off into some other place. Slowly, he seemed to expand and gain strength and when he looked back to Chris at last, there was the first faint glimmering of hope in his eyes. He reached out a hand like gnarled oak and placed it on his son's.

"It means a great deal to me, Christopher . . . a very great deal, indeed."

Tom Crowley was waiting in the library. There were others, milling about, smoking, drinking, or reading. They were the rest of Arthur's staff. Tom stood up at once when Chris entered.

"Relax, Tom. Somehow I was sure you'd be here. Care for a drink?" he asked while pouring a Scotch for himself.

"Got one already," said Crowley, sitting back in the armchair.

Chris seated himself opposite Crowley and looked over the rim of his glass.

"No bullshit, Tom. Just give it to me straight."

Crowley nodded, pausing only to light a cigarette and exhale.

"No bullshit, then. I loved and respected Arthur more than anyone I've ever known. He did his job, an important job, Chris. Now I'm not going to sit around and cry or moan. That's over. I've been on the phone to the governor all morning and he's prepared to appoint you to Arthur's seat, if you want it. Also, the party's policy committee has agreed to give you Arthur's committee assignments."

"What are your feelings? And theirs." Chris pointed outside.

"We all want to see as good a man as he was in the job. It's too important to let an asshole get it. I personally nominated you for Arthur's seat. You have all our support. Will you go to Washington, Chris?"

He thought of his father's words, and of his brother's, and of his own life. He was being given a chance, he knew, to enter the power center of the country. But he would have to earn it every single day. He thought of his secret desire to find those who had murdered Arthur. That would have to wait.

In the end, he realized that he had expected and had been fighting this moment from the start. And he knew from experience that the right choice was the one most difficult to make. He could not let Arthur's work end.

"I'll ask you for the last time," said Crowley. "If you need time to think, to doubt or to ponder, you're not the man I thought I knew. Will you go to Washington?"

Chris Leyland finished his drink, and his youthful face was hard with purpose.

"Wild horses, Tom," he said.

Crowley stood up and offered his hand.

"Wild horses, Senator."

PART TWO

PART TWO

1

The Pacific Ocean crashed incessantly along the rocky cliffs of the Torrey Pines Inn in La Jolla, muffling the radios which crackled communications to those who guarded the golfers on the celebrated course. Though all the club entrances, including the big stone main gate, had been closed off by chains for the past week, the fine old inn was filled to capacity.

The Jasons had assembled again in California.

There were no press briefings or reporters anywhere on the scene, and only those who played the course regularly would have noticed the dramatic increase in "gardeners" who had sprouted up overnight, eyes watchful, radios and weapons concealed, their overalls tailor-made to specifications from Langley.

The Jasons were established in 1960 and named after the mythical seeker of the Golden Fleece. They drew their membership, by invitation only, from the finest physical and computer scientists in the country. Every spring, their number limited to forty, these Nobel Prize winners, IBM Fellows, and professors emeritus gathered in the hope of finding answers to national security questions posed by the departments of Defense and Energy.

The Torrey Pines Inn had become one of the most scrutinized spots on earth. Every room was swept daily for "bugs"; scrambler telephones and secure computers were installed, and every person was required to wear special, coded ID tags. However, in many ways the scene looked as casual as a tropical resort in the off-season.

Generals and their aides, top-ranking NASA people, defense experts, and the Jasons mingled on the golf course or over lunches of Pacific prawns. Computer experts drank together on the terraced lawns. Two- and three-star generals descended from their helicopters, entered their rooms, and emerged in Lacoste shirts and plaid slacks.

This time, the subject was Space.

Senator Christopher Leyland had been invited to deliver the opening speech. Progressively more at ease with public speaking, he had found that an honest, reasonable tone and what Crowley called his "boyish charm" had gotten him excellent reactions in his first six months of public life. The initial reaction to his appointment had been positive and taking over Arthur's assignment to the Intelligence Committee had provided considerable opportunity for political maturation. He glanced over the gathering and got Crowley's nod that the speech thus far was going well.

". . . It must be seen, therefore," he continued, "that up until now, American defense policy has been based on the assumption that any nuclear exchange would be so disastrous that neither the U.S. nor the Soviet Union would be willing to risk such a conflagration.

"However, the illusion of Mutual Assured Destruction has blinded U.S. policy makers to the need for a potent defensive system. Consider the strategic impact of a workable Soviet defensive system capable of knocking out our ICBM's. The entire relationship changes. We would, literally, be at their mercy, vulnerable to attack by virtue of being unable to retaliate. The MAD doctrine depends on two cancelable forces. A working defense system makes MAD an unacceptable and unworkable premise.

"Our top military priority must be to accelerate the development of a modern defensive weapon—a space-based laser system that could destroy ballistic missiles launched from anywhere in the world. The Soviet Union has already outpaced us in their commitment to laser research, and it's only our greater technology and resources which have thus far maintained our superiority.

"The Shuttle program gives us an access to space undreamed of but a few years ago. Manned missions can fly again and again to support any goal we have the courage to attempt. But how can we feel truly safe without a concurrent military presence which guards our country and protects its investment?

"Again I stress the importance of lasers as primarily defensive weapons. They are not to be targeted on cities or people, but only on offensive weapons themselves. Thus, they serve two vital strategic purposes. First, to bring us away from the brink of nuclear war. Second, in one fell swoop to reduce the Soviet Union's massive ICBM buildup in the last decade to an obsolete, antiquated system that must be scrapped because it is useless. We could end the arms race in such a way as to have never fired a single shot in offense or having taken a single human life.

"Realistically, it is unlikely that space-laser defenses will end war. But at least they hold the promise of removing nuclear missiles from the arena of war. Is that not alone sufficient reason to proceed with this project?

"I leave the choice of chemical laser or X ray or others to the scientists, the choice of delivery systems to the military, and the choice of command to Washington. For myself, I take on the task of promoting this best way to protect our people and give safety to this country.

"Alone among you, I have been to space. The next time I go, I do not wish to ask permission of a Soviet Orbital Control. Thank you."

Returning to his seat on the panel, Chris was pleased by the enthusiastic applause from most sections of the audience. But others, he noticed, seemed to take no pleasure at all in his words. He anticipated a difficult question period.

The panel was composed of senior officials from the nation's space program. Three were from NASA, which was responsible, like a giant contractor, for the overall efforts in space. Three were from the Air Force Space Division, in charge of the military aspects of the space program, chartered by the Department of Defense. And two were Jasons, an astrophysicist and a laser expert.

The chairman of the Jason's steering committee commenced the question period. Dr. Paul Jeffers was in his seventies, sharp-eyed and hawk-nosed, dean of the School of Physics at Rand University.

"The chair recognizes Dr. Arielle Simmons," he said, and one of the most striking women Chris had ever seen stood up.

"I have heard Senator Leyland's thoughts before, and again, I must reject them totally. If we turn space into the arena for yet another arms race, we do it the greatest disservice. I remember the days when nuclear power advocates said it would be a source of energy, a boon to all humankind. Does anyone doubt the destructive power of Three Mile Island or multi-warhead ICBM's? What great promise, other than military, does nuclear power now serve, and look what the absurd arms race has done to both the U.S. and Russia. Now you propose defensive laser weapons. I tell you it will end in the same ugly way—a laser race in the sky and not one step closer to disarmament; secrecy and not openness; fear and not progress. We must oppose that kind of thinking here and now."

Dr. Jeffers turned to Chris for his response, but one of the generals, a burly man named Rogers, broke in, "All the idealistic wishing in the world is not going to change the fact of a hostile Soviet Union and its territorial aims. In the face of potential aggression we must be prepared to respond. I couldn't agree with the senator more. We have the capability to defend ourselves and our satellites. We must use it. I can understand your ideals but more important is the need for what works. Reality is the issue here, not idealism or romance."

Chris felt an unfamiliar tightness in his chest as he watched the emotions play over Arielle Simmons' face. Her voice was crisp and sure and her intelligent brown eyes blazed in a sensual face. Her impact on him was dramatic and unsettling. He leaned forward to his microphone.

"If I may be allowed to respond to Dr. Simmons . . ." He paused and the general sat back truculently in his chair. "I believe that the United States has lost the very commitment to idealism of which you speak. And perhaps the only way in which we differ is in our ideas of which ideals logically must come first."

"Your stated ideals are more arms and more secrecy," retorted Simmons.

"I think my ideals are peace and security and a climate in which we can grow and mature as a nation. I have found the strongest people to be the most compassionate. Only the weak seek to dominate others, perhaps to prevent their own victimization. I don't know, but I don't want to see the U.S. in that position, either dictating to others or allowing others to dictate to us," Chris said evenly.

"So we put up lasers and tell the Russians what to fly and what not to. I don't see that as compassion, Senator. I see that as a threat to which the Russians will have to respond. Crises escalate crises. And what new means are developed to counter lasers? Biological warfare? Weather wars?"

"You people at NASA are in a dream world where everybody is nice and helpful and logically kind," protested General Rogers, exasperated by the discussion. "Your launch sites aren't secure from attack; you open your data banks to anyone who asks; and the climate you create is wide open for foreign penetration. You just won't understand or appreciate military concerns."

"And you use top secret clearances to surround yourselves with mystique and protect yourself from public scrutiny," Simmons shot back. "Space is for the good of the people, not for the tin soldiers."

"Perhaps, in our infancy, we still need some people to be soldiers," Chris offered to ease the tensions and find some bridge between them.

But Simmons shot him a glance of pure hatred. Distracted, Chris tried to put her out of his mind as the conference continued. But he watched her for the rest of the discussion.

"Ladies and gentlemen," Dr. Jeffers announced at the end of the afternoon. "Dinner is at eight o'clock this evening. The conference on laser propagation is scheduled for tomorrow morning. Tomorrow evening is the conference on satellite command-and-control systems. Thank you and good day."

Three hundred miles off the California coast Kasimov waited for the submarine's captain to bring him news of the speedboat's arrival.

For most of the voyage, Kasimov had kept to himself. He hardly spoke to Captain Prilenko and he took meals in his cabin. In the mess, seamen swapped rumors about him. The tight little world buzzed with conjecture.

There were few, Kasimov knew, who had any idea of who he was. How many Russians had studied the Greek myths well enough even to understand the derivation of the name he had chosen; Eris, the goddess of discord, the personification of strife?

His thoughts drifted back to Egypt in 1967, where he had been doing routine KGB intelligence work. His successes had begun to

mount up and nearly outweighed his insolent treatment of those superiors he felt to be incompetent.

He would never know which colonel had assigned him to move
into Israel ahead of the advancing Arab forces; but cut off in the desert when the Egyptian army was routed by the Israelis, he soon realized that he was on his own, stranded and lost; the support he had
been promised never arrived.

When his jeep ran out of fuel, he walked over the merciless sands.
When his water ran out, he crawled. Blistered and feverish from the
unyielding sun, he could not remember when consciousness had
slipped away and blind instinct had taken over.

He woke in the cool shade of a tent, a prepubescent girl mopping
his skin with a salve that numbed the pain. Falling in and out of
consciousness for days, he woke at last to three hawk-faced Arabs
staring at him, menace evident in the knives they brandished. Every
language he tried brought no response other than a shifting of those
deadly blades.

Wearying of him, two of the Arabs left the tent; the third stayed
to stand guard. Kasimov doubted that he would survive.

Frantic, he tried to think of a way to communicate. He was yet
too weak to escape, too tired to fight. The guard, meanwhile, flipped
his knife in the air, catching it by the hilt, a diversion on a boring
day.

Suddenly, Kasimov's hand shot out, plucking the knife away in
mid-flip. The Arab froze, a yell forming in his throat.

Kasimov's hand came up rapidly, cutting off the scream at
knifepoint. Expecting to die, the Arab watched warily as Kasimov
drew a six-pointed Star of David in the sand, spit on it, and drove
the knife into its center. Then, motioning that the knife could be
taken back, he lay back down and waited.

Slow comprehension formed on the Arab's face. He ran from the
tent, and Kasimov heard excited discussions in Arabic all around
him. Shortly, the two Arabs who had previously questioned him
came in, and he had to repeat his performance. Later, he was
brought food, and the girl returned to tend to his burns.

For six months he stayed with the tribe, learning their language,
healing, sharing their ways. They were from Palestine, they told him.
They had been driven out by the Israelis, and many of their men had

been killed. He was offered a bride, a young, sultry girl of thirteen, and he accepted the gift. When the men attacked the vulnerable Israeli outposts, he soon rode with them.

Valentin Kasimov became a terrorist.

For two years he raided and killed as fiercely as any of them. Soon he came to meet other terrorist groups, and the name of Eris became well known among those who dreamed of Israel's destruction. He met the oil-rich sheiks who supported the terrorists with money and guns. He met the politicians who, disclaiming all knowledge, paved their way and supplied information. He met the European businessmen, fat on oil profits, who gave shelter in France and Germany. The name of the goddess of discord served him well, for strife and pain followed him closely.

That day in 1971 he was sitting in the shade of an oasis with other leaders planning a raid when the Israeli jets roared out of the sky. In the minutes that followed, half of Kasimov's group died, their tents in flames. The animals bolted in terror. In the embers, Kasimov found his dead wife. She had been six months pregnant.

He made his way to Europe and formalized his contacts with the Red Brigade, Black September, and the Baader-Meinhoff network. His hatred of the West, Jews, and democracy burned inside him like a furnace.

The next year he returned to Moscow. Believed dead, he received a hero's welcome and a promotion to major. He activated a network of international terrorists, and Russian gold and guns flowed out to his agents in Europe and the Middle East. The KGB promoted him to colonel, and the hidden terrorist armies did his bidding as his reach grew to North and South America.

The captain's knock interrupted his reverie.

"The boat is here, Colonel. We are surfacing now."

"Very good, Captain. Tell the Libyans to prepare to depart. I will speak first to Catera. Have him brought here."

"Remember," said the captain, "longer than an hour and we risk detection. The American antisubmarine helicopters do not scan this far out, but we must be prepared to flee should radar spot anything approaching."

"I have other things to concern me, Captain. The ship is your responsibility," said Kasimov perfunctorily, watching the captain's departing back with disdain. In the desert, he thought, the captain and all his crew would never have survived. "Where has the Russian spirit gone?" he wondered.

An olive-dark, young Hispanic entered his cabin, eyes still adjusting to the light from the night's darkness.

"Eris?" he asked doubtfully. He had expected a younger man.

"I am Eris," Kasimov replied. "Now sit down and let me explain your task."

Jorge Catera, self-styled general of the Mexican-American People's Army, sat down and listened to the terrorist master.

The Imperial Ballroom had been converted to a banquet hall for the Jasons' conference. Long linen-covered tables sat in rows before the dais, and waiters flowed endlessly around with trays of steaming food. Picture windows looked out over the rolling green fairways, the ocean radiant in the distance.

"It's the crewcuts that make the civilian clothing look so ill-fitting," thought Chris to himself, surveying the military people scattered around the room. He took another bite of tender abalone and turned his attention back to the discussion at his table.

"In the final analysis, it's computer technology more than anything else that holds back the Russians," Dr. Jeffers was saying, "what we call command-and-control systems. Putting up a laser system is impossible without highly sophisticated tracking, control, and target differentiation facilities. Otherwise, you have a giant gun in the hands of an 'idiot' brain. No control at all. Useless."

"That's why we're so interested to see your reaction to the new system DARPA and our Air Force boys have come up with," said General Rogers.

"Defense Advanced Research Projects Agency," whispered Crowley behind his napkin, unnoticed by the others. Chris nodded unobtrusively, grateful for his continuing education.

"I'm eager to see it. We all are," said Jeffers enthusiastically.

"The specifications will be brought over from the Scripps Institute tomorrow afternoon. We think that coupled with present design demands it could make a space-based laser satellite feasible. We'd like your people to check it for snags and run some simulations," said the general.

"We'll take it up in symposium tomorrow," agreed Jeffers, and the talk rolled on.

Chris's attention caught the movement of Dr. Arielle Simmons through the noisy room. The dark print silk dress she wore accentuated the subtle curves of her trim, high-breasted body. She plays tennis or runs, Chris thought, watching her.

She was tall—five eight or nine, he estimated. Her hair was black and fell in soft waves from a widow's peak to just past her shoulders, and her skin was white and flawless. Her features flowed in sensual lines. Her mouth was full, her forehead was high, and her neck was long and thin.

Most of all, he had been impressed by the passionate energy which supported her beliefs. He had always seen strength as a virtue, more so when coupled with intelligence. Dr. Simmons piqued his interest. When he saw her leave the dining room for the garden, he excused himself, disregarding Crowley's raised eyebrow, and followed her into the sweet-smelling night.

Arielle walked out onto the golf course, striding rapidly toward the ocean, and he followed, watching her hair fan out from the wind. Chiding himself for such an adolescent pursuit, Chris slowed down and saw her disappear over the dunes to the beach.

Women had not played a great part in his life. It seemed to him that he had always been running, chasing some goal that had claimed his energy.

But in his mind there was the vision of a relationship. He had tried to define it, to decipher the complexities that the vision incorporated, but he wasn't sure what he wanted in a woman.

Overruling his hesitation, he walked down to the beach, the vision acting as compass and guide. In the moonlight he saw Arielle walking near the water, shoes in hand. Still heeding his internal impetus, he followed, narrowing the distance.

She stood in the low surf, staring out at the moon-silver ocean as he came up behind her.

"Excuse me, Dr. Simmons," he said hesitantly.

She turned quickly, like a startled deer, then saw who it was and turned back to the sea.

"I can't imagine why you've followed me, Senator Leyland," she said coldly, "as we have nothing to say to each other."

"If we started with hello, who knows where that might lead?" he said.

"It would lead nowhere."

"Your optimism is boundless," he laughed, unoffended.

Arielle turned, frowning. "Save the schoolboy charm for the masses, Senator. I'm unimpressed with cute from a man that Attila the Hun would vote for. Why are you here? A little come-on and the lady mellows; I don't need it, Senator."

"I followed you because I felt badly about this afternoon. I hoped we might talk about our differences. But your attitude is as bad as your manners," he said evenly.

"My attitude stems from indignation and my manners from conviction. I'm not some child to be shamed into silence."

"It's just that I can't get past you," he said in frustration. "Talking to you is like flying through a tunnel; there's nowhere to turn. I came out to talk peacefully and I end up fighting for my life. What does it take to get a truce?"

"Change your views."

"Without any discussion? That's not a truce, Doctor. That's abject surrender and damn unfair of you to demand."

"But there is no gray here. It's black-and-white to me," she said with less rancor. "On some issues it has to be either one way or the other. Abortion, bigotry, capital punishment; where's the midground? How do you compromise? The fetus is alive or it isn't; people are equal under the law or they aren't; capital punishment is murder or it isn't. I'm really not trying to be difficult. But my views on space are just as fixed as yours are. For us there is only conflict."

"Not necessarily. Perhaps our views are not mutually exclusive," he said, glad of the sudden change in her.

"I'm surprised you could suggest that," she said thoughtfully.

"Not so surprising," Chris grinned. "I haven't been a politician for very long. I flunked demagoguery class."

She laughed, and it was like payday: worth all the effort.

"If you'd like, we can talk tomorrow over lunch," she said, and her mouth creased into a half smile.

"I'd like that. Is twelve all right?"

The scream that was her answer almost knocked him over. For a second he was totally confused as she fell into the water, wondering just what he had said to produce such an odd reaction.

"Arielle . . . I . . . ." he started.

"My legs," she gasped, grabbing at them, her eyes wide with fear and pain. "My legs," she shrieked.

And then he saw the floating blob that had wrapped around her naked legs. The jellyfish squished in his hands as he tore frantically at it, the stinger tentacles burning his hands and arms.

Arielle thrashed like a woman possessed. In the black water, he pulled at the fish until it separated from her and he could drag her onto the sand, sobbing with pain and shock, coughing up swallowed water.

He ripped away her sodden skirt and piled damp, cool sand on her bare legs. Then he held her until the pain subsided and her ragged breathing cleared. For a moment, she yielded against him and warmth spread through him. Then she stiffened. "Go away. Please, go away," she moaned, pushing at him, desperate to untangle.

"But . . . I'm sorry . . . I only . . ." Chris sputtered, confused. But he now held a stone. Releasing her, he tried to help Arielle to stand.

"I'm fine, really," she protested. "Just leave me here. Please do as I say. Just go. Go, damn you!"

Bewildered and hurt, Chris walked away. Behind him he could hear her crying as he stumbled back to the inn.

Arielle lay on the beach, hot embarrassment surging through her. The pain caused warm tears to course down her cheeks, and she bit her lips in deep self-loathing.

She knew that he wouldn't understand, couldn't understand what had taken place inside her. How the pain had awakened that part of her she feared most, the part she had had to deny. For a moment their bodies had touched while he held her. She had felt the sweet, wet warmth begin between her legs.

She fought a familiar battle for control, hands dug deeply into the damp sand, clenching hooks to anchor her. Bursts of heat traveled outward from her center and her brain was clouded with fog and fever.

Finally, she achieved a kind of victory in the struggle. The heat abated. Her breathing stilled. The wind and spray began to cool her skin.

Then, for a long while, she lay silent and alone on the dark, wet sand.

2

Though most of the next day was spent in discussions or on panels, Chris found himself unable to concentrate on the conference. Confusion about Arielle Simmons was foremost in his mind.

He looked for her quietly all afternoon when she failed to show up for lunch. But by the evening, he decided to give up. Now, lying in bed, shirt and pants flung carelessly over a chair, he reviewed the previous night for the hundredth time and still could not figure out what he had done to provoke her violent rejection. His hands and arms still stung slightly from the jellyfish. And he had only held her in the most fraternal, soothing way. Fatigued by the day, he drifted off into sleep, his questions unanswerable at one in the morning.

The old Ford van rumbled up Highway 5 and crossed over to Torrey Pines Road, its bald tires and ancient suspension squealing and creaking all the way. The woman who drove, called only Perez by her compatriots, was plump and dark haired, and she hung onto every word "General" Catera spoke as if each one promised to unravel the secrets of the universe.

In the rear of the van, six more men and women listened in silence. Each was armed, each was committed, and each one had a different motivation for hating the United States. Their rage bonded them together in an explosive alliance.

Eris had lit the fuse and provided the target.

General Catera again recited their assignments. He did so because he was nervous. The three Libyans Eris had recruited for the raid made him nervous. In a test of authority, he was not sure they would obey him. But Eris had said they had their own responsibilities, and Catera had little choice but to let it be so.

Half a mile from the inn, they parked the van and prepared. Perez would wait until they signaled and then come to get them at the pickup point.

Dressed in jeans and work shirts, sneakers and bandanas, the silent army checked its weapons and moved off toward the inn.

Usually a light sleeper, Chris woke immediately at the first ring of the telephone and glanced at the clock. It was 3 A.M.

"Senator Leyland?"

"Speaking."

"This is Arielle Simmons. I'm sorry to bother you but I thought . . . I wondered . . . if we could speak. I know it's late but . . ."

"In the garden in ten minutes," he said quickly. "Okay?"

"That will be fine." She hung up.

Chris bolted out of bed as if stung by a cattle prod. Amused by his own excitement, he ran a hand through his hair and threw some cold water on his face. Slipping into a shirt, jeans, and sneakers, he left the inn, feeling like a schoolboy meeting a girlfriend for a midnight rendezvous.

Arielle sat quietly on a stone bench amidst the trimmed hedges and giant jade trees. It was hard for her to be there, harder still to forget the previous night. He had ripped the animal from her at some considerable risk to himself, she knew. Her own legs still smarted, and she wore a gray cotton sweatsuit because it didn't chafe her skin. Her reaction had not been his fault; although she could not explain further, her dignity demanded that she at least thank him before leaving.

"Hello, Arielle," Chris said, sitting down beside her.

The familiarity disturbed her, but she had come to apologize, not to argue.

"Good evening, Senator. Thank you for coming."

"Are you feeling all right? I'm sorry about last night," he said. "You were hurt badly, and I must have said or done something to upset you. I'm sorry if I did."

"On the contrary, Senator . . ."

"Chris, please," he interrupted.

"On the contrary . . . Chris," she said, but it was still formal. "I wanted to thank you for helping me last night. You did nothing wrong, and I owe you a great deal. I was," she shuddered, "taken by surprise and I panicked. You acted quickly and bravely, and I treated you poorly. I'm sorry." She stood up to leave.

"That's all?" he asked, just as confused as ever.

"That's all. I have to go now."

"Please," he protested. "Just a minute. I seem to be at a total loss whenever we speak. Couldn't we just talk for a while? You moved into my life like a hurricane, and now you want to leave like a ghost. You make no sense to me."

"I don't have to make sense to you," she said stiffly.

"Not if you make sense to you," he agreed.

"That's rare enough," she said, and for the first time he realized that her anger was not all reserved for him, but in part, for herself. He sensed, however, that her mood was too fragile for him to share that insight.

"Please, sit down," he asked her. "I know this whole thing is crazy. We've had politics and jellyfish, gardens and 3-A.M. phone calls. Any minute I expect a small riot."

Her smile was brief, but it was there, and he was thrilled when she sat back down.

"What possible motive could you have for wanting to know me?" she asked suspiciously.

"Motive?" He snorted. "I'm really Chris Leyland's communist twin brother, and I want you to swim to China with me."

"Don't make fun of me," she warned, tensing again.

"I'm not, really," he said, chastened. "But it's just that I'm as unsure at this moment as you are. Couldn't it just be that you've upset my equilibrium and I'd like to get to know you better? Or that you're a brilliant, beautiful woman who strikes a chord somewhere inside me. I don't know. Not yet, anyway. I don't have enough to go on."

"I don't trust you," she said flatly.

"Correction, Arielle. I'm just one of the group. You don't trust anybody."

He waited for the explosion he expected to occur, but she absorbed the statement dispassionately.

"You know," she observed, "you don't fit the soldier mold I'm used to."

"Soldiers love the military. Pilots love the sky. There's a big difference. Politics aside," he said hastily, "you can understand commitment to task. For me, flying was everything. I was alive in the air in a way it's hard to communicate. No boundaries, I suppose. And the Shuttle was the ultimate. There's no other craft in the world that can do what *Constitution* can. To be part of it meant, well . . . everything."

"And yet you gave it up. Solely because of your brother's death?"

"I'm not that selfless, Arielle. There's always self-interest involved even in the hardest of sacrifices. It would have been years before I got another flight, and I was offered a pass into the Senate, the most exclusive club in the country. Now, I'm trying to earn my wings all over again, to make a difference in a different way.

"When you look at me, I think that you typecast me in a role that I don't deserve. I believe defense is a rational issue to discuss. And the military is not just a group of scheming psychotics aching to pull the trigger. There are bright, dedicated people in that profession as there are in doctoring, lawyering, or garbage collecting. Not all, surely, but that's true everywhere. Unfortunately, people get polarized by politics, and we forget that everybody is human and just as uncertain as we are. There are good people and bad people, but you can't tell which is which from their uniform, whether that's jeans or suits or dress blues."

Arielle sat quietly for a while, absorbing his words.

"You scare me when you try and reach inside me with that way you have. No, don't protest. You know what I mean, Chris. You don't push or grab at me but you . . . address my feelings, even when I don't want you to. It reminds me I have them and that's not good for me.

"You want me to see you, truly see the person that you are. Can you understand that I can't meet that kind of challenge? That the past pulls me up short like a brick wall and that I can't afford to share that way. I have my work, and I'm tops at it. It's always been enough for me. It has to be."

"Work's not enough for anyone," Chris said gently, wanting to pursue but knowing he could not.

In the quiet of the garden, the wind's rustle was faint and mild and the susurration of the night insects soft. Almost all the lights of the inn were out and Chris watched a lone sentry wandering past them down on the high dunes, silhouetted by the glow of false dawn in the sky beyond.

He would have missed it had he not been looking right at the guard, a few hundred yards away. But suddenly there was a brief, pointed flash and the sentry disappeared from view as if he had jumped.

"Arielle," he said in a whisper, "I think I just saw the flash of gunfire and a guard fall. I don't know what it means, but I want to look. Will you stay here?"

"No chance," she hissed back, and knowing how useless argument would be, he moved off, crouched and silent, Arielle behind him.

Wriggling over the crest of the dunes, they saw the fallen guard on the sand below them. Bent over him was a man in jeans with a silenced automatic rifle.

"We are under attack," she whispered simply, and he marveled at this no-nonsense woman. "We have to wake the others," she continued, "and call the police. I'll do the first and you the second. Go."

Chris moved to go, but suddenly the dune crumbled and they fell headlong toward the beach. He had time only to realize that they were falling as Arielle's involuntary yelp alerted the gunman who turned and fired in one startled motion.

Chris saw the flash of fire and dove as he fell. Rolling faster than the terrorist had anticipated, his combat-trained reflexes caused his feet to come up together and he slammed into the man, knocking him sprawling and throwing the gun from his hands.

The terrorist leaped up, his face transformed by fury, a knife in his right hand, slashing at Chris's face.

Chris sidestepped and caught the terrorist's wrist with his right hand in mid-swing, twisted with the motion, and smashed his left fist into the man's elbow. It broke with an audible snap. Still holding the wrist, Chris drove his foot into the man's rib cage and the terrorist went down in a heap.

He turned frantically, looking for Arielle, but she stood calmly, some ten feet away, holding the rifle. He held out his hand, and she gave it to him.

"There's very little time," he said urgently. "Would you have used this?"

She nodded tightly.

"Good," he said evenly. "But we may not have to. Help me here."

Minutes later, the terrorist was buried up to his neck in tightly packed sand. His mouth was gagged with a strip of cloth torn from his shirt, his hands tied to his sides. He was trapped by the weight of the sand and would be unable to free himself when he awoke or even to cry out.

They scrambled up the beach, over the dunes and back toward the inn. At the garden he stopped, senses alert for the slightest noise.

"I couldn't find the guard's radio on the beach. We don't know how many of the guards are left or if the inn's phone lines are cut. I'll try to call from inside, but you get to those houses on the other side of the highway and make the call just to be sure."

Without question, she moved off into the night. He had wanted to say . . . but she was gone.

He surveyed the inn. It was quiet yet, and he didn't know how many terrorists were on the grounds. He looked at the sky. There was less than an hour till dawn.

He crept slowly into the inn. The main lobby with its modern couches and huge freestanding fireplace was deserted. Behind the front desk, he found the night manager, a hole above his heart. The phones were just as dead.

A door opened to his right, and he crouched behind the counter. Three men, Arabs, he noted, passed quickly by him. They had a different look than the man on the beach. Something in him guessed *professionals*.

The Arabs disappeared down a corridor. He let them go, not daring to begin a firefight while so many slept unaware. It was five minutes since Arielle had gone. Ten more to the houses, he estimated. Another ten or twenty for the police to arrive. He needed half an hour. It could make the difference.

Crowley answered his door sleepily at the insistent knocking. Chris pushed his way in and spoke intently to his shocked friend.

"Tom. There's no time to explain, but the CIA guards are probably dead, and the inn's been infiltrated by some kind of terrorist group. I'm going to start a diversion on the main floor, and when I do, I want you to rouse everybody you can. The military people should have arms. Tell them to take over the upper floors if they can and work down to close up behind me in the lobby. These men are armed and dangerous. Make sure they understand that. Give me five minutes to get back down." He glanced at his watch. "Go at five-fifteen."

There was no time to argue so Chris left Crowley hurriedly dressing and moved cautiously down the fire stairs.

He heard voices on the first landing. Low, rapid-fire Spanish drifted up to him as he stalked down the steps. Straining, he could just see a man and a woman, dressed like the man he had killed, unloading explosive devices.

He underestimated their speed when he bounded down the staircase, rifle firing steadily. He killed the man as he turned, catching him high in the chest with his first burst, but the woman spun and her rifle spat flame. The first shot tore into his left shoulder, ramming him back on the stairs. But it saved his life, the other bullets passing over his head. Rolling, he fired again, and the woman fell, blood blossoming at her middle. Then, silence again.

He picked himself up, ripped off the woman's bandana and wadded it up against the bullet's entry hole. The shoulder was already stiffening up, and he fought off the dizziness of shock.

The main lobby was still deserted. Staggering across the room, the bright red fire-alarm box was like a beacon to his fuzzy senses. He reversed the gun, smashed the window and pulled the lever. Then all hell broke loose.

Bells went off all over the building. In the lobby they were deafening. He shook his head to clear it from pain and almost passed out. His blood soaked through the makeshift bandage and flowed down his side. He swayed dangerously.

Bullets blasted into the wall over his head, and he dove behind the twin-chimneyed fireplace. More shots pinged off its copper hood. From the upper floors, he heard yells and the thunder of running feet. He couldn't locate his attacker, and pinned down, his back to the open doors, he was an exposed target. Another fusillade of shots sent a spray of ash from the fireplace into his face.

Breathing heavily, fighting to stay conscious, he lay in wait.

The Libyans heard the alarm bells and knew at once that Catera's raid would fail. They didn't care at all. Catera and his band were a diversion, nothing more; their deaths were preordained. The Libyans were professionals, hand picked as boys by Qaddafi's CIA-trained agents and trained by the KGB at a camp outside Tripoli. Their only target was room 100.

The first man shot the lock on the door, the second kicked it open, and the third tossed in the stun grenade.

General Rogers and his aide were blinded by the intense light and sound which paralyzed their muscles. They died in a rain of automatic weapons fire, the look of disbelief on their faces frozen forever.

The Libyans found the general's briefcase, opened it, and satisfied that they had the documents they had come for, left the room, their incendiary grenades blasting it into flames. The entire operation had taken less than three minutes. In another ninety seconds, they were outside the inn, heading for the beach and the waiting speedboat.

A flash of color crossed his clouded vision, and Chris fired but missed. Even if the clip had been full when he began, he knew he had few rounds left. People were nearing the lobby as Crowley and the fire alarm emptied the inn. From upstairs, he could hear staccato bursts from automatic rifles and the return fire of Army .45s.

Suddenly, the room was filled with a stampede of people trying to get out. The terrorist's rifle fired, and Chris saw Dr. Jeffers spin around and fall, crashing into the panicked mob, which surged back into the corridor.

Slithering around the fireplace, he sought the terrorist with a fierce hatred that pumped energy into his body. An explosion in the far dining room sent sprays of plaster from the ceiling down on the lobby, and the crackle of fire and the smell of smoke wafted in.

Someone screamed, and the people surged into the lobby. Again the terrorist's weapon barked into life and more people fell, some finally reaching the exit doors. Chris spotted Crowley in the corridor and knew that he would be dead if he entered the lobby. He sprang up, rifle firing, and the terrorist leaped out to kill him.

Chris's gun clicked empty as he dove for the man suddenly before him, and he swung the empty rifle like a club, missing the terrorist but knocking away the rifle.

There was nothing in his mind but an all-encompassing rage as his hands found Catera's throat. Catera's hands clawed at his eyes and his knee knifed up into Chris's abdomen.

A black curtainlike fog dropped over Chris's eyes as he forced strength into his arms. Pressing, gripping. Blood flowed from his wound and soaked them. Catera's breathing grew hoarse and his chest heaved as he fought to stay alive. Chris's hands locked deeper into Catera's neck, the windpipe ribbed and soft under his thumbs.

Somewhere there were people yelling and sirens sounding far away. Catera died with a hissing rattle, and Chris Leyland slid unaware down a long, quiet tunnel where there was no pain and no death, and peace waited in the blackness.

3

Brendan Connors had not had a good morning. The UN peace-keeping force in the buffer zone between north and south Afghanistan was in danger of collapsing without more U.S. support. The Russian equivalent of Viet Nam was heating up. China's designs on Mongolia were becoming obvious; the morning's Prophet photos showed a buildup of Chinese infantry in the area. And the Libya/Syria/North Lebanese States Coalition was demanding still another OPEC price raise.

Every major newspaper from New York to Los Angeles carried the terrorist attack on the Jasons' conference as front page news, the stories screaming for explanations and accountability. So earlier that morning, Connors had told his secretary to change the setting of Monday's lunch from the Roosevelt Room to the Cabinet Room, signaling that business had ascended over pleasure on the agenda.

He strode down the West Wing corridor, loosening his tie, remembering his doctor's imbecilic admonition to relax.

The Cabinet Room was dominated by a long, oval mahogany table surrounded by dark brown leather chairs. Brass plaques with the names of Cabinet members adorned each chair's back. The green-and-gold carpet, matching draperies, brass chandelier and sconces added to the formality, and Connors saw that it had the intended impact on the waiting group. "Fine," he thought; "they're nervous as hell."

"I want a complete briefing," he said without preamble, directing his attention to Terrence Clancy, "on the Jason matter."

Clancy pushed a duplicate of his report across the table.

"It's all there, Mr. President," he said, outlining the main items verbally. When he finished, Connors sat smoldering, shaking his head in disbelief.

"We've got a top-secret conference, guarded by CIA, with the most important scientific and military people in the country, and some group of amateur crazies manages to break through security, disrupt the conference, kill Jasons and almost burn the place down . . . That's what you're telling me? How the hell could this happen?" he thundered angrily.

"We are investigating, sir," said Clancy evenly.

"Don't bullshit me, Terry. I don't want investigations that drag on till they're overshadowed by the next crisis. I want answers within the next forty-eight hours. The press on this is going to cost me ten points in the polls. Do whatever you have to."

"I understand, Mr. President."

"And where's fucking CIA in all of this?" Connors continued. "The conference was their responsibility. Who screwed up? I swear I'm going to have his ass."

Barbara Reynolds had been waiting for the question. The report she held in her hands was going to be a bombshell, and she wanted maximum effect when she presented it. In the uncomfortable silence that greeted the president's last question, her first words caught everyone's attention.

"Mr. President," she said firmly, "we have a leak in CIA."

Connors' eyes narrowed but she pressed on. She had wanted the stage to be hers alone, and now she held it.

"I've completed a study of CIA operations over the last ten years, and it leads me to the inescapable conclusion that there exists in CIA a highly placed executive officer who is a deep-cover Soviet mole.

"It is also my opinion that this mole is controlled by a Soviet agent who uses international terrorism to achieve his ends. We have had persistent rumors of this hypothetical agent and his code name, Eris, which have been consistently denied by CIA. I believe Eris is real."

"I'm still listening," Connors said guardedly. "Go on."

"As for the mole, in 1977 a CIA spy in the Kremlin, Trianon, was exposed by the KGB within months of his starting work for us. Before that, from 1965 to 1977, CIA had failed to establish a single productive mole in the Soviet Union. In 1978, a still undiscovered source leaked top-secret plans for the KH-11 satellite, one of Prophet's precursors, to the KGB. The presence of a Soviet mole, highly placed within CIA, is the only possible explanation for these kinds of events. Read, gentlemen. It's all in my report."

"I've heard rumors of this Eris for some time, especially in the Middle East," said Powell reflectively. "As far back as the early seventies. But no one has been able to prove he's more than a myth."

"Judge for yourself, Harold," said Reynolds. "We have the two latest instances of CIA failure, in Rome and La Jolla, both at the hands of terrorists who had information which could only have come from the CIA itself. The computers say the mode of operation fits our composite of Eris, and the operations themselves could not have been put together without some kind of hostile intelligence service's aid. In my mind, that means KGB."

"It's not news," Connors offered, "that the Soviet Union finances terrorists all over the world. But you believe that this Eris is vested with that control?"

"I do," agreed Reynolds, "and furthermore, that this pattern of activity holds a purpose which is decidedly not in our best interests."

"The possibility of a mole is my concern," said Parienne. "I've said before that the Soviets are up to something, but finding the mole has to be our first priority."

"We're faced with a classic problem, though," said Connors. "If the search for the mole is a failure, it will become a demoralizing witch hunt. If it's successful, it destroys our credibility, both past and present. I am certainly open to suggestions."

"We can't use any CIA people," Clancy said flatly. "That's obvious. How does NSA feel about conducting the investigation?"

"No, thank you," said Reynolds quickly. "If you use any branch to investigate any other branch, you're going to start the biggest scramble for power in history and make the whole thing political. It has to be someone outside of intelligence."

"Catch twenty-two," muttered Powell. "You've just ruled out our entire investigative apparatus."

"I think that there is a way out of this," said Parienne, organizing his thoughts. "If, as Barbara suggests, the death of Arthur Leyland and the attack on the Jasons' conference were politically motivated and run by the same man, Eris, then there's another person who is connected to both events. He's beyond reproach, holds high office, already sits on the intelligence committee, and this investigation could be seen as within his purview."

Parienne could see it in their faces, the idea catching on. Reynolds liked it, he caught her nod, and the president's furrowed brow indicated he was giving it serious consideration. Powell spoke openly in support.

"And let's not forget that the man is a national hero, the likes of which we haven't seen since John Glenn in the Kennedy days. Witnesses report that he single-handedly prevented a massacre at the conference. Use Leyland in two ways. Praise him and you take the sting away from CIA's failure, and if he'll cooperate, you have an investigator who throws back responsibility on the Senate and away from the executive branch. I must say, Mr. President, Jim's choice is damn near brilliant."

"But will he do it?" asked Clancy. "We have no leverage at all on him. He's too new. And Tom Crowley protects him like a mother hen. He'll know there's no political advantage in this for his boy."

"I don't think it will matter," said the president thoughtfully. "We'll have to give him something, I'm sure. But politics will not be the governing factor."

Connors walked over to the window and gazed reflectively out over the Rose Garden beyond, noting the first spring flowers blooming in profusion.

"He's been a combat flier, a NASA astronaut, and yesterday he risked his life rather than get his ass out of danger."

Connors turned back to the table, and the others could see traces of the predator that lurked beneath his polished political veneer.

"For Chris Leyland," he said with finality, "this is going to be purely personal."

Chris heard sounds first, but they were meaningless and seemed to be coming from far away. Slowly, the dreamlike state began to evaporate as consciousness returned.

Tom Crowley swam into focus standing expectantly over the bed, and next to him, a white-coated doctor stared contentedly at a bank of machines that bleeped and hummed.

"Welcome back," grinned Crowley broadly as the doctor stooped to examine his patient.

Chris began to speak but memory returned in a sudden flash, and the night at Torrey Pines raced through his mind.

"Just relax, Senator Leyland," cautioned the doctor. "You've had one serious trauma and a collection of minor injuries. You're going to feel like you crash landed for a while."

"Is Arielle okay?" Chris demanded of Crowley, ignoring the doctor's frown.

"She's fine, Chris. Just fine. Let the doctor examine you, and I'll fill you in on everything when he's done."

Suffering the examination impatiently, Chris reflected on the previous night. He remembered it all, up to the last moments of fighting in the lobby. Then, nothing but blackness.

The doctor left, seemingly satisfied, and promised to return later. Chris was restive in bed, but the dressings on his shoulder and head made movement difficult and painful.

Crowley tossed a stack of newspapers to him.

"It seems you've made the headlines again, Chris. According to the media, you're the greatest thing since sliced bread. Some very grateful Jasons didn't hurt that image any, either. Especially one Dr. Simmons."

"Who were they, Tom, and what did they want?"

"Apparently, they were a terrorist group led by a guy named Jorge Catera. He fancied himself general of the Mexican-American People's Army. It's all in the police report which you can see later.

"No one is certain yet what they wanted, but we're all hoping that, thanks to you, they didn't get it. We won't know for a while because some parts of the inn went up in flames, and all the rubble has to be sifted through. Rogers is dead. And Jeffers."

"How many were there?"

"Seven, including Catera, died at the inn. There was a driver who the police picked up waiting in a van."

"I remember three Arabs," said Chris, unsure of the memory. "At least, I think I do."

"No one of that description was found in the area or reported by anyone else."

Crowley watched Chris closely. There was something troubling him. His reaction didn't fit a man who had saved so many lives and for whom the public's reaction was so strong.

"What's eating you, Chris? No, don't shrug me off. I know it's something or I wouldn't be asking."

It took a while for Chris to answer.

"Have you ever killed anyone, Tom?" he asked at last. "I mean, not just thought about it or wished it would happen, but have you yourself pulled the trigger and seen someone die or choked the life out of someone and felt them die under your hands?"

"No. But you were a soldier. I'd have thought . . ."

"Not like this, Tom. And even so, that only adds to the difficulty I have with it. Everyone can yell hero as often as they like. But I killed four people. And now I have to live with it."

"You miserable son of a bitch," Crowley sputtered, astonishing his friend. "You want sympathy? Compassion? Well, you can stick that crap, pal, along with any other philosophy you care to indulge in. When those bastards invaded the inn, what the hell do you think they wanted? Forget about national security interests, forget about the theft of people's life's work; I'm not going to play some semantic game about paper versus lives. They tried to kill me, damn it. *Me!* And I take that personally. If you want to sit here and weigh the balance between some assassin and myself and who should die and what's your responsibility, you can do that. For myself, the man who took on Catera barehanded to save my ass has more meaning than all that inner-conflict bullshit. There isn't a person who's alive today because of you who doesn't feel that way. And if those aren't your priorities, then I have nothing else to say. I quit."

"Please, Tom . . ."

"Don't 'please Tom' me, Senator. Either you have the balls to back up your priorities or you don't."

"Did you yell at Artie that way?" Chris asked, his face creasing into a rueful smile.

"When I had to," admitted Crowley, softening his glare somewhat.

"Then consider me properly chastised. But not before you understand my feelings. I'm not sorry that I fought, and killed, to protect something that was important to me. Given the same situation, I'd act the same way. But I am sorry that four people died, any people, and presumably died for something that they believed in, too. Tom, we can't relegate any human life to so simple an equation that we don't have to care about it. There's always a cost, for every ideal. I'm just trying to figure out what, and who, to pay."

Crowley was silent for a moment. Then, "If it's okay with you," he said, "I'd like my job back."

Chris laughed. "And here I was thinking that I went to all that trouble just to break in a new adviser."

"You are a miserable, insolent . . ."

The phone rang and Crowley broke off in mid-oath to answer it, his expression changing from amusement to bemusement as he listened.

"Yes . . . I understand. That will be fine," he said. "Eight o'clock. Very good. Goodbye."

"Who was that?" Chris asked sleepily.

"You're going to have a visitor," said Crowley excitedly. "That was the White House. The president's coming here to visit you at eight tonight. National coverage."

"That's fine, Tom," Chris said, pulling the covers up to his chin and yawning. "Find Arielle and tell her I'll call later. I'm going to get some sleep. All this talking . . ."

Amazed, Crowley watched him snoring peacefully. He shook his head, smiling, and went out to meet with the reporters.

Chris was lying comfortably in bed when Crowley called to tell him that the president had arrived. Connors had requested a private talk to begin with, and for Crowley to join them later. Chris agreed that would be fine, and seconds after he had hung up the phone, a pair of Secret Service agents were ushered into the room.

"Good evening, Senator," one said, the other already in the process of making sure the room was safe. They left a few minutes later, wishing him well, and a knock on the door preceded Connors' entrance.

"I'm glad to see that reports of your recovery weren't exaggerated. You look well, Senator Leyland."

"Thank you, Mr. President. It's very kind of you to come," Chris said, shaking the offered hand.

Connors moved a chair close to the bed and sat down easily.

"This is the first time we've met, Senator Leyland. I'd like to con-

gratulate you on your appointment to the Senate and tender my
deepest condolences on the loss of your brother."

"Thank you, sir. The telegram you sent six months ago meant a
great deal to my family."

"I was very fond of your brother," he said.

"Thank you for saying so, Mr. President. But Artie was a pain in
this administration's rear end. I'm probably regarded the same way.
Even so, I do appreciate your visit."

"You know, I served under your father for a time during the Second World War. He struck me as the same kind of candid son of a
bitch you are."

"I'm glad we've reached an understanding, sir," said Chris guile-
lessly.

Connors' belly laugh was long and hearty.

"That we have, Senator. That we have. I was wrong. You'll be a
bigger pain in the ass than your brother."

"One tries, sir. Call me Chris."

"You did one hell of a job yesterday, Chris. Sincerely, I do hope
you're feeling well."

"I am. If I can just duck the reporters, I'll be out of here tomorrow."

"That's a wrong move, if you don't mind some advice from an old
pro. Never dodge the newshounds when they're on your side. If you
do, they'll kill you when they're not. Accept the praise. It's probably
sewed up the next election for you."

"Advice accepted, thank you."

"Don't mention it. I'm just grateful you're too new at this to go
for my chair," he chuckled. "Today, there's no one in the country
who could beat you."

"With that in mind, you know," said Chris casually, "that if you
supported it, I could manage a larger appropriation for space in the
Senate."

"What kind of money are we talking?" asked Connors, his expression as unreadable as a professional card shark's.

"Another billion. Half to laser research and half to systems development."

"It's possible we could come to a deal. What's in it for me?"

"What do you want?" Chris asked.

Connors stood up and paced. When he turned back to Chris, his tone was deadly serious.

"I want you to find a Soviet spy in the CIA, Senator Leyland."

For ten minutes, Connors talked. He repeated almost word for word Barbara Reynolds' arguments, seeing doubt grow into conviction on Chris's face.

"You'll have direct access to the NSA chief, Barbara Reynolds, and your authority will come straight from me," Connors continued. "I'm giving you access equal only to mine. Anything you need will be handled by one of my special secretaries, twenty-four hours a day, anywhere in the world. Choose your own staff, spend what you need, but we must have that mole."

"And the mole leads us to Eris," Chris finished.

"That is our working premise," agreed Connors.

"There's something more you're not telling me," Chris said suspiciously. "What is it?"

"I'd rather hold off till I have your answer." Connors looked uncomfortable.

"You'll get no answer till I have all the facts," Chris pressed.

"Stalemate," Connors sighed. "But remember I didn't want to say this till after you'd decided. We believe that your brother's death in Rome and the attack here yesterday were both set up by Eris using information supplied by his mole. Eris is the probable killer of your brother and, if so, is equally responsible for almost having killed you, too."

Chris heard the words and knew what his answer would be and that all the analysis in the world would fail to change it. He could relegate the major tasks to his legislative aides, most of whom were far more able to work the Hill than he. Crowley would object, but in the end would see his position.

"I'll take the job," he said at last. "I want a briefing set up in Washington on Thursday. Will you arrange it? Also, I want the same clearance and a special assistant's ranking for Tom Crowley."

"Done. I'm in your debt, Chris," said Connors, rising to leave.

But Chris was lost in thought. Consequently, he missed the president's self-satisfied expression when he left for the press conference.

Chris was still thinking about what Connors had told him when Crowley came in.

"I don't know what you said to him, Chris," he said gleefully, "but Connors just gave a speech about you to the media that rivals the Gettysburg Address. You're national news again. Anybody who reads a paper or watches television knows your name and connects it with bravery and integrity. Do you have any idea what this kind of attention can do for your political goals, not to mention your career? You sure must have sweet-talked that bastard Connors. I would love to have heard it."

"Maybe you'd better sit down, Tom."

" 'Senator Leyland represents the highest ideals of the American ethic in his steadfast determination to uphold the ideals of freedom and liberty regardless of personal cost.' That's only one quote, Chris," he chortled, happily.

"I think we have to talk, Tom . . ."

"As soon as you're out of here, we'll set up a press conference, maybe do a *Meet the Press* and some exclusive interviews . . ."

"If I could break in here for just a moment . . ." Chris interrupted.

"Yes?"

In a few sentences, Chris outlined his conversation with Connors.

"And you bought that nonsense?" demanded Crowley, angrily.

"Put like that I hardly think . . ."

"You didn't think at all. This is the hottest moment of your young political life, and in the middle of it you're going to go running off to chase some phantom mole and some mythical Soviet spy? I can't believe it."

"I'm going after the man who killed my brother," Chris stated flatly.

"You're going to commit political suicide," retorted Crowley. "This mole is his problem, not yours."

"Artie was my brother. Not his."

"What did you get from Connors?"

"Tentative approval for another billion for laser defense, backed by the White House."

"It's not enough," said Crowley, somewhat mollified.

"It's more than we could get without him. You of all people should know that."

"You were out-manipulated by a pro. I sure as hell know that.

If this blows up, you're the scapegoat. He's dumped the whole affair on you. I won't have any part of it. You're on your own."

"I need you, Tom. I need your support and your political savvy. A couple of hours ago you called me every name in the book and told me that you took the whole thing personally. How in the hell can I do less?"

"I loved him, too, Chris. Don't forget that."

"Then help me," Chris asked.

"Well . . . maybe we can press Connors for another half billion. And a speed-up in the development timetable . . ."

"That would be fine, Tom."

"And you'll do the television interviews?"

"Absolutely."

"Then it seems I have little choice but to eat my own words and go along with you. Are you ready for the press? No. Don't you dare," grumbled Crowley, putting up a hand. "If you say wild horses, I'm going to strangle you."

4

The doctors urged Chris to stay another day in the hospital, but a date with Arielle at her family home outside San Diego and his own restive nature forced a showdown. In the end, he compromised with the doctors, settling for a shoulder harness that secured his arm to his side.

He chose to drive down the coastal highway rather than the faster freeways to the east, enjoying the rugged Pacific cliffs and the blue waters beyond. Also, speeding along the narrow road was exhilarating after the days in bed.

The Simmons home was a rambling white, Spanish-style ranch capped by a red tile roof. A palm-lined driveway led into a tiled courtyard and to a large, central atrium beyond, fenced off by a black, wrought-iron railing. Behind the house, a deep green lawn sloped gently to the ocean.

Arielle came out the front door as he turned off the engine.

"What is that thing?" she asked, pointing to the harness as he stepped gingerly from the car.

"It constrains the shoulder. My doctor had to have studied with the Marquis de Sade, and it's obvious the bastard never wore one."

Arielle chuckled. She wore a light jacket, white shorts, and sneakers, her hair brushed back and pulled into a bun.

"The water is beautiful in the evening. Would you like to go sailing?" she asked. "The wind is up, and my father's boat is moored right behind the house."

I don't know anything about sailing; but if you're willing to captain, I could be persuaded to crew," Chris said warily.

"No problem. Just remember that mutinies are still punishable by hanging," she said brightly, "and I don't take command lightly."

"Good. That's how I feel about drowning," he said sincerely.

The sailboat was twenty-five feet long and single-masted, with a cabin below deck that slept four. Rocking gently on the low waves, it looked sleek and eager to run.

"I'll respect your invalid status," said Arielle, starting up the small but noisy outboard engine, "so I'll do the casting off. Just hold that line steady, and we'll be out of here in a minute."

"The crew gratefully accepts your offer," he yelled back over the noise.

She threw off the lines that secured them to the dock and jumped back into the boat. Releasing the line Chris held, she lowered the propeller into the water, and they chugged away from the dock.

"Take this, would you, and steer straight out," she said, handing over the tiller.

Chris watched her move about the boat, securing lines and unfurling the main sail. That marvelous sense of her competency filled him again. Arielle was lean and fit, taut muscles showing when she stretched, all her motions strong and precise.

She finished raising the main sail and moved forward to fasten the jib. Running the lines back to the stern, she settled in beside him, retook the tiller, and shut off the engine.

The abrupt silence was broken only by the slapping of the water against the hull.

"I remember a cartoon when I was a kid," Chris said as the last echoes of the engine died away, "where somebody yells 'Quiet!' in two long syllables, in the middle of Manhattan, and suddenly everything stops dead."

"It's a nice moment when you turn the engine off," she agreed. "You almost forget how peaceful the world can be. On land, there's always a car going by, a radio blaring, or some loudmouth yelling. Here, just the water and an occasional gull."

She turned the boat, and Chris settled back against the cabin with a cushion wedged behind his shoulder. He was content to watch her, totally absorbed, as she sought the wind.

The boat reared up on its side and cut sharply across the waves as she caught a gust and it slapped the sails taut. Arielle's hair came undone as their speed increased, wisps of it whipping around her face, now flushed with exuberance.

"We're going to bring her about," she called over the wind. "I need your help. Release that line when I tell you—it holds the jib in place—but watch the boom. That's this beam perpendicular to the mast. It's going to swing over the boat so keep the hell out of its way."

"Release the jib, watch the boom," Chris repeated, hunching over the line. "Got it."

"Now," she commanded, "more . . . all the way . . ."

He released the line rapidly, and Arielle hauled the jib over.

"Very good," she complimented him. "Would you like to try it?"

"Wild horses, Arielle."

"Come again?"

"Sorry. It's an old family custom. Whenever we want something very badly, we say it. You know the expression, 'Wild horses couldn't keep me away.'"

"It's 'drag me away,' I think," she said.

"Think of it as poetic license and don't get so technical," he said, shifting the harness to a more comfortable position and taking the tiller in his strong right hand.

Immediately, the sails began to flap and their speed decreased. Chris looked chagrined.

Arielle explained the principles of sailing to him, and he was surprised to find it somewhat similar to flying. He looked to the flag flapping at the tip of the mast, judged the wind's direction, and steered according to her instructions.

For almost an hour they spoke rarely as Chris sailed, improving steadily. They came about several more times and soon had it down to a smooth process between them, commands unspoken but understood.

Only friends can sail well together, Chris thought happily, as they made the wind and the current work for them. Their efforts united into a common purpose; more speed, smoother sails, and the world narrowed down to the sea, the setting sun, and each other.

Arielle settled in beside him. He slowed the boat and put his arm around her in the chill evening air. He felt her stiffen but then deliberately will herself to relax. He kissed the top of her head and smelled the fragrance of her hair and the salt spray. She gave only the smallest of shrugs and then nestled a bit closer to him.

"I'd like someone to pour amber over us now, sort of capture the moment," he said contentedly.

"But I could be breaking some maritime law," she responded mock-seriously, "being too familiar with the crew on the high seas."

"That only pertains to wartime," he counseled.

"Where did you get your legal training?"

"Same place you got your captain's license."

"It's my boat," she reminded him, "so I'm the captain."

"That's fine. I'm a colonel. I outrank you," he gloated.

"Showoff." She laughed. "Don't you suffer from doubts like normal people?"

"All the time," he said seriously. "But I figure that no one can predict the future, so why try? Feel; then do. It works or it doesn't. But to sit around and ponder everything beforehand is foolish. It's running your life like a feasibility study."

"I think that's possible only because you like yourself," Arielle mused out loud.

"Maybe. But there's something even more important that comes first."

"Which is?"

"Forgiving yourself."

Chris realized he had unwittingly come close to whatever she held deep inside her by the look on her face, the instant of pain. Then it was gone.

"I do," he continued. "For all the screwing up I've done, all the mistakes I made, and whatever pain I've caused, I forgive me. I'm human. Leave perfection to the angels and move on."

"That's too easy," she protested. "Every killer in history probably felt that way. It's positively psychopathic."

"Stop being sophomoric. I'm not a killer or a madman. That's the whole point. I'm not going to convict myself of crimes I didn't commit or of grandiose hurts I wasn't responsible for. You're the one with the absolutes."

"Another definition of absolute is truth, Chris. What if there are morals and rules that are right and true? Then what?" she demanded.

"Then my hell will follow death, Arielle, and yours will precede it. All in all, I don't care to trade," he said truthfully.

"I wish I . . ."

"Don't wish," he whispered. "Stay with me, and whatever you're frightened of, we can handle together."

"I can't, Chris. I . . ."

"You can do anything if you want to badly enough."

"Let's go back, please," she said, pulling away.

"If you want to," Chris said helplessly, and he turned the boat toward home.

The house was warm when they entered it. Chris sank into an armchair in the living room which was pleasingly furnished in contemporary prints and pastels. Large floor-to-ceiling windows looked out at the sea behind him.

"Drink?" Arielle asked from the bar.

"Scotch, please."

She made the drinks and sat opposite him, her feet curled under her on the couch.

"It's a pretty house," he offered, opting for small talk.

"My parents bought it when they moved out here a few years ago from New York. My father heads the computer research division of Lockheed."

"I'm impressed. I know that you work for IBM and that you're an IBM Fellow, but I don't know much more than that."

"Most of my research is in systems integration and miniaturization. The computers that make the Shuttle fly are partly my design. And as for the Fellow part, that's nothing but a fancy title meaning that my time is my own, and I work only on projects which I choose."

"You like your independence," he observed.

"I couldn't function without it."

"Then you'll understand what I'm about to say. I can't function without certain things either. One of them is honesty. We do this push-me-pull-me back and forth every time we're together. Now we're stuck at a point somewhere beyond attraction but still short of a relationship, and it's bad for both of us. I'm tired of always pushing, coming at you, and running into walls. Let me in, Arielle. Or maybe it would be better if I go."

"What do you want from me?" she yelled. "Should I sit here and spill my guts like some kind of emotional child? Who are you to come pulling at my insides?"

"You know that's nonsense," he said sincerely. "If there really is something between us, then I want to explore it. If not, then tell me to go. But holding back makes me feel like an adolescent. Adults talk, Arielle. They don't hide from monsters in the dark. Maybe I shouldn't be trusted. But how the hell are you going to know that if you don't try?"

"You make it sound so simple," she said bitterly.

"It is simple. You're not the kind of person to put any stock in candlelight suppers and halfhearted attempts to get you into the sack. What is it that draws you close and then frightens you away?"

"You're like a fucking boy scout. So pure and so brave. The goddamned astronaut conquering hero. What I am . . . where I've been . . . How can I share that with you?" she demanded, tears in her eyes.

Chris shrugged out of the harness and sat next to her.

"Go away," she cried.

"No. Not anymore. If a tsunami comes roaring in at us, I'm not going. You can reject me if you like, but I'm sure as hell not going to be the one to reject you."

"You will. You'll have to."

He looked directly into her eyes and held her gaze. The sun had almost set, and the room was darker. He sat, not reaching out, watching her tears glisten when they caught the fading light.

"Tell me," he urged softly.

Finally, she nodded slowly, head bowed, and her hands tangled tightly in her hair.

"I was . . . a very smart little girl," she began, her voice small and filled with pain. "The brilliant daughter of a famous scientist. Mathematical aptitude shows up early. Did you know that? If it isn't active by twelve years of age, it's assumed you don't really have it. I was studying calculus by the time I was eight. I went to special schools, took special classes; and when I wasn't studying, I was spending time with my father in his lab.

"Now don't misunderstand me. I *wasn't* unhappy. I had my work, supportive parents, and a list of honors as long as your arm. I just didn't think much about anything else. The very few dates I accepted were disasters, wrestling around in backseats with a pimply boy groping at my breasts, feeling prudish if I didn't let him and bored if I did. Believe me, I was just as happy without it.

"I was in graduate school at twenty, before I really took a look around me. The riots and marches and drug subculture in the early seventies hadn't held any fascination for me, but suddenly I wanted to get more involved. I started to come out of my shell. It wasn't hard. I know I'm attractive, and there was a long line of hairy students and professors newly discovering their hormones who were waiting to play guru. I had still never slept with a man."

She drew in a long, raspy breath, her body rigid from the pressure of her narrative. Chris felt her summon up the will to continue.

"There was a party, one of those gatherings of grad students where everyone just gets high and sits around being erudite. Maybe ten of us all together, smoking pot, drinking wine, and eating lousy cheese in a house off-campus.

"I remember it getting stuffy from all the smoke. I started to sweat. Sounds were also doing odd things. I opened a window to get some air. My skin felt funny, like plastic, smooth, but with no real feeling. I didn't know, Chris, that someone had put barbiturates in the wine till much later, but at that moment I don't think I would have cared if I had. I knew nothing about seconals and tuanols and quaaludes. All I did know was that for the first time in my life I was lighter than air, and I wasn't watching my every behavior, and I was free to laugh and sing and fall into laps and tease and play and it was glorious.

"The first man to touch me sent shocks up my spine. I was like an infant captivated by the newness. The air on my bare skin was cool, and the faces that grinned up at me were warm and sweet with approval. He took me in front of everyone, there on the floor. I remember screaming when the first orgasm hit, and I thought I would die from such pleasure. I yelled like a baby when he couldn't get hard again, yelled for the next one to give it to me. And then the next. The other girls must have left sometime in the night because I woke up later with only the men around me. The worst part was that I remembered every detail as if I had watched it. Except that it had happened to me."

She twisted her hair in her hands, curled on the couch as if seeking a second womb. Still, Chris held back.

"I went home and threw up. Then I showered again and again. I tried to excuse myself, blame it on the drugs. I succeeded partially. It was a once-in-a-lifetime mistake. Forget it, I said. So a few weeks later, I dated another man. I needed to try the whole thing straight. To start my life from that point forward. It was a catastrophe. We went to a motel, and I just couldn't respond. He told me not to worry about being frigid. I tried it again with a different man, and the result was the same. I couldn't turn off my mind. Couldn't relax. They hurt me . . ." She cried bitterly.

"I went back to drugs. Cocaine, speed, ups, downs, whatever I could get. There was always someone to help out a pretty lady. Just take this and lie down. And I did. I learned about pain, Chris, the kind I need to make it over. It's pain or drugs that make me release what I can't any other way. I have to be hurt. That's what happened on the beach the other night. The pain . . . started it, and I couldn't stop it. If you hadn't gone, I would have . . . I needed so much to . . . It won't stop once it starts. Please, Chris, I can't live with myself anymore. Just go away now. Go away and accept that I'm sick. I can't stop. All these years and I can't stop . . ."

His strong arms enfolded her, and she struck out blindly, flailing at his chest hysterically. Pain shot through his shoulder, but he ignored it, pulling her closer as she fought and scratched.

He covered her mouth with his and kissed her deeply. Her eyes were wild with fear, and he kissed them as well, forcibly, but with all the tenderness he possessed. Her struggles grew less intense as he pressed her body into his own, and his hands played across the bunched muscles of her back, stroking and soothing as she cried.

He cradled her in his arms and stood, lifting her as easily as a child. She clung to him, her arms tight around him, and her face buried in his neck as he carried her into the bedroom and placed her on the bed.

He undressed her slowly. Her blouse and bra came away in his hands, and he stroked down her long neck to her breasts. He placed his mouth on her flat stomach and licked upward slowly till he circled her hardening nipples with his tongue and a moan tore from her lips in spite of herself. He kissed her again and pulled off his shirt.

Her first touch was timid. She ran her fingers over the hair on his chest, hesitantly probing the hard muscles under his skin. Bolder, she cupped his face in her hands and drew him down to her, her lips warm and wet on his mouth and cheeks and eyes.

He saw her form unspoken questions, but he shook his head and stroked her hair and kissed her deeply again.

Arielle arched her back as he slid her shorts down her long, tan legs. When she was naked, he kissed her thighs, drawing them apart, and her fingers entwined in his hair, suddenly urging, insisting. He felt her hands at his belt and then he was naked, too, and his face brushed over the thick, coarse hairs of her pubic mound as her hands sought his skin.

Her nails raked the flesh of his back as he stroked the already opening petals of her sex. His tongue separated layer after layer, and he licked at the sides of her clitoris as it grew hard and engorged. Her buttocks strained upward, grinding into his slickly moist face.

She writhed against him, gasping and panting as his fingers probed her oily wet channel. She screamed when he raised her up and drove his tongue deep inside her. Her legs circled around his shoulders, and she clawed at her own sweating face.

When he entered her, his penis was a steel-cored shaft, and his chest crushed against her heaving breasts. Her arms pressed him to her, clutching in fevered madness.

"Oh yes . . . yes . . . more . . . yes," she cried as he stroked in and out again and again. Their mouths came together and his tongue sought hers, and she sucked on it and beat her fists into his sweat-drenched back.

He felt her tighten around him, and he drove deeper inside her. The pressure in his scrotum grew to an unbearably sweet agony, and his penis swelled against the slippery walls that held him viselike in their grip.

"Now," she yelled. "Now . . . Oh, now . . . Ohpleasegodnow . . ."

The first climax tore through her body as the inner chamber of her sex opened to receive the flood of his. Again and again her body hammered into climax as he came, groaning and panting, grinding into her hard and fast and over and over till they trembled in each other's arms, locked together, and the blood pounded in their heads, and the heat surrounded their bodies and they could, after a time, lie still.

"Chris?" she said later, calling him back to earth.

"I'm here, princess," he responded, rolling over to face her.

She lay across his chest, and he brushed damp hairs from her wide, happy eyes.

"I'm not sick," she said breathlessly. "I'm really not."

"Nope." He grinned affectionately.

"That was wonderful," she said wonderingly. "I feel like . . . like I want to thank you. Is that silly?"

"Sure. But I understand. How do you feel now?"

"Like it's Christmas morning." She stretched luxuriantly.

"No regrets?" he asked hopefully.

"How could you even think that? Chris, I feel like a weight's off me that I've been carrying for so long. I'm not crazy or sick or screwed up if I felt like I did or could feel like I do. And how I feel about you is so special and so big that it takes up all the space that all those other things used to. Oh, how can I explain it?"

He ran his fingers over her skin. "You don't have to," he said tenderly. "Not when you consider the lovely notion that I'm happy too."

"I hope so, Chris. I want you to be as happy as I am right now."

"Do you know when I fell in love with you?" he asked serenely.

"Oh, Chris . . ." She beamed.

"I think it was that second night," he continued peacefully, "on the beach. When I saw you standing there with the rifle in your hands, and you hadn't run or screamed or stood around like some harebrained movie female. I knew you were something special, Arielle. And I knew I could depend on you as a best friend, a partner maybe, and I think I loved you for it."

A light had gone on inside her, and the brilliance of it glowed from her features.

"Colonel senator, sir?" she said meekly. "I think we ought to consider the possibility of a relapse." Her hands slid down to his thighs and caressed him lovingly.

He reached for her.

"Somehow," he conjectured, "I just don't think that's going to be a problem."

5

The black Zil limousine swept toward the Kremlin. Kasimov regarded the briefcase next to him like a hunter's trophy. He had ordered the driver to take a roundabout route, savoring the pleasure of returning home. But soon that pleasure changed into contempt as scene after scene of corruption and criminality flashed before his hawkish eyes.

It was late, and the shops should have been closed. In fact, all the front doors were locked and their shades drawn tightly. But time and time again, in every corner of the city, citizens, coats drawn tightly around them, scurried briefly into pools of light in the alleys at the rear of the stores, packages quickly changing hands. Soon after, others whisked in to replace the comrades whose business was complete.

It was happening more and more, he reflected ominously, as food shortages grew more dire and consumer products disappeared from stores, impossible for all but the privileged few to obtain. The *Nachalstvo,* they were called. Literally, it meant the authorities. But idiomatically, "big shot" was the definition, a term of derision, of frustration.

So the secret economy flourished and grew. Factory workers stole products to trade for food and luxury items. A bottle of vodka was traded for cosmetics, watches for fabric. The rare new car was traded in at three times its original value, the owners buying a second, cheaper model and hauling the huge profit back to grimy apartments. Even the language had begun to reflect it as the verb *kupit*—to buy—was replaced by *dostat*—to obtain.

Kasimov watched with the emotions of a man who witnesses his wife being raped.

On Granovskovo Street, a different scene, no less appalling, lay before him. A number of chauffeur-driven Zils stood in line in the street outside the Bureau of Special Passes, a private Party store, from which men emerged in tailored suits carrying nondescript packages filled with Argentinian beef, Danish salamis, and Iranian caviar.

He noted that the license plates all began with the letters MOC, indicating members and staff of the Central Committee.

Kasimov saw more limousines waiting, as they turned onto Kalinin Prospekt, in front of the Kremlin Polyclinic, a special medical facility for the Soviet leaders. The clinic, Kasimov knew, was operated by the Fourth Department of the Ministry of Health, the department which serviced only the elite. Every major city had at least one Fourth Department Clinic, the level of treatment for every strata of the *Nachalstvo,* rigidly prescribed and written down in books which indicated what type of room, what kind of food, or the limits of care each level was entitled to. Kasimov bit back imprecations.

They passed without obstruction through the Borovitsky Tower gate into the red-brick-walled, pentagonal Kremlin citadel. Kasimov's relief at being home was soured. The city lay all around him like a body rife with cancer. He glanced at the briefcase once again. All that was left was Nightsight.

Inside the Arsenal, a long narrow building at the northwestern edge of the Kremlin, Vassily Komarovsky took his seat as the Politburo assembled. Risking a sideways glance at Dimitri Torgenev, he was rewarded by a covert nod from the marshal, who sipped water from a glass set on the table in front of him.

Komarovsky turned his attention hopefully to the man who sat at the head of the table. As contradictory emotionally as he was physically, Pyotr Meledov, president of the Soviet Union and Party secretary, shifted his bearlike head, with its blunt features and unruly shock of white hair. His head was at odds with his long-fingered, fine-boned hands, more appropriate to a concert pianist. The contradiction suited him, though, Komarovsky thought, for he had seen

Meledov survive endless challenges to his authority and knew him capable of both cleverness and brutality.

One by one, the fifteen voting members of the Politburo that ruled the Soviet Union fixed their attention on Meledov. Komarovsky drew in a deep breath and, with a warning to himself to remain calm, waited for Meledov to change the world.

"Some of you are wondering, no doubt, why this meeting was called and why no agenda has been presented to you," began Meledov, his voice silky and coercive. "I assure you that, in due time, all will be made clear."

Komarovsky could feel the tension of the other members. The nighttime session, the absence of the usual recorders and secretaries, the hidden agenda, all pointed to the unusual. In the U.S.S.R., he reflected, that was always a dangerous condition.

They sat, seven to a side, Meledov at the head of the long, ornate table. Komarovsky had the seat on Meledov's immediate right, and he concentrated his attention only on those members who effectively controlled the Politburo itself: Foreign Minister Viktor Grishen, whose seat was next to his own; Minister of Agriculture Mikhail Gorbach next; opposite Komarovsky, his ally Marshal Torgenev; newly appointed Minister of Science Vyacheslav Trapeznikov on his left; and Minister of Defense Arvid Telshe last. The remaining eight seats were held by Party secretaries, all of whom held enormous power in their regions of control but whom, Komarovsky knew from experience, would have little input into the decisions that would be made this night. They would, as always, side with the winners.

"It is essential, Comrades," continued Meledov, "that we face facts. It is a fact that we have enormous resources but do not have the capabilities to exploit them. The Siberian oil fields have posed greater challenges than we anticipated, and production is down. It is a fact that we cannot feed the people, and this we must fear. Revolution begins in the stomach, Comrades; the people grow restless.

"The empire is held together at this moment only by the momentum of seventy years. It is fraying at the edges, and we have been powerless to prevent it. We struggle to control Yugoslavia and Poland. We have lost half of Afghanistan. Czechoslovakia and Romania teeter. Their raw materials no longer pour in freely but are sold to the West for a profit. Still we stand by and do nothing.

"The people have been seduced from us," Meledov said, his voice growing stronger and more powerful. "It is time to act.

"Yet we cannot act. The Americans watch our every move from our very skies. The simplest troop movement is an open book to them. Force, we say. Where is the army, we ask. The erring states must be brought back into the fold, we decide. But again, we are an open book, and the American president counters with ease our every design.

"Lenin taught us that to shrink is to die. We are collapsing in on ourselves, and we must fight to stay alive, to grow once again.

"I am here to offer the only way I know to stave off our collapse. There is an idea called Operation Nightsight. It is our greatest hope, and I urge you to look upon it with favor."

Komarovsky listened breathlessly as Meledov played the assemblage like a master conductor. He had stirred their anger and their passion. He had slapped down cherished beliefs. We are losing, he had said, and the men at the table leaned slightly forward in the hopes of a savior to counter their fear.

"Who is responsible for this Nightsight? All I have heard is rumors," said Gorbach, the balding pragmatist, unhappy with subterfuge, more at home with his grains and weather charts.

"Nightsight is the combined effort of the State Security Committee, the army, and the Ministry of Science," Meledov answered evenly.

Gorbach nodded, looking first to Komarovsky and then to Torgenev and Trapeznikov. He read the conviction on their faces and was silenced by it.

One down, thought Komarovsky. Gorbach would acquiesce to their will.

"I, for one, would like an explanation," said Grishen, not one to be intimidated by a show of solidarity, his dark eyes challenging.

Meledov raised his massive head and nodded to Torgenev. The marshal stood and walked over to a large globe of the earth that spun easily when he slapped it with his hand. All eyes followed his movements.

"We have spoken of facts," he said in his terse style. "No one is more aware of facts than the military. If I thought that our missiles could destroy the West, I would launch them tonight. But they will not. If I thought I could invade and win, I would invade. But at this time we cannot win such a war. Not while the Americans outstrip us at every turn.

"But our enemy is not invulnerable. He is most definitely not. In one arena and one arena only he is as weak as a child. In space," Torgenev stopped the globe with another slap, "he is totally dependent and completely unprotected.

"The basis of Nightsight is this, Comrades; to place in geosynchronous orbit around the earth a series of laser platforms capable of destroying the American orbital satellites and holding the skies for the U.S.S.R. alone. In one instant of blazing light, we can destroy their damned Prophet network, their communications satellites, both military and civilian, and wreak such havoc that it will be years before they can recover. And then only as we permit. With lasers in orbit no ICBM could fly against us. With their satellites down no spy in the sky could detect us. Under cover of darkness we will be free to act, to take back what is ours. We cannot destroy the Americans, Comrades. We are going to blind them."

"It will mean war," insisted Grishen. "The West will never stand for it."

"And what will they do?" shot back the marshal. "How will they respond? Such an operation as this renders their nuclear forces useless, and their reliance on Prophet and satellite communications proves to be their greatest liability in conventional tactics. Further, we will invade no territory other than what is historically ours to avoid direct confrontation. Four weeks after we orbit our lasers, we will be in Poland. Another two, through Afghanistan. The rest of our client states will realign quickly enough with us, and we can force cooperation from the West on our terms. Even the Chinese will be helpless without the American-supplied Prophet information.

"Their planes can't fly without our permission," continued Torgenev with barely suppressed emotion. "Their ships can't cross the ocean. In the midst of their panic, we march into territory unimpeded. The empire will be re-created; the resources ours again."

"If such a strategy is feasible, why must we stop at restoring the Union?" asked the fervent Telshe. "Why would we not take Iran, Pakistan, Finland, Korea . . ."

The first smile slowly creased Meledov's thick features.

"In time," he said smoothly, "almost anything is possible. Is it not, Comrades?"

When he looked into the faces filled with sudden fever, Komarovsky knew they had won.

Receiving word that Kasimov had entered the Arsenal, Komarovsky caught Trapeznikov's eye and inclined his head toward the door.

"Comrades," he said, passing the note to Meledov, who nodded. "Please excuse the Minister of Science and myself. A matter of some importance calls us."

Trapeznikov stood along with him and followed out of the room to an office reserved for Politburo use.

Kasimov sat stiffly in a straight-back chair, the briefcase on his lap. He looked up sadly as Komarovsky and Trapeznikov entered.

"Tell me only one thing," he said. "Has Nightsight been approved? Because if it has not, we are a doomed nation."

"It has been approved," said Trapeznikov. "In part, due to your success."

"Then the inevitable conflict Marx predicted will come to be at last," Kasimov said with enthusiasm. "After my trip tonight, through this sewer of a city, that is good news, Comrades."

"This sewer of a city, as you call it, is suffering from strains that would have broken the back of a lesser people. You might do well to remember that," admonished Komarovsky.

"Perhaps," said Kasimov wearily. "It has been a long day. Here is the American technology we require."

Trapeznikov accepted the briefcase and scanned the view graphs quickly.

"It's all here," he said excitedly. "The specialists will have to go to work on it; but with this system, I believe we can orbit lasers. You are to be congratulated, Kasimov. This is splendid."

"Nightsight is the only congratulations I want," said Kasimov. "I'm going to sleep now, if that's all."

"But it's not," said Komarovsky to Kasimov's surprise.

"Excuse me, but I'm going to rush these over to the Academy," said Trapeznikov, closing the briefcase. "Our work is just beginning." He left the room, already selecting personnel for assignments, occupied with the enormity of the work still to be done.

Kasimov waited stonily.

"His work may be just beginning, but ours is not over," said Komarovsky.

"There is nothing left," objected Kasimov. "My mission is complete."

"Not yet. There is a loose end, Valentin. One you have helped to create. We cannot afford to have the Americans turn their attention to space in the near future. They must remain uncommitted to protecting their satellites. Even the slightest rumor of Nightsight and they can obstruct us. We cannot afford a race."

"How does this concern me? My operation was a perfect success. No one even suspects what we were after," he said hotly.

"It was your operation that promoted Christopher Leyland to political prominence," responded Komarovsky, "which I agree was not your fault and could not have been foreseen. But he has picked up his dead brother's standard, and again, Valentin, we cannot afford one of the Americans' famous 'crash programs.' Remember the Berlin Airlift, the Polaris submarine, and their lunar landing. Do not underestimate them. I want Leyland to be occupied elsewhere for the next few months."

"That should not be difficult," offered Kasimov, accepting the logic of the situation.

"It has not been," said Komarovsky.

"You use the past tense. Why?"

"Because the movement has already started. He is going to Rome to investigate his brother's death. He is searching for Pollux, and I want you to occupy his attention until Nightsight is operational. You see, he is also coming to kill you."

"Then he is a fool," observed Kasimov. "What is the time frame?"

"We need three months. Four, possibly. Can you do what I ask?"

"Absolutely. Only one question remains for clarification. Tell me how you manipulated Leyland to Rome in the first place."

"Your success in La Jolla started dangerous inquiries. I had to protect our greater assets by directing the Americans' attention toward our lesser. I decided to use Pollux."

"Pollux is too valuable," objected Kasimov angrily.

"Your perspective is limited. Pollux is filled with personal greed.

His age haunts him. Soon enough he would be reaching the end of his usefulness. You must see this operation in larger terms."

"I object to your using my people without my knowledge. It weakens my control and creates tension in them."

"If anyone else spoke to me this way . . ." threatened Komarovsky.

"I'm not anyone. I'm the man who just put Nightsight into your hands," said Kasimov, unperturbed.

"Don't make the mistake of believing your own propaganda. Comrade Colonel. The KGB can survive your loss."

"You still need me, I believe that."

"I suffer you. There is a difference," said Komarovsky, his gaze unwavering.

"Very well, then," replied Kasimov. "We understand each other. I will try and repair any damage you may have done."

"There has been no damage," Komarovsky said angrily. "Unlike some, Colonel, Castor is still the complete professional."

PART THREE

1

Chris reflected unhappily on the disadvantages of public life when he saw the surging mob of reporters and media technicians who surrounded the entrance to his father's house. Arielle, curled up beside him in the limousine, observed the furor with equally small relish but accepted it with her usual intelligent composure.

"I suppose I'm going to have to get used to this sort of thing," she sighed philosophically.

"This is Crowley's work, no doubt," Chris observed darkly. "He'd have the press in my shower if I didn't restrain him."

"Well, you can hardly blame him. The 'whirlwind marriage of the battle-scarred hero and heroine of Torrey Pines,' as the media has so subtly portrayed it, was just too great a temptation for him."

"Then you don't mind that we should stop and get our pictures taken?"

"Not really. Tom's right after all," she said. "Tell Franklin it's all right to stop."

"You and Tom seem to have formed a pretty amiable relationship," Chris said, arching one eyebrow. "I'm not sure I can handle being double-teamed."

"Don't even try," Arielle chuckled. "Tom and I have found we have something very important in common."

"I'd like to be privy to what that might be."

"We both love you, darling," she answered as the car stopped and the first flashes illuminated their embrace.

The ceremony was brief and informal. Crowley served as best man, and the Admiral joyfully gave the bride away.

Later, with Chris in the library tending to long-postponed business, Arielle wheeled the Admiral up to his rooms.

"You realize," he said warmly, when they were both comfortably ensconced, "that you're my first daughter. This is a very happy occasion, Arielle. Welcome to the family."

"Thank you, John. You've made me feel very comfortable, and I appreciate that."

"I'm sorry your parents couldn't make it, though. I'd like to meet them."

"Chris and I spoke to them on the phone before we left California. We'll see them as soon as we get back from Rome."

"Then you're going too?" the Admiral asked.

"I've found only one other thing in my life that makes me happy besides my work. I see no reason not to have as much of both as possible."

"But won't your work suffer?"

"Not at all." She shook her head. "It's mostly theoretical research, and if I need to I can use the computer facilities there."

"Chris has told me what he intends to do in Rome, and I'm worried, Arielle, worried about his safety," said the Admiral unhappily.

"As am I, John."

"Then why not stop him? You could, you know. He loves you."

Arielle phrased her reply with thoughtful precision. "Of his love, John, I am quite sure. And I'm equally sure that the day I use that love as a gun to his head is the day that I lose him. Because he wouldn't permit it, and I couldn't live with him if he did. And vice versa, I should add."

"I see," he said, nodding, and his bony hand reached out to rest on hers. "Then I'll ask you to forgive an old man's selfishness. You're a remarkable woman, and I'd be pleased if we could spend some time alone together when you get back."

Arielle leaned forward and kissed the parchmentlike skin of his cheek affectionately.

"Wild horses, John."

"Wild horses, daughter," said the Admiral, delighted. "Now go tell Chris I'd like to see him when he has a moment free."

Chris found his father at his writing desk when he came up later in response to the summons.

"Arielle said you wanted to see me, Dad."

"How familiar with Rome are you, Christopher? Please bear with me on this."

"Not very," Chris admitted. "I've never been there before, but I'll have a great deal of support from our intelligence apparatus."

"That's fine, up to a point," said the Admiral, "but I don't think it will be sufficient. There is so much of Italian society that goes on underneath the surface that an outsider, even with the kind of support you'll have, can rarely penetrate it."

"And you perceive this as a problem," Chris conjectured.

"I do. I was stationed there toward the end of the war, as part of the occupation government. I had a chance to see firsthand those levels of society.

"It was a painful time, Christopher. Famine, disease, shortages of every kind of vital supplies. And once the fascist government collapsed, there was no central authority to provide any relief for the population. The only force that held the country together were the local dons, the leaders of the Mafia, if you will, whose power was undiminished and dated back to medieval times.

"We had to cooperate with them if anything at all was to be accomplished, and they, in turn, had to cooperate with us. An uneasy truce was formed and, to be perfectly honest, I found quite a few who had a damn sight more honor and concern for the people than many of the duly elected officials.

"Now I don't condone that type of feudalism any more than I condone organized crime here. But try to remember the times and that feeding the people superseded any ideology. Satan himself would have been welcome if he sported a loaf of bread under each arm."

"I take it there is some significance in this for me," Chris prompted.

"There is. The end of the war didn't end the influence of the dons; just placed it back underground where it had always been.

The system still exists, and there's a man in Rome whose aid I think you're going to need. I've seen him only a few times since those years, but his power in Rome has grown since the war and his obligation to me is undiminished."

"What's the nature of this obligation to you," Chris asked, "that could hold up for almost forty years? I've never known you to step outside the rules with this kind of deal before, Dad."

"Morality," the Admiral sighed, "is often a function of circumstance, much as we might prefer otherwise. And the nature of his debt to me is up to him to share with you if he chooses to. I don't know if you'll require his services, but if you do, you'll have them for the asking."

"I hope your concerns aren't justified," Chris said pensively.

"So do I," responded the Admiral. "But I've played too many hands of stud poker in my time not to appreciate the value of an ace in the hole."

The cherry trees were in full bloom, their colors announcing that spring had at last come to Washington, D.C. The military jet which transported Chris, Arielle, and Crowley from Ohio receded in the distance as the staff car sped away from the airport toward the White House.

"I still say the bastard conned you," said Crowley stonily, staring out at the Potomac. "We could back out even now."

"Forget it, Tom," responded Chris. "I knew what he was up to at the time. Just consider that a billion more for space and Arthur's murderers constituted a deal I couldn't turn down."

"A billion and a half," said Crowley smugly.

The office of the National Security Adviser was only a few doors down the corridor from the president's Oval Office, and Secret Service personnel ushered them to it.

"Good morning, Senator, Mrs. Leyland, Mr. Crowley. I trust your flight was pleasant," said Barbara Reynolds cordially.

"It was," Chris said as they all sat. "And I trust that the arrangements for Rome are taken care of."

"They are. When you're through here, a plane will be waiting. All concerned parties have been notified of your arrival and your authority though, obviously, not of your agenda. I assumed Dr. Simmons would have an official capacity and have arranged for her security clearance as well."

"I'm going to handle the computer research," said Arielle. "I appreciate your thoughtfulness."

"Not a problem," Reynolds said. "IBM Fellows are not noted to be high-security risks, and we're grateful for your expertise." She handed Arielle a slim brown notebook. "These are your personal authorization codes and transfer relays to our operators at Langley, as well as tie lines into our NSA data bank operators here in D.C.

"Senator Leyland, this is a copy of my report on the CIA leaks as well as all our data and projections on Eris. Mr. Crowley, I would ask you to serve as liaison between the senator and the Special Secretaries who will tend to your needs." Another slim notebook was passed across her desk. "You'll find all the access numbers listed there. Is that acceptable?"

Crowley nodded stoically.

"I'm not familiar with the chief of Rome station," said Chris.

"His name is Henry Talon, and his file is included in your material," said Reynolds. "I've known Hank personally and, under ordinary circumstances, I would trust him completely. But this is a new game, and you'll have to write your own rules.

"I can't stress enough the urgency of your task, Senator. The Soviet Union has its back to the wall, so to speak, and the entire Communist world is watching their struggle to determine where the ultimate best interest lies. Without Soviet support, Cuba falls apart; without Cuba, the Communist strategy in this hemisphere is unworkable. It's the same in Africa. Without Soviet-sponsored support, Angola, Ethiopia, Mozambique, and Zambia fall and their base in the region disappears. Continue on down the line. If the Soviets allow even one of their client states to leave the fold, they may be unable to exert sufficient global pressure to control their internal regions.

"There are fifty million Ukrainians who could follow the lead of the client states into revolt; three million Armenians; four million Lithuanians. Like a silk stocking, if even one thread breaks from bondage to the others, the whole fabric unravels in time.

"We know that the Soviets cannot challenge us directly. But we're equally sure that they're not going to give up without a fight. Their weapons will be stealth, secrecy, and subterfuge; and the premise of a Soviet mole in CIA is quite feasible because it is so much their style of espionage. We use Prophet. They use people. Don't forget that, ever.

"Find the mole, Senator, before he turns us inside out."

Komarovsky's plane touched down in the Central Air Terminal of Novosibirsk, the largest city in Siberia. In the back of his mind was the realization that he could just as well have ordered Nikolai Mikoyan, head of the First Directorate, back to Moscow, but his own need to get away from the city had overshadowed expediency. And as Mikoyan's leave was so long overdue anyway, it suited Komarovsky to fly to him.

One forgot, Komarovsky thought, as the KGB limousine pulled out of the airport onto Krasny Prospekt, the wide central avenue which ran all the way to the banks of the Ob River, how much had been accomplished in the last seventy years. Every so often, he had to get out into the country itself to feel the heartbeat of the people, the rumble of the factories, and the sounds of the children to remember his purpose clearly. He had come to remember what he fought for. He had come on a pilgrimage.

This close to the river, Krasny Prospekt began to narrow; parks and well-tended squares bordering its sides. Almost every architectural style since the beginning of the century had left its traces here, from the opulent opera house to the constructivist-style State Bank and Central Hotel.

People sat in the parks eating lunch or talking, and the deep blue sky, for once, did not remind Komarovsky of American satellites. Rather, a feeling of peace settled over him. This was the Union; the heartland he had devoted his life to protect.

The limousine stopped in front of Mikoyan's father's home, a small house that looked warm and inviting. A brick chimney bespoke the fireplace inside, and the narrow front lawn was well tended, full with spring growth. He ordered his guards to stay in the car.

Mikoyan's wife, Inessa, opened the front door, startled to see him.

"Comrade Komarovsky? But . . . is anything wrong? Nikolai is not here just now," she said hurriedly.

"No, Inessa, nothing is wrong," he said kindly. "I must speak to your husband, and it pleased me to come here to do so. So rarely can I get away from Moscow, the trip was a pleasure."

Inessa's fear gave way to a hesitant smile. The notion of a purge was not unthinkable, and she had lived with fear all through her husband's working career. But Komarovsky's response calmed her even though his unusual presence was still cause for concern.

"Won't you come in for some lunch?" she asked, remembering her manners.

"No. I'm sorry, but I should speak to Nikolai first. Perhaps later? . . ."

"That would be fine, Comrade," she answered. "Nikolai is in the park with his father, Aleksandr, and our youngest son, Yuri. Would you like me to . . ."

"I will find them," said Komarovsky. "The exercise will do me good."

He walked off toward the park, Inessa's obvious fear on his mind. How unfortunate to create such tension in people. Yet it was so necessary to keeping order. Komarovsky felt like the worker who loved the finished product but hated the tools he must use. The age-old questions taunted him. Would there ever come a day when he and people like him were unnecessary? Perhaps, he consoled himself. With Nightsight, perhaps even in his lifetime. Still, the guards followed silently behind.

Putting such ominous thoughts out of his mind, he walked into the park. Citizens, young and old, sat on benches on the spotless grounds. One old man paused in his walking to snatch a piece of paper someone had carelessly tossed. Komarovsky watched him stoop to put it in his pocket. It was such a simple gesture, but it moved him nonetheless.

He saw Mikoyan almost at the same time Mikoyan saw him. Leaving his son and father, Mikoyan rose up and covered the distance between them in quick strides.

"There is nothing wrong, Nikolai," said Komarovsky to his tense subordinate, explaining his reasons for coming as he had to Inessa.

"Come meet my family," said Mikoyan. He knew Komarovsky had none of his own still alive and hoped the meeting would not awaken painful memories.

Introduced only as "Comrade Vassily, a man with whom I work," to Aleksandr and little Yuri, Komarovsky settled down on the bench in the warm afternoon sun.

"You must be an important man," said Aleksandr, eyeing the raincoated men who stood quietly nearby. He wore a faded jacket over a thin sweater; his pants and shoes were newer, but still those of a worker. He had an aged, lined face and wispy white hair, with eyes that were undimmed by age. Komarovsky knew him to be in his eighties.

Yuri, by comparison, was dressed in shorts and shirt, his brown hair flowing over an unlined, plump face. He was engrossed in a toy sailboat his grandfather had built for him.

"Father, your age is not an excuse for bad manners," said Mikoyan gently, but Komarovsky was not bothered.

"A moment ago I saw a man pick up some litter in the park," he said. "Compared to that man, I am very unimportant, Comrade."

"My son is an important man," said Aleksandr proudly.

"That he is," agreed Komarovsky, enjoying Mikoyan's pained look.

"Please, Father," said Mikoyan, "Comrade Vassily and I must talk."

"We have time, Nikolai," said Komarovsky. "It is not often I have the chance to speak with someone of your father's experience and wisdom."

Mikoyan's eyes raised in mock gratitude and he relaxed somewhat, letting Yuri run off to play.

"You work with intelligent people, my son," said Aleksandr confidently. He turned back to Komarovsky. "I like to come to this park, Comrade, especially with Yuri so he can see that monument and I can explain what it means."

Komarovsky's eyes traveled to where Aleksandr pointed. The war memorial that dominated the park stood almost thirty feet high and was hewn from a solid oblong block of stone. Roughly six feet on each squared side, it rose upward into the head, shoulders, and arms of a hooded woman whose hands clung to her mouth in a gesture of sadness and horror at so many who had died. Flowers had been laid at the monument's base.

"So many times," Aleksandr continued, "we have been invaded, so many times we have been at war. Someone must remember. The children must remember, as we old ones die, so it will never happen again."

Komarovsky nodded. It was true, he thought. Few of the world leaders understood the particular paranoia the Russian people felt about foreigners on their soil. The whole history of Russia was one invasion after another, each brutalizing the people and each repelled, some after centuries of occupation, at the cost of countless lives. In 800 A.D. the Vikings had invaded from across the Baltic Sea, only to be conquered by the Tartars and Mongols four hundred years later. Moscow recovered, after two hundred years, and finally, even the Golden Horde was defeated. But by the 1500s Poland had invaded Russia and wasn't forced back out until the early 1600s. From 1918 to 1921, France, England, Japan, and the United States sent troops to Russia in support of the Czar, leaving only after Lenin's triumph in wiping out the Kronstadt Island forces. During the wars of the twentieth century alone, Russia had lost almost twenty million citizens. Entire provinces had been decimated by the Nazis. And no Russian would ever forget that almost every invasion in recent memory had come across Europe.

Aleksandr's sentiment was a common one. The average Soviet citizen looked to the protective ring of client states that surrounded the U.S.S.R. as the most vital part of her defense strategy. With a fear bordering on the pathological, any possibility of a weakening of that land ring was unthinkable, cause for alarm. It was no small wonder, thought Komarovsky, that the Americans, with their single, paltry British invasion in 1812, could neither understand nor appreciate the Russian paranoia. For the last century, Americans had done their fighting everywhere but at home. Would they sit quietly if Canada and Mexico were to turn hostile? Yet with utter righteousness they said stay away from Poland, let Czechoslovakia and Hungary sway from the flock, ignore Mongolia, and sit by as Afghanistan falls to the enemy.

Perhaps, even more than an economic necessity, Nightsight's basis was grounded firmly in this fear of invasion if the ring should fall. For no citizen could feel safe if the country stood alone and naked, the ghosts of invading troops always uppermost in the Soviet mind, real and horrifying.

He looked at Aleksandr and nodded. "The young should remember, Comrade. I lost both my parents in the war," he said.

"You must not let it happen again," said Aleksandr, and for the first time Komarovsky wondered if he knew who he was. He rose and motioned to Mikoyan. "Can we talk?"

"Yes. Let me walk with you. My father can watch Yuri."

The soft earth, warm from the spring sunlight, pressed under their shoes as they walked. Sadly majestic, the war memorial stared down at them. Mikoyan waited, walking silently.

"Tell me, Nikolai," said Komarovsky at last, "what you think of Kasimov."

"There's little to think. Professionally, he is a master, and his international contacts give him hands where even I don't have hands, eyes where even I can't see. Personally, he's a disaster. His independence has grown into a complete disregard for authority and his insolence is unbearable. I wonder if he's not more of a risk than an asset."

"Yet, he gave us the command-and-control system that makes Nightsight a reality," said Komarovsky.

"Caracal has others to depend on," said Mikoyan. "Don't overrate his worth."

"I'm glad you agree, Nikolai, because I, too, have serious problems with Comrade Eris. His conflicting loyalties are becoming more and more an issue.

"I want a second Caracal team set up to watch him. He's too valuable to lose and too risky to leave alone. A backup is necessary. Second, I want Castor and Pollux brought under control of your directorate. Set up new lines of communication that exclude Kasimov. Leave his old ones in place, but in case he should fail, I want some safeguards."

"You're freezing Kasimov out," said Mikoyan.

"No. Not yet," said Komarovsky. "Merely being prudent."

"I'll return to Moscow with you tonight and attend to it at once."

Komarovsky turned to watch Yuri return and climb happily up on his grandfather's lap. The toy boat became animated as Aleksandr made it ride waves of air before his grandson. Conscious of both the war memorial and Aleksandr's words, he shook his head at Mikoyan.

"That won't be necessary, Nikolai. There is much to be gained here. It is for them," he pointed to the pair, "that we do what we do.

Stay another two days and let the boy learn. Then come back to Moscow."

"Very well, Comrade," said Mikoyan gratefully. "Is there anything else?"

"Yes, there is," said Komarovsky, wistfully. "I'd like to stay for dinner."

2

Henry Talon rose from behind his desk, and Chris felt an ill-disguised reticence when he was greeted.

"Welcome to Rome, Senator. I've been expecting you. Would you care for some coffee?"

"No thank you, Mr. Talon," Chris responded, settling into a chair. "I came alone for this first meeting because I want to get some things straight between us from the beginning."

"Honesty is the best policy, Senator," shrugged Talon noncommittally. "But rest assured that the president made it quite clear that this is your show."

"That's not what I mean," Chris said quickly. "What I want clear is that my investigation in no way implies any criticism of you or your office, and I hope you won't construe it as a threat."

"Where there's smoke there's often fire," observed Talon, "and since you're asking for honesty, station chiefs have made notoriously good scapegoats in the past."

Talon was a short man, not more than five eight or nine, but the breadth of his shoulders and his thick forearms gave the impression of strength. His curly hair was cut short, and gray had already begun to dominate the natural brown. His eyes were big and sad-looking, his features large.

"That's not going to happen here," Chris insisted. "I have no other motivation than wanting the truth. If that truth doesn't involve you, then you have nothing to worry about."

"I've been in this business too long to place a whole lot of faith in the notion of truth. Forty years ago the Russians were our allies; now we're pointing our missiles at Moscow. Thirty years ago we fought the Chinese; now we're building Coca-Cola plants there. You tell me, Senator, what the hell is truth?"

"Do you know why I'm here, Mr. Talon?" Chris said, sidestepping the question.

"If you mean have I been formally briefed on your purpose here, the answer is no. But the intelligence community is fairly close-knit and rumors precede you."

"And those are . . . ?"

"That ostensibly you're investigating your brother's death but that there's more to your agenda," said Talon.

"Both those rumors are true," agreed Chris, choosing not to amplify further.

"Then you'll forgive the less than enthusiastic reception. The mere mention of a congressional investigation makes us as jumpy as a whore in church. Everybody comes to the intelligence services with some ax to grind, wanting to bring back some headline-making dirt to the good old folks back home who think CIA should be run like the local grocer's."

"I'm not here for headlines, Mr. Talon, and I'm sure that you've researched me. I want no publicity whatsoever; no points for my political scoreboard. But if I'm to succeed here, I do need your trust and cooperation."

"Then be the first politician in my experience to level with me. The more you hold back, the greater is my desire to protect my ass. Sure, I've read about you. And your recent exploits are impressive as hell. But you're not here as a Navy ace or a NASA astronaut now; you're here as a political figure with presidential authority and that's a whole different kettle of fish. Trust works both ways, Senator, and I don't like working blind."

Chris glanced around the office before replying. It was windowless, being underground, but several paintings added color and dimension to the white walls. Talon's desk was large and made of mahogany with a green blotter at its center flanked by two phones, a pen-and-pencil set, and a picture of Talon's family, an attractive mid-fortyish blonde and two smiling, teenaged girls. Behind and to the right of Talon's desk were his computer terminal and teleprinter.

"I've got a limited amount of time to give to this investigation, Mr. Talon, as the business of the Senate can't be postponed more than a short while. Consequently, I've got to take some gambles that a more prudent investigator might not. I've read every report written by you or about you that CIA has on file. My own sources through the Intelligence Committee tell me that you're extremely competent, hard-working, intensely loyal, and overly independent.

"No outsider could possibly hope to get through the maze of intricacies built into CIA without inside help, and my first calculated risk is that by trusting you, you'll give me the support I need. Is that a fair assumption?"

"Or a very clever gambit. Little is what it appears to be, Senator. Only time can tell if you're an exception to that rule."

"Very well. I'm willing to stand on that. My alternative is to spend months discovering what someone in your position already knows." Chris looked deeply into Talon's sad eyes and hesitated, knowing that the investigation would be compromised from the start if he was wrong to trust Talon. But he sensed that Talon was reliable.

"The reason I'm here, Mr. Talon, is to uncover a highly placed mole in CIA who is controlled by a Russian masterspy called Eris. My brother's assassination was some of his work."

Talon rocked back in his chair and whistled in surprise. "Jesus. That's a mouthful all right. Who else knows about this?"

"No one else in CIA, if that's what you're asking. My liaison to the president is through Barbara Reynolds. Dr. Arielle Simmons will handle the computer work, and Tom Crowley, my chief aide, will coordinate with Washington.

"The man I'm looking for is probably no longer attached to Rome. We believe that he was also responsible for supplying information regarding the Jasons' conference in California, and that information was never stored out of the States. Likewise for the information on Arthur's visit here—the information was stored only in Rome. Dr. Simmons has already checked the computer records. Most likely the mole was here until August and back in the States by March."

"That narrows it down somewhat, I'd think," said Talon. "But it's still going to leave maybe a few hundred people. You'll be looking for a needle in a haystack."

"Just out of curiosity," Chris asked benignly, "do you always favor this many clichés?"

Talon's puppy-dog eyes grew rounder as amusement filled them. "I like clichés, Senator. One of the only things to withstand the test of time. Fixed truths, if you like, in a too mutable world. My life is a fucking cliché; everybody's is no matter how you try and avoid it. Work hard and get ahead; a penny saved; you'll understand when you're older; youth is wasted on the young. All true and all ignored till it's too late. As I've already said, in this business you cling to any truth you can get.

"I'll help you, Senator. Maybe cautiously at first, but that's more than you'd have got if you'd walked in here and thrown your weight around."

"Let's see what the future brings," said Chris adroitly.

Talon smiled for the first time. "Now you've got the hang of it. I'll have an office prepared for you and your staff. Will tomorrow at nine be all right?"

"Fine. There's only one more thing, Mr. Talon, and I hope you'll forgive my bluntness but I'm very new at this."

"Yes?"

Chris walked to the door but turned back. "Mr. Talon, if it turns out that I was wrong to trust you, that in some way you are connected to the mole and that someone is hurt because of you, then I will kill you myself," Chris said, shutting the office door quietly behind him.

"Out of the mouths of babes . . ." whistled a wryly astonished Talon to the empty room.

The private casino in the Roman suburbs was crowded. An almost endless array of jeweled bodies tossed money onto green baize tables and lived or died with the outcome of their wagers. The man Kasimov had been watching for days was dying.

Jack Greyson yanked the bow tie from his wilted collar. He pushed another pile of fifty-thousand-lira chips to the croupier to be bet on black. The wheel was spun.

Kasimov mentally congratulated Pollux on his selection. Greyson had every sign of the compulsive gambler, close to the edge of destruction, played out. Red came up and Greyson died a little more. Kasimov wondered what it was like to have a need one couldn't control. The idea disgusted him.

Greyson's pile of chips had dwindled to almost nothing and two large men in tuxedos came to the roulette table. When the chips were all gone, they gestured for Greyson to follow, unmoved by the fear in his eyes. They entered an office at the casino's rear.

Casually, Kasimov moved to the office door and pressed a miniaturized contact microphone onto its surface. Amplified by the battery pack he carried in his breast pocket, it fed the sound inside directly to the small receiver concealed in his ear.

". . . what you said last week, Signor Greyson," he heard. "But still you have not taken care of your debt."

"Please," said Greyson's voice, "just a little more time. I'll get the money. Just give me a little more time."

"But your debt is already greater than your yearly salary, and your assets are exhausted. When, Signor Greyson? There are nervous people who are waiting for you."

"Please, I'm begging you. Just forty-eight hours. That's not a great deal."

"Ah . . . but it is, Signor Greyson. And what will you do? The CIA looks poorly on debts such as yours. Who will you go to?"

"How did you . . . ?" asked Greyson's frightened voice.

"Don't be naive," said the voice harshly. "Please, Bruno, show him what naive people receive."

Kasimov heard the sounds of a struggle, the hiss of a zipper, and Greyson's strangled scream.

"It is so small an object, is it not, Signor Greyson? So small and yet so valuable. This knife could cut it off with less effort than it takes to slice sausage."

Greyson's cries were nearly hysterical as Kasimov removed the microphone and walked away.

Ten minutes later, a white-faced Greyson emerged from the office and staggered across the casino to the bar. Settling onto the stool next to Greyson's, Kasimov motioned the bartender to bring a second, and then a third drink to the shattered man.

"Excuse me," Kasimov said politely when Greyson looked up to identify his benefactor, "but I have a proposition which I'm quite sure will be of interest. Have another, won't you?"

Theresa Rennata's strong, young hands pushed the dust mop along the hallway. She understood little of what went on in the labyrinth of underground corridors, and though she spoke perfect English the snatches of conversation that drifted by her went, for the most part, unnoticed.

She moved virtually unseen past the men and women who rushed through the corridors with varying degrees of urgency. At the end of her work day, Theresa placed her cleaning supplies on the appropriate shelf, tossed her soiled uniform in the cleaning bin, and put her worn ID badge in the shopping bag she habitually carried. Fixing a scarf over her dark hair, she left the CIA station, grateful for the hot Roman afternoon after the too-cold air-conditioned depths.

Her home in a modest section of the city was cool, the old stone walls and marble floors providing thick insulation from the sun. In the kitchen, Theresa put on an apron and checked the tomato sauce which had been simmering on the stove since morning. Contentedly, she selected strips of pasta from the drying rack in the pantry and started a pot of salted water to boil. It was already six o'clock, and her husband and their two teenaged sons would be returning home for dinner within the hour.

Remembering that she had one final task before she could devote her total attention to the rest of the meal, she walked to her bedroom, opened the drawer of a cherished music box which sat near her bed, and stared for a while at the picture she withdrew. Satisfied, she lifted the phone receiver and, still distrustful of the newly installed device, gingerly dialed the only number she had committed to memory.

The voice on the other end was quite congenial, discussed the weather, and inquired after her health before asking the question she expected.

"He has arrived," responded Theresa Rennata. The voice thanked her politely, hung up, and Theresa went back to fixing dinner.

3

Arielle stood on the balcony of their hotel suite looking out over the city. Rubbing sleep from her eyes, she stretched luxuriantly in the morning breeze which billowed her loose robe around her long legs.

Chris came up behind her and put his arms around her waist.

"Good morning," he said, nuzzling the back of her neck affectionately.

"Good morning, my love. It's such a beautiful day. Let's not work today, Chris. I think we both need a holiday."

"I know it isn't one of the most romantic honeymoons. And I'm sorry."

"Don't be foolish. I wouldn't care if we sat around doing square roots as long as we were together. Honeymoons are for children. We're adults," she said.

"Then what would you like to do?"

"Play hooky," she grinned.

"I thought we were adults."

"We are. Let's play it in bed . . ."

She shrugged out of his arms before he could reply and scampered inside. With one fluid roll of her shoulders, the robe came undone and slipped to the floor. Naked, she stood waiting for him as the sunlight caressed her body, golden and warm.

Chris came to her with a wistful sigh, tossing his own robe away in loving haste.

"You've convinced me," he said happily, and then she was in his arms.

The following morning Chris and Arielle saw Crowley off on his weekly flight to Washington. Though he reported via diplomatic pouch to Reynolds every day, his presence in the capital was still required, for increasingly long periods, to manage the legislative aides who were guiding bills which Chris had sponsored through the Senate. He was always missed as his absence cut down their small group even further and added labor to an already herculean task.

The piles of documents, reports, and computer printouts had grown into stacks which covered every conceivable open space and finally forced them to expand into yet another room.

Talon, at first hesitant to commit his energies to the project, grew to trust Chris and Arielle. Soon, he had delegated many of his duties to his deputy chief and become a partner in the search for the mole.

Rome station was aware of the activity taking place within its midst, but the nature of the investigation remained camouflaged by rumors from "informed sources" who knew a Senate budgetary inquiry when they saw one. No one but Talon, Chris, Arielle, or Crowley was permitted access to their locked offices, and the one eager agent who had attempted to find out what was truly going on had been discovered and transferred to a detention facility for interrogation. His absence the next morning was most conspicuous.

Long hours at the station continued to take their toll on Chris, Arielle, and Talon. Thousands of reports were organized, collated, and selected for relevance as Arielle fed the numerous and ever-increasing data into the computer, endlessly checking for correlations and causalities.

Talon began to hate the computer.

"Think of it, Hank, as a brilliant idiot," Arielle said to him after he finally voiced his frustration, "capable of an almost limitless ability to retain data but lacking the ability to interpret what it knows. First, I have to make the data acceptable to the computer, teach it, if you will. Then it's essential to develop programs to allow the computer to interpret what it's learned, like teaching a child numbers and then, later, addition and subtraction. The computer can only be as intelligent as its program, regardless of its capacity; it's only capable of doing what I tell it to do. In the business, we refer to that condition as c-i-c-o, pronounced *psycho,* or crap in, crap out."

"I'm getting to feel like the damn thing's insatiable," said Talon, tensely. "We keep pouring data in but get nothing back. When does it get enough?"

"When it can solve for the numerous parameters I'm feeding it. Parameters are boundaries, like guidelines. The first parameter is time. The mole was here in August and in the States by no later than March. So, after programming in all of the comings and goings of relevant personnel, we solved for the first parameter—time. That program yielded a little over two hundred agents. Obviously, the trick is to narrow that number down. Sometimes, that's evolving the right parameters such as 'agents whose promotions have been related to success regarding the Soviet Union' cross-checked against the 'time' parameter. But remember, all the data on agent promotions has to be programmed in first."

"How many parameters are you operating with?" called Chris from over numerous reports scattered on his desk.

"About three dozen," Arielle answered. "The two I just mentioned plus 'agents promoted ahead of expectation,' 'contact with mole-type operations,' 'agent salary versus expenses,' to name a few. But every program I create yields either too many names or none at all. What we're looking for is a finding of two or three names who can satisfy enough parameters to indicate a high probability. Our mole should be in that group."

"No rest for the weary," grumbled Talon, settling back to read.

"How do you think I feel?" Arielle retorted. "If I don't ask the right questions—crap out."

"Let's break for lunch," Chris suggested diplomatically, exhausted himself.

Chris pushed lunch around his plate morosely, aware that the time he could spend in Rome was dwindling. "Maybe," he said to Arielle and Talon, "we aren't asking the right questions. Can we come at the problem a different way?"

"I'm at my wit's end," said Arielle. "If you've got an idea, let's hear it."

"I was remembering a lecture I once heard about the discovery of the planet Pluto," Chris said halfheartedly.

"If you can make some connection out of that, you've got my vote for life," said Talon morosely.

"Not exactly. It's the process they used that strikes me as analogous," Chris continued. "Pluto was too far out to see with a telescope, but they proved its existence by looking at the orbits of the visible planets and calculating divergences from what was expected. When the divergences were plotted, they realized some other object had to be exerting gravitational influence on those orbits. They couldn't see what it was, but it had to be there just the same."

"You're suggesting, then," said Talon with growing enthusiasm, "that we look for the mole by trying to spot his influence on other agents near him. If we find 'disruptions,' we verify his presence."

"It's possible," mused Arielle. "There's so much data in the banks already. We've got to have a parameter that the computer can operate with, though."

"If an agent were a mole—now bear with me—he might try to work the destruction of his superiors. Actually, he would benefit in two ways. CIA loses a valuable, loyal agent, and the mole rises to take his place," Talon suggested.

"That's close to what I'm thinking," Chris agreed.

"It's possible . . . just possible," offered Arielle, "that 'agents replacing immediate superiors' could yield something when computed against the other parameters. And if we add scandal, death, disloyalty, and the like as causalities . . . Suddenly I'm not hungry. Let's get back to station, gentlemen, right away."

"There it is," whispered Arielle as the data display flashed three names again and again.

"No clichés, Hank?" asked Chris elatedly.

Talon shook his head slowly. "I swear . . . not a damned one. You've made a believer out of me."

"Try 'nothing succeeds like success,'" suggested Arielle with unrepressed emotion.

Chris read the names from the screen.

PAUL SANDERSON, DEPUTY CHIEF—SOVIET DESK, LANGLEY STATION

PETER LAZARSKY, CHIEF—COUNTERINTELLIGENCE, LANGLEY STATION

JOHN MATHIAS, CHIEF—INTERNAL SECURITY, LANGLEY STATION

"The fucking apostles, that's what we've got," whistled Talon. "Peter, Paul, and John. The goddamned fucking apostles."

"Not quite, Hank," said Chris soberly. "Among them is a Judas."

"This isn't enough to go to Reynolds with," said Arielle flatly.

"No, not yet," agreed Talon thoughtfully. "We still need proof that one of these men is a mole. Only the first part of the investigation is complete. It may take just as long to narrow those three down to one. Chris, I think . . . Chris?"

Chris looked up from a concentration so deep he hadn't heard Talon at all.

"What were you thinking?" Talon asked, noting his friend's absent look.

"Just remembering something my father said," Chris responded, "about an ace in the hole."

Komarovsky could read the ecstatic expression on Trapeznikov's face as soon as he entered the Minister of Science's office.

"You look happy," Komarovsky observed with interest.

"The model is complete, Vassily," Trapeznikov chortled, "and it's everything we hoped for. The preliminary tests have all demonstrated complete congruity to our system."

"That *is* good," Komarovsky agreed, "but tell me about time. That's my concern."

"That's what I'm trying to tell you, Vassily. We took a gamble that has paid off. Assuming that the American system would be what it seemed, we built not just the one model but started production on all the hardware at the same time. They're ready, Vassily; all four command-and-control systems are built, tested, and ready to be installed."

"Excellent, Comrade, excellent," gloated Komarovsky. "That's going to make things easier. Give me an estimate, please."

"A week for installation, another for programming. All else is in a state of readiness due to Marshal Torgenev."

"Again, I congratulate you and the entire Academy. It makes Kasimov's report that much more of a minor matter."

"He's still in Rome?"

Komarovsky nodded. "Yes, and he reports that Leyland is getting very close to Pollux."

"Then that's not minor at all. If Pollux is taken, with his knowledge . . ." Trapeznikov barely suppressed a shudder.

"As I said, Comrade Minister, you have made that less of a problem. Now I can let Kasimov do what he has always loved to do."

"I was unaware that Kasimov loved anything," said Trapeznikov, scowling.

"Not so," objected Komarovsky with his face as hard as stone. "He loves to play the end game."

4

Arielle had protested and Talon downright threatened but Chris stood firm.

"We've got to continue to improvise," he insisted. "It's already worked once for us and if it doesn't pan out, nothing's lost. But we just can't afford the kind of time needed for an in-house investigation of each of the three men. I can't stay out of Washington much longer."

"It's totally against procedure," Talon insisted. "You don't even know who you're doing business with or whether you can trust him. Why ask my advice if you're not going to follow it?"

"I trust my father and you would too if you knew him. That's enough for now."

"I want some insurance before I agree to this," said Arielle emphatically.

"Agreed," Chris had said at last.

Now he stood alone on the Ponte Sant' Angelo, one of the ancient stone bridges across the Tiber. The instructions of the voice on the phone had been politely given but explicit.

He rested his arms on the iron railing between the bridge's concrete posts and looked up at the circular, medieval Castle Sant' Angelo, which loomed at the end of the bridge like a gigantic clenched fist over the river. Beyond, to the west, the lights of Saint Peter's were coming on, the dome glowing red, back lit by the setting sun.

At eight o'clock, a taxi stopped and the driver beckoned. Patting his pocket for the reassuring feel of the transmitter sewn into the lining of his suit jacket, Chris got in the back and was whisked off. As all his attempts at conversation were met with a shrug from the driver, Chris sat in silence as the streets sped by, and soon they had left the darkening city behind.

The villa to which they drove stood high atop a grapevined, terraced hill and was surrounded by ten-foot stone walls. Guards with caps and carbines met the taxi, ushered Chris out at gunpoint, and searched him. Then they led him into the courtyard after tossing the transmitter back into the taxi as it sped away.

A sense of having moved backward in time descended on Chris. Splashing fountains, formal gardens, marble statues, and heavy-bosomed women all defied the imagery of modern times. Chris had the distinct impression that he was not merely being escorted into a house; he was being presented to royalty. The realization sobered him.

The guards took him to an inner courtyard lighted by torches where a linen-covered table had been set for dinner. His feeling of the ancient persisted even after the guards left him alone.

"You favor your father, you know," said a voice from behind, startling Chris, but he remained stock-still.

"There are other similarities," he said evenly.

"I can see that," said the voice, amused. "He, too, realized the value of first impressions."

Chris turned slowly and looked at the voice's owner. Old, as old as his father, he judged, but radiating a different kind of presence. This was power.

Phrases like regal bearing were inadequate. The snow-white mane of hair that grew straight back from his widow's peak, the intense, almost-black eyes in the aquiline-featured face, the simple, perfect black suit and tie, and the arrow-straight posture all said "king" more eloquently than any coronation.

He stood unwaveringly against Chris's gaze and returned it with his own.

"I am called Don Pietro. Your father is my friend, Senator Leyland," he said after a while.

"Then it would please me if you'd call me by my first name, as I have found my father's friends are men to be respected."

Don Pietro inclined his head. "Such charm from one so young is rare. Please, Christopher, would you join me for dinner?"

"I'd be delighted, sir."

Seemingly without signal, servants appeared with course after course. Don Pietro spoke little during dinner but prompted Chris to talk about himself, his father, Arthur's death, even of the Shuttle flight. And at each turn of conversation it seemed to Chris that the don was weighing a tally of his own, judging Chris in some private way and arriving at a sum.

In the library, over brandy after dinner, Don Pietro settled into a deep leather chair and gestured for Chris to do the same.

"How much do you know of my relationship with your father?" he asked.

"Nothing at all except that in the past there was a debt between you. He said it was up to you to tell me more if you chose to."

Don Pietro smiled. "Yes. That would be expected. Your father has great personal integrity. I value that. It is, therefore, no surprise to me that his son has this quality as well.

"I am going to tell you a story, Christopher, and at its end you will give me your assurance that it will never be repeated. Not because I ask it, you understand. But you will give it nonetheless, I am sure.

"You know that I first met your father near the end of the war, but you don't truly understand what that means. Imagine a society totally broken down, where bands of children armed with broken glass fought over the rights to a pile of garbage. Where honest women sold their bodies for a bar of chocolate to feed their starving infants. Where even the vilest trash of an occupying army could dole out life itself with their food.

"Like your father, I was not a young man even then, but my power was just beginning, and it was difficult even to protect those for whom I was responsible. Just as your father was, I felt sickened by the atrocities committed by both conquered and conqueror. But I could not be everywhere. Nor could he. No, we could not be everywhere in those days . . .

"A company of American soldiers came to a village not far from where we sit now. They stayed for a while, bivouacked, I believe is the term, and then most moved on. Most, but not all.

Those who left had been generous. Their gifts fed the people of the village, some, for the first time in days.

"There were three who stayed, and they had sufficient provisions in their supply trucks to feed the villagers for weeks. And they gave, but just enough to still the hunger pangs and to quiet the infants. But when the people came to accept them as good and kind and generous, then the demands began.

"Small at first—an old heirloom, a uniform pressed, a boy to run an errand. Soon they became what they dreamed of, royalty to the peasants, tyrants. There was no one to stop them. The men of the village had almost all been killed in the war. The rest were old or feeble. There were no rifles, no police, nothing to make the three soldiers afraid . . .

"One night they got drunk and demanded a show for their food. They forced some of the women and boys into the square and commanded the others to watch. The soldiers had guns, those who resisted died. These . . . animals . . . forced the women to do what they wanted and no corrupt Roman emperor could have done worse. One woman was made to lie with her son, another with a goat. Rapes, beatings, perversions of every sort imaginable. But these men still had not had enough. In the end, they killed the women, calling them tramps and whores and spitting on them . . .

"The elders still speak of it in the village, Christopher. It is called the night God turned His back. They are ashamed of the memory.

"I found out about it, of course. It could not be kept secret. I had no choice but to go to the Americans and ask for justice. That is how I met your father, Christopher. He was appalled and tried to help me. But it was still wartime and who would convict a soldier of anything? Especially not of murdering the subhuman Italian peasants. They laughed at us, your father and I. And the animals were allowed to go free, rotated home to America.

"I can still see the looks on their faces at the hearing when they were pronounced innocent. Had it not been for your father, I would have leaped at them. But he sat beside me and held me back and took me to his home to talk . . . I can still remember all of it.

"The ship that was going to transport the soldiers out of Italy was under your father's command as naval chief. He ordered a small boat to pick up the three men at their assigned point. There was only one single sailor on the boat, instead of the usual three, all by your father's command.

"The small boat never reached its destination, and the ship finally sailed away. I was that single sailor, Christopher, and I cut the hearts from all three with my own hands and scuttled the boat offshore with the bleeding bodies inside. I murdered them, and I only wish I could have done it again and again for even that was not enough suffering to avenge those who had died the night He turned His back . . . on my wife and my only daughter."

Don Pietro's gaze was far away on some other place and time. By visible degrees, his breathing returned to normal, and Chris was drawn back to the present by the ghosts in his dark eyes.

"That is the nature of what I owe your father; the debt of vengeance, Christopher."

Chris was silent for a long moment, and when he finally spoke, it was barely a whisper. "I'm sorry, Don Pietro, truly sorry."

Don Pietro nodded slowly. "It was so long ago, Christopher. So very long ago . . . But now you have heard my story and may ask of me what you wish. I am content you are your father's son."

"First, be assured of my silence, Don Pietro. I respect that what had to be done was done. Mad dogs must be destroyed."

"You give your assurance as I said you would. Go on."

Chris handed him three eight-by-ten photographs.

"One of these men is a traitor to my country, but I don't know which one. An investigation of this sort can take months, even years. That's time I don't have.

"It occurs to me that the man I'm after must have had contact with many Romans during his tenure here and that if I could trace his movements through the city, then I might be able to spot something out of the ordinary, something that might give him away."

"Tell me more."

"If the man had a mistress, maybe some landlord will recognize his picture. If he did business under another name or held bank accounts under a separate identity, maybe that would lead us somewhere. Did he gamble, drink, whore? You have access to sources the CIA could never touch. I want the imprint these men left on Rome and its people. It's no sure thing, I admit. But this man is, in part, responsible for my brother's death, and I'll try any reasonable bet to find him."

"It will be done. Is there anything else?"

"Now that I've met you, Don Pietro, I'm thinking that there are a few things . . ."

Don Pietro listened quietly and finally, began to nod his head.

Chris was escorted out of the house by a single guard but not before Don Pietro handed him a black attaché case, his face twinkling enigmatically as he clasped Chris's shoulders.

"The second transmitter your friend Talon placed on the taxi is inside as well as the weapons he and your wife carried. They are waiting comfortably, if a bit unhappily, in my car outside. Please assure Mr. Talon that his skills are quite excellent but that we have had a two-thousand-year head start. He should not feel badly. And it goes without saying that a man whose woman would fight for him is a man to be respected indeed. I congratulate you, Christopher, on your judgment in people. Goodbye, my young friend."

Talon, indeed, was in a foul mood, sulking in the limousine when Chris tossed the case to him.

"I don't want to discuss it," he said disgustedly as the car sped back to Rome.

"He said not to feel badly," Chris needled, "but they had all the odds on their side. Where did they pick you up?"

"At the bridge," Arielle said. "Suddenly, we were staring at half a dozen guns. Hank wisely decided that discretion was the better part of valor."

"Et tu, Brute," grumbled Talon, sadly.

Chris recounted his impression of the meeting with Don Pietro.

"Now we just wait and see," he concluded, as the villa's lights faded and the night shrouded their journey back to Rome.

5

For a week they assembled every conceivable record on Sanderson, Lazarsky, and Mathias. Phone bills and checking accounts were fed into the computer under Arielle's orchestrating hands. Chris read supervisors' reports. Talon read those reports written by the agents themselves and then those, too, were programmed in. Like astute biographers, they built up profiles, researched pivotal career moments, and sought to understand contradictions in their subjects.

On the eighth day, a messenger arrived from Don Pietro.

"We've got someone above ground in Postelli's president's office," said Talon, coming into their office. "He says he's here to see you, Chris. My secretary just got the call. I swear your Don Pietro must have more tentacles into the city than an octopus if he could find us here."

"It doesn't surprise me at all," Chris said reflectively. "Let's see him together and hope he's got something we can use."

The messenger was elegantly attired in a three-piece suit, sitting comfortably in an armchair. Postelli's president hurriedly excused himself.

"I'm Chris Leyland. This is Mr. Talon and Dr. Simmons. How can I help you?"

"You may call me Mercury, and to the contrary, Senator Leyland," said the man in a lightly accented, cultured voice, "I am here to help you. A mutual friend has directed me to present the results of his quest in your behalf."

"I am pleased to know of my friend's continued concern," said Chris, the allusion not lost on him.

"I shall tell him so," said the messenger. He handed the photos of Lazarsky and Mathias over to Chris. "On these two men there is nothing in their stay in Rome to be of interest to you, nothing that would be considered outside of the guidelines of," he gestured downward, "the organization to which they belong."

"On what do you base that?" demanded Talon.

The messenger smiled politely. "Apart from the normalcy of their behavior, both were approached while in Rome, though at different times, by groups which sought their services. Lazarsky by a Swiss international banking firm, and Mathias by a Libyan concern. Both of these offers were rejected."

"I have no record of that," said Talon, eyeing the man narrowly.

"No record exists. Surely you know that an agent does not like even the smallest taint of being suspected as a weak link in his organization. It makes his superiors nervous. That is why you never reported the offer made to you by the West German Stangel Company which hoped you could get them a U.S. export license to buy the kind of mirrors sometimes used in laser apparatus."

Talon was openmouthed in shock. "That was . . . You couldn't . . . How did . . . ?"

"So often people in your profession forget about the people in mine," the messenger sighed. "You choose public places to meet, never thinking about the waiters and maids and taxi drivers and streetsweepers who are beneath your notice. What does it cost, Mr. Talon, to gain the loyalty of a domestic who must grovel daily before a rich mistress? Or a chauffeur who must listen to daily abuse from the owner of a car that costs more than he will earn in his life? You may protect the country, Mr. Talon, you and people like you, but we *are* the country, and we are never far away."

"Assuming what you say is true, then," spoke up Arielle, "it clears, in some ways, those two men. But only if you can implicate the third, Sanderson. Lack of evidence is not necessarily proof of innocence."

"That is also true, Dr. Simmons. But proof will still be up to you to find."

"Then you did uncover something on Sanderson," Chris said hopefully.

"We did. But again, what it means is for you to determine. There is a fine men's tailor shop on Embassy Row which serviced one Signor Martelli . . ."

Chris and Talon arrived at the tailor's shop and noted the quality of the fabrics and the understated air of wealth.

"We would like to speak to Arturo," Talon said as a diminutive Italian in shirt-sleeves came to greet them.

"I am he, signors. How can I help you?"

Chris showed him Sanderson's picture. "Do you know this man?" he asked.

Arturo took in the face on the picture and the folded money at the same time.

"I do," he nodded, taking both from Chris. "Signor Martelli shops here often. One moment, signors."

Arturo went to a desk and consulted a heavy, bound ledger. "The last time," he said, leafing through pages, "was in late July."

"What can you tell us about this man?" prompted Talon.

"What is there to tell?" Arturo shrugged. "It is always the same. Signor Martelli's office calls us, usually around 10 A.M., placing the order for that day and his arrival in the late afternoon around six o'clock. I always place the selections in our dressing room downstairs and leave him his privacy for the hour. He is very particular not to be disturbed and requires no help in making his selections. May I ask what this is in reference to?"

"I'm sorry," Chris shook his head, "but you understand . . ."

"Ah, well . . ." Arturo said ambivalently. "I thought as much. But we are a fine shop, and I don't want to be involved," he lifted both palms up, "in any type of affair."

"Rest assured, Signor Arturo, your shop will stay uninvolved," soothed Chris.

"How did Martelli settle his account?" Talon asked, unperturbed, exposing more money.

"In cash," Arturo replied. "Always as he was leaving. The garments were then sent to his home."

"I'd like to see the dressing room he used," Talon said. "You said it was always the same one?"

"I didn't. But it was. Come this way, please. The dressing room is below street level."

The mirrored room was identical to countless others of its type, but Talon insisted on checking every inch of it.

"I don't understand what you're looking for, Hank," Chris said as Talon swept the room with an electronic device he brought out from his coat once Arturo had left.

"An agent comes to a store under a false name, orders clothing too expensive for his salary, stays too long just to be trying it on, then leaves and pays cash for his purchases. What does that suggest to you?"

"Logically, a clandestine meeting and a payoff. But Arturo said Sanderson was alone in here."

"He did, Chris. That he did." But Talon was busy with his device near one of the mirrors, grunting intently as he read figures from its digital display.

"I think . . . yes . . . right around here . . ."

Chris was taken totally by surprise as Talon's fingers found and released the hidden catch. Smoothly the mirror slid open and Chris stared unbelievingly at what Talon's action had uncovered.

"The Roman catacombs," Talon gestured theatrically at the vast subterranean space beyond.

"Entering the times that the men's shop received the telephone orders," said Arielle, hands flashing over the computer's keyboard, "and checking that against Sanderson's duty roster and the station's telephone records, show two things, gentlemen."

She read the data aloud from the display. "First, Sanderson was here at station four out of six times the orders were placed, and second, no such calls went out from station. Conclusion—someone else made the calls at least sixty percent of the time."

"I've interviewed his driver," Talon added, "and he indicated that Sanderson never told him to go to the shop before they left station but did so only after they had been driving for a few minutes or so, as if he'd had a sudden thought. That suggests to me he received a signal of some kind en route. Very clever."

Arielle punched up another display.

"There is no record at his bank of any withdrawals of the size needed to pay the shop. A further analysis indicates his other expenditures leave no room in his salary, anyway. He spent what he earned and reports to IRS no income other than salary."

"I'm satisfied we have enough to ask Mr. Sanderson some very serious questions," said Chris.

"Then don't waste time," counseled Arielle. "Call Reynolds, tell her what we have, and demand that Sanderson be picked up. We can stay here until it's verified that he's the mole. If he's not . . ."

"Back to the drawing board," supplied Talon. "But the more I think about him, an episode last summer concerning an agent named George Williams comes under a different light."

"It's quite possible, given what we suspect, that Williams was manipulated by Sanderson to appear under the control of the Russians," Arielle said when Talon had finished recounting the episode.

"Or by Eris," Chris suggested. "If you reverse the positions, he gains one disgraced CIA agent and flushes out a traitor within the embassy."

"And promotes Sanderson," Talon said bitterly.

"Well, what does seem likely," said Chris, picking up the phone, "is that whoever he is, Eris is a master at human chess."

6

Brendan Connors looked up from the speech he was revising with Clancy, Powell and Parienne and immediately caught the excitement on Barbara Reynolds' face as she burst into the Oval Office.

"He's done it, Mr. President. Leyland's got enough to suggest a candidate for the mole in CIA. I've seen the data he's put together; Dr. Simmons sent it by satellite relay from Rome, and it looks to me like a pretty damn good bet to be Paul Sanderson, deputy chief for the Soviet Desk. He's right here at Langley."

"How certain of this man are we?" queried Connors.

"We can't be totally certain at this stage, of course," Reynolds replied. "Not without interrogating Sanderson himself."

"In due time," said Connors. "But first I want some thought given to using him against the Russians."

"We might be able to repair some of the damage," agreed Clancy, "funneling disinformation back through him."

"I disagree," said Parienne. "Take him, roast him, and let's see what he knows. I'd like the bastard hung."

"Terry, call Treasury and have a Secret Service detail put together," ordered Connors. "I want them to be able to pull Sanderson in on a moment's notice. Jim, get covert surveillance set up on every part of Sanderson's life within the hour; home, office, club, the works. Use FBI. Then, everybody back here in one hour for a strategy session, CIA's chief included. Barbara, you set it up. Harold,

you stay with me and coordinate. I want Sanderson, guilty or innocent, in a box so tight that he can smell his own breath."

Paul Sanderson had been aware of the investigation from its in-
ception. For weeks he had taken pride in the finest acting job of his
career. No one, neither superiors nor subordinates, friends nor family, had been aware of the surging tension which boiled within him.

He had always anticipated discovery. No one could cover his
tracks so thoroughly that detection was impossible when full govern-
ment-Intelligence resources were brought to bear. One month, one
year, twenty years; in the end it was all the same. Exposure was
inevitable. He had known that from the first day in 1965 when
Kasimov had confronted them in the Paris brothel. But the noose
Kasimov placed around his neck had been too tight, and the only
way to loosen it was to surrender.

Sanderson was prepared, had been for weeks. His "travel kit" as
Castor called it, was ready in his safe. Fake identity papers, a sum
of cash, and the numbers of his Swiss accounts, swollen far beyond
what he ever could have accumulated in his lifetime any other way.
All in all, he was as ready to leave the States as he ever would be.

Well past fifty, his once hard-muscled body had become soft and
even expert tailoring no longer hid the swelling paunch which folded
over his belt. His hair was still brown, matching his eyes, but only
by vestige of monthly dye jobs. He was a plain-looking person, he
knew, but with the money, he would be able to indulge in his rather
esoteric tastes. The future beckoned with greedy hands.

His private line rang twice, stopped, and then rang twice again a
minute later. So it may be now, he thought, turning on the scrambler
and lifting the phone.

"Sanderson here," he said calmly.

"Lifeline," said Castor's familiar voice.

"Gambit," responded Sanderson correctly.

Satisfied, Castor's voice continued.

"It's over, Pollux. You have less than one hour. Leave at once
and drive to number ten Kerrin Street. You will be met there. Travel
well, old friend."

The connection was broken and Sanderson replaced the receiver.
Opening the safe, he withdrew his travel kit and immediately left the

office. He took nothing with him, nor did he pause in his departure
for even the simplest of gestures toward the people he had worked
with for over thirty years. It was over and nothing of the past could
claim him now.

The guards passed him out of Langley without comment or delay.
It was less than five minutes since Castor's call. He carefully observed the highway speed limit and pulled without incident into the
underground garage at the address he had been given.

"Just leave your keys in the car, sir," said a junior attaché from
the Russian Embassy whom Sanderson recognized from diplomatic
receptions. "We will dispose of it."

The attaché motioned him into a Mercedes with diplomatic plates,
and they drove out of the garage back onto the streets of Washington.

It was the last time he would ever see the city, Sanderson thought
as they sped toward the airport; but that neither disturbed nor sad-
dened him. Nor did the loss of every possession he had accumulated
over the course of his life; more could be bought. The lack of feeling only strengthened the realization he had achieved so many years
ago; there was nothing more important than himself.

The attaché's diplomatic papers were checked at the airport, as
were Sanderson's. Both were accepted without problems, and the car
was waved through to the waiting Aeroflot jet.

Paul Sanderson boarded without a backward glance at the country
he had betrayed.

The calls came into the White House, one by one reporting that
Sanderson had vanished. Reynolds left the surveillance teams in
place, though with the ominous knowledge that it was a waste of
time. She said as much when the meeting convened.

"Somehow, he knew we were coming," she said to the president.
"He left his office, drove out of Langley, and no one can find him
now. He could be anywhere."

"Do what you can, Barbara," said Connors wearily. "Notify all
services, call Customs, and start a net for Sanderson. Get Interpol
on it in Europe. I want Sanderson found."

"Do we recall Leyland?" asked Reynolds. "I suppose his job is
over."

"I'd rather see him there," offered Parienne. "He's deeper into this than anyone, and if Sanderson should surface in Europe, we have Leyland already in place. Another week or two won't hurt him."

"Okay. Brief him then," Connors directed Reynolds, "and see if he can come up with anything."

"Tom Crowley's still in town," said Reynolds. "I'll speak to him and fly him back to Rome by military jet."

"Fine, but Sanderson is our number-one priority," said Connors bitterly. "Use what you have to, do what you have to, but no matter where on this planet he may be, find him."

The military jet roared over the airfield, banked steeply, and dove in for a landing. On the field, Chris, Arielle, and Talon were already waiting when Crowley emerged. He peeled off the flight suit with obvious gratitude and walked to them, still shaken from the ride from Andrews Air Force Base to Rome.

"Washington believes you got the right man," Crowley said to the others as they drove back to the city.

"Now that's good news," said Talon gratefully.

"I don't think that's all, Hank," said Arielle, observing Crowley's frown.

"It's not," he said. "In between the time Chris called Reynolds and the time the president authorized the arrest, Sanderson flew the coop. The man has completely vanished."

"It's not over then," Chris shook his head, chagrined and frustrated.

"Not by a long shot," Crowley agreed unhappily.

The Aeroflot jet began its final approach to Paris, and Sanderson interrupted his fantasies long enough to hand the remains of his bland meal to the waiting steward and buckle his seatbelt. Less than three hundred miles away, his money rested in the vaults of the banks in Zurich. A short ride by plane, he conjectured, a handshake with whomever the Soviets sent to transport him, and then he was on his own, free and wealthy. "I deserve a little celebration," he thought. His personal contacts were still operable and, for the right price, drugs and young girls shouldn't be too difficult to procure. Maybe a few boys for spice. He was going to enjoy the next twenty years.

After the landing, he waited patiently in the empty plane for his contact to arrive. Though he would be searched for over the next few weeks, after Nightsight was launched it would all be academic. The U.S. would have its hands full, and he would revert to being a minor matter. Just a few weeks of seclusion in Europe and then he'd be free to move. Nightsight would bury him as effectively as it would his ex-country, he thought to himself.

"Welcome to Paris, Comrade Sanderson," said a voice, interrupting his reverie.

"Is that you, Kasimov? I'm . . . surprised to see you here. I thought you were still in Rome with Leyland. I expected . . ."

"You expected some minor official to transport you to Zurich, yes?" interrupted Kasimov. "But we couldn't let so important a man as yourself leave our employ without some words of appreciation."

"That's not necessary, Colonel. Your country has rewarded me well enough. All I require is the freedom to enjoy my later years as agreed."

"And you will have that, Comrade. You most assuredly will, but you must accept all the rewards due you. To be decorated at the Kremlin is an honor few men ever receive."

"The Kremlin? What are you saying, Kasimov? I don't want to go to Moscow," said Sanderson, the first tendrils of fear brushing against him.

"You will be our honored guest, Comrade. Everything we have to offer is yours. After Nightsight is over, you will be free to stay or go as you please. Surely you can see the sense of this."

Sanderson felt walls closing in around him. Once in Moscow, a dreary, depressing city, he might never get out. Endless debriefings on CIA—for his own protection, they would say. A dismal apartment, broad-faced ugly women, and all his money waiting far away, impossible to get at, unable to be spent. No one got out of the U.S.S.R. unaided, and he was totally alone. He fought back the panic that threatened to overwhelm him.

"I'm all done, Kasimov. Let me go," he insisted.

"The matter is settled, Comrade. I will accompany you myself. We will be leaving shortly," responded Kasimov coldly, brooking no further discussion.

"In that case, I accept your gracious invitation," said Sanderson.

"Excellent." Kasimov smiled. "I have some matters to attend to. I'll be back in a few minutes. Why not have a drink?"

Kasimov left the plane, smiling, and Sanderson watched him enter the terminal from the window by his seat. The steward was busy in the galley restocking provisions, and the single guard paid Sanderson only perfunctory attention until he rose from his seat.

"The men's room," Sanderson said, pointing, and the guard nodded.

"Excuse me, please." Sanderson wriggled past in the narrow aisle, and the guard turned his back to let him pass.

Sanderson struck him at the base of the neck with all the force he could produce. The guard dropped, unconscious, and Sanderson removed his gun and levered him into a seat. The steward continued to work, unaware of his exit.

The terminal was crowded, and Sanderson walked unnoticed to Customs. His false passport was stamped by an ambivalent agent, and he walked quickly outside. Selecting a taxi, he ordered the driver into Paris. Three hundred miles, he reminded himself. Three hundred lousy miles. He had to get to Zurich.

7

Chris lay quietly next to Arielle, lost in thought, while she slept. Sanderson was gone. Later reports confirmed that. Crowley had spoken in favor of their return to the States, claiming their job was done and Sanderson's capture was best left to the professionals. In the end, even Talon had agreed.

Growing restless, Chris tossed off his blankets and padded silently into the living room. Something was tugging at his subconscious, but it failed to emerge as a concrete thought. Through Sanderson, he had hoped to find the reasons behind Arthur's death. Further, he had hoped to find the man directly responsible. All he had now was a name, Eris. Frustration made him angry, and the anger only increased his despair.

There had to be a link between Arthur, the Jasons' conference, and, quite possibly, himself. Space suggested itself immediately, but the thought went nowhere from there. In the scheme of things, he was a relatively unimportant junior senator from Ohio. Arthur's influence had been greater, but even so it hadn't been enough to generate the changes he had sought.

The city that had once conquered the world looked cool and silent from the balcony's lofty perspective. Now Rome remembered its glory only in museums and ruins. But still there was a sense of power here, in the knowledge that it had ultimately conquered in more lasting ways. With its law, its literature and its roads the

Roman Empire created the European civilization that later replaced it. Rome had the pride of a successful parent, the wisdom of age.

Arthur, the Jasons, and himself, he thought again. It was still uncertain if anything had been stolen from the Jasons' conference; the destruction of the inn had been too extensive. He sought again for a connection, but the night gave no easy answer.

It was something Crowley had said that tugged at him, he decided. Something he said when he was angry. Something about . . . manipulation. Chris began to look at events with a different perspective. *Manipulation.* With a growing assurance, he sat down to call Don Pietro.

Sanderson walked along the cobblestone streets of the Left Bank, passing in and out of the lights which emanated from the countless cafés in the area. Voices flew out into the night, students arguing politics, sexual repartee, drunken literary criticism.

This deep in the student quarter near the Cité Université, the streets grew narrower, unevenly flowing downward toward the Seine in Paris' center. Bookstores, art galleries, and cheap student hotels predominated, all old buildings of three and four stories which gave the impression of wear and fatigue.

Loud applause and the noise of a crowd reached Sanderson's ears. Turning a corner, he saw fifty or so people gathered about a show that was taking place. Tourists mostly, with a sprinkling of students sitting on the damp cobblestones, watched the small street circus, the "ringmaster's" strident voice calling their attention to the shabby foursome's next feat of "death defying" acrobatics.

Sanderson flowed easily into the crowd, moving closer to the front as it shifted constantly, tired from standing so long on the hard street. Lighted by torches, the scene could have been transposed from some olden country fair, the paraphernalia of the performers handcrafted, with colors and banners faded by time and weather.

The ringmaster, another man, and two women were all clad in formfitting, often-mended leotards with gaily colored scraps of cloth sewed to their sleeves. The costumes showed the fluid bodies of the performers to maximum advantage. Oiled muscles and deep, open cleavages glistened in the flickering torchlight.

Sanderson watched the performance until its conclusion, a

"deadly and dangerous" acrobatic leaping through hoops of flame complete with fuzzy music from a phonograph and the release of balloons. After the final bows, the ringmaster, a dark man with curly black hair, passed the hat through the crowd. Most of the tourists, happy with such an unplanned surprise and already thinking of the story it would make back home, tipped generously. Sanderson waited until the hat was thrust into his reach and dropped a hundred-dollar bill into it. The ringmaster looked up in grateful surprise. Then he recognized Sanderson and his eyes shadowed.

"Twenty minutes, Henri. La Tristesse," Sanderson whispered. The ringmaster nodded quickly then danced away to reach the last tourists before they wandered off to other pleasures.

Sanderson walked unhurriedly to La Tristesse, a dark, quiet café bar two blocks away. He took a booth in the back, ordered wine, and then spent five minutes checking the rear exit and the alleyway onto which it opened. Satisfied, he checked the phones, returned to the booth, and placed the gun he had taken from the Russian guard comfortably on his lap.

Ten minutes later, Henri, now dressed in sweatshirt, jeans, and sneakers, came into the bar, saw Sanderson, and slid into the booth. Hastily removed greasepaint still clung in smudges to his ears and neck.

"Bonsoir, Henri. Ça va bien?"

"Your French stinks, Sanderson," Henri replied easily. "I'm still comfortable with English, and I'm fine, thank you."

"And business is good? I enjoyed your performance," Sanderson said.

"Business stinks. But it's still the best cover I've ever had. We can go just about anywhere, and the border guards rarely bother us. My employers value that." He filled his glass with wine and sat back in the booth.

"I'm told the Third World people pay quite well," Sanderson offered.

"It's the old trouble," Henri said. "They need Caucasians to work for them in Europe. Orientals and Africans are just too easy to spot. They certainly pay better than the CIA used to. But who am I to tell you that?" he said slyly.

"Then the word is out," Sanderson said uneasily.

"Out? You've become the Typhoid Mary of our little world. There are so many agents looking for you that I'm amazed you're still walking around."

"I've got a job for you," Sanderson said. "I have to get to Zurich."

"Not a chance in hell," said Henri quietly. "The borders are sealed, and your picture is hanging in more places than Jesus Christ's. Three, four weeks maybe. But not now. It can't be done."

"I can't wait, Henri."

"I don't see what choice you have."

"Would a hundred thousand dollars American increase my chances?" Sanderson said, leaning forward.

Henri bolted down more wine and indecision crossed his face. He pulled at his chin in conflict.

"Ten now and the balance when we're in Zurich," Sanderson pressed.

"Let me think, damn it," Henri said with agitation. "I don't know, Sanderson. It's a good price but unspendable if I'm rotting in some French pisshole of a prison."

"You said before that the border guards will pass you through," Sanderson insisted.

"True enough. But your escape has changed conditions drastically. Stay here, I've got to make a phone call."

Henri left for the back of the bar, and Sanderson waited quietly. After sixty seconds, he left the bar, pistol concealed under his jacket. Outside, he hurried around the building, ran through the alley, and nudged open the rear door, careful to make no sound.

". . . Sanderson, I tell you. Yes. Here now," he heard Henri say into the phone.

"No. Not till I have a commitment on the money . . . Bullshit! Your cut's too big. I want sixty-forty or shove it."

Sanderson pushed gently at the door and slid inside. He was blocked from Henri's view by the side partitions that bracketed the phone.

"That's more like it," Henri was saying.

Sanderson moved behind Henri and shoved the barrel of the gun hard into his spine. Henri stiffened and froze.

"You'll call back," Sanderson whispered angrily.

"I'll . . . I'll have to call back later. Yes. Goodbye." He hung up the phone.

"Come with me," Sanderson ordered, and he pushed Henri out into the dark alley beyond the back door.

"How much is being offered for me?" he demanded, the gun rising to Henri's chest.

Henri looked at the gun, his muscles tense and his face a desperate mask.

"Two hundred and fifty thousand," he said in a whisper.

"That is considerably better than a paltry hundred thousand. And almost no risk to you. So much for esprit de corps, old brother from the Company. And I do understand, Henri. Believe me, I do."

Henri permitted himself to breathe again. "I knew you would, Paul. It's not personal. Surely you know that I'll get you to Zurich. You can trust me."

"I don't think so," said Sanderson wearily, and the gun flashed twice in the night. Henri was rammed back against the old brick alley walls, blood turning his sweatshirt dark and glistening wet. Sanderson reached down and made sure there was no pulse.

"You were right about one thing, Henri," he said tonelessly to the corpse. "It isn't personal."

He left the alley quickly and walked out of the Quarter. A taxi returned him to the dock area where his hotel was located, and he walked the remaining blocks, circling the hotel until he was certain he was alone.

In the ugly, dilapidated hotel room, he sank exhaustedly into a chair and pulled hard on a bottle of whiskey. It burned his throat, but the harsh liquid returned some calm to his shaken nerves. For two hundred and fifty thousand dollars, friendship and the ethics of business dealings ceased to exist, permanently. Henri had proved that he was alone, the borders of Europe sealed, Zurich impossible to reach.

The Russians were looking for him, too, he was certain. He knew the basic concepts of Nightsight and, even at this stage, a leak would be considered disastrous. With respect to the KGB, he was a dead man. Kasimov would see to that, and Kasimov knew he was in Paris.

He knew it was only a question of time before he was caught, and by whom became academic. The Russians would kill him, the Americans would lock him up. Both avenues were unacceptable. He had to act while he still had the ability.

In the afternoon of the third day, he called Rome station.

Chris was sitting in the office pulling together a final report for Reynolds when the call came through for him from the unidentified caller. Curious, he had the communications room transfer it to him.

"Senator Leyland?" asked the voice.

"Speaking."

"This is Paul Sanderson. Is your phone secure and are you alone?"

"Yes, to both questions," Chris responded. "Can you verify you are who you claim?"

"You've been trying to expose me for almost two months. I've been a Soviet mole for almost twenty years, code name Pollux. My Soviet control is code-named Eris. Sufficient?"

"For now. I assume you called with something in mind."

"I want a deal, Leyland. First, protected transportation to a city of my choice. Second, total immunity; and third, protected transportation from that city to a safe haven. In return, I'll tell you what I know about your brother's death, Eris, and a Soviet operation called Nightsight. Do we deal?"

"I don't have that kind of authority," Chris said, stalling.

"Don't play games with me, Leyland. I know your authority comes from the president himself. Here's a tidbit to sweeten the deal. Eris operates in Rome through the Red Brigade. A man named Renard killed your brother. Now make your decision. Do we deal or not?"

"I thought your partners were Russian," said Chris. "Why come back to us?"

"I don't like the climate in Moscow," said the voice flatly, "and I don't give a rat's ass for either country. But I do care about my life. You need me, Leyland, for what I know. The Russians are close by, and if they take me, you'll never learn about Nightsight till it's all over but the counting."

"I want the person who gave you the word to run," Chris added, fishing.

"Code name, Castor. I'll throw that in as a bonus," agreed Sanderson mirthlessly.

"You have a deal, Mr. Sanderson," Chris agreed, his stomach tightening in anger.

Sanderson gave him an address in Paris.

"The only coin I have left is my own life, Senator. And if anyone but you comes through that door, I'll kill myself. No hesitation, just one bullet in my brain. I hope you understand that and believe it. It'll work out the same anyway if the Russians get to me. I've got nothing to lose."

"It's a deal, Sanderson. Midnight, tonight," Chris said in acceptance.

"I'll be waiting." The connection was severed.

Chris looked at his watch. It was five o'clock. He sent for Talon, Arielle, and Crowley, and within half an hour they were deep in conference.

Sanderson replaced the phone and sat down heavily in one of the soiled brown armchairs. Each of the faded flowers on the peeling gray wallpaper seemed to reflect his darkening mood. Through the soiled windows, the sounds of traffic and the occasional singsong whine of police sirens drifted in. He thought about Zurich.

The soft crunch of footsteps on the old wood floor spun him around.

"Good afternoon, Pollux," said Valentin Kasimov, holding a silenced automatic.

Sanderson sagged deeper in the chair. The gun he had taken from the guard was across the room. Despair flooded over him along with a realization.

"You set me up," he said tiredly, past emotion.

"Of course," Kasimov nodded. "It took no great insight to know you would sell us out if you perceived gain in it for yourself. We simply arranged a set of conditions."

"To get Leyland here," Sanderson said, understanding dawning.

"In part," agreed Kasimov. "The Soviet Union can't kill a United States senator with impunity, even now. His death will be just one more black mark on your record."

"Is there anything I can do to buy my life?" pleaded Sanderson.

"I'm sorry, Pollux," Kasimov shrugged. "Nothing at all. But you knew that from the start, didn't you?"

Talon and Arielle drove Chris to Aviano Air Force Base, a short distance north of the city. In the distance a military jet was being readied for his flight. Crowley had grudgingly stayed at the station to handle communications and whatever else Chris might need when he got to Paris.

Chris would fly the plane himself. It glistened on the runway like a jewel. The sky beckoned to him like an old friend, and his hands clenched reflexively, anticipating the feel of the jet's controls.

"Be careful, Chris," Arielle said, tugging her coat closed tightly against the wind that whipped across the field.

"You too," Chris said. "Stay close to Talon. No one's out of danger yet."

The crew chief helped him into a flight suit and then into the cockpit. Closing the canopy, he gave Chris the go-ahead.

Chris informed the tower that he was ready and got the green light for takeoff. Turning for one last wave to Arielle, standing with Talon by the car, he taxied out to the runway, bore down on the throttle, and shot off into the darkening sky.

Talon made coffee for them. Most of the station personnel had gone home, and the corridors were darkened and quiet.

"I still don't like this, Hank," said Arielle. "Too much risk."

"I've gotten to know your husband pretty well," Talon mused, "and he strikes me as someone who's damn steady under pressure. He's not foolish. He just does what it's necessary to do with a minimum of fuss."

"Flying to Paris and bringing Sanderson in alone is not minimizing risk," she insisted.

"He hasn't been wrong yet. I'd say we could give him the benefit of the doubt."

"I'm going to do some work in the office. Keep me posted, Hank."

"I'll be here, Arielle. We're all in this together."

Sitting at her desk, she began to study some of her own work that had been postponed since they had come to Rome. Distracted at first, she began to make headway on a set of equations and soon was lost in the world of theoretical mathematics, oblivious to anything else.

A knock at her door startled her, and she noticed that over two hours had passed since she began working.

"Dr. Simmons?" The knocking continued.

"Come in," she called.

"Excuse me, ma'am. I'm Agent Greyson. There's been an accident with your husband's flight, and Mr. Talon has a car ready outside. Please, come at once."

Arielle's hands flew to her mouth to stifle her involuntary cry.

"Is he hurt?" she demanded at once, grabbing her coat and scarf.

"I don't know, ma'am. Mr. Talon said to hurry."

They raced down the hallways to the station exit. Abruptly, Arielle grabbed at Greyson's sleeve.

"Please, I think I'm going to . . . be sick. I need . . ."

Greyson had seen the reaction before. "It's all right, ma'am. Right in there. Just hurry, please."

Arielle fled into the bathroom and Greyson heard her violent gagging. A minute later she came running out, a damp paper towel held to her face.

"This way, ma'am," Greyson said, taking her arm.

The air was cool outside in the street as Greyson steered her toward the waiting car.

Suddenly, three men emerged, grabbed her roughly, and pushed her inside. Greyson walked quickly back inside as the car sped away.

"Please don't scream, Dr. Simmons," said Renard happily, pushing his razor-sharp stiletto against her neck. "I would hate to cut your tongue out."

8

The lights of Paris spread out beneath Chris like diamonds on black velvet. His radio suddenly crackled with the voice of a Paris air controller who gave the priority flight immediate clearance to land on a reserved, cordoned-off runway at Orly.

Alone in the night sky, Chris wondered again if he had done the right thing. But he had lived by his judgment all his life, and it was too late to second-guess. Arielle would be safe at station; he trusted Talon without reservation.

Banking sharply over the airport, he turned into the landing path. The white-blue runway lights came into focus, two parallel lines before him, and he dove toward the ground. The jet struck the runway perfectly, tires smoking, the screech of the engines penetrating the cockpit as he poured on reverse power to cut his speed. At the end of the runway, a U.S. military police patrol waited to guard the plane.

"I can't stand this any longer," exhorted Sanderson in a trembling voice. "We've been sitting here for hours. Let me go, Kasimov. I can still be of use to you."

"Look at yourself," Kasimov said disgustedly. "You are of no use to anyone."

"Then why are you torturing me? Get it over with, damn you."

Kasimov sat calmly in his chair and motioned with the gun for Sanderson to remain in his.

"A coroner can pin down time of death to within one hour. Leyland is due at midnight. Detail, Pollux. Always remember detail."

"You aren't human," spat Sanderson.

"Thank you." Kasimov smiled. Then he saw it in Sanderson's face, the doubt growing to conviction, the preparation for a last effort to survive. But it was eleven-thirty, far too late for an attempt at bravery to have any effect at all.

As Pollux came out of his chair, Kasimov pulled the trigger and watched the body jerk violently with each explosion. Paul Sanderson died slowly, as badly as he had lived.

Chris drove to the address he had been given in a poor section of the city by the docks where the smell of water and rotting dock timber suffused the air. Narrow cobblestone streets glistened wetly and shone with reflections from garish neon bar signs that lit up the night.

The Hotel Quai was a four-story, wooden building, paint peeling off its sides like some leprous disease. The windows were darkened by brown, greasy shades, and moisture hung from its iron fire escapes, dripping into brackish pools below. An odor of decay was everywhere.

The stairs crackled under Chris's feet as he ascended to the third floor, rising through a miasma of oily cooking odors and harsh, unshaded light. He knocked on the door of Sanderson's room and pushed it open.

"Come in, Senator Leyland," called a voice inside. "I've wanted to meet you for some time."

"Sanderson?" Chris called in return, entering hesitantly.

Abruptly, the door was shut behind him, and Chris faced an armed man he had never seen before.

"Sanderson is in hell, Senator Leyland, where he belongs."

"I came here to meet him," Chris insisted.

"Very well," Kasimov shrugged. "Come here and have your meeting."

On the floor of the small foyer, Sanderson lay in a pool of blood, his lifeless eyes dull with death.

"You're Eris," Chris guessed with sudden understanding, as he was searched for hidden weapons.

"Colonel Valentin Kasimov."

"All this," Chris's gesture included the room and Sanderson, "just to get me here?"

"You came to get Sanderson, he resisted, you both died in the struggle. Not an eventuality, I assure you, merely an option," Kasimov said comfortably.

Chris nodded. "Very neat. No connection to you or KGB. Still, it does seem a bit of overkill."

"Perhaps, Senator. But I want you to know that I can kill you with total impunity."

"I can't believe I'm all that important, Colonel. Forgive me, but I still don't see what's in this for you."

The phone rang, but Kasimov's gun never wavered.

"It's for you, Senator. Please answer it."

Chris picked up the phone, listened, and his face drained of color. Wordlessly, he hung up and stared at Kasimov.

"If you hurt her, I'll have your heart," he said hotly.

"Your wife is well. Overkill, you think? I consider it just another option. Sit down."

Chris dropped helplessly into a chair, his muscles knotted in rage, struggling for control.

"I can kill you. I can kill your wife. Don't even think of stupid heroics," Kasimov ordered.

Chris said nothing, but his eyes never left the Russian's.

"You're going to work for me, Senator Leyland. Just as Sanderson did. Things are about to change in the world, and we have need of another set of eyes and ears in Washington. As long as you please me, your wife stays alive. Extended vacation, you'll call it when you return to the States."

"I won't let you blackmail me," Chris said flatly.

"Please examine the alternatives."

Chris bit back curses. "You left me none," he said at last.

"It's always pleasing to talk to an intelligent man. I was reasonably certain you'd risk your own life. But not your wife's. The Greeks, whom I'm fond of, called it tragic flaw," Kasimov said smugly.

"Spare me the lectures, Colonel. It seems I have no choice but to work for you," Chris said, wretchedly. "But someday you'll make a mistake, or turn your back, and I'll be there waiting. I promise you, Kasimov, you'll be paid back."

"I detest grandiose speeches," Kasimov said coldly.

"Remember it, Colonel. It will come to pass."

"But it won't, Senator. I can guarantee that."

"Because of Nightsight?" Chris said, guessing.

"That's just a name Sanderson mentioned on the phone," Kasimov said with assurance. "You know nothing."

"Then tell me."

"I'm not a fool, Senator. You provide the information, not I," Kasimov stated.

"Who is Castor?" Chris asked.

"You'll meet Castor when it's time for you to be contacted. Not before. Your subterfuge is transparent and this discussion tiring. I want you to return to Rome, report Sanderson's death, and then return to Washington. Your job in Europe is over."

"I didn't really think you'd tell me anything."

Chris stood up abruptly and walked to the window.

"What are you doing? Sit down at once," Kasimov demanded.

"Don't threaten me unless you intend to use that gun. And you don't, yet," Chris said, raising the shade to open the window. "I need some air."

"You walk a fine line," Kasimov threatened angrily.

"I can afford to, Colonel."

Kasimov looked narrowly at Chris, sensing something in his attitude changing subtly.

"Your wife can be tortured for many hours before she dies," Kasimov reminded him. "I'll send you a recording of her screams."

"Did anyone ever tell you that you have particularly noxious sensibilities?" Chris said, tensing.

"What game are you . . . ?"

The loud crash at the door took Kasimov's attention from Chris for one split second, and Chris dove over his chair instantly, rolling as he hit the floor. Kasimov was already to his feet, but the window exploded and the stun grenade burst into blinding, muscle-paralyzing sound and light, fixing Kasimov where he stood. His gun discharged from reflexive spasms.

But Chris was already moving off the floor and charging for the

fast-recovering Kasimov. He hit him like a defensive tackle with all
the fury of an avenging angel moved by the ice-cold rage reserved
for his brother's killer.

Kasimov still held his gun. Chris grabbed at it and locked on to
Kasimov's arm as it swung toward him. Chris twisted aside, but the
Russian's strength was enormous. It was like wrestling with a writh-
ing boa constrictor, and the gun drew closer in line with his head.
He kicked out viciously for the Russian's groin, missed, and saw the
insane rage that contorted Kasimov's features turn to animal glee as
Kasimov forced the gun toward him. Chris strained and forced his
failing muscles as he fought to turn the hand back. But Kasimov
feinted, his other hand spearing into the nerve bundle under Chris's
solar plexus, and the world grew darker. Kasimov grunted in anticipation of triumph. But then came the sharp hiss of compressed air
and the simultaneous, soft slap of an anesthetic dart and Kasimov
collapsed onto Chris in an unconscious heap.

Chris pushed Kasimov's senseless body from him and got groggily
to his feet.

"He has much strength for a man his age," observed Don Pietro's
messenger from Rome, breaking open the tranquilizer gun and shaking out the spent gas cartridge.

"If there's ever a next time, I want to take him from behind, with
a club," Chris admitted, rubbing his sore chest.

"It has been a pleasure working with you," Mercury said light-
heartedly. "You have some of the quickest reactions I have ever
seen. The operation was perfection itself."

"Except the patient almost died," Chris said dryly. "Let's get them
out of here."

Mercury nodded happily, and soon his men had transported Sanderson and Kasimov downstairs to a private ambulance which sped
off, siren wailing, to the airport.

Chris dialed Rome station and Crowley answered at once.

"Eris down," Chris said.

"Good work. Are you all right?"

"Just a few bruises. Don Pietro's men did their job excellently.
Sanderson's dead; Kasimov's on his tranquil way to Rome. Is your
end ready?"

"All set. Their location is within the city, and Talon's already
there with the troops."

"Fine. Just tell him to make sure no harm comes to our girl. We already owe Don Pietro too much."

"He knows that, Chris. We all do," answered Crowley.

"I'll be airborne in an hour. See you by morning."

"We've still got a ways to go," Crowley reminded him, and the connection was severed.

Chris walked over the dried bloodstain. His plane was waiting, and he had no time for pity.

"Just sit quietly, Dr. Simmons," Renard said, putting his hands on her shoulders, pushing her down. She resisted and squirmed uncomfortably, as before, when Renard had first touched her.

He enjoyed her distress. From time to time, to amuse himself, he poked the stiletto's point into her breasts. She cried at first, then sat resolutely with her arms drawn about her, silently hating him. He enjoyed that, too.

Most of the other men sat playing cards. Curses and loud, raucous joking accompanied each hand. Much of the humor concerned the woman, all of their comments degrading.

"They would like you to themselves for an hour," Renard told her, grinning.

"You're a pig," was the only response. Renard poked her again, harder.

"If you insult me, Dr. Simmons, I will cause you pain. We are going to be together for some time, you and I. Don't insult me again or my friends will protect my honor."

"You have no honor. You're just a little boy playing in an adult world. The violence in you is an infant's rage, spiteful and ugly. I am sorry for you."

"If Eris hadn't said . . ." Renard hissed, struggling for calmness.

"Renard, come here. Quickly!" called the guard on watch at the window.

Renard raced over, the card game abruptly dissolved by the anxiety in the guard's voice.

"What is it?"

"Look, there. And there," the man pointed. "There are men in the streets. Police, I think, with rifles. They're moving into position on the roofs of the other buildings, too."

"Don't panic. We have the girl. They can't attack us," Renard said confidently. "Get everyone into position. Rico, check if the escape route is clear. We're going."

Rico vanished out the door. Hastily, the other men drew their weapons and stood ready by the windows and the door.

"Get up, woman," Renard ordered, pushing her to her feet.

Rico returned, panting and wild-eyed. "There are police everywhere, Renard. The whole block is surrounded. We can't even get to the catacombs; the police have found the tunnel."

"Stay calm," Renard demanded. "They can't shoot if we have the girl. I tell you the hostage will protect us. Let me think. Quiet, all of you. I need to think."

But the men were agitated, unsure. They looked from one to the other with the dawnings of fear. Terrorists were treated very harshly when they were caught. The courts would look aside . . .

"Someone is coming up," yelled the guard from the hallway.

"Let him pass," Renard yelled back. "See?" he told his men. "I told you. They come to offer us a deal. We have played the hostage game before. They will deal on our terms. Just stay alert. Let me negotiate with them. If we keep our heads, we can get away with both the girl and our lives."

He smiled, again in control, and the men relaxed. Renard stood in the center of the room, hands on his hips, and waited to show them how a leader functioned.

Then, with utter weariness, Jack Greyson walked into the room, and Renard felt his heart grow cold in his chest.

"What went wrong?" he demanded. "Why did they send you?"

"They knew you'd believe me," Greyson said sadly, "and maybe I'll get some time off from my sentence. That's all that's left for me. For any of us. Give it up, Renard. There's a goddamn fucking army in the streets."

"But the girl," Renard insisted. "Tell them we'll kill Dr. Simmons. They must want to save her. We have a hostage."

"You still don't see," said Greyson emotionlessly, eyes fixed on the woman. "You have nothing at all. We, all of us, Eris, too, have been played for fools. Outguessed. That's not Arielle Simmons. She's outside with Talon. I don't know who the hell this woman is!"

Renard looked at him blankly, refusing to comprehend. Greyson continued.

"They must've pulled a switch when she got sick and went to the toilet. I didn't notice with that towel held to her face. Believe me, that's not Leyland's wife."

"You can believe him," said Theresa Rennata, her voice amused. "I am no one at all. Just a person who cleans." Then she said it again in Italian to remove all doubt.

"We can still use her," Renard sputtered. "They won't risk a young girl's death. They can't . . ."

"They don't have to," said Greyson bitterly. "Look in the street, fool. He said she belongs to him and to remind you of your family. All your families," he said to the other men.

Renard looked out the window. There, alone and elegant, stood Don Pietro, ramrod straight in the glare of the spotlights. Renard choked on the bile which rose in his throat.

"Give it up," said Greyson, softly.

Theresa Rennata walked out of the room and no one stopped her.

The fear was back in the men's faces. But this time it was fueled by hatred for the leader who had failed them. Renard felt it and drew back.

"I have to think," he pleaded. "Listen to me . . . I'll find a way . . . Eris will . . ."

"He's the one they want," Greyson said flatly.

"That is acceptable," acquiesced Rico, and he and the other men drew closer to Renard.

Greyson nodded dispassionately and walked out of the room.

The stone path which led to the storehouse near the villa was worn by age and countless footsteps. Naked bulbs suspended from a ceiling conduit cast glaring shadows throughout the cavernous building.

Walking past cobwebbed wine racks and piles of obscure bric-a-brac accumulated over centuries, Chris saw Don Pietro sitting in an antechamber past the main room. Beyond him was a medieval-looking oaken door which was guarded by two men.

"Ah, Christopher. Things worked out as we planned. You should be pleased," said Don Pietro at his approach.

"Your debt has been paid many times over. Thank you . . . my friend."

"That is trivial." Don Pietro waved his hand airily, pleasure in his voice.

"I'm going to talk to Kasimov," Chris said. "I trust you can record our conversation?"

"The room is wired. I will listen also. Perhaps an old man can add something."

"Good. I value your experienced ear."

Don Pietro motioned to the guards, who unbolted the thick wooden door.

The room beyond had a single, barred window and was lit by an unshaded pair of bulbs. Iron bars bisected the chamber, set from the stone floor to the ceiling, and the block walls on the other side were completely unadorned. There was only a cot, a water pitcher, and a chamber pot behind the bars. Kasimov's clothing had been taken, and he wore a faded cotton shirt and pants. He stood up sharply when Chris entered.

"Have you eaten?" Chris asked.

"I have," he said coldly.

Chris pulled over a wooden chair and sat quietly, contemplating the Russian.

"I haven't the slightest idea how to go about interrogating you," he said at last.

"And I don't believe in your naiveté," Kasimov said.

"I told you before. I'm just not all that important. Being here is as new to me as I'm sure being there is to you."

"This act of yours, the boyish innocence, is as fraudulent as your claim to lack of skill in trade craft."

"I think you can't accept an amateur on this side of the bars," Chris prodded.

"I am a colonel in the Soviet Committee of State Security. This accommodation is an insult, these bars an offense."

Chris fought down his sudden rage. "These bars keep you alive," he said coldly. "Remember my brother."

"I haven't forgotten. There is a war going on, whether or not your citizens accept it. He was a soldier, an enemy soldier. There was no alternative." Kasimov shrugged.

"Terrorism is not war. And assassinations are never valid alternatives for civilized nations. But I'm not here to argue politics. I want Nightsight. And Castor."

"That is out of the question."

"That is the question, Colonel. When you killed Arthur, you

voided the rules. Eris bred discord, lack of order. That's your particular gift. You can depend on reciprocity," Chris said evenly.

"You mean torture. Or drugs."

"I mean my friends detest animals."

"Then call them. They can't break me. Not in sufficient time. You'll achieve nothing but my death," Kasimov said calmly.

"Your arrogance is amazing." Chris shook his head. "You spoke about tragic flaw. Well, that's yours, Colonel. Pure and simple arrogance. It would surprise me if you ever even contemplated a snag in your divine plan."

"Utter nonsense," Kasimov said angrily.

"Is it? You're so used to using flawed people like Sanderson and Greyson, or that rabid dog, Renard, that you think all people are just as flawed. Except for you.

"If you had settled for Sanderson's escape, or even his death, it would have been over. No one could have found him or you. But your arrogance, your obvious self-love, wouldn't let you waste a piece on the game board. Sanderson's call was just too easy, Kasimov. It had to be a manipulation. And going for Arielle to bind me was so much your style it seemed crazy not to prepare for the possibility. We had Crowley protected the same way. With your obvious inroads to CIA, and all of us in station most of the time, we suspected a turned agent almost at once. Patterns, Kasimov. George Williams, the Jasons' conference. Each time a manipulation, always a counterpoint. If you had humility enough just to vary your style even one iota, our positions right now might be reversed. You're a complete failure at being a human being, and that's what brought you down."

Kasimov's face was suffused with deep color, and his fist hit the bars furiously. "You taunt me from behind a wall. And even so, you think that you've won. But it's you who will be brought down, along with your decadent cesspool of a country."

Chris shook his head sadly. "It seems that any understanding . . ."

Suddenly, a deep bass roar shook the building. Dust shook loose from the ancient stones and a gleam of triumph flashed over Kasimov's features. The unmistakable sound of automatic weapons fire filled the small room. Chris pulled open the heavy door and peered into the dimness beyond.

Don Pietro's men were pinned down behind overturned tables by three men firing steadily into the anteroom. Don Pietro lay wounded, clutching at his shattered right arm. Chris ducked down beside him.

"You see, Leyland," called out Kasimov from his cell, his voice filled with maniacal glee. "You see? I am not alone. Eris is never alone. You will never beat me, Leyland."

Another explosion shook the building, and Chris watched helplessly as the wall behind Kasimov disintegrated into a pile of stone. The dawn sky and more men showed beyond. Kasimov scampered to them over the rubble. Chris searched for a weapon, but was pinned down and couldn't reach one. Bullets pounded into the wall behind him.

"Remember, Leyland," he heard Kasimov's voice call as he ran toward freedom. "Remember that Eris left laughing at you!"

Don Pietro's men had come from the house at the sounds of the fighting. Slowly, they circled the remaining enemy. Wine bottles exploded into shards of flying glass as bullets hit them. The noise of a grenade burst over the room.

Equally as sudden, it was over. Don Pietro's men rose slowly and walked to the bodies of the attackers, turning them with hot rifle barrels and checking to be certain of death.

Chris helped Don Pietro to his feet. A doctor was called to staunch the pain and the flow of blood as Don Pietro listened angrily to the report of his guards.

The doctor walked over to the men who lay still on the cold stone floor.

"*Morto*," he pronounced, sending men for blankets to cover the corpses.

Chris walked away, fatigue crashing over him like a wave. Don Pietro laid a hand on his slumped shoulders.

"Forgive me, Christopher. My men tell me these were trained troops. They would have to be to have taken us by such surprise. Kasimov is gone but take comfort that no harm came to your wife and friends. Forgive me, Christopher. I am truly sorry. I am to blame."

"No one's to blame," Chris said tiredly, "least of all you."

"You are worried," Don Pietro said. "I heard his final words also."

"He was right. In the end he did win. We couldn't hold him."

"What will you do now?" asked Don Pietro.

"Sleep. Then go back to Washington to report. It's just beginning, whatever Kasimov worked so hard for. And Castor knows what it is, what all this means. He's our last chance at stopping it."

"What can I do to help?"

Chris looked deeply into his friend's face, trying to read some portent in its ancient lines and wise eyes.

"Help? For all I know it's too late for help."

"It's never too late," the old man said firmly.

"Then pray for us, Don Pietro; pray for us all."

9

Vassily Komarovsky looked through the giant, steel-louvered windows of the Launch Center and watched the sun rise over the desolate scrubland surrounding the Baikonur Cosmodrome. Ignoring, for the moment, the launch team's steady, measured preparations in the Launch Control Center behind him, he regarded the sun, and its red color, as an omen. With a deep sense of mystery, which could no longer be called religion in the modern State, he believed in portents as completely as his ancestors must have, riding hot-breathed horses across the endless permafrost.

Komarovsky had seen work begun on the sprawling Baikonur Complex, now far bigger than the Kennedy Space Center, as a young KGB lieutenant in 1955. Begun as a testing facility for the earliest ICBM's, within two years the outpost of tents, shacks, and caravans had been replaced by huge concrete launch platforms connected by a mile-long railway to the assembly buildings. Later, the base was extended northward in a Y-shaped system of roads and railways linking other launch pads east and west of the original site, till almost a hundred miles separated the top points of the Y.

At the southern base of the Y stood Leninsk, the Science City, whose population of over fifty thousand was kept alive by endless trainloads of consumer goods, now only sporadically arriving in the service town of Tyuratam, to the south. He remembered Leninsk, interlaced with a complex irrigation system to feed the barren land, as beastly hot in the summer and killing cold, sometimes seventy degrees below zero, during the long winter. But like other cities of the "new era," Leninsk had constructed countless schools, several palaces of culture, movie theaters, pools, stadiums, and hotels. There was even a local radio and television station.

Komarovsky had spent the past week in Leninsk, responsible for the security of Nightsight. Always aware of the eyes-in-the-sky looking down at them, even Pyotr Meledov and the other Politburo members arriving to watch the launch were shuttled north to Baikonur in ordinary, nondescript vehicles. How often Komarovsky had seen their eyes look upward, then be quickly averted, replaced by hard looks in anticipation of the future.

Tensions were growing, too, emotions long smoldering coming dangerously close to the surface as launch time grew near. Those scientists, technicians, and launch personnel who understood what was taking place, the goals of Nightsight, knew the risks as well. Slowly, their fever spread, carried by rumor, until the Cosmodrome buzzed with speculation. Three days earlier, Komarovsky had ordered the Cosmodrome sealed. No one gained entrance or exit and no one communicated with the outside world without his permission.

At the extreme eastern end of the facility was the industrial support complex, in which the laser stations and the two launch pads for the giant proton rockets which would send them into orbit had been built and tested.

Komarovsky looked into the morning sky and thought again of the Prophets which scanned the area continuously, twenty-four hours a day, and of the deceptions they had made necessary.

It was standard procedure to notify the Americans, and vice versa, of launches to take place. That minimized the risk of setting off their nuclear attack detection systems. However, regardless of the notification, the launch would be monitored from ground to orbit by spy satellites whose lenses could spot the unusual configuration of the payload and discern its purpose long before insertion into orbit. Merely a hint of offensive weaponry would be enough to bring on American missiles to destroy the payload before it could be deployed. Nightsight would be over before it had begun, powerless to defend itself from nuclear-tipped ICBM's.

To this end, an elaborate ruse had been planned months before under the guise of the Salyut Space Station program. Each of the configurations of the Salyuts were well known to the Americans.

Salyut 9 and 10, as these launches were named, would be the first Soviet attempt to orbit two stations, and join them in space into one much larger station. This was a credible, understandable mission, given the restrictions on payload capability of the launch vehicles, also well known to the Americans.

What the Americans could not, must not know, Komarovsky thought again, was that the Salyut stations were facades, mere shells which would be jettisoned in orbit to deploy the laser platforms, two in each payload, on the first orbital pass. There was still a risk, though, he thought ruefully. At the orbital height of five hundred miles, the platforms would each orbit the earth in under an hour. But after insertion, when the facades were discarded, it would take precious time for the platforms to align themselves ninety degrees apart at the twelve-, three-, six-, and nine-o'clock positions with respect to the earth. For those minutes, two of the four stations would be vulnerable. They would have to be protected by the remaining two. Everything depended on the element of surprise. Once inserted into position, anything thrown up against the lasers could be vaporized. But until operation, the lasers were vulnerable. Komarovsky knew it would be the longest minutes of his life.

A hand on his shoulder startled him, and he turned quickly.

"You are worried, Vassily?" asked Pyotr Meledov gently. Vyacheslav Trapeznikov stood next to him, a sympathetic expression on his haggard face.

"No, Comrade President," said Komarovsky. "I am prepared."

Meledov nodded. "That is as it should be. From you, I would expect no less. We are about to make history, Comrade."

"A long road comes to completion today," Komarovsky agreed softly, "but another begins."

"It is almost time," broke in Trapeznikov, tension apparent. "Perhaps you would both go to the viewing section? I'll be along shortly."

"How much time remains?" asked Meledov.

Trapeznikov glanced to the launch clock. "Less than half an hour."

"You go, then. We will be along presently," said Meledov, and the Minister of Science nodded and hustled away to confer with the launch team. Turning, Meledov walked to the far window and motioned for Komarovsky to follow. In the distance, the two proton rockets and their payloads, almost three hundred feet tall, stood on the twin launch pads like slim needles dominating the flat plain.

"May I confide something to you?" Meledov asked quietly, his gaze never leaving the distant rockets.

"I would be honored," said Komarovsky, staring at the bearlike visage beside him.

"I have looked into my deepest thoughts and tried to foresee where we will all be twenty-four hours from now. But it is dark, and I cannot see the way. Have you done this also?"

"I have. And for me, too, the end of the path is unclear. But there is no other choice for us . . ." said Komarovsky slowly.

"I agree. And I offer you this, Comrade, for whatever it is worth," said Meledov. "I came to watch the rockets being readied as they were transported to the launch sites from the assembly buildings. For all the space programs I have supported over the years, for some reason, I had never personally seen that phase of a launch. You know how the rockets are transported horizontally by rail and then elevated vertically by the transporter-ejector mechanism to the gantry? How tall they then stand?"

Komarovsky nodded, "I do."

"Well, then," Meledov continued. "Then you may not find it so strange if I tell you what it reminded me of to see the rockets erected into place and how I felt for the State at such a rising. Tell me if you know, Vassily."

"I know," said Komarovsky as Meledov turned to him and their eyes locked. "You saw . . . manhood."

"Yes," sighed Meledov. "I thought you could understand. Come now. It is almost time."

On the wall, the launch clock showed only minutes remaining before Nightsight would begin. The steel shutters on the windows began to close. In the distance, the giant proton boosters roared into life.

Fourteen hundred feet below Cheyenne Mountain in Colorado, the North American Air Defense Command tracked the Soviet launch. Ground stations in Guam and Australia were the first to pick it up and verified the already received Prophet data that the launches were congruent to the published Soviet schedule.

Members of NORAD's battle staff tracked the rockets as they

passed through the atmosphere. Prophet's photos of the payload configuration were fed into the massive computers and matched with the established configurations of other Salyut launches. The alarms were silent, the tracks on the screens in the combat operations center all showing a launch within predicted norms.

"Look like good birds," commented Major Ron Brandon, his tracking console below the director's. "Both of them."

"Punch it over to my screen," said General John Blaire, director of the COC. "Sure do look fine," he commented when the tracks appeared on his own panel. "What's the projected orbit?"

"DOD says five hundred eliptical."

"And the tracks match that?"

"Absolutely," said Brandon.

"Okay. Stay on it," ordered the hawk-faced general scanning the large, multi-screened room, satisfied that the situation was being handled.

Throughout the combat operations center, soldiers sat at their consoles keeping track of every one of the thousands of satellites and assorted space "debris" that orbited the earth. The command center looked much like Mission Control in Houston or Canaveral, save for the military personnel. But here, the tracking was unceasing, continuous every hour, twenty-four hours a day. At the top of each console, a lettered plate identified the targets of each tracker, NAVSAT, VELA, TACSAT, NATO COMSAT, DSCS, PROPHET. And for those who tracked the Soviets, VOSTOK, SALYUT, COSMOS . . .

General Blaire leaned back, sipped his coffee, and ran a hand over his steel-gray crew cut. None of the easy banter that characterized NASA facilities was allowed here. This was the nerve center of the entire air defense establishment. Should the onslaught of nuclear war ever begin, it was NORAD that would detect it first. No one who sat in the director's chair, Blaire thought for the countless time, could laugh in the face of that.

"We have orbit insertion on Salyut 9 and 10," Major Brandon called out

"Very good, Major. Keep on it," Blaire acknowledged.

The rhythmic slaps of the ribbons flapping over the air conditioning ducts were punctuated by data relays and the hums and clicks of computers. One soldier took off his headphones to scratch an ear.

Blaire caught the movement and buzzed the soldier's console impatiently. The soldier jumped, fumbling, and replaced the headset at once. Blaire permitted himself no smile. They could not afford sloppiness here where seconds counted. Like an unforgiving father, he took his children to task every second of his watch.

"Sir?"

Blaire looked up and saw a frown cross Brandon's features.

"Yes, Major?"

"Something on the Salyut 9 over the North Pole, sir. It's on your screen now. Looks like . . . looks like it's breaking up! I've got some kind of separation showing . . ."

Blaire's screen accepted the data display, and the general shook his head in confusion.

"Never seen this before. Where's Salyut 10?"

The major's hands played over his console, and new data flashed on the screen.

"Jesus," he swore, "Salyut 10's over the South Pole. Same thing's going on. What the hell are they up to?"

"Keep tracking, Major. Get a computer check on it."

General Blaire hit the Condition Yellow alert button with one hand and reached for the phone with his other. The alarm flashed on every console and on every screen in the COC. It galvanized the room. Emergency procedures were activated. The Department of Defense Console operator began the chain of command that would alert the military. The assistant director slapped on the recorders.

"General Blaire, DCOC. Get me Air Force Sat Com. Condition Yellow," Blaire said quickly into the phone. The com center relayed the call via the Fleet Satellite Communications System, in geosynchronous orbit, through to the Air Force Satellite Command near San Francisco. Five seconds later the director of AFSATCOM was on the line.

"General Parkins here. Go ahead, NORAD."

"Blaire here. We've got some strange pictures on the Salyut 9 and 10. I need corroboration, General. Can you re-angle the Prophets and get us a look?"

"Can do, NORAD. Hold at Yellow."

Blaire heard orders being shouted. The Air Force Satellite Command was in direct control of the orbits of every American satellite in the sky. They would plot the Salyut orbits and guide the Prophets in for a direct look. Yellow lights still flashed all over the COC. Blaire tapped his console in frustration.

"Let's get on it." He swore silently under his breath. He knew every military base in the free world would be on standby by now. SAC crews would be racing for their planes. Missile silos would begin preliminary operation. God, how he hoped this wasn't some freak computer ghost. Then, in almost the same breath, he prayed that it was.

"Check your screen, sir," Major Brandon called out. His voice was tense, his breath drawn unsteadily. "I've got eight separate blips showing. Looks like . . . four blips falling back into the atmosphere. Can't get a handle on this."

"Plot reentry points," commanded Blaire, fingers hammering on the phone.

Again, Brandon's fingers played over his console.

"Two into the Atlantic, fifteen hundred miles offshore, two into the Indian Ocean, five hundred miles offshore. No danger at all. No priority," he read out.

"What the fuck is going on?" demanded Blaire hotly. There was no danger from whatever it was that was falling into the ocean. But what was still left up there? Accident or design? They had to know damn soon. His finger hovered over the Condition Red signal.

"Two blips in stationary orbits a hundred and eighty degrees apart," called out Brandon, "two others still maneuvering. Could be going for ninety degrees, sir."

"Keep it coming, Major," barked Blaire.

"NORAD? Prophet data in line to you. Computers checking configurations now. Go to Red. Repeat. Condition Red," ordered General Parkins.

Blaire's hand shot out, and the red glow filled the room, bloodlike on their faces.

"Start intercept tracking on those four blips," ordered Parkins again "The Situation Room is on top of this. We are waiting for identification of target. Stand by NORAD, Situation Room coming on."

Blaire relayed the orders to his deputy, who began a course interception analysis at once. Then he punched in the AFSATCOM data onto his screen. At once, the Prophet view of the Soviet blips came into focus. Blaire drew in a sharp breath. The blips were not debris from a broken-up Salyut. Each one was twenty feet long and cylindrically shaped with the great bell of a rocket engine at one end and a swivel-based gunlike apparatus on the other. Radar antennae jutted out from the center of the cylinder. Blaire looked up in shock.

"Is the intercept course plotted in?" he demanded.

"Plotted in and continuous tracking on," confirmed Deputy DCOC Colonel Atkins from the console next to the general's.

"Good. Stand by to feed it to SAC. Those things up there sure aren't debris," Blaire said.

"NORAD? This is General of the Army Peterson," came a new voice over the phone. Peterson was the four-star general who commanded the military, head of the Joint Chiefs.

"NORAD here. General Blaire, DCOC," he said in response, controlling his terror.

"Those devices in orbit are identified as laser battle stations, General Blaire. Go to Code Green. Repeat, Code Green."

Blaire's hand shot out again to his console, and the color in the room changed again. Green, the faces became the color of sickness and fear.

"Code Green acknowledged," said Blaire, his hand gripping spasmodically at the phone. He began to pray.

"Blips at ninety degrees diametric and one-eighty degrees diametric," called out Brandon. "No further maneuvers."

"On screen," Blaire called back. "We are tracking blips," said Blaire into the phone. "All on screen."

"Very well, then," said General Peterson. "SAINT is authorized. Can you supply data?"

Blaire had anticipated the use of the Satellite Interceptor Program. He looked up at the deputy DCOC. "SAINT. Are we ready?"

"Yes, sir," barked the colonel.

"SAINT program rolling," said Blaire back into the phone. "On your order."

"Commence program," ordered Peterson.

The Strategic Air Command base in North Dakota had been on alert since Code Yellow. From dormitory-type barracks, pilots and their crews had jumped into flight suits and had run to their waiting planes.

The SAC commanding general received the order for SAINT and gave appropriate commands from the control tower.

Thirty seconds later the first of the F-15 Eagles shot off the runway into the sky. Within minutes, the F-15's were at squadron strength blazing through the cold Dakota air.

The squadron leader's computer officer, in the seat behind his, accepted the computer data from the NORAD facility, five hundred miles distant. The squadron converged on the SAINT squadron leader. On command from NORAD, the planes turned in unison. Each carried a two-stage SRAM/THIOKOL-ALTAIR 3 missile underneath its fuselage. These Boeing short-range attack missiles had first-stage Altair boosters and second-stage self-homing warheads carrying cryogenically cooled infrared telescopes to home in on the target using NORAD data.

Three other squadrons of this type took off concurrently from SAC bases throughout the world. All used NORAD data. Each had a separate target to destroy. Unmindful of danger, the Soviet stations continued their orbit.

On squadron leader's command, the F-15's began a zoom climb straight up. Their engines pouring out hot exhaust, they tore up through the sky toward the target like banshees straight from hell.

General Blaire watched it on the big screen in COC. Supplied by tracking stations all over the world, the big board glowed with the four targets and the squadrons of F-15's that flew at them in sharp, full-power climb.

Colonel Atkins watched the flights climb. He called out the seconds remaining to missile launch, controlled by the computers.

". . . two, one . . . Missiles away!"

Blaire looked at the screen and saw the missiles separate from the F-15's. The planes began to descend as the missiles raced toward their targets.

". . . Separation," called out Atkins.

Blaire watched the screen, transfixed by the flight of the missiles.

"Twenty seconds to impact," called Atkins, his voice faltering.

Soldiers rose out of their seats. Blaire gripped the phone and almost yelled out loud for the birds to make it, to get there, to blow the lasers out of the sky.

"Ten seconds," Atkins called out. The men were on their feet now.

Blaire watched the missiles race along projected tracks. Closer . . . Closer . . .

The missile tracks vanished off the screen.

Wide-eyed and shaking, Blaire spoke into the phone, and his voice was a whisper. "General Peterson. NORAD reports SAINT negative. Repeat. SAINT negative."

"Acknowledged, NORAD," said Peterson's now harried voice. "We've got it on our screens."

"What do—"

"General Blaire!" yelled Major Brandon. "We're losing satellites . . . They're going off the screen one by one . . . My God, General!"

"Keep tracking, damn it!" yelled Blaire, but in his mind's eye he watched the laser beam flash out again and again and again. A beam of light so hot and deadly that steel vaporized into fumes. SAINT negative, he kept repeating. What the hell was left?

"NAVSAT down," called a console operator, awakening to terror.

"Fleet SAT Com down," called another in a voice barely audible.

"Defense Command Sat Com System down."

"TACSAT down."

"LANDSAT down."

"British Skynet down."

"NATO 2 down."

"Nuclear Force Com Sat down."

"Bell System down."

One by one every console went blank, death-knelled by its operator. Blaire stared in horror at his command console. He saw the lasers flash and flash again.

"All essential systems down, sir," Atkins reported in a voice dull with shock and disbelief.

General Blaire picked up the phone to report, but it was dead. He dropped it from nerveless fingers. It was all there on his screen, every system down and out. He saw it but couldn't imagine, refused to believe. And there, flashing insistently on his display, over and over again, were the words he dreaded most to see, the words that could cripple the American military to which he had devoted his life. Again and again it flashed, like an unceasing death knell . . .

PROPHET BLIND . . . PROPHET BLIND . . . PROPHET BLIND . . .

PART FOUR

PART FOUR

1

The White House was under siege. Reporters and cameras mobbed the press section and, despite the best efforts of the Secret Service, crowded in on the stream of military and civilian personnel who passed through the north entrance on their way to the presidential briefing.

Entering the State Dining Room, the only area large enough to contain the number summoned to the briefing, they were ushered into seats that had been hastily erected earlier that morning. Uneasily, they glanced around, their eyes recording the staggering array of power in the room.

Almost all of the Joint Chiefs were assembled, sitting stiffly in the straight-back chairs with hats held firmly in their laps. Most of the Cabinet, the secretaries of the Interior, Treasury, Agriculture, Labor, Commerce, Transportation, Energy, and the Attorney General were present. Business, too, was well represented—by the chairmen of TRW, Boeing, Lockheed, Grumman, ATT, IBM, COMSAT, McDonnel Douglas, General Dynamics, Hughes, Litton, and Rockwell, all major defense contractors.

When the last person was seated, the doors were swung back by uniformed guards. Attention turned to the podium at the front of the room which bore the presidential seal. Conversations began with whispered conjecture. They all hoped the president would be arriving soon with answers to the question on everyone's mind—just what the hell had happened "up there"?

Several stories below the dining room level, Brendan Connors stood staring at the small group of men at the conference table in the Situation Room. Around them were screens depicting the total military posturing of the United States throughout the entire world. Slowly, communications had been restored using older ground and underwater cable systems. But the damage was extensive, the situation unpredictable.

Senator Chris Leyland, General of the Army Bennett Peterson, and Secretary of Defense Arnold Dupont stared back without giving ground.

"Even to ponder such an option is insane," said Connors in disbelief.

"That may be, sir," said Peterson, a short, wide man with gray hair growing sparsely on the sides of his head and bifocals perched upon his thin nose. "But I urge you to accept our counsel. We see no other alternative."

"The United States signed a treaty in 1972 outlawing this kind of thing. And even before that, in 1970, we dropped the whole program. What you're suggesting is goddamned illegal as well as insane," said Connors hotly.

"The means still exist," said Secretary Dupont, his spare, ascetic face more like that of a Trappist monk than a retired Naval admiral. "They are stored in the Utah desert with the other remains of the program. Frankly, I see no other alternative, no other way to buy the necessary time. The plan is sound, the meteorological conditions appear to be perfect. In a few days, that may no longer be so."

Connors turned to Chris. "You know as much about Nightsight as anyone. Do you support this strategy?"

Chris rubbed the stubble on his face. Almost forty-eight hours had passed since he'd last slept or shaved. Flown hurriedly back to Washington after reporting the results on the Rome investigation to the president, he had been rushed down to the Situation Room to join the crisis management team. His revelations concerning Castor had been essential to the team's successful planning. Now, sitting with the team's leaders, Dupont and Peterson, he regarded the president slowly.

"We've been over this again and again. The Soviets have all the power right now, and we are vulnerable to a nuclear attack. That alone is enough to drive any sane man to desperate acts. Every form of tactical warfare is nullified by their lasers. Forget about long-range bombers, ICBM's, cruise missiles, conventional weaponry of every kind. You tell me if you've got some kind of miracle weapon in the arsenal. This isn't some science fiction movie. We've got to restore a tactical balance at once, and I don't see any other way to do that."

Connors hit the table in frustration. "I'm the one who has to face the public. And don't tell me that I can approach them honestly with this. I've got to go on television in under two hours, and I can just see it now—We're okay again folks, but most of Europe and Asia could be uninhabitable at any time."

"Use the solar flare story. I believe it will hold up for a while. Don't tell them the rest," said Dupont.

"That won't wash for those upstairs," Connors said.

"They get the truth," agreed Chris, "but not including our response. They have to know what we need, and no bullshit about solar flares is going to satisfy them. Classify it National Security. For once, at least, it is."

"Look, Mr. President," said Peterson, "I'm not saying I like this either. But we got caught with our pants down. Leyland here has a right to gloat if he wants to. It's my responsibility to advise you on military matters. I've just done that. We have no choices left."

"I've said all I can," agreed Dupont.

"We've still got Castor to worry about," said Connors bitterly. "I can't believe he could be one of my people. I've trusted them all for years."

"And now we have Soviet lasers in orbit," said Chris wearily. "Your people have to be frozen out, isolated to give the rest of us time to come up with a way to destroy those lasers. Sanderson told me he was alerted by Castor. No one else but your people and mine knew that we'd found him. You said so yourself this morning. I can vouch for my people . . ." He left the implication hanging.

"But I can't for all of mine," conceded Connors unhappily, "with

the exception of the Secretary of State. He was in my presence from
the moment Barbara announced that you'd found Pollux till long
after the discovery of his escape. Powell had no opportunity to alert
anyone."

"That still leaves Clancy, Parienne, and Reynolds," Chris said.
"No one else had either the information or the opportunity. They
must be frozen out of the planning of this operation for security
reasons—at least during the next seventy-two hours. If the Russians
get wind of what we're planning to do, we'll have no chance at all."

"Your oath of office impels you to preserve, protect, and defend
this country, Mr. President," added Dupont not unsympathetically,
"even at the sacrifice of personal considerations. I know how
difficult it is for you to endanger some of your closest friends and
advisers; but contrasted against the disaster this country surely faces
if our security is further compromised, the choice is clear: Castor
must be uncovered."

Connors looked away with an expression that asked for divine
guidance knowing none would be forthcoming.

"What is your plan?" he asked finally.

Chris explained the necessary details, seeing the president's
distaste for treachery, knowing that the pressure of time and events
had left them little choice.

"They'll be part of Powell's team, at least for seventy-two hours.
Then they can be brought back to Washington along with Talon and
closely watched. When Castor makes his move—we'll be there,"
Chris finished, staring into Connors' stony silence.

"If I could see any other way to go on these issues, any alternative
at all, I would gladly take it," said Connors slowly. "But the fact
remains that I do not. Leaving this country, even for a short while,
open to a Soviet nuclear strike would be criminal malfeasance."

For a moment Connors weighed conflicting responsibilities in his
mind. Dupont was correct, he decided; his oath demanded that there
could be no higher law than protecting the nation.

"All right then," he said at last. "Get the ships moving and the
people prepared. You have my authorization."

The announcement rang out over the room and silenced all.

"Ladies and gentlemen. The president of the United States." The assembly stood, and then sat down with the rustle of paper as Brendan Connors strode into the State Dining Room and up to the podium.

"I thank you all for your prompt response to my somewhat hasty summons, but I can assure you that it is in the best interest of this nation that I have called you here today.

"In times of crisis, the country has always had to call upon its finest men and women to shoulder a load that is perhaps disproportionately heavy. That is certainly the case today. I am, however, confident that you will do what can be, what must be done.

"Twenty-four hours ago, without warning and in violation of every international code of conduct, the United States was attacked by the Soviet Union. In an engagement which lasted only seconds, the Soviet Union, by means of four orbital laser stations, destroyed almost our entire satellite network, both military and civilian. The damage done is inestimable, but it is not, I repeat, it is *not* irreparable. Already, measures are being taken to guarantee the safety and security of our nation. We are not defenseless. Make no mistake about that.

"What is required of you here today, our foremost military figures and defense industry contractors, is an effort so massive as to rival the Berlin airlift in scale and the Lunar landing in cost. Within three weeks, twenty-one days, we are going to rebuild and replace every single satellite that was lost. Every single one!

"The logistics of such a massive effort will be coordinated by the Department of Defense under Secretary Dupont. Shortly, I will turn this meeting over to him for particulars.

"What I have just told you must now be classified under the highest provisions of National Security. Press Secretary Lawford will provide you all with copies of the announcement I will be televising to the public. We must avoid a panic which could result if the truth were known prematurely.

"Again, it must be stressed that security in this matter is paramount. Should anyone doubt that, they would be well advised to review the importance of government contracts to their respective companies. I have no doubt that I can count on all of you to cooperate fully with this administration in a time of crisis.

"Ladies and gentlemen, the task ahead is enormous, the hours

long, the cost high. Such is freedom's unchanging price. Thank
you."

One hour later, the hot lights of the television crew burned down
on Connors and he felt sweat combined with makeup run down
under his collar. He had been speaking to the public for ten minutes
already and knew he had to maintain his composure for the "big lie"
to succeed. He smiled warmly at the camera lens.

". . . The solar flares which have destroyed the satellites are not,
I am assured by our top scientists, harmful to those of us on earth.
Our atmosphere protects us completely. But the high level of radiation has reduced the complex circuitry of our satellites to worthless
scrap.

"For most of us, this will result in difficulties with our television
cable systems, long-distance phone calls, data relay systems, and
with our weather forecasting. Even this speech will reach many of
you on videotape. Rest assured that other, more sensitive areas,
such as national security are being well tended to by the nation's
peacekeepers. I know that the American people will bear these burdens as we have always borne them, with the sure and certain
knowledge that no obstacle can stand for long against American in-
genuity and perseverance . . ."

Connors continued his speech, hoping to God that the people
would buy such utter nonsense. Somewhere in the back of his mind
was the frightening realization that they had before.

In the Situation Room, Leyland, Peterson, and Dupont soberly
regarded the chief of the Military Weather Division, Dr. John Whitney. Whitney, though head of a military unit with the equivalent
rank of full colonel, was totally unused to the battle-command envi-
ronment in which he had suddenly found himself. Every so often, he
would pause, raise his glasses up from his blue eyes to rest them on
his pink, freckled forehead, and scan the room nervously as colonels
ran from station to station, barking orders and re-establishing communications links with the global allied commands. Generals sat at
desks marked SACEUR, SACLANT, MALCOM, PACCOM (Supreme Allied Command Europe, Supreme Allied Command Atlantic, Military Airlift Command, Pacific Command) ascertaining
strength of forces and conducting battle feasibility studies in light of

their downed surveillance and communications networks. The room made Whitney, a scholarly little man happiest with air flow charts, isobars, and temperature gradients, inordinately nervous.

"Just ignore the commotion, Dr. Whitney," counseled Secretary Dupont. "To most of them, your weather stations would be equally confusing."

"Quite so . . . I'm sure," said Whitney hesitantly, pausing to mop his forehead with an old shredded tissue he pulled from a pocket of his baggy corduroy jacket. He and the meteorologists who composed his division did not wear military uniforms.

"Do I understand you to be saying that conditions are near perfect for the type of operation we've described?" prompted Peterson.

"Yes, indeed, they are quite what you want," said Whitney, his speech growing stronger as he retreated to familiar topics. "It's a condition which occurs in that area of the world quite often. The prevailing winds over the Soviet Union during this season blow from west to east. Actually, slightly northwest to southeast is more accurate. Now, there is a high-pressure 'ridge' sitting over the British Isles and a similar high-pressure ridge over Japan. As the pressure is higher in those ridges than in the wind, they act somewhat like walls, forcing the wind to make a kind of U-turn, if you like, and reverse direction. These ridges, coupled with the low-pressure 'trough' which is currently sitting over the northern Soviet coast, make the weather ideal. The trough, again due to pressure differences, pulls the wind into it and directs it southwesterly where it hits the Japanese high ridge, turns, and blows back into the Soviet Union. In short, General, any winds going into the Soviet Union will, at least for the near future, stay in the Soviet Union."

"What about China?" asked Dupont.

"The Gobi desert is a more or less permanent high-pressure ridge. The Chinese wind pattern comes northerly from southeast Asia, not south from the Russias. China is not a problem, gentlemen. Your worry should be the Japanese ridge. If that dissipates, and well it might at any time, the wind blows out over the Pacific toward Hawaii and our West Coast. Alaska and Canada will surely be in its path."

The pronouncement was met with stunned silence. Faces turned to each other, and receiving no answers, looked away in growing horror of what they contemplated.

"If the British ridge dissipates completely," Whitney continued, "or moves eastward, toward the Soviet Union, it could redirect the winds back into Europe. Now, please understand, gentlemen, our forecasting abilities are severely curtailed by the loss of the Meteosats. We have no satellite data to use in our computers. We're back to old-fashioned methods, augmented by the computers surely, but nowhere near the accuracy the satellites gave us."

"Then what is your projection if both ridges dissipate?" asked Chris, his question betraying the fear he felt.

"In that case, Senator Leyland," said Whitney softly, "God help us all."

The hot water swirled around James Fuller's waist as he settled gingerly into the hot tub in the backyard. Immediately, the frothing water relaxed his tired muscles, sore from the morning's exertion in the garden. His two children, Sean and Kathleen, ages four and six, were already in the tub with their mother, making distorted faces to mimic their father's. They playfully splashed water at him. He smiled and kissed them as they swam into his arms. His wife, Beverly, fifteen years his junior, sighed appreciatively and sank farther down into the steaming water.

"Let Daddy relax, children," she offered halfheartedly, knowing there was little hope of controlling them. Daddy's return was too recent for their joy and affection to be suppressed so easily.

Fuller held his children in a great bear hug as they poked at his darkly glistening full beard. He watched Beverly's pert breasts rise and fall in the water as his family and the hot tub reduced his aches and restored his equilibrium.

The rocky Swedish mountains, sheer and pine-forested, rose up behind the house. It overlooked the water which ran, miles distant, past Stockholm and into the Baltic Sea. During the long, cold winter, Fuller moved the family back to the U.S. but, stationed as he was on a ship in the North Atlantic, when the family was in Sweden, he was usually less than a few hours' plane ride away. His visits could be longer and more frequent. Having married late in life, he treasured his family dearly.

Later, the children asleep, he and Beverly lay locked together in bed. The first time they made love when he returned was always fast and hard, passions stored over solitary weeks needing to be abated. The second time was softer and more gentle. As were the times after that.

"I missed you," Fuller said, turning languidly to face her.

"Such is the lot of a captain and his wife," said Beverly easily, her voice still husky from the lovemaking.

"Another few years, honey. Then Rear Admiral Fuller retires to a desk," he promised.

"I'm not worried, Jim. We have all the time in the world," she said comfortably. "And the children are just fine."

"You do a wonderful job with them," he said sincerely. "I want to . . ."

The roar of a helicopter descending covered his words. Fuller grabbed a robe and walked downstairs to open the front door as a naval pilot strode up the walk.

"I'm sorry to bother you, sir. But your presence is required back on ship at once. I'll wait outside, sir."

"I just got home, son. Why wasn't I radioed about this?" Fuller demanded. In this area, satellite-linked radio was the only method usable.

"I don't know, sir." The pilot shrugged. "Could be the problem we're having with all our communications equipment. President says it's some kind of solar flare-up."

Fuller heard the words and sensed at once that something more serious than solar flares had transpired. He hastened inside and told Beverly. They decided not to wake the children.

Fuller's face was lined with worry as he reached for his uniform with its four half-inch gold stripes on the sleeve and the silver eagle on its collar.

"Ready, Captain?" asked the pilot when Fuller was inside the helicopter.

"Son," said Captain Fuller, "I don't really think that matters. Let's get out to the *Tarent*."

The helicopter leaped into the air and raced for the ship.

The communications officers were just finishing setting up the hotline equipment in the Oval Office. Connors came in, hastily toweling streaked makeup from his face. He took in the red phone, with its auxiliary lines to the translator, and seemed to shrink a bit, to compress, as if marshaling his strength for yet another effort in the counterwar they were so desperately waging.

Chris noted the strain in Connors' expression. "If it's any help, Mr. President, both speeches seem to be having the desired effect. Your press secretary was just in to tell you that the papers are giving you high marks for leadership, and the public reaction is to take this thing in stride. You've bought us some time, sir; no one could have done better."

"Thank you, Senator," said Connors, settling into his chair. "But you know, too, that this is only a temporary state of affairs. There are just too many ways this could leak out. Amateur observers, ham radio operators, defense industry workers. Don't fool yourself; it's just a matter of time."

"We'll make the best of it, sir," said General Peterson. "Security's as tight as we can make it."

"Five minutes, Mr. President," said the head communications officer, placing the last contact into the system. He and the other officers left at Connors' satisfied nod.

Secretary Dupont broke the silence created by the com officers' departure.

"Mr. President," he said slowly, "I don't want to add to the strain you're already under, but this conversation with the Soviets is critical. Whatever else you say, whatever else you do, the *Tarent* must be allowed to proceed to the Gulf of Finland. Once there, it can be secured. But if the Russians suspect a trick or a ruse of any kind, and don't give it permission to enter their waters, we are finished before we begin. That is the bottom line, sir."

"Very well, Mr. Secretary," said Connors.

"One minute, sir," said the translator, Aaron Barrows, a former Soviet affairs scholar, now permanently in government service. Though Meledov spoke fluent English, translators were still necessary for finer points.

"Thank you, Mr. Barrows. You may proceed," said Connors.

Chris watched the president draw a deep breath. It made him realize he was holding his own.

The red light suddenly blazed from the phone's console. Barrows picked his phone up, spoke swiftly in fluent Russian, and nodded to the president.

"Mr. Meledov is on the line, sir."

Connors activated the speaker system and put forty years of political experience into controlling his voice.

"Good afternoon, Mr. Meledov. I trust you've been well since our last conversation?"

"Very well, Mr. Connors. You appear to be well yourself, judging from your televised conference earlier. I commend the discretion you displayed," said Meledov, his voice cordial but restrained, emanating from the amplified speaker.

"I believe we all wish our present . . . interaction . . . to be kept within manageable boundaries," said Connors.

"Yes," affirmed Meledov's voice, "that is agreeable. The Soviet Union has no need to capitalize publicly on your discomfort."

For now, you son of a bitch, thought Connors. He heard the implied threat clearly.

"Then surely you will agree that negotiations on the highest level should begin at once to minimize that discomfort," said Connors.

"That is acceptable to us," said Meledov, "but may I remind you that negotiations imply a state of equality which may no longer be a realistic approximation of international affairs."

Connors grimaced but kept his voice calm, ignoring the rage and the humiliation that was its source.

"That is precisely why they are so necessary, Mr. Meledov. We wish to avoid any possible escalation . . . on both sides."

"What is it you wish?"

"Unfortunately, my advisers tell me that our own satellite communications are no longer controllable from this end. I am . . . asking . . . in the interests of continued global peace, to send a negotiating team, headed by the Secretary of State, to confer with your chosen delegate. The secretary will carry my personal message to you and await your response."

There was silence on the line, and Connors heard voices speaking in Russian on the other end. He looked to Barrows.

"I think he's checking out your request with his people," said Barrows, listening intently. "Hard to make out. Sounds like they disagree on a conference."

Connors waited. In the faces of Leyland, Dupont, and Peterson, he saw his own frustration mirrored. In the picture of George Washington, over the marble fireplace opposite his desk, he saw only history's condemnation if he were to fail.

"That is acceptable," came back Meledov's voice. "There is much to discuss between our nations."

"Very well then," said Connors. "I will order a military flight to transport the Secretary of State to Moscow where . . ."

"That is unacceptable," said Meledov's voice at once. "We will not permit armed forces in our air space."

"We have no intention, Mr. Meledov, of doing anything to jeopardize the sanctity of our mission to you."

"Nevertheless. Our position is final."

Connors heard it at last, the power come into Meledov's voice. It was the sound of a man who held all the aces. Connors retreated diplomatically.

"Would you allow an unarmed communications ship far enough into your waters to make a meeting possible? Again, Mr. Meledov, I think flexibility is essential," he paused, "on both sides."

Again there was silence. Then, "Will this ship submit to an inspection?"

"Agreed," sighed Connors.

"Then you may have your conference, Mr. Connors. We will await your signal."

"One of our ships can be in the Gulf of Finland by tomorrow. Her captain will be under orders to permit the inspection. Secretary Powell will be en route within the hour. Thank you, Mr. Meledov."

"Good day, Mr. Connors."

The light on the console blinked out. Connors slumped back in his chair.

"They seem to have bought it," he said quietly.

"Well done, Mr. President. There remains then only one more detail," said Dupont, already out of his chair. "This operation must have a name. Do you have one in mind, sir?"

"Indeed I do, Mr. Secretary," said Connors, "as we may be letting at least one of the four horsemen loose into the world. You will call it Project Apocalypse."

The Politburo heard Meledov's report on the conversation with the American president with unrestrained glee.

"They are crawling to us with tails between their legs," said Viktor Grishen, the Foreign Minister, happily.

"What can they say to us but to accept our superior position?" gloated Trapeznikov, fingering his newly gained Order of Lenin.

"Conjecture is pointless," said Komarovsky, hoping to dampen premature celebrations. "It would be a mistake to underestimate the Americans. Even now."

"I agree," said Meledov, his long fingers drumming over the tabletop. "Which is why you will be in charge of the meeting with his envoy, Vassily. Comrade Grishen will accompany you as chief negotiator. We must still be wary."

"I will select the inspection team at once," said Komarovsky, "but there is something else I must report."

"Proceed," signaled Meledov.

"The mole Pollux has been killed. Kasimov's target, Senator Leyland, was responsible for the disruption of the operation. We have lost a very valuable agent, and Leyland has returned to Washington."

"The mission was successful in my mind," said Trapeznikov. "We had the time we needed to launch Nightsight. Kasimov should get a hero's welcome."

"It's not Kasimov's welcome I'm concerned about," said Komarovsky. "It's Leyland's continued interference in our plans. It is KGB's recommendation that he be terminated."

"Can this be accomplished quickly and quietly?" asked Meledov.

"It can be," assured the KGB chief.

"Then do it," said Meledov, already moving on to other matters. "What is the state of our military expeditions?" he asked Torgenev.

"Given that we could not betray our intentions by moving troops while the Prophets were in the sky, it will take another three to five days to stand at invasion readiness," said Torgenev.

"I must have support soon," said the Party secretary from Czechoslovakia. "The people have rioted twice already over food cutbacks. We must show them the State will respond to such behavior."

A chorus of such requests followed, demands for troops, consumer goods, foodstuffs, all necessary to quiet the epidemic of unrest.

"Comrades," Meledov said sharply, and the Party secretaries were silenced. "In three weeks you will have your troops. Soon after, the goods you require. You must remember, Comrades, military superiority has always implied concessions."

". . . That is the current state of affairs," finished Connors with little power left in his voice.

"What you're saying," Powell hesitantly summarized, "is that we've lost the war without ever having fired a shot."

"Not the war, Harold," offered Connors, "just its first battle. That's why your assignment is so critical. We must establish a direct channel to Meledov if this thing is to be prevented from spreading to a nuclear disaster."

Parienne, Clancy, and Reynolds had, as yet, said nothing. The shock of understanding had silenced them as effectively as a bullet.

"Leyland's actions in Rome bought us nothing of value," said Parienne bitterly.

"Not quite," said Reynolds. "Sanderson is no longer a problem, and our internal security is re-established. That's a great deal, Jim, from my point of view."

"I need people I can trust on that ship," Connors said. "You three will make up the team under Harold. Communications facilities to your offices will be made available to all of you until your return. The *Tarent* can reach us by radio, regardless of the loss of satellites. The situation will be made clear when you reach the ship. Sealed orders for all of you have been delivered to the captain. I needn't remind you that I'm counting on your success. Cancel that—I'm praying for it."

"Can you give us any indication of what we'll be dealing with?" Parienne inquired.

"I'm sorry to be so high-handed about this, Jim," said Connors, "but for security reasons, it must be this way."

"You look tired, Mr. President," said Clancy paternally. "Some sleep would help."

"When there's time," said Connors. "Get your affairs in order and be ready in an hour. Your jet is waiting at Andrews. Godspeed."

"Very well, sir," said Powell, and he and the others left the office.

Connors watched them leave. He knew well what he was consigning them to, the position they would be in. At least three of the people he was sending to the *Tarent* were loyal friends, no better to be found. The fourth . . . he didn't know at all.

He felt the crushing responsibility that had been placed on him grow heavier. Project Apocalypse was a desperate last resort. To its end, he had lied to the people, to the other branches of government. About his personal friends, he wondered painfully, if he would have to sacrifice all four to eliminate the threat of Castor's continued influence. He felt alone and unwise.

The soft knock at his door startled him out of his reverie. Barbara Reynolds came in, files in her hands, and closed the door behind her.

"I hoped you'd come back, Barbara," he said. "It's been a long day."

"It may be some time before we see each other again," she said, coming behind him, kneading his tired back muscles with her hands.

"God, that feels good," sighed Connors, head lolling forward.

"I always know what you need, Brendan."

Coming around him, Reynolds drew the blinds and locked the door. It was late. No one but the secretaries would be in the outer area. And the Oval Office was soundproofed.

Standing before him, she pressed his head to her chest as his hands slid up her legs, under her dress. Slowly, she reached down and raised it above her waist. She wore nothing underneath.

Connors' hands went round her, clutching at her skin as she pressed closer to him. A moan passed his gritted teeth when she grabbed at his hair, grinding him hard against her. He felt the tremble in her legs and the heat that rose from her.

He stood as she clawed open the fastenings of her dress and tasted the hot, sharp sweat when his mouth crushed down on hers. She forced his hands hungrily to her breasts and then her own hands moved agonizingly lower, kneading, demanding. The cool air on his exposed flesh, the rake of her nails, the urging of her finger; he stiffened . . . and heard the sharp increase in her breathing as if the object of her hunt had suddenly burst into view.

She tore off the dress and pushed him back onto the couch. When he was naked, she bent over him and drew the hard points of her breasts across his thighs. Holding him like a pommel, she mounted and slid him inside her. Already slick and wet, she needed no further foreplay than that of her own hunger released. Her knees held him viselike and her buttocks rose and fell in frenzied jackhammer motion as he groaned and flexed under her assault.

He felt her open wider to receive him as he swelled into orgasm. Cries tore from him when hot fluid leaped from his organ into hers. Shivering and groaning, she slammed against him as the first waves of climax roared through her taut, stretched body again and again.

For a long while she lay against him, savoring her release. He could not move as she now did. He had been eaten; he had been consumed. Finally, he slept.

Barbara Reynolds held him as he dozed fitfully on the couch, listening to his dreamy mumblings and stroking his head until she had to leave for home to pack for her journey.

The park was quiet at night. In years past, casual strollers and young couples would have dotted the lawns, but now the threat of muggers and rapists had closed the park to all but the street people who slept on its benches. Most of the lights had been broken and graffiti was scrawled across the concrete paths.

Parienne entered the park, his light raincoat pulled close around him, his other hand in his pocket, holding a small package. Approaching him from the park's opposite side was the man he had come to meet.

The transaction went quickly. The man took the package, and Parienne received a manila envelope in return. Both continued on, Parienne to a coffee shop across the street.

In a booth, he ordered coffee and glanced at his watch. He had little time before he had to leave for Andrews.

He withdrew the documents from the package he had received.

"Something the matter, sweetie?" asked the waitress who arrived with his order. "You look like you've seen a ghost."

"What? No . . . I'm all right," said Parienne, startled, shoving the papers back into the package.

The waitress shrugged ambivalently and served the coffee. Parienne waited until she had gone to pick up his cup. He didn't want her to see his shaking hands.

Terrence Clancy still waited patiently across the street from the almost deserted park. He had followed Parienne from the White House, curious when his friend had driven in the opposite direction from his apartment. The president's briefing turned the mildest deviation from the norm into reason for closer scrutiny.

He witnessed the transaction between Parienne and the unknown man, the exchange of envelopes, and watched Parienne enter the café alone. The other man left the park hurriedly, passing less than twenty feet from Clancy, ignoring his presence as would any chance passerby.

Coming to a sudden decision, Clancy followed the man. His scholarly, disciplined mind began to select what he would pack at home even as he walked through the shadowy streets in pursuit.

Captain Fuller's second in command, Commander Paul Newton, was waiting on deck as the helicopter settled onto its pad.

Formalities observed, Fuller motioned him to his cabin after ordering a status report from the bridge.

The *Tarent* had begun life as a heavy cruiser of the Oregon class in 1945, but the war ended when she was only half built. In 1948, she was ordered completed by the Navy Department, converted to a Task Force Command ship and fitted with an elaborate command information center, electronic equipment, and flag accommodations. Until 1971, *Tarent* was used as the flagship for the commander of the Second Fleet.

Withdrawn from service, *Tarent* was given a complete overhaul and the latest in communications equipment was installed. Data processing relays and data displays were added, along with tropospheric scatter and satellite relay facilities. Her foremast was the largest ever to be built, almost one hundred and twenty-five feet high, and served as a radar installation-radio antenna.

Almost all of *Tarent*'s armament had been removed to make room for communications and radar facilities. All that remained were two five-inch guns, one fore and one aft. As a flagship, *Tarent*'s job was to command, not to fight. Sprouting radar dishes and antennae all over her decks and superstructure, even on her two stacks, *Tarent* now served as the command ship for the North Atlantic Fleet.

Fuller passed through the offices below the superstructure, noting the absence of activity there. Rooms, usually filled with technicians and their computers, were now empty and silent. *Tarent* had a crew of sixty officers and eleven hundred enlisted men. Where were they? Fuller could barely restrain the questions that clamored through his mind.

In his cabin, Fuller noted at once the sealed orders on his desk. They bore the code that meant he and he alone could open and decode them.

"First things first," he said to Newton as he closed his office door. "What the hell are we doing in the Gulf of Finland, Paul?"

The commander tossed his hat onto the desk and sat down. He was brown-haired and brown-eyed, six feet tall, and had the lanky body of a swimmer.

"We tried to radio you, sir, but your setup at home is a satellite relay. Sir, there are no satellites anymore."

Fuller listened to Newton explain what he knew of the Soviet attack.

". . . then, about twenty-four hours ago we received sailing orders, direct from the Pentagon, to head for the Gulf of Finland. Most of the crew, high-tech gear, and the administrative personnel were taken off in Copenhagen, and three crates of some kind of machinery parts were put in storage.

"We also took aboard a man named Henry Talon who was flown in from Rome with Navy Department authorization. I've settled him in one of the officer's cabins. Now let me ask you, sir, do you know what's going on?"

Fuller shook his head. "No, I don't. But if I had to guess, I'd say we were going to find out pretty soon. For now, I want to see this Talon fellow at once."

"Right away, sir."

Fuller tore open the seal on his orders and retrieved the code books stored in the locked safe inside his desk. Ten minutes of rapid calculations and he read the orders, even more puzzling than the ship's position.

TO: James E. Fuller, Captain, C.C. Tarent

FROM: Alfred R. Hill, Admiral, Chief of Naval Operations

(1)   Tarent is relieved of all duties with respect to North Atlantic Fleet.

(2)   Tarent is reassigned to special duty on assignment to President/Project Apocalypse.

(3)   Tarent will proceed all haste to position reference A467353.

(4)   Tarent will accept Soviet inspection team boarding at point A467353.

(5)   Tarent inspection completed, proceed to point A467932.

(6)   Tarent will there accept and accommodate Presidential negotiators:

    1. Sec. of State, H. Powell
    2. Nat'l Sec. Adv., B. Reynolds
    3. Sp. Asst., J. Parienne
    4. Sp. Asst., T. Clancy

(7)   Tarent security will be governed by Henry Talon, Special Asst./President.

(8)   Tarent Captain will deliver additional sealed orders to team listed (6).

(9)   Tarent will remain position A467932 until further orders.

                        (signed) A. R. Hill, Admiral

Shocked, he unrolled a map on his desk and plotted the coordinates twice, just to be sure he had envisioned them correctly. Finally, he was forced to accept that the chief of Naval Operations had just ordered the *Tarent* to sail into Russian waters, alone and unescorted, after an inspection by the Russian authorities.

Suddenly, the removal of some of the crew and much of *Tarent*'s radar and communications equipment made sense. But little else did. Someone knocked on the cabin door.

"Captain Fuller? I'm Henry Talon, CIA. Commander Newton said you'd asked to see me."

"I did, Mr. Talon. Perhaps you would care to explain to me why my ship is in this godforsaken place and who exactly you are."

Talon reclined in one of the chairs. "You received your orders, Captain. I received mine. That's why we're both here."

"I want an answer, Mr. Talon," demanded Fuller angrily. "I'm responsible for this ship and its crew."

"And this ship is part of an operation for which other people are responsible," retorted Talon, "and which I cannot discuss until the Secretary of State arrives."

"What cargo did we take on in Copenhagen? Please don't tell me machinery parts."

"Classified, Captain. I'm sorry."

"Mr. Newton!" Fuller bellowed.

Newton hurried into the cabin. "Yes, sir."

"Mr. Newton, you will take sufficient crew members to storage, armed with axes or whatever is necessary and open those crates we took on. Understood?"

"Yes, sir."

Talon jumped to his feet. "Wait, please. You don't know what you're doing."

"Then answer my questions, Mr. Talon."

"I can't. Surely you can see that," he pleaded.

"Mr. Newton, you have your orders," said Fuller again.

For the second time Newton turned to leave but Talon stopped him.

"You drive a hard bargain, Captain. Very well, in the future I will know how you operate. I'll tell you."

"Cancel my last order and return to the bridge," Fuller said to Newton, "and lay in a course for point A467353, flank speed."

Newton's eyes widened.

"But that's almost in . . ."

"You have your orders, Commander," said Fuller sternly.

"Yes, sir," said Newton, and he left the cabin.

Fuller settled back and watched Talon, who was clearly unhappy about the situation. Fuller said nothing, but waited.

"Well . . ." Talon sighed at last, "as God said to Adam and Eve, 'Don't say I didn't warn you.'

"You are aware by now that we lost our entire space presence due to a Soviet attack. But what you don't know, Captain, is that there are right now four Soviet laser battle stations in orbit around the earth which effectively nullify our conventional and nuclear forces.

Nothing we have, nothing we can put together, can change that right now."

The blood drained from Fuller's face; a career military officer, he understood immediately the implications of what he had just heard.

"Then what are we—" he began, but Talon cut him off.

"We are making a move of such desperation that the slightest leak of this operation would cause a global panic which could engulf us all in nuclear war. A war the United States cannot, at this moment, win."

Fuller leaned closer, unconsciously, as Talon continued.

"There is a substance known as PA II, evolved in the days before saner heads prevailed in the government. It has been stored in the Utah desert for almost fifteen years, too dangerous to use, too unpredictable to destroy.

"In *Tarent*'s storage, we are now carrying almost a thousand ounces of PA II in the warheads of a hundred short-range Army Orion missiles, stored in three rapid-fire portable launchers. We can only hope the Soviets won't be looking for anything like it, Captain. It must go unnoticed during inspection.

"PA II is a variant of the deadliest plague ever developed, pulmonary anthrax. Airborne, this amount could kill over a billion people in three months. Later, it settles in the ground and is eaten by animals or absorbed by plants and continues to kill for years. There is no antidote.

"You are, Captain Fuller, in command of a plague ship."

2

The weather had worsened steadily over the past twenty-four hours, and Komarovsky sensed that the rainstorm which pelted the windows had yet greater force to reveal. Alone, in his office, he reflected that it was probably an accurate prediction for the forces Nightsight had released as well.

The American president's posture had been surprising, keeping Nightsight hidden from the public. Surely he would know that such a secret could not be kept for long. But if the Americans were to agree to a lengthy list of demands, ultimately, it didn't matter a damn if the people knew the reasons behind that agreement or not. Still, it bothered him, the uncharacteristic secrecy, the lack of the traditional call for unity in the face of foreign aggression, the atypical response.

The Secretary of State would soon be on board the ship, the conference scheduled for tomorrow. The Politburo, he decided, had taken the wisest course: wait and see. He shrugged mentally; if Nightsight could be used as a lever rather than as a club, so much the better.

Earlier that morning he had met with the International Department of the Central Committee, which maintained Moscow's relations with the Communist parties of other countries. Unaware of Nightsight, the Party secretaries from the client states had painted a gloomy picture indeed. He had longed to tell them that deliverance was near at hand. But Meledov's instructions were firm: wait until the situation was stable.

It was the Party secretary of Poland who had been most eloquent.

"Tell me, Comrade Komarovsky," he had said, "how to maintain order. In one breath we rebuke the West as decadent, yet we owe their banks over thirty billion dollars, more money than we can ever hope to repay. If they now called due the debts, our economy would be bankrupted overnight. We call our State a workers' paradise yet it is from the workers' continued threats that strife occurs, and we must face a world that watches us cart them off to jail. They threaten strikes every day now. More food, shorter hours, free press, no press, different government, less government . . . you must realize that it is falling apart. We cannot demonstrate that Communism works and that is the root of the problem. In Poland, it hasn't worked! And unless Moscow does something soon, it may find itself a head with no body, controlling only the remembrances of past glory."

"It is the same in Czechoslovakia," said that country's Party secretary. "People cannot eat words. They cannot heat their homes with words, and Party indoctrination speeches will not clothe the children. The situation makes it impossible to be a good Communist and place food on the dinner table as well. So the weak become bitter and the strong become black-market capitalists. We must have more than words, Comrade Komarovsky."

"And there is another problem which stems from the roots of economic despair," said the Party secretary of Romania, "which is not limited to our countries but exists in the U.S.S.R. itself. We have the world's steepest rise in alcohol consumption and fully a third of our consumer spending goes toward the purchase of alcohol. We alone among modern countries have an increasing male mortality rate. Who'll get the vodka and how to find the money for it are topics of greater concern than Marx or Lenin! But these are only symptoms. Moscow must cure the disease itself or we will surely collapse from within."

How he had longed to tell them of Nightsight. Komarovsky sighed. To tell them that the tide had been turned, that a secret war had been fought and won above their heads in less than a single hour. To tell them that the balance would indeed change, that Russian troops would soon walk proudly through their streets and the stores would be filled with goods. But he could not. Soon, he promised himself. Soon, they would have more than hope.

His secretary came into the office. "The travel arrangements have been made, Comrade Chairman. Your group will assemble at the naval base on Kronstadt Island in Leningrad Harbor, then be helicoptered out to the American ship."

"Thank you. That is fine," he said.

"Colonel Kasimov is still on your agenda. Do you wish to see him now?"

One more thing to do before he could leave the city, Komarovsky thought. He had summoned Kasimov hours earlier and then let him wait. It was an obvious gesture of disapproval. Kasimov would recognize it and be furious by now.

"Send him in."

Komarovsky rose from behind his desk and poured himself a glass of vodka. Reseated in a chair by the window, he waited. The rain had grown stronger, he noticed.

"Why was I kept waiting?" demanded Kasimov upon entering, his loose posture reflecting his usual disregard for the chairman's authority.

Komarovsky continued to stare out the window. When he spoke, his voice was detached and quiet but his tone was hard-edged.

"You have two choices, Colonel. When you address me, it will be at attention and by my proper rank. The other choice is immediate dismissal from KGB. Don't take too much time deciding; I am quite busy."

He imagined the rage that must be contorting Kasimov's features and heard the hiss of quickly indrawn breath. But when he turned, Kasimov was indeed at attention.

"Very good, Colonel." He nodded.

"May I ask the Comrade Chairman why I am being treated in such a fashion?"

Komarovsky heard the anger underlying the politely phrased question but ignored it.

"You, Colonel," he said, "have committed the one mistake unpardonable in an arrogant man . . . you failed. Had it not been for Mikoyan's team set up to cover you, you would still be rotting in that cell Leyland put you in. We lost several very good men getting you out, Colonel. I do not intend to lose any more because of your incompetence."

"May I remind the Comrade Chairman that I delivered the American command-and-control mechanism? And that Leyland was effectively out of the way during the period the Comrade Chairman required."

"True enough. Did you know that the Minister of Science wants you decorated for that? Well, no matter. It does not justify your failure. Or your attitudes. I am giving you one final chance to mend the damage you've done. Castor reports that Leyland is increasingly active in the White House, but his purpose is unclear. No matter. Like his brother, the purpose he serves is not in our best interests. And if he uncovers Castor as he did Pollux, our security will be compromised. Find him and kill him, Colonel. It may do both your humility and your career much good."

"Do we know where Leyland is?" Kasimov asked.

Komarovsky looked up sharply.

". . . Comrade Chairman," Kasimov added, teeth clenched.

"In La Jolla, California, Mikoyan reports. You will be assigned to our Diplomatic station in San Francisco as a low-ranking trade expert. You may go now, Colonel."

"Yes, Comrade Chairman."

Kasimov shut the door behind him and walked stiffly out of the building. In his mind burned a rage the likes of which he had not felt since he held his dead wife in his arms after the Israeli air attack. His sinewy muscles were knotted so tightly that spasms shook his body. "Leyland," he thought. "Leyland did this to me."

For the first time in his career, he realized, he was going to kill not for the State, but for personal satisfaction. He ordered his driver to the airport and sat trembling all the way there.

"All engines stop," commanded Captain Fuller. The order was relayed to the engine room, and the four giant propellers ceased. Fuller lifted binoculars to his eyes and scanned the horizon beyond the inspection point but it was empty.

The bridge was semicircular with wraparound panoramic windows, broken only by the doors which opened onto the observation wings that surrounded it. The highest level of the superstructure which sat amidship, it was crammed full of the most sophisticated radar, tracking, and communications equipment ever developed.

The helmsman sat directly behind the captain and the executive officer at a wide console, steering the ship on command. Brass plates underneath every control switch gleamed against the battleship-gray paint underneath. Color-coded emergency signals—red for general quarters, green for "gas" attack, and yellow for collision alert—also sat atop the console. On the right side of the bridge lay the radar officer's station; on the left, course plotting, with its lighted map displays and, until Nightsight, a direct link to the naval satellites which pinpointed position to within thirty feet anywhere in the world.

Almost the entire rear of the bridge was dominated by the communications section, with relays down to the command information center below deck. Though the actual radio equipment was operated in its own section below deck, serviced by a crew of engineers and junior officers, control originated in the bridge.

The heart of the ship, providing her lifeblood, the energy to power all her electronic systems and to drive the mighty turbines which propelled her, was the engine room, deep in the interior. Commands from the captain or the exec were "telegraphed" to the engine room officer through the intercom widely known as the "bitch box" and converted to action by the crew. Triple backup systems ensured the delivery of power. Ever watchful vigilance ensured the backup system. A powerful giant, the well-integrated systems of the *Tarent* functioned like muscle and nerve cells and cooperated in movement.

Talon stood stiffly in his new naval uniform, silently watching the smooth operation of the ship with a look of approval on his face for the crew, one of wariness for the captain.

The weather in the gulf was holding steady, slightly overcast with winds from the northwest. Talon had explained the necessity of the current weather pattern holding, and Fuller had ordered a twenty-four-hour-a-day watch on it. Communications had also been set up, through unaffected ground stations, to the two weather monitoring ships, the *Vycore* off Japan and the *Blake* off the northern coast of the Soviet Union in the Barents Sea. Data was relayed every hour to the *Tarent,* the slightest change in pressure readings fed into the computers to be analyzed and new predictions forecast.

"Picking up helicopters, sir," called out the radar officer. "Looks like three, sir."

"Ready the pads," Fuller ordered, and Newton left the bridge to supervise reception of the Soviet inspectors. Fuller lifted his binoculars again and saw the small dots on the horizon grow larger.

Every instinct, trained over thirty years of naval service, rebelled at the notion of permitting soldiers of a foreign, hostile government to board, much less inspect his ship. A ship at sea was as much a piece of its sovereign nation as was New York City, or the White House for that matter. To allow boarding passively signaled to Fuller the seriousness of the global situation more effectively than Talon ever could have.

He shook his head to clear it, mindful of Talon's watchful gaze. The helicopters were landing, and he motioned to Talon to follow him down to the flight deck.

The wind whipped around them as they approached the Soviets, who had unloaded their equipment and gathered on deck. He counted thirty in all, in naval uniforms, as he threaded his way past radar turrets and ventilating grilles to his officers by the pads, Talon a few paces behind.

"Captain Sergei Kalinskya, commanding the official inspection team," said one of the Soviets in perfect English, stepping forward with a sharp salute.

"Captain James Fuller," he responded, returning the salute. For a moment, he locked eyes with the Soviet captain, who must have understood his distress.

"These are difficult times, Captain," said Kalinskya softly, for Fuller's ears alone.

"That they are, Captain," said Fuller as quietly, then louder, "very well. How would you care to proceed?"

"I have two teams. One can go aft and proceed forward; one can start forward and proceed aft. We anticipate that two of your officers will guide each team. I will remain here in radio contact with our base. Agreed?"

"Acceptable," said Fuller. "Commander Talon and Commander Newton will guide the forward team; Lieutenant Brown and Lieutenant Horley will guide the aft team. You may proceed, gentlemen."

Fuller gave a final salute and walked stiffly back to his bridge.

Every inch of space below *Tarent*'s decks were checked and rechecked by the Soviet inspectors. Sophisticated Geiger counter-like instruments checked for any sign of the radiation that would indicate the presence of nuclear weaponry. Crew lockers were opened, berthings checked, storage facilities were inspected. Diligently, the Soviets continued aft, working slowly but efficiently through *Tarent*'s cavernous interior.

In the storage bays, they passed their instruments over crate after crate of foodstuffs, tool replacements . . . and machine parts.

Talon, not even daring to look at Newton, held his breath, feigning a calmness he didn't feel.

"What are these?" asked the supervising Soviet lieutenant. "These three large crates?"

Talon checked his roster. "Machine parts. Replacement pieces for the turbines which drive the ship," he said nonchalantly.

"Open one, please."

"Lieutenant, we've been at this for hours. If you start opening everything in storage, we'll be at it for days," he objected.

"No matter," said the lieutenant. "I am under orders. Anything of this size must be looked into. Please open it."

Talon reached for a crowbar, icy sweat running down his sides. The crates were nine feet high so he pushed a mobile flight of metal stairs against one and clambered up.

The Soviet lieutenant stood quietly watching, his instruments at his side. The rest of his team gathered behind him, drawn by his obvious interest in the crates.

Talon rammed the crowbar under the top planks of wood and pushed downward. The wood splintered and came loose. Again, he rammed the bar home, the sound echoing off the metal walls. With a final effort, he pulled free the last plank and lifted the top off the crate, ready to use the crowbar if . . .

The lieutenant sprang up beside him and looked inside.

"Very well, Commander Talon. We can continue," said the lieutenant, and his men returned to their duties.

For a long moment, Talon just stared inside the crate at the battleship-gray, metal engine housing that lay inside. In a moment of realization he almost laughed out loud but recovered sufficient presence of mind to climb down and mask his surprise.

"Seal it up, Mr. Newton," he ordered and went to follow the Soviet lieutenant, praising whatever gods existed that his side was as good as the Soviets in building facades to conceal their weapons.

Fuller watched the helicopters leaving from the bridge. He had been given the signal from Captain Kalinskya to proceed into Soviet waters.

"Proceed to point A467932," he ordered, and the four huge General Electric turbines spun into life as the anchor was winched out of the choppy, gray sea.

The Secretary of State and his negotiating team, already in Copenhagen, would be arriving soon, now that the inspection was completed.

Fuller thought again of the bacteriological holocaust he carried in the hold. Then the image of his family, so near to *Tarent*'s position, appeared vividly in his mind.

"We have all the time in the world," Beverly had said.

Foolishly, he now realized, he had agreed.

3

Chris, Arielle, and Crowley drove past the armed guards to the temporary buildings put up to house the Department of Defense investigators who poured daily through the wreckage of the Torrey Pines Inn.

It was the first time Chris had seen the inn since the night of the terrorist attack, and the scene produced conflicting emotions in him. Here he had met Arielle; but here he had seen men die. It was true he had saved lives, but it was equally true he had taken them.

"I feel like we were last here years ago instead of just weeks," said Arielle pensively, echoing his feelings.

"So much has changed since then," agreed Crowley, "and not all for the better."

"Unless I'm wrong about what I saw that night," Chris said, "we should find some of the reasons behind those changes here."

They walked toward the inn looking for Pete Renquist, the man in charge of the investigation. They spotted him standing in a burned-out section of the inn, carefully supervising a group of Army Engineers who were laying out a series of rope lines to divide the area into manageable search sections. He turned when one of the engineers pointed to the approach of Chris, Arielle, and Crowley and scampered over charred beams and loose stone to meet them.

"Senator Leyland," he said, "I was told you'd be out sometime today."

"Pleasure to meet you, Mr. Renquist. This is Dr. Simmons and Mr. Crowley."

Renquist was in his late forties, Chris judged, angularly featured and tan from outdoor work. He was dressed in jeans, construction boots, open-collared shirt, and a light jacket. A bright yellow hard hat adorned his head.

"Pete, please," said Renquist. "They tell me you three saved what's left of this place from total destruction."

"Total luck," said Chris, glancing at Arielle. "If I hadn't been wakened by a late call, the terrorists would have taken all of us by surprise."

"How can I help you, Senator?"

Chris looked at the inn, trying to force his memories of the night into sharper focus. Somewhere in his fuzzy remembrance, three Arabs raced through the lobby, intent on some purpose he had come here to discover.

"How much of the inn has been checked already?" he asked Renquist.

"Come over here. I've got a blueprint that has it laid out."

They followed Renquist to a sheet of plywood which rested on sawhorses near the section just roped off.

"Normally," Renquist began, "in a situation of this much structural loss, the most reasonable approach would be to bulldoze everything and start over again from the ground up.

"But there were so many research files and classified reports in the Jasons' rooms that we need to excavate every single section to find whatever may be left."

"You're functioning more like archeologists than construction engineers," observed Arielle.

"Exactly," agreed Renquist, "which slows everything down. We can't use heavy machinery to move rubble because it would pulverize the more delicate objects and might shake loose the upper stories which are tottering right now anyway."

"I'd like to see your list of the guests and their room numbers," Chris asked.

"No problem," said Renquist, flipping through the blueprints. He spread a new page out on the table.

Chris placed himself mentally in the lobby of the inn. He remembered checking the phone lines and the manager and finding both dead. The Arabs had come into the lobby from his left and darted into the wing that began to his right. He scanned the list of names from Renquist's chart for those rooms: 100 through 120 on the first floor; 200 through 220 on the second.

"How difficult would it be to shift the operation over to this area?" He indicated the wing he wanted on the blueprints. "I may be able to narrow it down, but I think we lost something of value in this area."

"Can't you be more specific?" Renquist said, frowning.

"You've got to understand the confusion taking place that night," objected Crowley, "and the concussion he suffered at its end. He's being as specific as he can be."

"What Tom says is true, Pete," Chris said. "A lot of the night is still pretty hazy to me."

"Okay, Senator. Washington says you get what you want. We can be shifted over there by late today and start tomorrow. You can take this room chart. I have a copy."

"Fine," said Chris. "We'll be back in the morning."

Over dinner in their motel, the Seaside, a few miles away from Torrey Pines, Chris looked at the list of names Renquist had supplied and frowned. "This wing suffered more damage than any other part of the inn. We're looking for an unknown needle in a rather large, chaotic haystack."

"If you're correct," said Arielle, "that the attack here had to do with some phase of the Nightsight operation, it might make sense to disregard any room that held occupants not directly related to aerospace research."

"That's going to be a problem," Crowley said, pulling his lobster apart with fingers slick with melted butter. "Everybody at the conference was connected in some way to aerospace. That was the whole agenda."

"There's got to be some way to narrow it down," Arielle insisted. "Otherwise, we've run into the same problem we had in Rome. Except that time is even more severely limited now."

"I don't see a way," said Crowley, spearing another bite. "Even the military people were bringing over their new C&C system from DARPA for . . ."

Chris grabbed Crowley's arm in mid bite. "Wait a second, Tom. Say that again."

"Say what again? Let go of my arm. Don't you remember? We were talking about it at dinner the first night. Or were you too pre-occupied with the former Dr. Simmons?"

"Please, Tom. The lobster and the leer will both wait. What were we discussing at dinner?"

"It was Rogers and Jeffers talking mostly about how the Russians couldn't orbit laser platforms without . . . Jesus, Chris—without far more sophisticated command-and-control systems than they had presently developed! And Rogers said he was having the newest C&C system from DARPA sent over from Scripps for a look-see by the Jasons."

"I worked on the design of that system," said Arielle excitedly, "at least on the computer end of things. Do you think that's what Kasimov wanted in La Jolla?"

"I think we'd better find out if Scripps did send it over. Because if they did, then," he quickly scanned the room list and saw Rogers' name on it, "Room 100 is where we begin."

"Finish your lobster, Tom. I'll buy you another myself," Arielle said as Chris raced off to call Scripps's director and find Renquist.

The next morning saw the area that corresponded to Room 100 roped off, and Renquist had his men carefully sifting through the rubble, lifting out charred fragments of wall and ceiling and placing any items of interest on white sheets spread out on the grass beyond.

Chris's request to Washington had produced the necessary verification of his authority to convince the director of the Scripps Institute to open the top-secret projects vault and verify that a copy of the command-and-control system that General Rogers had spoken of in such glowing terms at dinner had indeed been sent over to him, in a high-security, fireproof briefcase, at Torrey Pines the afternoon before the terrorist assault.

Chris and Arielle, now wearing jeans, boots, flannel shirts, and gloves, sifted through the rubble. Every so often, one of the crew would call for help moving a slab of stone or a heavy beam and work would concentrate on cooperating to disgorge the object and carry it aside.

Crowley, appalled by physical labor of any kind, "supervised," cataloging objects as they were placed on the sheets.

Chris wrestled an electrical conduit pipe out from a tangled mass and tossed it aside. The sun was high in the sky and the heat and dust made it difficult to breathe.

He glanced at his watch, half an hour till lunch. Ignoring the aches in his tired body, he bent again to the task of uncovering Room 100.

"Good morning, sir," said the naval officer to the desk clerk at the Seaside Hotel. "I have an urgent message for Senator Leyland. Is he in his room?"

The desk clerk lazily scanned the rows of cubbyholes behind him and saw that both keys to Room 216 were there.

"I'm sorry, but the Senator isn't in now."

"That's too bad." The officer frowned. "Do you know how to reach him?"

"I'm sorry, but I don't. Would you want to leave a message, Admiral?"

"Lieutenant Commander Donaldson," said the officer without annoyance, opening his attaché case and handing the clerk an envelope. "Yes, please. Would you see he gets this?"

The clerk shoved the letter uninterestedly into slot 216.

"Done," he pronounced.

"Thanks again," said the officer.

Outside the hotel, he doubled around to a side entrance and went quickly to Leyland's room. From his attaché case he withdrew a ring of keys the diameter of a dinner plate and studied the lock for a few seconds. Selecting a key, he inserted it in the lock, which opened at once.

The maid, he was relieved to see, had not yet been in. The bed was still unmade and rumpled from the Leylands' occupation of it. He tossed the covers to the floor, removed the bottom sheet, and folded it carefully into a plastic bag he took from his case. Then he replaced the sheet with another he had brought. The plastic bag back in his case, he left the room and relocked it.

Returning to his car, he drove a few miles down the road toward Torrey Pines. Pulling off the main road, he entered a driveway which led to a small, rented cottage. A station wagon waited outside, wire cages in the rear.

In the cabin, he took off the naval uniform and replaced it with a jacket, shirt, and slacks. He tossed the uniform into the fireplace.

Opening the door to the bedroom, he was inundated by a cacaphony of growling and barking. He crooned to the two muscular, black Dobermans, teeth bared, insanely trying to chew through the steel cage they had been in for two days without food. Spittle sprayed from their moist red gums.

Tearing the sheet he had taken from the hotel into two, he fed one half into each of the cages. Ten seconds later, the halves were in shreds on the floor of the cage. But the dogs were now bright-eyed, feverishly slavering.

"So you've got the scent now, my pets. Soon, very soon, you may go hunting for its source. No guards can stop you, and there will be one Leyland for each of you," Valentin Kasimov said happily.

The KGB-trained dogs caught his tone and whined with blood-lust and excitement.

"Hey, Senator," called one of the workmen, pulling two gray, metal objects out from under a pile of blackened wood, "I haven't seen anything like these before."

Chris stepped carefully through the ruins to take the objects. Burned and blackened, there was still no doubt as to their original use.

"This one is a part of a stun grenade," Chris said, shaking his head. "I think the other is from an incendiary bomb and that we've found part of what we're looking for."

They concentrated efforts on the general area of the find. Half an hour later, someone uncovered the remains of a second incendiary device. Half an hour after that, they found blackened cartridge casings. Chris peered at them closely.

"It will take a ballistics report to confirm this but," he held them out, "I don't think these are standard Army or CIA issue. Rogers may have been dead before the flames ever touched him. We must find his briefcase. That's critical."

Chris walked away from the inn. Then he walked to the crest of the dunes where Arielle had come to clear her head after the hot, exhausting work. Breathing deeply, they looked out to sea before turning to the inn to search for the briefcase.

The dogs were fluid motion along the forest floor. Scent was everything as they sniffed and tested and moved on in silent tracking. They had been trained to perfection, each one a hundred and thirty pounds of teeth and bone and muscle.

One stopped at a tree near the wood's edge. He sniffed carefully, unsure at first, and whined to his mate. They sniffed the urine together, growing more certain as somewhere in the primordial brain mass, synaptic relays closed and confirmed the odor. A trail led away from the tree, and they moved toward their quarry, certain now. Hot-breathed and fever-eyed, they ran, teeth needing flesh to rip and tear. They burst from the woods in rambling motion, legs pounding on the ground, ears pulled back by the wind. Hungrily, they followed the trail to the dunes and there found the second scent. Training took over again. They fixed on the smells, each targeted on its prey like a hunter-seeker missile of destruction.

Renquist looked up from the work to wipe the sweat from his face with a dirt-streaked handkerchief. Blotting the back of his neck, he glanced idly at Chris and Arielle walking back from the dunes. Suddenly, he saw the dogs. The Leylands, he realized at once, were unaware of the Dobermans racing toward them. Something clicked in his consciousness, perhaps the intensity of the dogs' motion, or the vulnerability of the Leylands, backs turned, but all at once he was racing over the debris, shouting and waving furiously at Chris and Arielle to turn around, to look out, to see what was behind them . . .

Two hundred yards away, Arielle caught sight of Renquist's frenzied motions. "I think Pete wants us," she said unconcernedly to Chris.

"Maybe a phone call," Chris said, continuing to walk unhurriedly across the grassy knoll toward the inn. He waved back to signal that he was aware of Renquist, but the wild gesticulations and shouting continued.

"He sees that we've seen him," said Arielle. "Why is he still pointing?"

"I don't know. Maybe we dropped something. Wait a minute."

Chris patted his pockets and found his wallet. Turning idly, he looked back at the way they had come . . . and saw the dogs racing at them. Their snarls reached him now, and there could be no mistaking their purpose as they ran toward them, less than a hundred yards away.

"Dogs behind us. Run!" he shouted, pushing Arielle into movement. They ran, searching for weapons or shelter to protect them.

"Get to the inn," he yelled as he ran beside her, measuring distances and speed as only a pilot could, suddenly realizing that the dogs would be on them before they could reach the inn or help could reach them.

Mounds of debris that had been carted away from the inn lay all around them as they ran for shelter. Chris could hear the dogs, closer now, and yelled for Arielle to run faster.

It was hopeless, no way to reach the inn in time. And the dogs were unstoppable if he had only his hands to use. Arielle would be dead by the time he could reach her even if he killed one of the dogs. He ran in desperation, throwing frantic looks over his shoulder. The dogs were closer still. Only twenty yards separated them.

A pile of rubble loomed up before them, and Chris saw their only chance. He yelled to Arielle to follow him, and they darted around one of the giant mounds. Panting, they yanked wood and concrete away to clear a space. The dogs, sensing their prey gone to ground, howled in anticipation.

The hole was bigger now as they tore at the loose rubble. But not big enough for two. Chris pushed a wildly protesting Arielle roughly into the hole and covered her, pushing and tearing at the pile to place things between her and the dogs. He heard them pawing and scampering over the pile. He had just finished enclosing Arielle, coughing and wheezing from the dust of the hole when the first dog's head appeared over the crest of the mound.

Frantically, he searched for a weapon, seconds left till the dog sprang. He spotted a length of wooden two-by-four, broken and charred at the end into a splintered point. He pulled at it, but it was wedged tightly. He pulled with all his strength, the dog above him crouching to leap. The wood moved but did not come loose. He pulled again, muscles straining with every ounce of force, yanking again and again at the wood.

Fangs bared and gleaming, the dog sprang . . . and the wood came loose.

Slower reflexes would have been fatal, less strength would have been useless. But as a hundred and thirty pounds of killer dog leaped down at him, Chris thrust the length of wood, spearlike at the Doberman, falling back as the weight hit him, jamming the back end of the spear against the ground. It caught the dog in its chest and the tip, flame-hardened and deadly, impaled the Doberman as if it had fallen six stories onto the point of the wooden shaft. The dog died, convulsed in spasms of frothing, howling fury, the two-by-four tearing out its heart.

Chris dove to the side as the second dog leaped at him. He saw only the eyes and teeth as it passed over his head and struck the mound violently. Dazed, it rolled off the stones and turned to attack again. Chris waited until the last possible moment, crouched low, and again dove as the dog leaped. For the second time the dog passed over him and landed helplessly, rolling into the stones at the base of the mound. But now it held back in its charge, circling warily, working its way closer to Chris, growling steadily.

An idea borne of desperation struck Chris, and he tore the belt from his jeans. Holding it by the end, he flicked it like a wet towel, the heavy buckle whipping out at the dog with a snap. The buckle caught the dog in the mouth, and Chris felt the vibration as the metal connected with teeth in a crunching, breaking sound.

The dog yelped and leaped backward, stung by the belt. Blood welled up in its mouth and poured over its black muzzle.

Chris advanced, his mind oblivious to anything but destroying the dog. Enraged, he faced the animal, belt in his hands and white-hot fury in his mind.

The dog sprang forward and again the belt whipped out into the dog's face. It flicked into one of the dog's eyes and the Doberman fell backward, half blind and bellowing in agony.

Chris pulled the belt back and rammed the tip through the buckle to make a noose. But the moment's inattention cost him dearly. The dog's teeth closed on his calf, pulling him down in searing pain. Punching and kicking, he dislodged the dog and thrust the loop over its head. Pulling tightly on the choke-leash the belt had become, he rolled onto the dog's back and thrust out with his booted feet against its head. The animal clawed madly at his legs to dislodge the belt, but Chris bore down, ignoring the pain in his legs, too maddened to feel the teeth that bit again and again into his flesh.

In a final moment of straining effort, Chris wrenched with the last remaining bit of his strength . . . and the Doberman's neck broke with a terrible, audible snap.

Chris rolled exhaustedly off the dead animal. His legs were bleeding, but he could stand after a while and limped over to help pull Arielle free of the rubble that had covered her.

Renquist and Crowley suddenly appeared, each holding a pickax, with other men from the site similarly armed. Chris looked at them with a weary grin, realizing that it had been only a matter of minutes between Renquist's frantic signal and the animals' deaths.

Crowley rushed past the dogs to Chris and Arielle. He shook his head in grateful disbelief that it was over and they had survived. He sent a man for an ambulance.

"Are you both all right?" he demanded.

"We are now," said Arielle quietly.

"I'm sorry we couldn't get here to help sooner," Renquist said ruefully.

"Without your warning, Pete, we'd have been killed," said Chris gratefully. "You did save our lives. That's all that matters."

Renquist looked at the wooden spear that had impaled one dog and the belt around the neck of the second.

"Sorry, Senator. But when this story is retold, it'll be pretty damn clear that you saved your own lives without any help from us."

"It won't be retold," said Arielle. "The less said about it the better. It's over now, and we haven't located what we came here to find. We can't have press all over the place calling attention to our presence here."

"Someone is already aware of it," said Renquist pointedly.

"Maybe so," admitted Chris. "But whoever it is will be uncertain now. Let's keep it that way." Renquist nodded in agreement.

The ambulance arrived, and the emergency medical technicians cleaned and bandaged Chris's wounds and gave him pills for the pain. The bodies of the dogs were taken away to be checked for rabies and other diseases.

"No permanent harm done, sir," said the EMT. "If the dogs check out clean, the wounds should heal nicely in a few days. But you should go to the hospital for tetanus shots and rest."

"No, not now," said Chris. "Later, perhaps."

The EMT began to protest, but Chris cut him off. Shrugging, the EMT got back in the ambulance and drove away.

Chris and Arielle returned to the inn, helping Crowley catalog the remains of Room 100, for the rest of the afternoon. Chris thought of the dogs and of who could have sent them. Kasimov, he decided, had the wherewithal to be responsible. He had certainly been around La Jolla before, wreaking the havoc that lay before them now. Crowley now insisted on Secret Service protection, and Chris had acquiesced. It could have been Kasimov, he decided. He felt it with greater and greater certainty.

A silent vow passed through his mind. Not only had Kasimov tried to blackmail and now to kill him, but he had also come twice at Arielle. Mad dogs must be destroyed, he remembered saying to Don Pietro. So it might have to be in Kasimov's case, he realized. Angrily, he thought of what the Dobermans could have done to himself and Arielle.

He vowed to remember today if ever again he encountered Kasimov.

Later, Renquist uncovered Rogers' briefcase. Fireproof, it was still intact, damaged only by water and falling debris.

The briefcase was empty.

For the second time that day, the flight deck of the *Tarent* received a military helicopter, this time a Navy Sikorsky which brought the Secretary of State and his group. Coming in through overcast skies, it landed on the swaying ship, whirling rotors flattening the hair and clothing of the attending crewmen.

Harold Powell, immaculately attired in a business suit, pulled his tan cashmere coat close around him, clutching a briefcase to his chest. He descended first, followed by Reynolds, Clancy, and Parienne, all similarly well dressed.

From the bridge, Talon watched them, thinking they would be more suited to a stockbroker's convention, so striking was the disparity between their sartorial elegance and the Navy uniforms that ushered them to their cabins.

"They don't know yet?" asked Fuller quietly beside him.

"Not yet," replied Talon. "And if you hadn't jumped the gun, you wouldn't either. I'd like to give them a few minutes to rest and then meet in your cabin. If that's all right with you," he added unnecessarily.

"Quite all right, Mr. Talon," said Fuller, unperturbed. "But answer one question for me. How is it that you have been the recipient of a presidential briefing on the nature of Project Apocalypse before the Secretary of State, two presidential aides, and the National Security Adviser?"

"I have friends in high places, Captain," said Talon enigmatically.

"I'm beginning to wonder if you've told me—" Fuller began, but was cut off by the anxious voice of the radar officer.

"Captain, we've got company. Two miles off starboard."

"Can you make it out?" asked Fuller, lifting binoculars to scan the area.

"It's got the radar signature of a *Sovremennyy* Class, eight thousand tons, steam-powered, guided-missile destroyer. Running configuration ident now."

Fuller put down the glasses, frowning. "Go ahead, Lieutenant, but you'll find it's the *Ural.* We've seen her before in the North Atlantic. She carries four thirty-millimeter Gatling guns, medium-range surface-to-air missiles and, most importantly for us, a full complement of surface-to-surface missiles and attack helicopters."

"Nice company you keep," said Talon.

"Radio message from the *Ural,* sir. Open channel," said the communications officer.

"Read it, Lieutenant."

"To Fuller, Captain, *Tarent;* From Kalinskya, Captain, *Ural* . . . URAL WILL REMAIN ONE MILE DISTANCE AT ALL TIMES . . . STAND BY TO RECEIVE DELEGATION.

"They request confirmation, sir."

"Send it," ordered Fuller, "and inform them we will leave this channel open for ship-to-ship."

"Aye, sir."

Talon regarded Fuller slowly. "It's time to bring up the machine parts, Captain."

For a moment Fuller thought of refusing. Madness, absolute madness, even to consider releasing such a horror into the world. But his responsibility was clear. Policy was made by the president and Congress, not the captain of the *Tarent*. He gave the necessary orders.

"We'd better get to your cabin," said Talon.

"Inform the Secretary of State and his party," Fuller said to Newton, "that their presence is requested in my cabin in five minutes. Mr. Talon? Please, follow me."

Secretary Powell, Reynolds, Clancy, and Parienne were already in the conference room in the captain's quarters when Fuller and Talon arrived.

"Hank Talon!" exclaimed Reynolds. "What are you doing here? This is a long way from Rome."

"It's good to see you, Barbara," Talon responded warmly.

"I see you two know each other," said Powell.

"Intelligence is a small community," Reynolds explained. "Hank did a fine job assisting Leyland in Rome." She turned back to Talon. "But you still haven't explained what you're doing here now."

"Security officer," Talon said. "But let me introduce Captain Fuller. He has your orders. I think Mr. Powell should read them quickly. The Soviets are on their way."

"Here you are, Mr. Secretary," Fuller said, handing him the sealed orders after introductions were completed.

Powell slit open the packet and withdrew the sheets of paper inside. Reaching inside his jacket for his glasses, he began to read.

Talon studied him closely. It seemed as if the color vanished from Powell's face. Clancy and Parienne, Talon noticed, had spotted the reaction and eyed the Secretary of State curiously. Reynolds waited expressionlessly. Wordless minutes passed as Powell read on. Then, with an expression that would suit a man who had just seen a report of his own terminal cancer, he spoke to the group in a voice dulled by shock.

"The content of these orders, signed by the president himself, is so unexpected, so . . . appalling, that you must forgive my obvious reaction. We are all aware of the Nightsight operation and its consequences for the United States; but we have been deliberately left in the dark concerning the president's response to it.

"I must inform you that we four, and every person on this ship, have been placed in extreme personal danger. The *Tarent* is carrying aboard her a huge quantity of a plague substance and the means to deliver that plague into the Soviet Union. We are here, not to negotiate with the Russians, but to deliver an ultimatum . . . if they will not remove the laser stations from orbit, we will be forced to release a bacteriological holocaust upon them."

Talon studied the reaction closely. Of the group, only Parienne greeted the announcement with a reaction other than disbelief. He was not shocked at all. Reynolds and Clancy were horrified, mouths agape and eyes wide.

"It is safe to say," Powell continued, putting his glasses down on the table, "that if the plague is released, the winds will pick it up and disperse it over the entire area of the Soviet Union. The weather is of great consequence to us now, for the prevailing winds and the current pressure patterns protect Western Europe, China, and Japan."

"But not for long," said Clancy hotly. "If the weather doesn't hold, we could be responsible for destroying God knows how many in Europe and even in the U.S. as well. This is madness!"

"This is desperation," said Parienne quietly. "And is it truly less horrible to contemplate America's destruction by a preemptive nuclear strike?"

"There are moral issues here," Reynolds said, her voice rising. "These weapons were outlawed over a decade ago. We cannot use them—"

"Just a minute," interrupted Talon. "These choices are no longer ours to make. I've never believed in an 'I was only following orders' philosophy, but we're here with a job to do because there's a loaded weapon pointing at our country. Does anyone really think that we'd be here in this place with this ultimatum if there were any other way . . . any other response possible?

"Delegates of a nation that attacked the United States are now on board this ship . . . that is the reality. You can weaken our response to restore the military balance essential to our survival if you quibble among yourselves . . . that is the reality. And if the Russians don't believe we mean every goddamn word Mr. Powell is about to say to them, then their missile ship lying two miles off our bow is going to blow us the hell out of the water. That is the reality. So choose quickly. The Russians are waiting; and they won't have any trouble at all choosing for you."

They assembled in a conference room on the level beneath the bridge, large enough to accommodate both groups and whose windows overlooked *Tarent*'s flight deck below. Beyond the helicopter pads, Commander Newton and a dozen crewmen waited by three six-foot-high rectangular "boxes," each covered by green, waterproof tarpaulins strapped to the boxes by ropes threaded through the eyelets in their hems. The wind had increased markedly.

Powell knew both Vassily Komarovsky and Viktor Grishen. He had sat on opposite sides of tables, much like the one at which they now sat, before. He remembered a vodka toast to Grishen at some diplomatic function. He shook hands gravely with both and nodded curtly to the aides who flanked them.

Clancy, Parienne, Reynolds, and the support staff sat alongside Powell, who took the chair opposite Grishen's. Fuller, as captain of the ship, sat at the head of the table, and Talon took the opposite foot.

The atmosphere in the gray, metal-walled room was taut, as if, at any moment, matched pairs from opposite sides might be selected to fight in the arena, the last left alive victorious. Talon had once been present, as a youth in New York City, when the rival gang leaders met to conduct the business of a truce. The feel was similar, undertones of violence masked by polite phraseology, ancient grudges subordinated by ritualized forms.

"If there are no objections," said Grishen in English, "we can proceed."

"No objection, Minister Grishen," said Powell, reflecting for the hundredth time that Russian should be taught in America's schools as English was in the Soviet Union's.

"Is there an agenda for submission?" asked Grishen.

Powell took a deep breath. "There is only one agenda, Mr. Minister. And that is whether or not the Soviet Union is willing to remove its laser stations from orbit around the earth and return to peaceful, political means to resolve our differences."

Grishen's posture became rigid. He regarded Powell with the diplomatic equivalent of shock. He ignored the question.

"I have not heard an agenda in your response, Secretary Powell. I remind you that it was your president who asked for this meeting to, as he put it, prevent any escalation in this conflict. If you wish, *we* have an agenda."

Powell understood Grishen's meaning well enough. Now it was time for Grishen to understand his. He summoned every ounce of his skill with words and every subtle manipulative strategy that he had learned in a life of diplomatic service, and when he spoke, the sound of his voice was deep, vibrant, and strong.

"It takes little ability to predict your agenda, Mr. Minister. It will be what an aggressor's agenda has always been. Demands for wealth unearned and territory undeserved, for stability by external acquisition and political growth by subjugation of others.

"The United States has never in its history acceded to demands made at the point of a gun. It matters not whether that gun is a cast-iron cannon or a laser battle station. The principle remains the same. We will not accede now."

Powell looked to Fuller who nodded to a waiting ensign and his order was relayed to Newton.

"What charade is this?" demanded Komarovsky angrily, getting up from his chair. "You have no interest in saving yourselves or your countrymen. You shall be ours. We are leaving."

"I suggest you look out the window behind me, Mr. Chairman, to those rather large objects in the bow," said Powell, "before you do."

On deck, Newton snapped a smart salute in the direction of the conference room and shouted orders to his men. The tarps were stripped away with a matador's flourish. Underneath, each missile launcher looked like a tall rectangular box filled with long, thin gray crayons in individual tubes. Drab green, each bore, in white-stenciled letters on its sides, U.S. ARMY.

"You all have sufficient data on our military weapons to know that what you are seeing are TRV portable rocket launchers which can fire their hundred surface-to-air missiles in under five seconds.

"As I have already said, the United States will not submit to blackmail of any kind. It is my sad duty to tell you that each missile contains in its warhead several ounces of the most virulent plague ever devised by the Bacteriological Warfare Division of our Army. Nightsight has begot Apocalypse, gentlemen. Our intent should be clear.

"If the Soviet Union attempts any military intervention outside of its borders or seeks to use its lasers for any purpose detrimental to the United States's interests, the plague will be released. Further, the Soviet Union will remove its lasers from orbit within fourteen days or the plague will be released. If any attempt is made to board, damage, or attack this ship, five seconds later, there will be plague on your shores.

"I urge you to remember your own city of Sverdlovsk where thousands of Soviet citizens died of an accidental discharge from one of your bacteriological research stations. By your actions you have released forces into the world which now threaten to consume us. In the name of the threatened billions who could fall victim to either burning beams of light or the burning fever of disease, I ask you to reconsider what you have done.

"There can be no turning back from our response, no submission now or ever. And what happens in the next few days may well decide the future of the entire human race.

"Be it on your conscience, gentlemen, and may God help us all."

The Russians sat down.

4

The White House physician completed his examination of the bites on Chris's legs and arms, pursed his lips, and confirmed that no serious trauma would result from the wounds. Antibiotics and tentanus shots were dispensed to prevent infection even though the lab tests from La Jolla had discovered no communicable diseases in either of the dead animals.

"You may run a slight fever for a few days, Senator, and I recommend some bed rest," said the doctor, "but, considering the source of the wounds, the damage is minimal."

Chris dressed and took the security elevator down to the Situation Room level where the crises management team's operations center had been set up.

Arielle had been in conference all day with the scientists who composed the technological staff for team leaders Dupont and Peterson. The stolen command-and-control mechanism was the first solid discovery concerning the nature of the Soviets' laser system, and Arielle's prior work on it made her the logical choice to discern flaws that might prove susceptible to exploitation. Additional experts, including fellow Jasons, had been flown in from all over the country to aid in the research.

As Chris entered the Situation Room he noted that the activity was only slightly less frenetic than days before. Now, however, the postures of the general staff were analogous to those of top athletes who knew that a contest was forthcoming but who had lost faith in the team's ability to meet the challenge. He heard harsh commands as the tension frayed tempers and saw bleary-eyed colonels in crumpled uniforms who fought to maintain composure.

He found Arielle in a room that resembled a college lecture hall, seats ringing a small platform surrounded by green chalkboards covered with equations. Tables had been set up by the chalkboards, and Chris saw that Dupont, Peterson, and others had already arrived. Arielle stood apart with the scientists, intently discussing a set of diagrams on the board.

Dr. Whitney, in his ever-present corduroy, walked into the room and nodded to Chris.

"Senator Leyland, Dr. Whitney," hailed Secretary Dupont, rising to make the necessary introductions. "This is General Parkins, head of the Air Force Satellite Command, and General Neill, chief of staff of the Air Force. Dr. Simmons informs us she'll be ready to begin in a few moments, gentlemen. There's coffee set up if anyone would like some."

Parkins, a tall, suntanned, well-built man, ambled off to get a cup of coffee while Neill pushed his cap back from his high, domed forehead and deep green eyes and returned to his conversation with Peterson.

Minutes later, Arielle and the other scientists joined them. Chris tried to read her facial expression but, cloaked as it was in professional lines, he could not.

"Gentlemen," Arielle began, "my colleagues and I have gone over every facet of the C&C system stolen from General Rogers in La Jolla. You are familiar by now with Senator Leyland's search to verify that the theft of the device was the motivation behind the raid on the Jasons earlier this spring. I can now add that there is further information which, we believe, proves that our system is indeed being used by the Soviets.

"Before its destruction, the electronic surveillance satellite system was charged with monitoring electronic signals emanating from the Soviet Union in order to decode high-level military communications. One of the ElecSurSats was in position over the Baikonur Launch Complex when the laser stations were sent into orbit. Until it was destroyed, our satellite intercepted signals from Baikonur to the lasers themselves.

"We've replayed the last transmissions NORAD received, and

they match exactly the frequencies that our own system uses. We have no doubt that the command-and-control system in the Russian lasers was designed in the United States—and that gives us our first edge.

"The laser stations are controlled from a single ground station, in this case, at Baikonur. Additional tracking data is supplied by Soviet ground stations throughout the world in the same way as NORAD is supplied. The electronic transmission from Baikonur to the lasers is almost instantaneous so there is no effective lag time or delay. Questions?"

"Shouldn't the use of a single control ground station make the lasers vulnerable?" asked Dupont.

"Not in the sense that any of the lasers are unmonitored at any time," Arielle responded.

"Down to brass tacks, Dr. Simmons," said Neill. "Either there are weak spots in the system or there are not."

"There may just be, General. But I think a bit of background may be necessary.

"Up until 1975 or so, satellite communications systems used low frequency microwaves, around four to ten gigaherz. However, these bands were also reserved for common carrier use and soon became quite congested. Interference emerged as a tremendous problem. Then, we discovered the benefits of using high frequency microwaves, in the range of eighteen to thirty gigaherz.

"At present there are no land-based systems operating in that range. So there is no congestion or interference. Second, high frequency microwaves are highly directional and easier to control. In addition—and here is the beauty, gentlemen—the size of all the components—including waveguides and antennas needed for transmission or reception—is proportional to signal wavelengths. Simply, the higher the frequency, the greater the gain. Antennas on satellites can be dramatically smaller using higher frequencies, which reduces the total weight and size. High frequency microwaves appeared to be a godsend."

"Forgive me, Dr. Simmons," said Neill impatiently, "but this doesn't appear to be a vulnerability at all. It seems like an asset."

"All scientists learn a basic rule early in life, General Neill," sighed Arielle sadly, "which is that benefits do not come without penalty. There is one major limiting factor in the use of high frequency microwaves. Above ten gigaherz, the signal size becomes comparable to the size of a raindrop. As a result, currents are induced on the drops and a significant amount of the energy is lost to absorption. In addition, energy is reradiated from the raindrops in a 'scattering' effect, and the signal is diverted from its intended path. The high frequency microwave signal, gentlemen, cannot pass through a simple, ordinary rainstorm.

"Our position is unanimous," said Arielle soberly to the stunned group. "Short of a nuclear bomb, the only force that will interfere with the C&C signals is rain. That, and that alone, will cut off control of the lasers. It's the exploitable flaw in the system."

"But surely DARPA must have known about this," Chris said, "and developed a strategy to counter it."

"Site diversity. Duplicate ground control stations over a hundred miles apart," Arielle responded. "That way one station would always be out of the rain. Costly, but effective."

"Then why wouldn't the Russians have built duplicates as well?" demanded Neill.

"I think I can answer that," said Dr. Whitney very quietly. "You see, ladies and gentlemen, it never rains in Baikonur."

For the third day in a row, the temperature in Black Mesa, Utah, had climbed over the hundred-and-ten-degree mark. Tom Crowley mopped his forehead continuously and pulled at his shirt as the heat rose off the desert floor in waves of asphyxiating fire.

A few hundred miles away, he knew, tourists were basking in air-conditioned rooms at the hotels in Grand Canyon National Park, but at the Echo Air Force Missile Station, the only relief to be found was underground, in the vast complex of cool tunnels and command stations which serviced the over two hundred Minutemen ICBM's. Almost a fifth of the nation's ICBM force lay here, in concrete silos spread over hundreds of acres of desert floor.

Normally, Echo Station would be lying quietly in the shimmering air, silos closed, showing only a forest of green conical covers on the shifting gray-white sands. Now, however, over half the silos were opened, huge cranes and derricks dipping into them like giant birds wrenching hard-shelled insects from the bone dry earth.

All over the range, military personnel and technicians from the enormous defense contractors, Lockheed, Grumman, Bell, TRW, and others, combined their efforts in a race no one had ever thought would have to be run. Hundreds of long-bed, sixteen-wheeler trucks converged on Echo Station, day and night, until they formed a convoy almost thirty miles long. From factories in nearby states, helicopters swooped in to unload their gleaming cargoes and then sprang out again to make way for others to land.

One by one, they brought the new satellites.

It was an effort as big as the Berlin Airlift, Crowley thought, as he surveyed the range with binoculars. At first, the plan was opposed by those responsible for the Nuclear Deterrent Force, but finally, the president himself had given the go-ahead.

This phase of Apocalypse was, in reality, simple in concept. It was just so much more logistically complicated to bring it into reality.

It would be impossible to make the required number of launchings necessary to replace the downed satellites into orbit in a short time, even using the combined facilities of every launch site America possessed. Vandenburg, Canaveral, Walops Island, and others would be too few by far.

The solution was "simple"—to replace the satellite presence of the United States in one fell swoop, the nuclear warheads of a large percentage of the Minutemen missiles would be removed and replaced by multiple satellite payload packages. Ready to be launched at a moment's notice, twenty-four hours a day, it was the Minutemen which would deliver Prophet, and a hundred others, back into the skies.

A colony of ants would have been staggered by both the furious pace and the intense cooperation of the work force and their machines. There was no time for delicacy, no grades for neatness, and debris piled up all over the range. Work was done in eight-hour shifts, round the clock, the night lit up by massive floodlights throwing eerie shadows onto the surrounding craggy hills, lead shielded receptacles for the warheads sprouting up like mushrooms.

Moving back inside the concrete blockhouse, one of the few aboveground structures at Echo besides the gatehouse and the towers which guarded the perimeter fences, Crowley settled in at his desk to recheck the growing number of refurbished missiles.

The staff Dupont had assembled from the Department of Defense to supervise the project had done an amazing job so far. Every hour saw more satellites loaded. In three days the project would be completed. They would be ready to launch if, he reminded himself, the lasers could be destroyed. He reached for his half-finished report to Secretary Dupont.

"You were right all along, Arthur," he whispered to himself. His thoughts ran back to a street in Rome, an explosion, a loss. So much affection and so great a burden they had handed to Chris Leyland.

Crowley walked over to a window and watched the work continue. Sounds still reached him; the clang of hammers, the roar of diesel engines, the camaraderie of hardworking men. Profoundly moved, he bent back to his task.

Inside the Arsenal Building at the Kremlin, the Politburo had been in session for almost three hours. Faces flushed with triumph just one day before now held the vicious tinge of those who sought blame and those who knew fear. It had taken all of Meledov's skill, with constant support from Komarovsky, to hold the group together.

". . . The weather is unquestionably on their side," finished the Minister of Agriculture, Mikhail Gorbach. "If the plague were to be released from the Gulf of Finland, it would indeed blanket us within a week. Our hope is that either of the two high-pressure ridges will move. If that is the case, the Americans won't dare release it. It would end up covering the northern hemisphere."

"What is your best prediction for the duration of the ridges?" Meledov asked.

Gorbach shrugged. "A few days, a week, maybe less. No one knows. There are changes that will signal their attenuation, but they have not yet occurred. If they do, I can predict to within seventy-two hours the destruction of the ridges. Our weather stations are tracking the pressure systems every minute. That, right now, is the best I can do."

"The longer we wait, the more credence we give to this bluff!" said Grishen hotly. "We cannot believe that the Americans would release such a thing. It violates their every tradition of warfare, and it would be suicide."

"They have never had their backs up to the wall like this before," argued Komarovsky.

"The *Ural* is standing by one mile from the *Tarent*'s position. I say give the order and let her missiles fly. It is a bluff. We must not be fooled by it. Destroy the *Tarent!*" Grishen demanded.

"But if it is not a bluff?" asked Meledov quietly. "Can we afford not one but a thousand Sverdlovsks? Could we survive the decimation of our crops and our livestock? You know the answer as well as I do, Viktor."

"We must bring to bear a nuclear weapon large enough to vaporize the *Tarent,*" said Defense Minister Telshe, his face set in hard lines.

"Impossible!" shouted Trapeznikov. "We can't know if the disease would be eliminated or spread by such an explosion. And anything large enough to blanket the entire area would destroy Leningrad! You must be mad."

"Watch your words, Minister," said Telshe angrily. "It was not I who put Nightsight together and brought us here."

"Comrades," said Meledov in a plea for order. "This is not the way out of our dilemma. If the American countermove can be neutralized for even one day, we can guarantee that it never surfaces again. We were fooled. I admit that and take responsibility for it. But," and his voice grew hard, "this is not the time for recriminations. We must know what type of plague *Tarent* carries and whether or not they will release it. That is critical. Crying like old women is not!" He smashed his hand down.

Komarovsky had waited for just such a moment. Cowed into silence by Meledov's stinging fury, the group waited, factional disputes still simmering.

"There is one avenue left undiscussed," Komarovsky said slowly, the weight of his years hanging like lead upon him. He looked to Meledov, who nodded.

"Castor," Komarovsky said, unequivocably.

The name brought heads up and a host of statements flew at him. He allowed Trapeznikov to speak.

"Good news at last, Vassily," said the Minister of Science. "If Castor can obtain a sample of the plague for us to analyze, we can discover its nature."

"Which means," interrupted Telshe, "we may be able to vaccinate against it. Our Civil Defense is the best in the world, and we can have ninety percent of Moscow in shelters within six hours. The other cities are nearly as organized. If the Army can transport the Party apparatus into the country, we could save the livestock as well."

"But the grain will die," countered Gorbach.

"The Americans will replace it," thundered Grishen stonily.

"It is possible," agreed Meledov. "In any event, it would break the stalemate."

"Where is Marshal Torgenev now?" asked Komarovsky.

"Less than a hundred miles from the Polish border," answered Meledov. "He stands ready to invade within three days."

"Hold him," said Komarovsky. "I must have time. Castor must have time. We cannot invade until either the weather breaks or Castor delivers to us the plague and the rest of the Americans' plan. We must not provoke the Americans till we are secure."

"Can you contact Castor," asked Grishen, "as well as providing a communications system and a means of delivery? Security will be monumental regarding Apocalypse."

"No one knows Castor as I do," said Komarovsky. "In fact, Comrade Grishen, Castor was at our conference on the *Tarent*. One day I hope to have the pleasure of introducing you.

"The negotiating team, all except their Secretary of State, will be returning to Washington tomorrow. Due to their hasty departure from Washington to board *Tarent,* there was no opportunity for Castor to gather information on either the plague or the rest of their plan, Apocalypse. That can be remedied now.

"Something is brewing in Washington, Comrades. The Americans are not acting as we thought they might. Give me two more days, three at the most, and I believe Castor can deliver Apocalypse to us. Then, we can protect Nightsight and proceed with our plans. But I must have time."

"Marshal Torgenev will not be happy if we restrain him. He has lived for this hour," said Grishen, "and will strain against the leash."

"He knows I have lived for this, too," Komarovsky sighed. "But he is a soldier and will have to do his duty."

Meledov ran a thin hand through his snow-white hair. "You will proceed, Comrade Chairman, with your plan to use Castor. But Grishen has a valid point. We cannot delay our response forever. If the Americans believe that Nightsight can be neutralized, they will attempt other dangerous moves as well. It is time to stop them permanently.

"You have seventy-two hours to operate Castor, Comrade Komarovsky. And you must be successful. Because, at that time, I will order the destruction of *Tarent* and our nuclear forces will launch a limited preemptive first strike to cripple the United States."

The signals officer jogged across the length of the mobile command post and handed the cable to Marshal Torgenev, who read the contents quickly.

The command post was poised at the head of Torgenev's combined forces like the hood of a cobra. The army he would lead into Poland consisted of eight motorized rifle divisions, six tank divisions, three artillery brigades, and numerous chemical, engineering, and signal units. It also had frontal air support and an advance intelligence corps. Stretching back ten miles toward Moscow behind them, more units arrived every day, transported along the Moscow-Warsaw rail lines.

For days, Torgenev had been a man possessed. Racing up and down the lines of bivouacked troops, he shouted encouragements to brigade commanders and herded the enormous force together like a militant shepherd.

Poland would be only the start of this campaign. Torgenev intended to secure the country to its East German border, and then pivot back through Czechoslovakia, Hungary, Romania, and Bulgaria to secure the western front. Meanwhile, a second army would be gathering in Turkestan to invade south Afghanistan and swing west to take the Persian Gulf, joining the first force at the Black Sea, placing Turkey between the armies. It, too, would fall in a matter of days. Without the Americans' Prophets, there would be no warning, nothing to reduce the vital element of surprise.

Torgenev read the cable ordering the army's halt a second time, masking his shock and anger from the signals officer, who awaited a response.

"When did you receive this?" he demanded.

"Only a moment ago, Comrade Marshal. It was priority coded so I rushed it to you."

"Eliminate any indication in your log of having accepted this transmission. It was too garbled to decode. Do you understand me?" Torgenev fixed him with a pointed stare.

"Yes, Marshal. Transmission garbled," said the officer, eyes averted.

"Very good. Resume your post."

Torgenev watched the officer race back to his radio console. Then, deliberately, he crushed the cable into a crumpled knot of paper and tossed it into the shredder.

Valentin Kasimov had followed the ambulance that wailed out of the Torrey Pines Inn. Perplexed by the dogs' failure to return when he had blown the recall on an ultrasonic whistle, his inquiries at the hospital turned up two distressing facts: the dogs were dead and Leyland and his wife were not.

Bitterly, he had reported his failure to Moscow from the San Francisco station and awaited Komarovsky's response.

Now, in his fist, he held the cable, frayed by the twisting of his strong hands. Recall! Recall, he read again. Disgrace and dismissal from KGB after a career that spanned over thirty years. It could not be tolerated!

As much as he despised Komarovsky and the weakness of his superiors, he was forced to admit that he, himself, had given the chairman the means to destroy him. Eris *had* failed. And now, like buzzards circling over a wounded man, they sought to pounce on him. Only one option remained; finish the mission, even without KGB support, and return to accolades rather than disgrace.

His hatred for Leyland rose up within him and almost blotted out his disdain for the Moscow bureaucrats. Leyland had cost him his position. It was Leyland that Komarovsky and the Politburo would use as an excuse to remove him. He could count on no support from the sycophantic Mikoyan nor could he rely on the useless Trapeznikov. Komarovsky alone could restore him to power. The key was Leyland's death as had been ordained.

The identity papers he had ordered from the documents section had already arrived. Three separate sets would have to be enough. He made out a requisition for sufficient cash and booked a flight for Washington.

He would have to be certain this time, he realized. He alone would have to see Leyland in the cross hairs of a telescopic sight and watch him go down when he pulled the trigger. He relished the moment in his imagination.

Tossing the cable into the garbage, Kasimov walked out into the brisk San Francisco night.

Hank Talon had many things on his mind as he left the morning watch on the bridge and descended to the helipads below.

The report from the *Vycore* off Japan had not been encouraging. Pressure readings and upper atmospheric high winds both seemed to indicate that the ridge was weakening. It took little effort to visualize the frantic concern on the faces of the men in Washington and the crafty hope on the faces of the men in Moscow.

Stuck right in the middle of the standoff were *Tarent* and everyone aboard her. No one needed to be reminded that if the ridges dissipated, or if the Soviets sought to break the stalemate, the guns and missiles of the *Ural* pointing at them would be unleashed in a fiery array of destruction.

The flight crew was finished preparing their helicopter when Talon arrived on deck. Luggage had already been stowed, and the long blades began turning slowly in the wind.

Clancy, Parienne, and Reynolds stood braced against the cold breeze talking quietly to Powell and Fuller. Each one had the oppressing awareness that these two, and the rest of *Tarent*'s crew, would be the first to die if Apocalypse provoked, rather than subdued, the Soviet aggression. Talon walked over to the group, his face bearing no trace of his internal disquiet.

". . . I appreciate your feelings," Powell was saying, "but the president is correct. You're all needed back in Washington, and you've already served your purpose in coming here. I had your moral support and your political skills, and the Russians could not doubt that this team operated with the full authority of the executive branch. All of our relationships to the president are well known."

"You know any of us would willingly stay in your place," said Reynolds tightly.

"I know that, Barbara. But my place is here. As Secretary of State, only I have the necessary authority to carry on diplomatic initiatives if the Russians will go that route. As I've just said, you three must go where you're most needed. And that's home."

"Our thoughts will be with you out here," said Parienne, clasping his friend's hand and then the captain's.

"Make that your prayers, too," added Fuller soberly.

"You've got them," agreed Parienne.

Clancy stepped up and shook hands with both men silently. His concern was in his eyes, in the firm clasp of his hand. There were no words that could alter what he felt, or lessen the danger of the situation.

"I'm sorry," said Talon, catching the helicopter pilot's signal. "I believe we're ready to go. Goodbye, Mr. Secretary, Captain Fuller."

His handshake was met with a grim nod from each. He was still the outsider, the man who knew more than he should, and they were still cautious around him. Regardless, Talon respected both.

The others boarded the helicopter, and Talon followed. Crewmen cast off the restraining lines as the pilot brought the engine up to full power, and the craft sprang from the rolling deck into the air.

Talon looked down at the *Tarent*. Gradually, the two figures on her top deck dwindled to small specks. Then, *Tarent* herself grew small, dwarfed by the cold, gray sea around her. The *Ural,* a mile off her bow, stood ominously silent and deadly, till it too shrank finally into the distance.

So far below them, Talon thought, a battle was being fought. Brave men had placed themselves into jeopardy in order to hold back a greater threat. This one small spot in an unimportant body of water became the nexus for tensions which threatened to engulf the world. And with the simple motion of getting on an aircraft, he had left it all behind.

A kind of delayed shock settled over Talon. He wondered if this was what soldiers had felt in Viet Nam, suddenly transported out of the steaming jungle and brought home by jet less than a day later. It seemed impossible that he had not left some indispensable part of him behind. By an act of will, he turned his thoughts forward. Only the beginning of his assignment from the president was over. The critical part was still ahead.

The military jet which would take them to Washington was fueled and ready at a NATO base. The helicopter settled down less than a hundred yards from the jet and its passengers disembarked.

Walking across the runway to the jet, Talon observed the three who walked ahead of him. Still forming a tight group, perhaps even closer for having left one of their own behind, they did not invite Talon to join. Their trust and faith in one another was obvious. He wondered what it would do to the remaining two when they discovered that one of them was a traitor.

Talon boarded the jet thinking dark thoughts. His surveillance teams would be ready and in place by the time they returned to Washington. The mole had to be uncovered—a single slip and he would be.

5

"The weather situation is deteriorating, Mr. President," said Defense Secretary Dupont. "Our best estimate is another forty-eight to seventy-two hours for the Japanese Ridge, a bit longer for the British. You know what that means, sir."

Chris Leyland watched the interplay of emotions across the president's features. Everyone else assembled in the Cabinet Room—General Peterson, Dr. Whitney, General Neill, and General Blaire—listened intently.

Arielle was deep in thought, preparing to deliver the synopsis of the only workable plan to be generated during the long, painstaking hours of the night.

"It means," said the president soberly, "that the Russians could believe that we won't dare release the plague if it means mutual suicide."

"Yes, sir," said Dupont. "It is our belief that as soon as the ridge goes, so goes the *Tarent*."

"And the balance of power," finished Peterson.

"Unless we release it now," argued General Neill. "The Soviet Union has declared war on the United States. Militarily, politically, and historically we are justified in responding! Release it now, before we no longer have the capability to do so."

"Vetoed," said the president immediately. "We are vulnerable to a nuclear attack. I will not push the Soviets into a position where they are forced to respond. Absolutely and unequivocally, no."

"I support that decision," said General Peterson clearly. Connors nodded.

"There is an alternative, Mr. President," said Dupont into the silence created by the disagreement. "If Dr. Simmons will explain . . ."

"You have the floor, Dr. Simmons," said Connors.

"The crises management team has conceived of an alternative to the release of the plague—a release that could possibly destroy us all. Clearly, our need is to destroy the Soviet lasers. Should that be accomplished, the balance of power can be restored, the *Tarent* withdrawn.

"It must be understood at the outset, however, that our proposal contains a high element of risk. It relies on some procedures which are still experimental in nature."

"Understood," said the president. "Go on."

"The command signals which aim and operate the Soviet lasers," Arielle continued, "can be interfered with by the commonest of nature's elements—rain. But the Baikonur complex, from which the control signal originates, is in a region of almost no rainfall, shielded as it is by the Ural Mountain range and the high altitudes of the Kazakhskaya Plains. The gist of our operation is simple, Mr. President. It is our intention to make it rain on Baikonur."

"And just how do you plan to accomplish that feat of magic, Dr. Simmons?" asked Connors, disbelief evident in his tone.

"Not magic, sir. Merely the application of experimental technologies developed over the last decade," Arielle responded. "Allow Dr. Whitney to explain."

"Clouds form," Whitney began, "because air containing water vapor is forced to rise upward in the atmosphere as a result of convection, orographic uplift—that is to say, terrain features like mountains—or large-scale cyclonic motions. As the moist air rises, it expands due to the decrease in atmospheric pressure and its temperature falls. Since the amount of water the air can contain decreases with the decrease in temperature, a point is soon reached where the water vapor contained therein is sufficient to saturate the air, and further cooling results in condensation—a cloud forms. It is the nature of the uplift, its size and strength, which determines the lifetime and the vigor of the cloud.

"Finally, the nature and concentration of the submicroscopic particles around which the water vapor coalesces, called condensation nuclei, determine whether or not a cloud will form raindrops of precipitable size over a period of time. Is that clear, sir?"

"Clear enough," said Connors. "But I still have no idea where we're going on this." His tone indicated that they had better get there quickly.

"In the late seventies," Arielle said, "a device was invented called the Meteotron, which consists of six jet engines, ground-mounted in such a way that their exhausts are combined into a single, vertically directed stream of superheated air. It can produce a vertical wind current with a temperature in excess of fifteen hundred degrees Fahrenheit and a speed of over fifteen hundred miles per hour.

"The Meteotron has been used to study the degree to which it is possible to initiate the actual development of rain-bearing clouds."

"I am going to assume a high degree of success in such tests," said Connors, his interest growing.

"Then you would assume incorrectly," said Arielle, pulling no punches. "There has been a fifty-percent failure rate in producing a viable rain cloud. Experiments have continued using various condensation nuclei, such as silver iodide and dry ice pellets, but we're banking on a compound just developed composed of acetylacetonate copper, AAC for short. When AAC is dispersed within the air-water current by means of an electric arc, it has the highest efficiency of condensation nuclei production ever achieved, or so Dr. Whitney assures us."

"Using AAC," Whitney said, "has given us a much higher success rate. And the newest generation of computers have allowed us to tie down the incredibly complex set of variables necessary for control of cloud production. It can work, Mr. President."

"Where will you locate the Meteotron?" asked Connors.

"As close as possible to Baikonur," said Arielle. "General Peterson is ready to transport the device to the shores of the Caspian Sea on the Iranian coast and secure it there. The entire operation should take approximately twelve hours, in and out."

Connors looked to Peterson.

"We can do it, sir. The Iranians haven't had an effective air defense mechanism since the theocracy executed most of the technicians for heresy. We can protect our people. Political repercussions I won't speak for, though."

"If we don't pull this off, political repercussions won't mean a damn thing," said Connors. "For the moment, an incursion into Iranian territory is an acceptable premise."

"The final problem becomes one of steerage," continued Arielle. "Without the MeteoSats, we're going to need three of our AWACS to monitor the prevailing winds and triangulate the proper formation point. Releasing several tons of tiny carbon filaments will allow us to track on radar the wind speed and direction. Without computers, the entire operation would be impossible. I'll supervise that end of things; Dr. Whitney, the meteorological.

"With a little bit of luck, sir, we can create a storm over Baikonur and cut off the signals to their lasers."

"That's the first phase of the operation, sir," said Peterson. "The second phase is more direct. We plan a simultaneous launch of two of our Shuttles from Canaveral, armed with heat-seeking missiles, to destroy the lasers in space. Once the signal is interrupted by the rain, the lasers will be vulnerable."

"Phase three will involve the launch of the Minutemen to replace the downed satellites," continued Dupont. "That's what we have, Mr. President—an operation of a size to rival the lunar landing. It can go wrong at any of a dozen points. A slight miscalculation, a failed computer, a loss of communications, and we could fail. Far from being a harbinger of doom, I want to give you a realistic picture of this undertaking. If we fail, sir, it will be on your head alone when it comes to the public's reaction."

"I see no alternative, Mr. Secretary," said Connors slowly.

Dupont shifted uncomfortably. "There is one, sir. And I would be remiss in my responsibility if I didn't bring it to your attention." Dupont paused for a long moment and then looked directly into Connors' deep blue eyes. "We could surrender, Mr. President."

Connors looked away for a moment, ignoring the sharp look from General Neill, and cut off all comments with a wave of his hand.

"Thank you, Arnold," Connors said softly. "I understand your motivation for suggesting such a settlement to our problem. And it would indeed lessen the risk to the country. But we both know it's impossible, a betrayal of principles we've always believed in. Suggestion vetoed."

"Then you approve our operation, sir," said Dupont.

"One question first. Why use Shuttles and not the SAINT program a second time?" Connors queried.

"Because there's one factor that's been left undiscussed," said Chris, speaking for the first time. "Even if we can place a cloud over Baikonur, Mr. President, we have no way of predicting the duration of the rainfall. The SAINT missiles would be destroyed if the storm is too short. But the Shuttles can at least make it into orbit, and if control returns to the Russians, we'll need pilot-guided flight. There is a possibility of destroying at least some of the lasers before the Shuttles are destroyed. No missile can maneuver like a Shuttle in the hands of a skilled pilot. As you said, sir, it's an all-or-nothing game."

"You're describing what could be a suicide mission, Senator. Who do we have to fly it?"

"I've already conferred with NASA. Major William Cooke has volunteered to command the Shuttle *Independence*. He was my copilot on the last NASA mission and as good a man as ever flew. We can depend on him absolutely."

Connors saw Arielle's features tighten and her gaze stray off into a private place of her own. Abruptly, he saw the strain she was under and in a flash of insight, understood its source. He considered the courage of the men and women who faced him and knew that he was seeing something that could never be defined, only marveled at.

"You mentioned two Shuttles, Senator," he said, knowing what was to come.

"Yes, sir. *Constitution* is mine, Mr. President, till the job is done."

Connors looked slowly around the table. Each of the faces was stern and drawn, each one waiting for his decision. They had offered him their best, he knew. Technical expertise, military judgment, and in Leyland's case, perhaps his life itself. He straightened in his chair, and when he spoke, it was with dignity and humility.

"We can no longer count on the weather to protect *Tarent*," Connors began, "and CIA reports that Soviet troops are massing on the Polish border in unknown strength. Further reports indicate a similar buildup in Turkestan province. The Soviet intention is clear, an invasion is in the making. CIA projections indicate less than a week remains, and without the Prophets, our military is blind to the Soviet movements.

"Here, security leaks concerning the Soviet lasers have already begun. Soon, very soon, the truth will come out. Public reaction will be swift and unmerciful, and we cannot be found wanting.

"We have reached the crises point, ladies and gentlemen, where we must act—or be doomed to face consequences which will change forever the nature of the world as we have known it. Mindful of the dangers in your plan and mindful of its risks, I am certain that what you have offered is the only option left, the court of last resort."

The president rose and stared down the length of the table.

"It is the business of great nations to accept great challenges," he continued slowly, "and it is the duty of all people to rise to those challenges when the call to action sounds. You have all answered that call. Let this be our final pledge: this nation will continue to live freely, or it will perish in the attempt.

"Your plan is approved. For the next sixty hours, the fate of the United States is in your hands."

The long flight from Scandinavia wore on, and Talon continued to observe and analyze his three suspects. There were no other passengers on the plane, and with the exception of the flight crew, no one had stirred once the plane was in the air.

Reynolds sat in quiet conversation with Parienne. Across the aisle, Clancy sat alone, his gray briefcase open on the seat next to him, writing a report for Connors. Talon had chosen to sit behind them, keeping all in view as he marshaled his thoughts.

Talon thought of the dossiers that had been compiled on each, resting innocuously in his briefcase under the seat. Even the most detailed investigation and computer search had failed to reveal any clue as to Castor's identity. Had it not been for Pollux's mention of Castor to Leyland, and the subsequent alerting of Pollux by Castor, even now the presence of a second, more highly placed mole might have gone unsuspected. But the record of times matched Pollux's claim that he had been alerted by someone. Only minutes after Reynolds had made the announcement to the president, Pollux had left his office in Langley and disappeared. The conclusion was as unavoidable as it was unsettling; the leak was certainly at the top.

On board *Tarent,* Talon had been given an opportunity to observe and study his suspects under unusual conditions. He watched carefully as they had reacted to the situation into which they'd been so suddenly flung, but no definite pattern appeared. He failed to spot any attempt at communication with the Soviets. Nothing out of the ordinary had transpired. He needed more to go on.

"Excuse me, Mr. Talon."

Talon looked up into the haggard but smiling face of James Parienne. "Yes, sir?"

"There hasn't been much of an opportunity to speak to you on less than formal terms. I thought I'd like to remedy that. May I join you?"

"I'd be delighted. Pull up a chair."

Parienne slid into the adjoining seat and then paused to breathe deeply for a moment. The slight effort seemed to drain him. Talon noticed too that his complexion was rather sallow, with the scars of old acne visible under scrutiny this close.

"You did a fine job in Rome, Mr. Talon."

"Hank."

Parienne inclined his head in acknowledgment. "You did a fine job in Rome, Hank. The president was quite pleased. And your work on board *Tarent* was top-notch. All our reports will state that."

"It's kind of you to take the time to tell me that, sir. Praise isn't exactly endemic in my business."

"It's true that the intelligence services have received their share of criticism these past ten years," observed Parienne with a smile tugging at the corners of his mouth. "But that's equally true of almost every other branch of the government. You mustn't take it personally."

Talon looked into the kindly face and came to a sudden decision. "So they said to the starving man," he said sarcastically. "I'm certain it was a great comfort."

"It can be," said Parienne, unruffled. "One recognizes dissent as part of the political process, sometimes painful but always necessary."

"Often absurd and almost always uneducated," Talon countered.

A shadow crossed Parienne's face, "Surely you wouldn't advocate putting curbs on first amendment rights?"

"Maybe there can be too much of a good thing."

"And who would decide that?" said Parienne, his voice rising. "Curb that right and things will be better, neater, more controllable, someone always says. And then someone else says maybe we should put some good old limits on that other little old right as well—just a bit, in the interest of order. And then why not fool just a bit more with the most basic right of all, the right to cast your vote. You know, get those poor lazy, uneducated riffraff who don't look like us out of the way . . ."

Abruptly, a look of amazement broke over Parienne's face. "You're testing me!" he said, astonished. "You're actually examining me. You don't believe the rubbish you were spouting. It was only to anger me enough to lower my guard so you could . . . probe me!"

"I confess," Talon admitted ruefully. "I hope you understand that it was in the interest of security. It's my job to make certain of things twenty-four hours a day. I have to understand the people I'm assigned to protect. There are no excuses, no time off while an operation is on, and no one we're allowed to take for granted."

"Why me, then? I mean specifically."

Talon shook his head. "You're missing the point. There are no specifics. You've been at the center of power for a long time now. We're familiar with power's ability to change a man. It's nice to see that it hasn't in your case."

"I don't know whether to be flattered or furious," said Parienne, rising.

"Pardon my alliteration, but why not settle for secure, sir?" said Talon, smiling disarmingly.

It was not lost on Parienne, who shook his head in mock defeat. "I'm just glad," he laughed, "that you're on our side."

Parienne returned to sit with Reynolds. Clancy continued to write. In the silence which ensued, Talon reviewed his conversation with Parienne.

The cues and responses had all been right, the outrage properly intense. But Talon couldn't escape the feeling that there was something bothering Parienne very deeply. It made him want to dig deeper into the man's life, deeper into his psyche.

People in less sensitive positions, with less support from the president, might have found themselves transferred at once to Langley for interrogation and internment solely on the grounds of these suspicions. But at least two of the three suspects were loyal and trustworthy, highly ranked members of the administration. If they were wrongly accused and their constitutional rights denied, the political repercussions would bring further damage to a suddenly precarious presidency.

There could be no publicity on this one, no mistakes or false accusations either. Castor had to be eliminated as a security risk or Apocalypse would be compromised as easily as the nation's satellite defenses.

But it was equally clear that Castor would be after the exact nature of Apocalypse. Talon had little trouble visualizing the demands for information that the Politburo would have thrust upon the KGB. And given that only the highest ranking officials in Washington had access to Apocalypse, the KGB would have to use its mole once again. Or so the thinking had gone, Talon mused fitfully. If, he frowned, Castor was indeed one of his suspects. But if somehow Castor had managed to cleverly divert suspicion, or if the KGB had wisely told him to lie low until other agents could be brought into play . . . Too many ifs and not enough facts. He sighed.

He watched Reynolds get up and make her way to the forward galley for coffee. Parienne reclined his seat and closed his eyes after putting his brown leather briefcase in the aisle next to him. Clancy kept on writing, politely refusing the coffee Reynolds offered him.

Reynolds glanced back to Talon and made the same offer again. Talon accepted and she brought it back, sliding into the seat across the aisle next to him.

"It's been a long time, Hank. How are you these days?" she asked, warmth in her voice.

"Pretty much the same, Barbara. A little more gray, a little more tired. Just now I think I'm feeling it more than usual."

Reynolds nodded in understanding. "This kind of situation gets to all of us. One mistake, one wrong judgment, and the world could be at war. It's too heavy a responsibility."

"You appear to handle it well enough," he observed.

"More practice," she shrugged. "But it never gets any easier. Inside, I'm scared as hell. What got you into the middle of this in the first place?"

"Security was needed for the *Tarent* operation. I assume Leyland must have had some influence on the president. One day I was sitting in Rome, the next day special orders came through, and I was flown to Copenhagen to take charge."

Strictly speaking, what he told her was true, but only the partial truth. He omitted Leyland's briefing on the nature of Apocalypse and Talon's role in it. And he omitted Castor.

"That's quite a vote of confidence," Reynolds said appreciatively. "If we get through this crisis, Hank, I wouldn't wonder if advanced postings won't be possible for you. Sanderson's discovery was quite a coup."

"We'll cross that bridge when we come to it," Talon said philosophically.

"Still the clichés, I see. I'd forgotten."

Talon smiled, "The more things change . . ."

". . . the more they stay the same," Reynolds finished with a grin. "What do you think of Apocalypse, Hank? Do we have a chance to bring down those lasers?"

Out of the corner of his eye, Talon saw Clancy close up his briefcase and put it in the aisle next to Parienne's. Someone's going to trip and go flying, he thought idly, but ignored it as Reynolds continued. He returned his attention to her, the not-so-subtle probes as yet unanswered.

"You know more about it than I do, Barbara," he lied. "What's your opinion?"

"Frankly, Hank, I'm not as well briefed on this as I'd like to be, though I'm certain the president will remedy that when we get back. We left Washington so quickly that there wasn't time for a full briefing."

"So you're pumping me," Talon said, his sad eyes twinkling.

It appeared that Reynolds was going to retort angrily, but her face creased into lines of amusement.

"As you might say, old habits die hard. Sorry, Hank."

"Perfectly all right. It's an occupational hazard. In our business, knowledge is not only power, it's survival. And it's been a lot of years for you."

"Almost twenty-five, counting my time in CIA. Cost me most of my personal life, including a marriage, to get to where I am now."

Talon heard a note of sadness in her voice. He surveyed her fine, intelligent features and decided that she was still a very attractive woman. Time had woven little gray into her lush brown hair, and her manner and style befitted one of her rank and power.

"I meant to ask you about the 'Mrs.' When did you get married?"

"Married and divorced the same year, 1975," she replied. "Too much distance between us, too much pressure from different careers; he was a civilian, owned his own business. I think we saw each other a total of ten weeks out of that entire first year. You know the harsh reality, Hank. We just couldn't hold it together."

"My wife and I came close to divorce two or three times over the years. If not for the kids, we might not have made it," he said with sympathy.

"I wonder what motivates any of us to stay in this business," she sighed. "Most people get up, go to work and at five o'clock close their office door, or punch the time clock and that's it; all over. No watching over their shoulders, no suspicion of the casual approach of an acquaintance at a party, no sifting through every conversation to find the truth amid the lies. I swear, sometimes I envy them."

"Their problems and responsibilities are as weighty to them as yours are to you. Is it any easier to worry about the mortgage payments and college for the kids?"

"But lives don't depend on that."

"Theirs do," Talon said flatly.

"I suppose. Maybe I'm just tired of the responsibility."

"Come off it, Barbara," Talon said, more sharply. "You could resign in a minute and make three times your salary in private industry. You stay because you love being at the center. If the world is composed of the actors and the audience, you need to be one of the actors. Everything you do is front-page news—your meetings with the president, your statements on world conditions, your part in molding foreign policy. You're too good a student of history, Barbara, and you want your own chapter in the books."

Reynolds hadn't winced under his verbal barrage, but he saw again the sadness whose source he could not identify.

"It's a trade-off then," she said quietly. "Personal isolation for a place in the history books; the illusion of being important."

"That seems to be the way it works," he agreed. "But you still have choices."

He saw the sadness again as she placed a smooth, manicured hand on his shoulder.

"My dear, old friend," she said at last, rising to return forward, "choice is the greatest illusion of all."

Talon watched her walk forward, turning to slip past Clancy's briefcase in the aisle, and slide tiredly into her seat next to the still-sleeping Parienne. She was a different person than she had been when last he knew her. She had aged, and her priorities had changed. Was it her office that had done that, he wondered, or was it just the years that do it to us all?

She looked so tired when she had walked away, psychologically brittle and . . . alarm bells suddenly went off in Talon's brain. Reynolds had twisted to avoid a single briefcase in the aisle where there should have been two! Clancy's gray one was still there but not Parienne's brown. It had been there when Reynolds came back with the coffee and Parienne had been dozing all during their conversation. He obviously hadn't moved it in his sleep.

Talon drifted up and out of his seat. Ten feet ahead in the aisle rested the single case. Shuffling forward, he timed his steps so that his foot intercepted the briefcase in mid-step. A loud crack followed as he tripped over it and his forward momentum took him careening wildly into the bulkhead beyond the seats. As Talon sank to the floor in what he hoped was a realistic tumble, Parienne woke with a start at the noise, and Reynolds was already out of her seat to help him up.

"Son of a bitch!" cursed Talon angrily, rubbing his head.

"Give me a hand, Terry," Reynolds called out, unable to lift Talon alone. Together, they hefted him into a seat.

"I'm truly sorry, Mr. Talon," said Parienne solicitously. "I shouldn't have left my things in the aisle. Are you all right?"

"I think so. Forget it. No damage done."

"My fault, too," said Clancy. "I left mine there as well. Sorry."

Talon rose and dusted himself off. A few more words of assurance, and he returned to his seat.

But his purpose had been accomplished. As he "tripped," he'd seen Parienne's case on Clancy's lap, and he was attempting to open it surreptitiously. The noise of his fall had interrupted Clancy. When Talon had stood up, both cases had been back in the aisle, as if he'd tripped over both.

What was it that Clancy had wanted from Parienne's case, he wondered. Something he already knew was in there or something he hoped to find? Perhaps, Talon ruminated, he had wanted to place something of his own inside; a "plant" of some nature. He continued to dwell on it.

Talon was like a prospector, searching for a vein of truth in a hard mass of Castor's lies and deceptions. To him, Clancy's actions were like finding a gold nugget on hitherto desolate ground; he had to uncover what might be underneath.

The surveillance he had ordered on his three suspects would be well in place by now. Every action of the three would be watched; every phone call, cable or radio transmission possible to monitor would be. One single mistake and Castor would be caught in the net Talon had devised and strung so tightly.

Perhaps, Talon thought, as the captain came back to report their descent into Washington, the first mistake had already been made.

6

The first tendrils of light crawled across the dark sky, and gradually the room at Andrews Air Force Base began to lighten. Chris felt Arielle stir and the rhythm of her breathing quicken as she awakened against him.

He didn't move. This last, quiet time together would have to sustain them both during the days to come. He wanted to savor it, to solidify the memory in his mind as one might carry a picture or a lock of hair.

Arielle's soft fragrance wafted up to him, and he felt the moistness of her skin where her head lay against his chest. Often, during the night, each had looked at the other with unspoken concern wanting to ask, to appeal, to demand even, that the other forgo the task ahead and remain safe. But knowing they could not ask, restraint had augmented the passion of their last hours, as resistance in a wire builds up an electrical charge. Finally, exhausted, they had slept.

The now normal rhythm of Arielle's breathing told him she was fully awake. He pressed his face into her hair and lay still.

"You're not sleeping," said Arielle, her voice husky and low. "Is it time yet?"

"Soon," Chris murmured regretfully. "An hour or so."

"I'm frightened for you, Chris. I can't help thinking that you'll be depending on how successful Whitney and I are. If the rain doesn't last long enough . . ."

"It will be no fault of yours," Chris finished. "We knew the risks when you presented the plan, and it's still the only way. I'm just as worried about you. Your team will be vulnerable sitting that close to Russian territory. A chance patrol . . ." He left the thought unfinished.

"We'll have squads of marines around us," Arielle protested. "You'll be alone."

"In the final analysis," Chris spoke softly, "I suppose we're all alone. What you and I have found together is rare, a gift of sorts. But it's a gift with a price. For the first time in my life, I'm frightened because I want so desperately to come back to you. For the first time, I have something to lose."

"I know, my darling. I have this pit inside me that's opened up again, and I'm afraid I'll fall back in."

Chris took her head in his hands and lifted her face to his.

"Never," he said forcefully. "Never again. You've learned too much, Arielle. You're different now and always will be. Whatever happens, whatever the result, you'll be able to live with it. What we've experienced is . . . a standard. And neither of us will ever accept less."

"I will try, Chris."

"I know, love." They reached for each other one long, last time.

The Lockheed C-5 Galaxy transport's massive bulk filled the runway as Chris and Arielle drove toward it. The largest cargo plane in the world, its wingspan was over two hundred and twenty feet wide and its overall length over two hundred and fifty feet. The cockpit stood three stories off the ground and the tail over six. Carrying a crew of five, the Galaxy also held seats in its upper deck for seventy-five troops and cargo space in its hold for two of the huge M-48 tanks or three CN-47 "Chinook" helicopters. In fact, the Wright brothers could have made their first flight inside the hold of a C-5 Galaxy.

All around the giant transport, myriad piles of equipment were being carefully tallied by support crews with long checklists in their hands. Over to one side, the contingent of battle-ready marines stood checking their gear, ready to board as soon as the plane was loaded.

Whitney was in frenzied motion around the sixteen-wheeler which held the Meteotron, supervising its backup into the cargo hold.

Chris stopped the jeep near Whitney. His own plane, an F-15, was ready on another runway, but he wanted to stay with Arielle till the last possible moment. Whitney, engrossed in his task, didn't even notice Arielle step down from the jeep.

"I've got to check the new computer installations," she said to Chris. "It will be a few hours before departure and then we'll hold at the base in Turkey till Peterson gives us the green light. From then on . . ." But her voice threatened to break and she looked away.

Overhead, a jet plane tore through the sky, its roar deafening. Chris put out his arms and she tumbled into them.

"Wild horses, Chris," she said desperately.

"Wild horses, my love."

The F-15 which carried Chris Leyland from Washington to Cape Canaveral touched down on the long runway, number thirty-three, north of the Kennedy Space Center launch complex. In the distance, the five-hundred-foot-tall vehicle assembly building towered over the flat landscape and the low buildings of the center, dominating the horizon.

A car was waiting at the end of the runway. The hot Florida sun caused convection waves to rise off the grooved concrete, making it appear as if it stood in the center of a vast puddle. Beside the car, Chris saw the familiar face of Barney Swanson, whose usually placid expression now seemed worried and strained.

"Welcome home, Stick," Swanson called out.

"Hello, Barney. It's good to see you again," Chris said, climbing into the car.

"We've got to talk," Swanson said as soon as he drove off the runway and onto the highway that led to the center. "Do I have enough credit with you for some straight answers?"

Chris turned back from watching the canelike brush flow past from which, he knew, Canaveral had derived its name when the Spanish first explored the cape.

"We go back a long way, Barney. If anybody's got the credit, you do."

"Just days ago, Chris, we got orders to prepare for the first double Shuttle launch in the history of the program. Normal astronaut rotation goes out the window, and we're told Cooke flies one and you're resigning from the Senate to fly the other.

"We've been on triple shift since that moment; no one's slept in days, and we've taken shortcuts in setup and fueling that are so risky as to be downright dangerous. I've complained, the other directors have complained, and we're all told the same thing—*Constitution* and *Independence* fly on the specified date or we explain why not to the president himself."

"I'm sorry it was handed to you that way, Barney. But as a friend of mine would say, we're shooting the works on this one."

"That's my point, Chris. You know as well as I do that all of us have friends in the aerospace industry. For God's sake, Rockwell owns the damn Shuttles. Rumors are all around. Bad rumors; that the solar flare-up is bullshit and that there's another reason why our satellites are down."

"The rumors are true, Barney," Chris said after a while. "And security's been tighter on this one than on the Manhattan Project. Would it help if I told you that I'm behind this all the way—that it's essential we fly this mission?"

Swanson looked uncomfortable. "It helps, Chris, but it's still not an answer. Not when you consider that those Shuttles are being armed! You know that violates everything NASA stands for and every space treaty signed by the United States. Why arms, Chris? I don't understand what makes this mission need heat-seeking missiles in the cargo bays. We all need to know if we're starting a war! That's the bottom line, Stick."

"No, Barney. We're not starting a war," Chris sighed. "We're trying to prevent one. We held the winning hand with our satellites. The Soviets couldn't breathe without our knowing. But they came up with better cards. Two pairs of Russian lasers, not a solar flare, took out our satellites, Barney; and if this mission fails, you'd better be ready to ask Moscow's permission for any future flights because that, old friend, is the real bottom line."

"Jesus Christ, lasers . . ." Swanson gasped in full understanding.

"We're only a part of the countermove," Chris said soberly. "As launch director, you'd have been filled in anyway. Timing for this one is crucial and will have to be very closely coordinated. I want you to keep a lid on this till the preflight briefing. The cape's been sealed but we still can't afford leaks. Agreed?"

"Agreed. And thanks. Even though I don't know whether to feel better or worse."

"Worse, Barney. Much worse," Chris said, and Swanson heard the fear in his voice. The car picked up speed as if it, too, caught the sense of urgency.

Driving past the VAB, with the orbiter processing facility and Launch Control Center stacked up against it in attached blocks, Swanson pulled the car onto the road running parallel to the crawlerway. The VAB area of Complex 39, the Shuttle preparation and checkout center, connected to the twin launch pads, some three miles distant, by the crawlerway, two forty-foot-wide lanes separated by a fifty-foot-wide median strip. It was on this crawlerway that the two crawler-transporters moved the Space Shuttles from the VAB—where the orbiter was mated to the external fuel tank and the twin solid rocket boosters—to the launch pads themselves.

The Shuttles had already been moved to the launch pads, and Chris saw that the giant crawler-transporters were now parked and at rest. The size and scope of the vehicles, like so many of NASA's projects, never failed to startle him.

The fully mated Shuttle was first placed on the mobile launch platform, a two-story, eight-million-pound transportable launch base built of six-inch steel. Both were then carried to the pads by this single, enormously powerful vehicle.

The transporter itself weighed over six million pounds, each of the forty-eight steel plates in the eight tanklike treads weighing over one ton each. Powered by twin 2,750 horsepower diesel engines, which drove four one-thousand kilowatt generators providing electrical power to the sixteen traction motors, the transporter had to have a special roadway designed for it. Using river stones like an oil lubricant on top of six feet of solid concrete, the transporter could move at almost one mile per hour and keep the Shuttle upright on the five-percent grade to the launch pads with less sway from the vertical than the width of a soccer ball.

Totally loaded, Shuttle, mobile launch base, gantrys, and crawler-transporter rose over two hundred feet tall and weighed just under sixteen million pounds—before fueling.

Chris was reminded of the timeworn in-house joke which held that an elephant, originally, was a mouse designed by NASA.

Stopping at the security station at the base of the upgrade which led to the pads, Chris and Swanson were identified and their security badges placed on the security board. Anyone entering or emerging from the pads was subject now to rigid checks.

Walking up the grade, Chris was struck by two things: the stark beauty of the Shuttle *Constitution* and the incredible activity of the men and women who labored under the herculean task of launching her.

Hundreds of hard-hatted technicians clambered over the twelve work levels of the fixed service structure which stood on the west side of the 125,000-square-foot "hardpad."

The rotating service structure, which swung out from the fixed one to mate with the Shuttle for servicing of payloads was already in place. It was from here, Chris knew, that the Shuttle had been fitted with its missile payload. Incredibly, the same scene was taking place on the second launch pad, two miles north, where *Independence* was being readied under the watchful gaze of Bill Cooke.

For a long moment, Chris stopped to stare at *Constitution*. The sun had dipped close to the ocean and back lit the scene in a glory of reds and gold. Lights began to blink on all over the gantrys, and floodlights shone from beneath the Shuttle itself. Billowing clouds caught the sun's final colors, setting golden islands behind the ship's fluid shape.

He noted the single line which ran from the Shuttle, past the fixed service structure, down to the earth, a quarter of a mile away. Like a slender spider's thread, the Slidewire system provided an escape route for the astronauts in case of emergency. Now it caught the last light and reflected it. Two flat-bottom baskets made of heat resistant fiber could slide down the wire to the bunker built into a hill to the west of the pad.

The light grew redder, and the Shuttle was bathed in ruby fire. Not even the gravity of his mission nor the crushing weight of world events could diminish *Constitution*'s beauty for him. More than its sleek lines, its raw power, and its physical grandeur, there was magnificence in the very notion of its creation. A tribute to the skills of the human race, it existed to fly, to carry the human mind that much farther than was possible before the Shuttle's birth. And in that achievement the mundaneness of greed and petty squabbles was shown for what it was: far less than what we are truly capable of as a people.

For a moment, as he reveled in the splendor that was *Constitution,* Chris Leyland knew hope.

Nightwatch on board *Tarent* became a waiting game. With a pair of binoculars focused on the *Ural* till it seemed as if they grew out of his eyes, Fuller's terse orders and hunched shoulders betrayed the tension that he felt but could not reveal.

The Secretary of State, powerless to alter their circumstances, waited alongside the captain, also staring out the bridge windows at the lights of the ship whose slightest movement might portend their destruction.

"Still no change in position," Fuller observed, lowering the binoculars to look at Powell.

"Every minute we survive here strengthens our position," offered Powell. "If the Russians were going to come against us, they would have done so by now. The longer they have to mull over the possible consequences, the less certain they'll be."

"Then you still think they're uncertain. I'm not so sure of that. The weather conditions are still holding, barely, and that lends credibility to our threat; but could sane men truly believe that we'd release such a plague into the world?"

Powell shrugged. "Under normal conditions, probably not. But these are not normal conditions. Right now, this minute, the Soviets could launch a preemptive nuclear strike that we would be powerless to defend against. The president *must* deter that threat, and the Russians know it. To gamble that the U.S. would fail to retaliate, given a nuclear strike, is a fool's gamble for the simple reason that, at that point, Captain, we'd have very little left to lose.

"But you can bet that the psychological profiles that KGB compiles on all senior U.S. officials are right now being pored over with every resource at their command to decide the question of whether we will or won't release the plague if sufficiently threatened."

"And the answer is," Fuller said, raising the binoculars again, "that we would."

"We would have to," agreed Powell, shaken by the undeniable logic.

Fuller nodded slowly, still intent on watching the *Ural,* death's messenger just a mile away.

The phone woke Foreign Minister Viktor Grishen out of a dream-filled sleep. Wiping a hand across his forehead and feeling it come away damp with sweat, he rolled over and stabbed for the phone, realizing groggily that it was the line reserved for Politburo business alone. It startled him the rest of the way to consciousness.

"Viktor? This is Telshe. I must see you now," said the voice.

Grishen looked at his watch, frowning. "It is three in the morning, Comrade Defense Minister. Why not wait till morning?"

"Now, Viktor. It must be now."

"Very well. Ten minutes," said Grishen.

"I'll be there." The connection was broken.

Grishen hung up the phone wondering why Telshe should be so insistent. This could not be regular business or Meledov himself would have summoned them all to the Arsenal. Very curious, indeed.

Tossing on a robe, he had but a few minutes' wait before his guards announced Telshe's arrival. Grishen rose and poured two glasses of vodka as Telshe strode in.

"Now, Arvid, tell me what is so urgent that it cannot wait," he said, handing a glass to the other man.

Telshe settled himself in an overstuffed chair in the center of Grishen's opulent living room. Once the residence of the Czar's nephew, the building now housed only the highest officials of the government.

"I am worried, Viktor. Deeply worried. I was not one who originated Nightsight, but, like you, was persuaded to adopt it."

"And now you regret that?" Grishen pursed his lips quizzically.

"No," said Telshe emphatically. "I do not. I was convinced and remain so. What worries me is that I believe Meledov is weakening our position by succumbing to the Americans' threat."

"You don't think the Americans would release their plague?" said Grishen, interest quickening.

"No, and neither do you. You said as much to the others. We must prevent Meledov and Komarovsky from tossing away the strategic advantage Nightsight has given us."

"What do you propose?"

Telshe drained the vodka in one long swallow and looked up to meet Grishen's gaze. "The ridges have almost dissipated. We must destroy the *Tarent* at once and launch a first strike."

"Impossible," responded Grishen. "It would take a vote to do that, to override Meledov. He has already spoken against doing so until Castor has had a chance to operate."

"Every hour gives the Americans strength. You know them," Telshe protested. "They cling to any hope. Only total defeat will convince them of our superiority."

"Even if I were to agree with your logic, Arvid, we are powerless to move."

"Not if we act . . . independently," said Telshe with an air of finality.

"So," Grishen thought. "That's what he's after: an accomplice. He's afraid to act alone, afraid to be wrong." Possibilities emerged.

"You would order the *Ural* to release its missiles at once, without Politburo approval," Grishen said calmly.

"Yes. And when the *Tarent* is down and all this nonsense of a plague is over, we stand as heroes. We can act while the others continue to talk themselves into impotence."

"And Torgenev?"

"Signal him to invade," said Telshe unequivocably.

"You realize," said Grishen after a while, "that we are talking about a . . . change in leadership. Think, Comrade, before the current grows too strong to swim against it. Think hard."

"I think," said Telshe, "that we have much to discuss."

"As do I, Comrade Minister," said Grishen, lifting the bottle. "More vodka?"

The military jet carrying Talon, Reynolds, Clancy, and Parienne was given priority clearance to land and soon taxied to a halt on the runway. Cars were already waiting for them, and Talon watched each of his companions get in and drive away. They would be followed, he knew, twenty-four hours a day if necessary.

Out on the concrete, Bill Menzel, the CIA agent to whom Talon had given the job of setting up the surveillance, waited by the car provided for Talon. He got in and received Menzel's report. Satisfied that all was in place, Talon rubbed his tired eyes and thought out his next moves carefully.

Clancy's attempt to get into Parienne's briefcase still weighed heavily on his mind. But he could not fathom a reason behind the action and that gnawed at him.

"Where are they now, Bill?" he asked as Menzel drove the innocuous gray Dodge from the base onto the highway toward D.C.

Menzel picked up the microphone from the car's radio and called for check-ins from each of the surveillance teams. One by one they radioed back in their positions.

"Otter . . . at home." Reynolds' address and prior movements followed; she had gone straight to her apartment in the city.

"Dolphin . . . at home." Parienne's address at the brownstone he owned followed. He, too, had gone directly home, had made no stops.

"Tiger . . . cruising . . . no destination as yet," came the final report, and a position followed.

Talon hit his hand into the dashboard. Clancy was the only one not to have gone home after the long flight. He was still acting oddly.

"Get us near Clancy's position," he told Menzel. "I want to be around wherever he finally comes to rest."

7

Lift-off posed no serious problem, and now all Chris's indicators showed green lights. Checking fuel reserves and computer systems, he replotted the first intercept orbit. A quick glance out the port window showed a pale gray Baja California jutting into the bright blue Sea of Cortez.

Coming up . . . coming up. Slowly now, he cautioned himself. No time for second shots. The fire-control screen, with its etched concentric circles, showed the laser station as an off-center blip of light. Brief orbiter engine burn . . . steady . . . the target moved closer to the center of the screen. Chris nudged the controls. Closer to center . . . still closer . . . There! The blip began to flash as the computer confirmed intercept plotted to target.

Chris's hand shot out and slapped down the missile release switch. One second; two; three; the missiles rode on trails of exhaust fire. Chris urged it to the target, already using the computers for course selection to the second laser . . .

All at once the lights came on.

"No good, Chris. Too much time," said Swanson's voice from the speaker above Chris's head.

Chris muttered an oath under his breath and slapped the orbiter simulator into down-power mode.

"Was it a hit?" he asked, rubbing eyes which were bloodshot from constant hours of simulator practice.

"It was," Swanson confirmed. "But you used too much fuel. Left yourself short for number two. If the rain doesn't hold, you're going to need even more."

"Even with the auxiliary tanks in? Shit, Barney. I'm not sure I can shoot any faster and be certain of a hit," he said into his microphone.

"I know," Swanson sighed. "Cooke has the same problem. Keep at it. We'll try another round."

"Give me a short run, Barney. I'm not worried about lift-off or orbit insertion. I want to try the shoot again.

"One more time," Chris muttered as the lights went out and the target blip appeared on his screen again.

The sequence was faster this time, but Chris felt more confident when he released the missiles. His reaction time improved slightly. He was, however, still not satisfied.

"We may make a pilot out of you yet, Stick," said Swanson as the lights came on again.

"I'd like to try it again," Chris said tiredly.

Swanson yanked open the hatch and beckoned for Chris to climb out.

"No time," he said. "Briefing in ten minutes. Grab a shower and work out your kinks. I'll meet you there."

Bill Cooke had already emerged from the shower when Chris walked into the locker room and began stripping off his gear.

"Stuck around for one more, I see," Cooke said, toweling his lean body.

"When I'm in the simulator, I don't worry as much," Chris said honestly.

"Who else knows what this mission is all about?" Cooke asked.

"Barney knows. And some of the top brass. Apart from you and I, that's all. The briefing in a few minutes will take care of that, though. Is there a problem?"

"I'm worried about our copilots. Barney's picking from kids so green that they'd bleed chlorophyll if you cut 'em."

"I know, Bill. I argued against it, but he bought the argument that risking two more trained pilots would be foolish, in case they have to try again."

Chris stepped into the shower and ran hot water across the bunched muscles of his back.

"Have the copilots been notified?" Cooke called in.

Chris rinsed soap from his face. "After the briefing. That'll give them time to withdraw their applications if the mission scares them."

"Makes sense," Cooke agreed, tossing Chris a towel as he stepped out of the shower.

"Besides," Chris continued dryly, "I'm sure everybody figured that if I could fly with you, I could fly with anyone."

Cooke's wet towel hit him in the chest. "Isn't that strange? They said without you, my insurance premiums were lower," Cooke retorted, ducking as the towel came flying back.

But the horseplay belonged to another time and another type of mission, one with lower stakes and less risk. Now, it could not be sustained, and in the pause that followed each man felt the weight that he carried and the terrible responsibility.

"We'll be on our own again, Bill," said Chris quietly.

His friend nodded in the now quiet room. "Frightened?" Cooke asked gently.

"I can live with it," Chris said evenly. "You?"

"The same."

"Said your goodbyes?" Chris asked.

"The ones that mattered. And you?"

"Same ones," Chris replied.

There was little left to say, each reading the other's thoughts as the final hour drew near.

"Let's get to it," Chris said, finished dressing. "Ready?"

Cooke paused for a moment, and when he finally spoke, it was in the drawl of his adopted Texas. "Well, son," he grinned, "a lady of the evenin' once asked me that very same question, and I'm gonna tell you jes' what I told her."

"Which is?"

"I may not be entirely ready, but nobody's gonna accuse me of a lack of tryin'."

For a room sufficiently large to contain the NASA personnel to be briefed on the mission, an auditorium in the Launch Control building had been appropriated. Every one of the two hundred seats was filled as Swanson began his opening remarks.

Tired men and women, many who had not had the chance to change from their work coveralls, listened intently. From the raised stage, Chris saw in them the strain that triple shifts and dangerous shortcuts had caused. He wondered why so many of NASA's people had such enormous dedication to their work and to the total effort of the group that was so rarely found in other fields. Could a dream be so infectious? He decided that it could.

Swanson finished the general outline. He motioned for Chris to come to the podium, and the audience leaned forward.

In clear, concise language, Chris explained the nature and positions of the Soviet lasers. He spoke of their own part in the three-pronged mission to remove them, and he spoke of the necessity for success.

". . . As soon as we have confirmation that the microwave command signals have been blocked, we will proceed to launch. That means we must be ready and holding at less than T minus 3 minutes, just before ignition, until we receive our signal from the group in Iran.

"I cannot say this too strongly—timing is critical. We don't know how long the rain will block the signals. Therefore, every second counts. A delay could prove fatal to the success of the mission. I emphasize that again.

"Once we have destroyed the lasers, our Minutemen will be cleared to fly. Both Shuttles are going to land at Vandenburg, just as we did last mission. As you all remember, Cooke and I are familiar with the terrain.

"No one could ask more of you than you have already given. Your fatigue is evident and will only increase till we launch. But what we do here is vital, failure unthinkable. Plant that thought solidly in your minds.

"Improvise if you must, scavenge if you have to—but I tell you the Shuttles must fly tomorrow. Eat when you can and sleep when you can't stand on your feet any longer—but the Shuttles must fly tomorrow. Let this, then, be the final, overriding commandment: in the name of everything we hold dear—tomorrow, the Shuttles must fly."

Brendan Connors regarded the display map in the Situation Room. General Peterson made final calculations. General Blaire, back at NORAD, had already reported that the linkups to Canaveral, Washington, and the group heading toward Iran had been coordinated.

General Neill's fighter squadrons were in readiness, the general in constant communication with his second in command in Turkey.

"Mr. President," said Peterson crisply, "our Echo Range Minutemen are loaded and on line. Canaveral reports they will be ready within the specified time. NORAD is prepared to feed data, and the C-5 has left our base in Turkey and is approaching Iranian airspace. You have less than ten minutes to cancel the incursion, sir."

"Are the fighters in the air yet?" Connors asked, eyes never leaving the map.

"No, sir. We need your direct order to commence military support."

For a long moment the president of the United States was silent. Once committed, he knew, there could be no turning back. The proper phrase, words of wisdom, bits of speeches whirled through his mind. The horror of a world at war swam over him. It all came down to his command.

"Sir, I need your order . . . Sir?"

Connors looked into the face of the general and finally found the words he sought. "Shit, Ben. Kick the piss out of 'em."

The cockpit of the C-5 was crowded. Behind the pilot and copilot, the navigator was crouched over his chart table. Arielle and Whitney stood next to him, ready to make last-minute changes should the proposed landing site prove unacceptable.

Marine Colonel Jack Bradey, in command of the troops, stood nearby, coffee in hand. Behind him, the computer officer scanned his instruments incessantly.

"We've just received authorization to proceed into Iran. Fighter squadron is on its way," said the pilot, Captain Collins.

"Have we heard from the AWAC's yet?" asked Arielle.

"Yes, ma'am," Collins responded. "They'll be in place by the time the F-15's reach us. Had to be refueled."

"That's fine," Arielle said. "Make certain that 'A' squadron goes in well before us to drop those filaments. They've got to be in the wind at least an hour before we arrive."

"Picking up the squadrons now, Dr. Simmons," the copilot announced. "As ordered, 'A' squadron's peeling off to go in now. 'B' stays with us."

"I'm glad to hear it," said Whitney, unabashedly.

"Amen," said the copilot.

The F-15's formed up around the C-5 as they entered Iranian airspace, flying as low as possible across the vast desert to avoid radar.

Arielle busied herself amidst the newly installed computers which she would use to select the correct "birth-point" for the cloud, using information on wind speed and direction supplied by the AWAC's that tracked the carbon filaments.

Checking and rechecking her programs, she tried to put all thoughts of Chris from her mind. Though the steady drone of the C-5's engines hammered unceasingly, her disciplined mind concentrated. When she looked up again, Whitney was engrossed in his charts as well.

"Dr. Simmons, Dr. Whitney, we need you up front. Landing soon," called the copilot.

They scrambled back to the cockpit to look down at the undulated gold-brown waves of sand beneath them.

"Just over these hills," Captain Collins pointed, "is the site you selected. I'm going to go in low, circle, and take a look-see. If we're all in agreement after that, I'll take her down."

The low hills sped toward them, and Arielle experienced a wrenching in her stomach as the land dropped abruptly away beyond. Stretching out ahead was a long, flat strip of desert, crossed distantly by a one-lane road. Whitney nodded as the plane circled over the area.

"Looks good, Captain. How far to the sea?"

"Under ten miles."

"Then I'm satisfied," Whitney pronounced.

"So am I," the captain agreed. "Let's take her down. You and Dr. Simmons get strapped in. This is going to be a bit bumpy."

"Just remember we have a hold full of delicate cargo," Arielle cautioned and then returned to her seat by Whitney.

The plane banked steeply and swung around for a final approach. Arielle found her hands gripping the arms of her seat as if a dentist were about to drill. A bad landing, she knew, and they were finished before they started.

A jarring thud cracked her jaws together as the plane hit the ground. Skewing at an angle, the pilot fought to keep it straight. Clouds of dust and sand billowed by the windows and the fuselage groaned with strain. The engine noise rose to a steady whine as the giant plane slowed and finally ground to a crunching halt.

Almost before the plane stopped, the marines were exiting to set up perimeter positions. A long, green-brown line streamed out onto the hot sand to orders barked sharply by the colonel and his officers.

The two loadmasters, in charge of loading and unloading the cargo hold, extended the ramps from the rear of the plane down to the sand. Already, the C-5's nose cone had been elevated to permit frontal access to the hold. From both ends, crewmen and material flowed out under the loadmasters' directions.

Cylinder after cylinder of fuel for the Meteotron was carted out and placed in pyramidal mounds on the ground. Almost half a mile of fuel hose followed. Inside the plane, crewmen began fitting the connections to the massive tanks which would pump water into the Meteotron. Whitney was busy supervising the setup of the AAC condensation nuclei spreading device, powered by the electrical generators of the C-5 itself.

Two hours passed while the site was readied. Arielle sat fixedly inside the plane, her computers steadily tracking the carbon filaments as they rode the winds toward Baikonur. Concurrently, Collins received status reports on the airspace around them from the distant AWAC's and the F-15's, which circled overhead.

Finally, the Meteotron itself was ready to be unloaded. One load-master drove the diesel truck on which it was secured while the other, outside, directed his progress. The truck left the plane slowly, the ramp underneath digging deeply into the sand as it rolled out.

With effort borne of urgency and time constraints, Whitney's crew began the complicated task of hooking up the Meteotron to its water and fuel sources as Whitney himself saw to a myriad of final, minute adjustments.

Thousands of pounds of concrete were forklifted out to the sand to anchor the Meteotron. Though the direction of the hot air current would, in part, counterbalance the thrust of the engines, vast weight was still needed to hold the machine in place. At last, the specially designed truck on which the Meteotron sat was bolted to the ballast and the final connections established. Whitney rushed back inside the plane.

"We're ready to go when you finalize the coordinates," he told Arielle.

"Look here," she said, and Whitney stepped up to peer over her shoulder. The computer display was lit up with ebbs and swirls like a tidal pool. A sweeping line, radar tracking, circled the screen every ten seconds.

"We've got a wind current tracked to Baikonur," she said succinctly, pointing to the screen. "This one here. Computers say our point of dispersion is here." She pointed again and then punched in a series of commands. The swirling tides vanished from the screen to be replaced by sets of numbers in equations. "This takes into account picking up the water vapor from the Caspian Sea."

"Looks very promising," agreed Whitney, studying the display.

"We won't know for sure till you begin. If a cross wind picks up, the cloud will be dispersed," Arielle said.

"I say we take it," Whitney said firmly. "If there's dispersion, we can recalibrate. Time is pressing on us. If we go with this one, we may have time for a second run."

Arielle glanced at the screen for a final time. The coordinates remained clear. But if there was no cloud, Chris would remain safe . . . Angrily, she thrust the weakening thought from her mind.

"It's a go," she said at last, and Whitney hurried outside.

The Meteotron's six jet engines were horizontally mounted, their separate streams combined into a single blazing current by means of an electronically aimed "muzzle" apparatus of ceramic-coated steel. It looked somewhat like a stack of cylinders attached to a snub-nosed cannon which pointed skyward, with electrical cables leading from the machine to an operating console some sixty yards away. The AAC and water were pumped into the muzzle under high pressure.

Whitney climbed into the operator's chair and donned the headset which would allow him to communicate with Arielle. Checking his board, he saw that fuel was being pumped into the engines and internal temperatures were right for ignition.

Carefully, and with an almost fatherly devotion, Whitney ignited engines one and six and brought them up to half power. Satisfied, he brought engines two and four roaring into life. Steadily whining, the sound was overpowering even at that level. Technicians clutched at their ears as Whitney ignited the final two engines, three and five, and carefully rechecked the indicator gauges. In balance, the engines continued to roar. Slowly, he brought the Meteotron to full power.

"We're on full, all engines," he transmitted to Arielle. "Standing by for coordinates."

"Coordinates on line," Arielle called back. "We're on automatic—computers locked in."

"Got it," Whitney acknowledged as the muzzle swiveled to the computer's command. The column of super-heated air began to shoot up into the desert sky at a speed of over fifteen hundred miles per hour. Whitney began the water flow into the column of air.

"My screen looks good," Arielle called in.

Whitney activated the AAC feed.

Inside the condensation nuclei device, an electric arc sprang into life. Vaporized AAC particles barely larger than the molecule itself, each gram of AAC forming ten trillion condensation nuclei, flowed into the air current and up into the sky.

On Arielle's data display, the hot air rose and then billowed outward like a mushroom cloud. Ascending upward of twenty thousand feet, finally the hot, moist air started to cool and flatten out in a broad "cauliflower" head. A cumulus cloud began to form.

The Meteotron continued billowing its rage upward to the heavens. The next few hours were critical. If the cloud broke up or if it failed to pick up and retain additional moisture, it would never survive the journey to Baikonur.

On her screen, Arielle watched the cloud form. Already, the high altitude winds tore at it. But more and more super-hot air fed it. She could visualize the AAC spreading inside like dust in the air, water vapor coalescing around the countless tiny nuclei.

She could neither directly see it nor feel it, but above her head the cloud continued to grow, wispy, white tendrils bound together by a force of nature diverted for their purpose. Her screen showed the cauliflower head growing on top of the long "tail" which led down to the Meteotron.

"I think we're okay," she called to Whitney, the first sense of hope growing that they could do what they had come to do. Overhead, the F-15's, out of fuel, flew off toward their refueling point.

Five minutes later, Arielle saw the blips on her screen where there should be none. Somebody, she knew, had found them.

Talon tossed down the remains of the tasteless hamburger Menzel had brought him while Clancy ate his dinner. Clancy still hadn't

gone home, and his stop at the diner seemed like an afterthought
when Clancy's car had braked abruptly after passing it. Inside, he
made no phone calls nor any attempt to speak to anyone. They
watched him pay the check and return to his car.

"I think he's aware he's being watched," Menzel muttered as they
followed Clancy in a new direction.

"I doubt it," mused Talon. "But make sure that everyone's well
back. Give him room. He's going somewhere he doesn't want anyone to know about. And it must be somewhere important if it has to
be tonight."

Menzel gave the orders as he allowed more cars in between him
and their quarry.

For nearly an hour Clancy drove aimlessly around the city. No
pattern was discernible. Sudden turns, quick stops; all bore out
Menzel's notion of a man checking to see if he was being followed.

"He's very careful," said Talon admiringly as Clancy cut across
traffic in a U-turn.

"No one's careful enough to get past a three-car pattern with
radio communications," said Menzel. "When he stops, we'll be there
right behind him. Car two's got him now."

The streets had grown less crowded as dusk fell. Trees hung
limply over side streets in the absence of winds. A thought occurred
to Talon.

"I think he's waiting till there are fewer cars on the road. That's
when he figures on spotting us. Make sure the others know that."

By eight o'clock Clancy had obviously decided he was alone.
Talon heard the voice on the radio, elated even over the static.

"He's stopped! Pulled in next to a park, and he's walking across
the street," radioed the agent in the third car.

"Get a house number," called back Menzel, anticipating Talon.

"Six twenty-four Mason. There's a nameplate on the building, but
I can't read it."

"Don't lose visual contact," radioed Menzel. "We're almost
there."

Talon leaned forward in anticipation as they pulled onto Mason
Street. He could see Clancy climbing the stairs and entering the
three-story brick building, indistinguishable from the others of the
same type that surrounded it on the tree-lined street.

"Cover all the exits and get men on the rooftops," ordered Talon, throwing open his door as the car slid to a halt a hundred yards from Clancy's. Menzel relayed the orders, and Talon heard car doors slam at the far end of the block as he walked up the steps to the building's entrance.

He could read the brass plaque now, and his brow furrowed as it raised more questions than it answered.

LEONARD T. BRISBANE MEDICAL PAVILION
PRIVATE CLINIC

Someone of Clancy's rank would be treated by the White House medical staff. More serious problems would be handled at Bethesda. And Talon knew from Clancy's dossier that his own private physician of many years was a Doctor Haldine, whose practice was on the other side of the city. Why such a convoluted trip to get here? Talon paused to tell Menzel that he wanted a complete check run on the clinic at once. Then, he pushed open the wood-bordered, glass-front door and entered the lobby as Menzel took up position outside.

A nurse in a white uniform stood behind the reception desk, medical chart files, telephones, and a variety of forms stacked in neat piles behind her. The lobby was furnished with some chairs and a couch on a marble floor of alternating black and white squares. An oaken staircase led upward from the rear of the large room, corridors on either side led into the wings.

"Can I help you, sir?"

Talon pulled his identification from his jacket and held it up for the nurse to see. He described Clancy to her.

". . . a minute or two ago. Did he have an appointment with anyone?"

The nurse took a step backward, intimidated by the man, his ID, and the rapid-fire questions.

"He . . . he said he was from the White House," she faltered. "He showed me identification, too. Is anything wrong . . . I wouldn't . . . I mean . . ."

"You did nothing wrong," Talon soothed. "His credentials are authentic. Please, just tell me who he's here to see."

"He asked for Doctor Radow. I called the doctor, and he agreed to see him. These are his evening hours."

"Have you ever seen the man here before?"

"No, never. And I've been here for over two years."

A sudden thought struck Talon, and he walked back to the door and conferred briefly with Menzel. A minute later, the agent returned with the dossiers from Talon's briefcase. Placing the dossier photographs on the counter, Talon asked the nurse if she had seen any of the faces before.

"Well," she hesitated but pointed to Clancy's picture. "He's the one who came in just before you. But you know that."

Talon nodded. "And the other two?"

She suddenly bobbed her head enthusiastically. "Yes, that one. Mr. Parker. I've seen him here several times." She picked up Parienne's photo and handed it to Talon, anxious to please him, trained to authority.

"Thank you, nurse. Now please tell me where I can find Dr. Radow."

"Room 227, second floor. Just go up those stairs and turn right."

"Excuse me, sir," cut in Menzel. "Report just in. Clinic checks out A-1."

Talon nodded and gestured to Menzel, who understood. No one would be alerted by the nurse. No one would follow. He walked up the stairs.

The second floor was still and quiet. Carpet padded his steps as he walked through the green-painted corridor toward Radow's office. He could hear voices arguing behind the door to 227. A small plate on its front read simply, DR. A. RADOW.

Talon could barely hear the voices. Words came through when tones were raised; some phrases. He heard, ". . . national security . . . matter of utmost importance . . . privileged information."

Talon came to a decision. Whatever Clancy was after, it must be important. The time for subtlety was over. He had enough to question Clancy directly now.

Talon opened the door and walked in.

Barbara Reynolds shut the door to her apartment behind her and dropped her bags on the marble floor of the foyer. The maid had already gone and a pile of mail from the past days was stacked neatly on a polished wooden table by the front door. Sorting through it carefully, Reynolds walked into the bright, modern kitchen and disposed of the junk mail in the basket under the sink.

Rifling through the personal correspondence, she came to a

thicker envelope, greeting-card sized, that caught and held her attention at once. This one she placed on the counter, all the rest set aside. Now, there were things to be done.

In each room of the apartment she checked that the telltale signs she'd left, a hair across a doorjamb, a ball of crumpled paper, a trail of dust, had not been disturbed. Satisfied, she returned to the kitchen, took a razor blade from the "junk drawer" and broke open the envelope.

The card had been mailed the day before from a local Washington address—a simple "Thinking of you" with a short note from an old friend with whom she had corresponded frequently for over twenty years. They had never met.

Holding the edge of the top flap of the card, Reynolds took the razor blade and cut carefully along the outer edge. Neatly, the cardboard separated, and Reynolds extracted the single piece of paper inside, thinner than onionskin, and took it with her into the bedroom after disposing of the remains of the card and envelope in the garbage disposal.

From her night table, she withdrew a book of poems by T. S. Eliot and a calendar. Then, she began to decode.

Half an hour later she'd almost completed the message. So absorbed in her task was she that the soft pad of footsteps along the hallway carpet failed to reach her ears. She finished decoding and read.

Suddenly, she was aware of a presence in the room with her. Not a single muscular twitch betrayed her awareness as she replaced the book and the decoded message within it into the night table. Her hand grasped the .25 automatic as she did so, and in one quick motion she turned, weapon first . . .

"How nice to see you again, Castor," smiled Valentin Kasimov.

"You! How did you get in here? If anyone saw you . . ."

"No one saw me," Kasimov replied calmly. "And you forget who taught you all your little tricks. I avoided them as easily as I avoided the covert surveillance that has been set up on you. Are you aware of it?"

"Ridiculous," snorted Reynolds.

"Not so, my dear. Leyland was told of Castor's existence by your old friend Pollux before he died. And Leyland is surely aware that only you or your closest associates could have warned Pollux to escape. Think hard over the past days. Has anything out of the ordinary occurred?"

Reynolds sat down hard and thought over the past seventy-two hours. At last, she nodded angrily. Tersely, she filled Kasimov in.

". . . which could explain why we were flown out of the country without a briefing and then flown back. We were all isolated, Clancy, Parienne, and myself. What a fool I've been not to see it! We've been kept far away from Apocalypse, and Talon must have known it. Damn you, Kasimov. I told you to get Sanderson out long before you did."

"It was a calculated risk. We needed Leyland out of the way. Too soon would have been too obvious. Besides, Pollux was becoming less of an asset. Greed does that, you know. All his dreams of villas and feasts. In the end, he was useful only as a lure. Nothing more." Kasimov shrugged.

"So now I'm in danger. And you no longer have any authority."

"I see," Kasimov said coldly. "Komarovsky told you that, too, in the communication you just deciphered. No matter. We will help each other get what we want. What else did he ask for?"

"Details on Apocalypse, the nature of the plague, and parameters for its release." She paused. "But what makes you think I'd help you? No one could be more pleased at your failure. I'd see you rot in hell first."

"A quaint notion. But you're in no position to dictate to me. If I have nothing left, I would gladly see you exposed."

"You would be tracked down and executed."

"But that wouldn't help you in prison, would it? I offer you a deal: help me find Leyland to finish my task, and I'll help you get what you've been asked for and allay all suspicions of you."

"How? If what you say is true, I'm being watched. So are the others."

"This apartment itself has not been wired, only the phones and your private car. I checked them all thoroughly. We can safely assume the others' homes are covered similarly. That makes what I have in mind possible. I will operate in your behalf while you are dining somewhere in full view of your watchdogs. No stronger alibi can be found than that. By morning, you will have your Apocalypse, and Talon will have Castor."

Reynolds knew there was little hope for success without Kasimov.

She simply couldn't be in two places at once. Finally, she acquiesced.

"I'm willing to listen. What is your plan?"

Kasimov explained. Her part was simple. One phone call to bring Dupont out of the White House to Parienne's home would do it. The rest was up to Eris. She had little doubt he could bring it off.

"Very well. I agree. When do you want it done?"

"There is time, my dear. Plenty of time. I trust you can make me quite comfortable till then."

Reynolds tossed her head back haughtily, and her flared hips jutted forward. She lifted the .25 and pointed it. "I choose my own partners, Kasimov. All of them."

"You forget where I first found you." He laughed coldly and held out his hand. The .25 caliber bullets gleamed dully. "And I warn you not to underestimate me again. The president is not the only one with a claim to your wares."

Reynolds looked into the frosty eyes and remembered his peculiar desires. She savored the internal heat that those memories generated. "Connors is business."

"And he has been a very good source of information," he added. "Come now, I am not a patient man. There are things I would have you do, things you have loved to do before . . ."

Sweating, she dropped the empty gun and reached for him.

"Hard," she whispered.

Much later, he covered her head with a pillow to stifle the screams.

The Zil limousine sped through the moon-filled Moscow night. The rain had let up and oily puddles filled with spectrums of color had collected in the streets.

"I tell you it can be bloodless," said Grishen to Telshe, in the rear of the car. The glass divider had been raised, the chauffeur isolated from their conversation.

"Meledov will not resign," Telshe reaffirmed his objection.

"He won't have a choice," Grishen argued. "Once *Tarent* is destroyed and shown for what it is, Meledov will be ousted by the vote I will call, and you will support. He won't be able to argue with fact."

"A dead man can't argue with anything at all," said Telshe softly.

"It's impossible," said Grishen categorically.

"I am scheduled to have breakfast with him tomorrow," Telshe said, "and one of his house staff is mine. The KGB is not alone in its access to lethal drugs. First, *Tarent*. Second, Meledov. Third, Torgenev invades, and we launch a first strike. We must be bold, Comrade, a whole world can be gained. We stand at the pivotal moment where individuals can influence nations. Let it be our influence that governs."

"It could be as you say," mused Grishen as the car pulled into the special garage under the Ministry of Defense.

No one barred the progress of the two ministers as they ascended to the War Center, analogous to the Situation Room in the White House. Staffed twenty-four hours a day, the room was ordered into the commands of each military zone throughout the world. Grishen noted the concentration of forces on the twenty-foot global projection screen which represented Torgenev's army and the Gulf of Finland where the *Tarent* lay so vulnerable.

Telshe conferred with his battle staff and composed the orders to *Ural*'s Captain Kalinskya. A second, more involved cable went to Marshal Torgenev, "for his eyes only."

Grishen's mind was filled with plans and people. Control of certain vital Party functions would have to be established. So little time left to ensure support. Yet, in the U.S.S.R., he had seen it before—things could change overnight. The military would follow Torgenev, whose support Grishen was sure they'd receive. The Party bosses would side with the winners, as always.

Komarovsky might be a problem, though. Grishen wondered if Mikoyan had ambitions. Perhaps, with a little pressure, Mikoyan might exert some influence of his own.

So involved in details was Grishen that he was startled when Telshe returned to announce that the orders had been sent under Politburo authorization.

It took Grishen a moment to fully realize that they had just begun a revolution.

Marshal Torgenev read the cable and understood at once its significance—a power play in the Politburo had begun. He wondered if Meledov would survive it and who was responsible for so sudden a change in policy.

It didn't matter, he reasoned. In the cable were the orders he wanted to obey. His slight trepidation at ignoring the "halt" order vanished. He did worry that Komarovsky would end up on the losing side. But even the loss of an old friend could not stand in the way of his need to invade.

Implicit in the order, he realized, was a request for his support. So be it, he decided. His support would go to the faction that supported him. Basic self-interest would rule his choice.

Marshal Torgenev called for a jeep to make a final inspection of his troops.

Captain Kalinskya read the orders handed to him by his second in command, Lieutenant Gregor.

"Have you checked the codes on this?" he asked Gregor.

"No, Comrade Captain. Is there reason to do so?"

Kalinskya frowned. He was not privy to policy, but someone must be totally certain to risk *Tarent*'s destruction with the plague on board her. So sudden a change in orders concerned him deeply.

He looked out to sea. The *Tarent*'s lights were visible in the darkness. He wondered if he should request confirmation of the order.

Perhaps it was the anticipated dissipation of the high-pressure ridges that had sealed the *Tarent*'s fate, he decided. Moscow must believe, plague or no, that *Tarent* was rendered ineffective. Surely that was it. Kalinskya felt much better.

Still, confirmation would remove any indecision. But he wondered if a captain who questioned orders would ever see sea duty again. He made up his mind.

"Tomorrow, Comrade Gregor. The orders say tomorrow we attack. Prepare the missiles."

Then Kalinskya gave the order to reposition the *Ural*—upwind.

Captain Fuller was very cold. Standing on the bridge observation wing, he shivered as the chilly wind penetrated his dark blue overcoat.

He saw the *Ural* begin to move and understood the significance at once. Time for all of them was running out. Morning probably; afternoon at the latest. They'd need the light to observe the missiles they would launch to counter *Tarent*'s release of its plague carriers.

Striding onto the bridge, he ordered the ship readied and the missile systems checked. He had no doubt that the *Tarent* would survive only slightly longer than it would take to launch their deadly cargo. He summoned the Secretary of State.

Powell came up to the bridge bundled in a coat identical to the one Fuller wore. The captain's explanation was quite short.

"The *Ural*'s moving, sir, upwind. That's the firing position I'd choose if I were Kalinskya. He wants the wind blowing away from his ship to avoid contamination."

"Are we secure, Captain?"

Fuller nodded gravely, "Tight as a drum, sir. Gas attack has been sounded as well as General Quarters. Every space exposed to the outside has been sealed."

Powell looked around the bridge at the taut faces. Death hung in the air.

"Get the president on the radio," Powell ordered, and Fuller gave the command.

Connors received the news of the *Ural*'s movement with angry despair.

"It could be a bluff, sir," counseled Peterson. "They might want to see how we react."

"I don't think so, Ben. But we have no choice. *Tarent* has to stay where she is. If the *Ural* goes against her, we have to release the plague. I see no other option."

"Do you wish to speak with Meledov again? It might buy us time."

Connors shook his head. "To what purpose? Only someone unsure threatens twice. I can't allow us to be perceived that way by him."

"Then *Tarent* is still on her own," said Peterson.

"As she has always been, General," Connors observed grimly.

The maître d' at La Pavillon on K Street knew Mrs. Reynolds well. A private booth was provided at once, a drink arrived soon after, and a telephone was provided at her request. She had made no move at all to dodge the surveillance, wanting them to see her at all times. The restaurant phone could not have been tampered with in the time she had given them. She had made no reservation nor any predictable movements.

Reynolds dialed the private White House number, conferred with the special operator, and waited while Secretary Dupont was located.

"Dupont here," came the voice two minutes later.

"Arnold? Barbara Reynolds. Something has come up that we need to discuss at once. Can I see you tonight?"

"I'm sorely pressed for time as it is, Barbara. Is this official or personal?"

"Official. I think I've just turned up something that . . . I'd rather not talk on an open line. But it involves someone named Castor. Do you understand, Arnold?"

There was a hesitation. Then, "I'll clear the time. Your office?"

"It can't be at the White House. When we meet, you'll understand. Just don't mention the subject of this call to anyone there. Can you meet me at Jim Parienne's in an hour? He's the only other one who knows about this. I have proof, Arnold. Please."

"Very well. Parienne's in an hour. And Barbara?"

"Yes."

"If you've got what I think you've got, it's damn good work."

"You won't be disappointed, Arnold."

Barbara Reynolds hung up the phone and ordered dinner.

8

Kasimov located the agents around Parienne's brownstone and ascended to the roof of the adjoining building, slipping past their vantage points. He was concealed by cover of the cloudy night, darting from shadow to shadow like a wraith, fluid and without form.

Old lessons, well learned and practiced during his terrorist years, flowed through his mind in precise patterns. People see what they expect to see, he thought again. The agents on watch were waiting for Parienne to come out; they would not be expecting anyone to be going in.

Threading his way through the maze of television antenna masts and ventilation shafts, he padded noiselessly over the soft, thickly tarred roof. Crouched low to take advantage of whatever protection the low walls around the rooftop offered, he came to the edge, Parienne's brownstone now eight feet away and six feet below.

Selecting a point on the roof out of the line of sight of those watching, he backed away ten feet from the edge. In the cool night air, he began to breathe deeply, evenly, clamping an icy calm over his thoughts. Concentration was everything. He tightened the straps on his nylon backpack. Breathe. In for five seconds, out for five . . . Again and again till the energy built within him and came to a head, ready to burst . . . Glance at the moon covered by clouds; darkness would continue . . . In and out; in and out . . . Muscles locked in a sprinter's crouch . . .

Kasimov burst across the distance to the roof's edge. His lead foot rose to hit the top of the low wall, and he catapulted his body into space. For a split second he was like a bird in flight, freed from earthly restraints. Then his feet hit the opposite rooftop, and he landed, rolling to absorb the shock of the fall.

For a while he lay still, listening to the night sounds around him. No clamor reached his ears, no sudden blare of radio chatter. He was still safe. A smile creased his lips, but he forced it back. Not yet, he cautioned himself.

Quickly, he slithered to the roof door. It was locked, hooked from the inside. He fished out a padded chisel and a rubber mallet from his pack. Ten seconds later, the doorjamb was separated from the frame, and Kasimov reached through with the chisel to unlatch the door. Freed, it swung open.

Senses alert for the slightest noise, he came down the steps into the attic. Below, he could hear a television set blaring some news show. He checked his watch and saw he was on schedule. Dupont would not arrive for a half hour.

A second set of steps descended into the kitchen. Kasimov eased himself down after making certain that it was empty. Gun drawn, he moved from room to room till the sounds of running water from a bathroom brought him up short. Inside, he could hear someone humming tunelessly. He pressed back against the wall and waited silently.

The sounds of the water ceased abruptly, and the humming grew muffled as if a towel had been brought up to dry a face. Kasimov tensed. Inside, the lights snapped off.

When the man emerged, towel indeed held to his face, Kasimov took a quick step behind him and struck brutally with the edge of his hand into the base of the exposed neck. The man collapsed like a deflated balloon.

Spinning, gun still drawn, Kasimov peered into the bathroom. Empty. He stepped over the unconscious body and checked every other room in the house. All were empty.

By the time he'd located the entrance buzzer for the front door, Parienne was beginning to come awake. Lifting the moaning head, Kasimov made certain the man matched Reynold's description and, satisfied that he did, struck him again. The moans ceased.

He dragged Parienne into the bedroom, tied him with rope from the pack, and tossed him easily into the closet. Again he checked his watch. He prepared to receive Dupont and withdrew what he needed from his pack.

The door chimes sounded precisely at the appointed time. Kasimov was pleased; he liked promptness. He answered the ringing with a long buzz and heard the door open downstairs; one set of footsteps followed.

"Jim? Where are you?" called out Dupont. "Barbara?"

"C'mon up," Kasimov called out, slurring the words to imitate the vernacular.

Dupont ascended the stairs, took two steps into the room, and Kasimov struck for the second time. There was no mistake. The Secretary of Defense slumped to the floor.

The doctor was a study in outrage, but Clancy's expression changed only slightly.

"You're a hard man to lose, Mr. Talon," he said simply, returning to his seat.

But the doctor was still standing. "Who are you, and how dare you walk into my office while I'm in conference. If you'll please wait in the reception area . . ."

"Just relax, Dr. Radow," Talon cut him off. He tossed his ID onto the desk and settled comfortably into a chair, ignoring the doctor's glare.

"I don't care if you're J. Edgar Hoover," said Radow angrily. "Get out of my office."

"He was FBI," said Talon calmly, retrieving his ID.

"Fussy bastard," observed Clancy dryly.

"I like to keep the record straight," Talon said with no hint of amusement. "Like, for instance, what this conference is all about."

"I'm calling the police," said Radow, yanking at the phone, fingers poised over the dial.

Talon shrugged. "Suit yourself."

When the tactic failed to produce the desired effect, Radow turned angrily to Clancy. "Do you know this man?"

"I know him," Clancy said easily. "We have the same employer."

"Then I'll tell him what I've just finished telling you. Medical information is privileged. I won't discuss my patients."

"Dr. Radow," said Talon soothingly, "if I could have a moment to confer with Mr. Clancy, we might be able to resolve this issue without taking up much more of your valuable time. Is there somewhere we can talk?"

"Across the hall, 224 is vacant. You can use that."

"Would you wait for us, please?"

Somewhat mollified, Radow agreed. Clancy followed Talon across to the vacant office, almost identical to Radow's.

"So I *was* being followed," said Clancy as soon as the door slid shut.

"You were," agreed Talon.

"Care to tell me why?"

"That depends on why you're here. Offer me a good enough explanation, and I could be persuaded to answer your question. But not until then."

Talon watched the brief play of emotions on the big man's face. Penetrating intelligence shone from his clear gray eyes, and his mouth twitched with unspoken wit. Clancy was quick, strong, and clever, Talon knew, and he reminded himself not to underestimate him. Clever enough to be the mole, too, he realized. He would have to be cautious.

"I understood long ago," Clancy began, "that people of my particular physique are often assumed to be less bright than our smaller-statured cousins. It's an antiquated notion but it allows those of us with adequate brain masses an opportunity to study our fellow humans without some of their usual camouflage on. Follow?"

Talon nodded. "People underestimate you. Go on."

Clancy smiled. "I've been aware for some time that all is not as it should be at the White House. Our group of advisers seemed to spend more time and energy convincing the president of what course to take than advising him. Further, it takes no great insight to see that in the matter of space lasers, we have advised him incorrectly. But that's hindsight now. We'll get back to it later.

"About a year ago I began to suspect that high-level leaks were taking place. There was little to go on, but our intelligence apparatus seemed to be less effective as time wore on, and technology had been pouring out of the country to the Soviets at an alarming rate. We no sooner invented a new process or assembled new hardware than it popped up in Russia. My estimate is that we've saved them over a trillion dollars in research and development costs."

"And this leads us where?" Talon prompted.

"It leads us to the most interesting notion that either the Soviets are so much better at espionage than we are, or someone in a very important position is not what he seems to be. Someone is allowing us to be given away from the inside."

"All speculation. You haven't given me a shred of proof of this. And I still haven't been told how your visit here ties in."

"You're my proof, Mr. Talon. You and that whole absurd episode on board *Tarent*. For the first time in my experience with this administration, none of us were briefed on a top priority issue—the response to Nightsight. I'd say that's conspicuous by its absence, wouldn't you?"

"I understood there to be no time."

"There's always time, Mr. Talon. It was a deliberate omission. Plausible perhaps, but deliberate. It came to me we were being isolated. Your being here—obviously meaning I'm under surveillance —clinches the matter. *Others* suspect the hierarchy as well. As I said originally, the president has been advised poorly. In light of recent events, I think that advice was a deliberate attempt on someone's part to set us up for Nightsight. And so, Mr. Talon, do you."

Talon said nothing. If it was true that Clancy had worked it all out from hints and suspicions, the man's intellect was staggering. But, he reminded himself again, Castor would know all of this.

"I'll tell you why I'm here, then," Clancy continued, "because your presence here convinces me that I'm correct. You can trust me if you want to, or not. It doesn't matter. I know we're on the same side on this so I trust you."

"You have the floor, Mr. Clancy."

"Jim Parienne's an old friend. I know him like a well-read book. And he's been . . . well, not himself lately. Withdrawn where extroversion was the rule, nonchalant about matters that used to infuriate him. Jim's changed, and I wanted to know why.

"Before we were sent to *Tarent,* we had only an hour to get our gear together. Fine. The usual thing would be to go home, pack, and race for the plane. We do it so many times that no one even considers it unusual anymore. But that night Jim didn't go home. He met a man in a park who gave him something that upset him deeply. I know because I followed him. Maybe it was wrong to do that and maybe I should have respected my friend's privacy. But I didn't. This was too important. Hell, maybe I just wanted to prove it *couldn't* be Jim.

"Anyway, the man he met came back here, and I followed him. An orderly told me his name, Dr. Radow. Without time I couldn't pursue it. I resolved to do so as soon as we returned."

"That explains the briefcases on board the plane," Talon mused out loud.

"You caught that? I . . . oh, I see."

Talon remained noncommittal. "Radow won't open up?" he asked.

"Like a clam," Clancy responded.

"Whatever he's hiding, Parienne must have wanted to hide it too. Otherwise, he'd have used the White House medical staff."

"That's why it interested me," Clancy agreed.

Talon reached for the phone, dialed, and waited for the connection.

"Who are you calling?"

"You need a sharp knife to open a clam. It will take a bit of time, but I'm calling ours."

He grew conscious of the black void around him only when it began to dissipate. His neck hurt, he realized. Pain seemed to grow larger, spreading all around him. He was confused, disoriented.

Dupont opened his eyes and stared at himself.

Full consciousness returned in a rushing wave and with it, more pain. He looked again into the full-length mirror before him at the bloody, naked man. Horrified, he emitted a strangled sound. He tried to move his legs but could not. He tried to lift his arms but could not. Terror overcame him when he saw the reason.

His arms and legs had been nailed to the wooden chair underneath him. Blood seeped from the deep, crucifying wounds and half covered him, pooling around his genitals. He tried to scream again but fainted.

He awoke. The mirror was gone, but the pain was still there. A gag covered his mouth. The suddenness of the attack, the thoroughness of his restraint and finally, the total helplessness of his position all conspired against him. He cried in great tearing gasps. He struggled, but the nails rent his flesh, and he screamed again into the gag till his throat was raw. There was no relief. Then, the voice began, behind him. He could not see the source, all the more terrifying for its anonymity.

"I am Eris," came the harsh whisper. "I have come for you in the night, and you are mine. Your wife is dead. Your son is dead. I have raped your daughter. I have eaten your dog. You are mine. I am god and the devil, and you are mine."

Again and again the voice repeated the chant. Hypnotically, irresistibly; Dupont could not focus, could not resist.

". . . Your wife is dead; your son is dead. I have raped your daughter . . ."

And later, over and over, ". . . are mine. Tell me of Apocalypse. I am Eris. I have come for you in the night. Tell me of Apocalypse . . ."

Dupont broke totally. The cassette recorder caught it all. When Dupont was done and the incoherent moans of insanity began, Kasimov quietly slipped a plastic bag from a cabinet drawer over Dupont's head and smothered him to death. The artistry pleased him, but there was more to do. He left the corpse in the kitchen chair, staring into infinity.

He dragged Parienne out of the closet into the kitchen. The man was awake and cuts on his arms were testament to his efforts to free himself. Kasimov tightened the ropes before slinging him into a chair in front of a table.

Parienne's eyes were open, and he was fully conscious. He had no name for the face in front of him.

"Who are you?" Parienne wheezed through sore lips, tearing his eyes away from Dupont.

"I am Eris. You should know that name."

Parienne nodded, in spite of the chill that clutched at him.

"I know it. What do you want from me?"

"Something very simple. Yet quite important for you. Did you hear what took place here in the last hour?"

Parienne nodded.

"And you see the results?"

Again the nod. "How can you live with yourself after that?" He motioned toward Dupont.

Kasimov smiled. "Quite easily. Your friend died most disagreeably because he would not do the simple things I asked of him. I trust you will not make the same mistake."

"I don't want to be tortured," Parienne said grimly.

"A sensible man. You are going to write a letter to explain your, shall we say, hasty departure. Also, you will make certain admissions. Afterward, I will end you life . . . gently. If you refuse, you will be tortured like your friend till you do as I ask anyway. Then you will be killed. The choice is yours."

"What am I admitting to?"

"Your identity as a mole, code named Castor," Kasimov stated simply.

Parienne sat for a moment. His mind raced to put together Eris' presence here, Dupont's death, and the demand now for the letter. Abruptly it became clear to him. The Russian wanted, and had gotten, the plans for Apocalypse from Dupont. Now, the letter would camouflage Castor by exposing Parienne as the mole. Thoughts whirled through his mind. It could explain much, the presence of a second mole who was Pollux's accomplice. No wonder Sanderson had escaped so easily! And it could explain the lack of briefing on Apocalypse. He was already under suspicion. Perhaps, Reynolds and Clancy were, too. Incredibly, Eris was protecting someone Parienne had trusted for years.

"My patience is not inexhaustible," Kasimov said finally. "Choose now."

There had to be a way to thwart Eris, Parienne thought desperately. The letter, if he wrote it, could bury the mole past all detection. But his position was totally helpless, and he was forced to accept that his death was inevitable. Eris would never let him live to expose the falsehood. Die now or die later; in the end it was just a matter of time.

But he knew something that Eris did not. It was ironic, he thought, if the simple fact that had threatened to shake his personal world apart could prove to be of some greater consequence after all. Irony, he thought again. It was the only way he could think of. There would be an investigation afterward, he was certain. He could only hope that they discovered the vital piece. It would have to do, for now. It was all he had left.

He had never thought of himself as a brave man and now, facing certain death, he was sure that bravery had no part in his decision. It was all anger. Anger that he should die so easily at Eris' hands; anger that it should happen in this way; anger that made him hope he would have the last, bitter laugh as Eris killed him.

Picking up the paper, he began to write the letter.

Talon and Clancy walked back into Radow's office just as he was finishing the phone call he'd received.

"Yes, John. I understand. No, I don't like it either, but I agree. All right, I'm sorry you were bothered. Fine. Goodbye."

Radow replaced the phone and glared angrily at his visitors. But the glare was modified by a new emotion—fear.

"That was my lawyer," he said, "but you already know that. He informed me that five minutes ago he received calls from no less than the IRS, the AMA Ethics Committee, and the Justice Department. It seems I am being investigated for tax fraud, violations of ethics, and failure to cooperate with a national security investigation. His advice is that I cooperate with you. I think you're both cold-blooded bastards."

"I'm sorry, Doctor," said Talon, "but I've got no time to fool around. I have too much respect for medical ethics to use anything but big guns. Please accept my assurance that we wouldn't have put you against the wall if we didn't have to."

Wordlessly, Radow went to his files, extracted one, and passed it to Talon.

"He gave his name as James Parker. I agreed to his rather strange terms for testing and treatment when he convinced me that his position would suffer if the truth about his illness were known. The reason should be apparent when you read the file. Goodnight, gentlemen. And goodbye."

Talon walked out of the office with Clancy. Moments later, they were in Talon's car, the overhead light on to read the file.

"No wonder he used a private clinic," Talon said when he was finished reading.

"Any government facility would have had to report it at once. Especially for a man in his sensitive position," Clancy agreed. "It explains quite a bit."

Talon ordered Menzel to take them to Parienne's and sat quietly, thinking over what he had read.

The diagnosis on James Parienne, adviser to the president of the United States, was lymphoma—cancer. Tumors had already been found throughout his body and had proved resistant to treatment. In less than six months the normal functions of his brain would be overrun by the growing deadly masses. Insanity first, then total loss of bodily control, and then death would take him completely.

Kasimov placed the letter in full view on the kitchen table. Dressed in Dupont's clothing, he made certain no signs of his prior activities were discernible. The pack and everything in it had gone into the furnace. All that remained was the cassette of Dupont's voice.

The furnace in the basement had been made to order for his purposes. Hefting Parienne's corpse over his shoulder as easily as a normal man might lift a child, Kasimov had taken it downstairs and pushed it into the furnace. There would be traces, of course, but no one would be looking. Dupont's corpse upstairs would account for one body, and when Kasimov left the house as Dupont, the assumption would be that Parienne had made good his escape in disguise. Expectations, he thought again. No one would suspect a third man.

Pulling the collar of Dupont's coat high against his cheeks, he walked out of the house. Dupont's car was waiting. He got inside and the chauffeur shut the door solidly behind him.

"Where to, sir?"

Kasimov pressed the gun barrel to the back of his head. "To the corner and make a right turn. Then, just drive."

The big car rolled away from the curb.

Talon pressed the buzzer on Parienne's front door again and again. Still no response.

"He has to be in there, Mr. Talon," said the agent in charge of the surveillance. "Secretary Dupont left almost an hour ago. No one else has entered or left."

"You're certain?"

"Absolutely, sir."

"Then break it down," ordered Talon.

He stood back as two of the agents hit the door with burly shoulders. Inside, all was quiet. Clancy followed Talon.

On the second floor, they found Dupont.

Talon heard Clancy gag behind him as he tried to sort out the scene before him. The plastic bag over Dupont's head stuck to his gaping mouth and terrified eyes like a macabre gift wrapping.

"No one else in the house, sir," said Menzel, returning from upstairs.

"Put out a bulletin for Dupont's car immediately. Check the airports, too," Talon ordered, turning away from the corpse. He saw the letter almost at once and picked it up with a handkerchief. Clancy read it over his shoulder.

To those I leave behind,

It saddens me to think of how you will react when you read my farewell and understand the reasons for it. Though I have done my duty, for over twenty years, I can even now regret the deception that I had to force upon you.

Castor was created to do a job. Now that job is done, and I must return to the country which has afforded me so great an opportunity to be part of the unending class struggle which must ultimately bring down the capitalist system. I have done what I have done for the people.

In my new home in the Soviet Union I will be honored for my part in what has been. I look forward to years of contentment in the workers' paradise. The time stretches out in front of me with great promise, days of camaraderie, years of harmony. I will live long among my brothers and sisters, dedicated to working for the future of Communism . . .

Goodbye,

(signed) James Parienne

Talon read the letter a second time and then a third.

A CIA team, in three white vans, was arriving to go over the house. He walked outside into the glaring lights of the van's beacon. The street was already cordoned off.

"Excuse me, sir," said Menzel. "We just received a report that Dupont's car has been found, the chauffeur dead of a gunshot wound. Instructions?"

"Bring it in and have it gone over," Talon instructed him. Evidently, Parienne had made his escape dressed as Dupont. No one would have followed the car; Dupont was not under suspicion. Parienne could be halfway to Russia by now. Probably by way of Canada or Cuba. It was hopeless. All he could do was put out the alert, like closing the barn door after the horse had run off.

Dupont would have revealed Apocalypse. A man of his age, of his lack of training would have broken under treatment such as he'd received. Talon faced the fact that he had failed. And that failure had placed the entire country in jeopardy.

He turned to Clancy, about to offer his apologies for the way he'd been treated, but the man's face held a strange, pensive expression.

"What does a dying man not do?" Clancy asked softly.

"I don't follow."

"Ask yourself that question. What does a dying man not do?"

Talon shrugged, "I'm too tired for riddles. Parienne knew he was dying. He chose to spend the rest of his time in a place where he'd be a hero. He's gone and so is Apocalypse."

"You're not thinking, Talon. Maybe it's easier for me because I knew Jim so well. I just don't believe he's capable of doing what we saw upstairs. Ask yourself again, what wouldn't a dying man do?"

"All right, all right," Talon said getting angry. "A dying man doesn't take a long lease. He doesn't make long-range plans. He doesn't . . ." He stopped as the implications hit him.

"That's right, Talon. He doesn't plan on years of enjoyment in the workers' paradise! Everything in that letter says over and over again that he's got lots of time, loads of time. But Jim didn't. He was dying of a disease that was rotting every system in his body, and he knew it. Blindness, insanity; ultimately death. And incurable. Does that kind of man write this kind of note?"

Talon shook his head to clear it. He looked long and hard at Clancy.

"Then who tortured Dupont and where is Parienne? Only one man entered this house, and he's dead."

"But that still doesn't prove that Parienne is the one who left."

"The house was watched. No one else entered," argued Talon.

"You can't be sure of that. Agents are fallible; even yours," Clancy insisted.

"Look, Clancy. I'd like to buy your premise even more than you would. If you're right, we might still have a chance. But the facts remain. Unless you can produce Parienne's corpse, we have to assume he's the killer. The house has been searched, every corner of it. No corpse, no body, no Parienne. Unless . . ."

Talon began to think along Clancy's suggested lines. What if Parienne had been set up to look like the mole? The note *was* odd. Could a third person have gotten in? Whoever left had done so alone. Where could you put a body to avoid discovery? Where would no one look. Suddenly, an idea crossed his mind. It was just possible . . .

"Unless what?" queried Clancy.

"Come with me," Talon said, racing back into the house, downstairs to the basement. A lab team was still dusting for prints, examining every corner.

"Have you checked in there?" Talon demanded of one, pointing to the furnace. It was possible, he decided.

"For what?" asked the confused technician.

"Kill that fire and check for human remains," Talon ordered. "I want an answer in five minutes."

"That could be it," said Clancy excitedly, as they went back upstairs. Dupont's body had already been removed.

Talon paced back and forth across the room. "If it's not," he said, "it's over."

The technician returned in less than five minutes. He held out a small plastic sample bag to Talon wordlessly.

In it were charred human bone fragments. The technician verified it.

Talon was up at once and racing for the phone, dialing a special number.

"Get me the president," he ordered, praying that there was still time.

Fuller handed Washington's response to the Secretary of State without comment.

"His face says it all," thought Powell as he read the paper.

"Remain position; stand by," was all it said. In truth, he had expected nothing very different.

Less than two hours remained till dawn. The *Ural* had moved to her new position, and the waiting game had begun again.

"I'm impressed that your crew is handling the situation as well as they are," he said to Fuller.

"They're Navy," was the all-encompassing reply as Fuller resumed his watch.

Powell looked to the first light that had begun to separate sea from sky and then to the *Ural*.

"Time," he thought for the hundredth time that night. "We must have time."

Apocalypse was already in operation by now, he was sure, though he had no knowledge of the specifics of the countermove. Whatever it was, it needed time to operate. But if the *Ural* fired upon them, even Apocalypse could not forestall the holocaust that would follow.

"You will have plague on your shores," he had said to the Soviets. God, how the thought repulsed him. Would they truly risk that threat coming to pass? Perhaps it had come to that. Two nations, almost acting like opposing individuals, locked into the conflict by forces that had been decades in the making.

He pondered his own death. Would he be as stoic as Fuller seemed to be? Or would the first explosions on *Tarent*'s massive frame send him screaming for a reprieve that would never come? He wondered if it took courage to face death, or merely disinterest. With each increase of light of the sky, he tried to cultivate both.

Harold Powell hoped it would be one hell of a sunrise.

Barbara Reynolds walked out of her apartment building into the warm, moist air of a bright summer morning.

Her meeting with the president was scheduled for later that day. It would be her sad duty to receive news of Parienne's defection, Dupont's death, and to carry out the subsequent investigation that would surely be thrust into her hands now that the mole had been "discovered."

Long practice at receiving news she already knew would keep from her face any betrayal of her awareness. Then the years of deception would begin again. As always, Castor had survived. The cost was inconsequential.

The tape Kasimov had made of Dupont's knowledge of Apocalypse lay snug in a small envelope in her handbag. Her weekly information drop would prove no more difficult than any of the others over the years. Kasimov had confirmed that the surveillance on her had been withdrawn.

She had been able to locate Leyland at Canaveral, and Kasimov had left several hours before dawn. His mission became even more important when he'd heard the plans. In killing Leyland, he would stop Apocalypse cold. Getting out alive would be a separate matter, but Kasimov had done it before, she decided ruefully. He probably would again.

She thought about him as she turned up Fourth Street, toward the Air and Space Museum, one of the Smithsonian's biggest summer tourist attractions. The huge modern building saw dense crowds every day, pouring past countless relics of the aviation and space age, from the Wright brothers' plane to the Apollo II command module. For the past twenty years, crowds had protected her. They would continue to do so.

But if Kasimov had not arrived to help her, she might now be under arrest, her future a long term in prison. So many mistakes she might have made had she remained unaware of the search for Castor.

She entered the building along with the stream of tourists, less dense at this hour than later in the day. Casually, she took a brief walk through the gigantic main gallery where aircraft and spacecraft were suspended like huge model toys from the vaulted ceiling. Soon, she would be able to go to the walk-in model of the Skylab orbital station to deposit the tape under an overhanging console. Then out. Ten minutes later someone would walk in to the mock-up and make the pickup, signaling to her that it was complete by placing a broken English Oval cigarette into the first ashtray by the elevator. After that, she could leave, the information safely on its way to Moscow. She glanced at her watch. It was time.

She followed a Japanese family up the ramp into the cylindrical Skylab model. Walking raggedly as the children excitedly poked at and gestured to tolerant parents, she slipped the small, prepared envelope out of her purse and into her hand.

In the wardroom section of the Skylab, she paused to examine closely the food heating apparatus. Observation blocked by her body, she slipped the thin envelope under the crew table, where it stuck firmly. Quickly, she was moving forward again, children underfoot. Their happy chortling caused a brief pain within her. Then they were all outside, and Reynolds began the ten-minute wait.

She moved back to the large flight gallery and stared at Glenn's famous Mercury capsule. She had survived again. No one could . . .

Abruptly, a man's hand caught and encircled her arm, and she started violently. But another was behind her.

"It's over, Castor," said Henry Talon quietly as she was propelled forward to the museum office. There was no place to run, no place to hide, and she sagged against her captors in the wood-paneled rooms, despair and fear flooding over her.

Talon motioned the others out and stared sadly at her. One hand reached into his coat and withdrew his gun. His face creased into hard lines, and he tossed the tape Reynolds had left in the Skylab onto her lap. She made no move to speak.

"Listen carefully, Barbara," he said in cold, emotionless tones. "There is very little time left. Help me, and I swear I'll help you get the best deal possible. Refuse and I swear I'll kill you here and now. There are no witnesses, and that tape's all I need. Mr. Yamato, the man in front of you on line, works for me. His family did quite nicely, I think. Witnesses and proof, Barbara. How long till pickup?"

"Give it up, Hank," she said softly. "Apocalypse has no chance."

Her face bore no readable expression. But the cocking of Talon's .45 was very loud in the small, tight room.

"Now, Barbara. It's got to be now."

Reynolds heard the words and understood the futility of further protest. Talon meant what he said, and she believed him.

"You have less than eight minutes," she said at last.

"You had less than that," he said, lowering the hammer. He walked to the door and summoned the men who waited outside with several large suitcases.

"Mr. Menzel," Talon ordered. "It's a cassette. Get me a match."

Menzel opened the suitcase and selected a matching brand of cassette. He inserted it into a recorder and passed it to Talon.

A second man had been rerecording Reynolds' original on his machine. He looked up at Talon. "Code to open, code to close, message in the middle. Computer will have a breakdown in sixty seconds. You can start, sir."

Talon took a deep breath. He handed a sheet of paper to Reynolds.

"That is the message you're going to record and send back to Moscow. Use the correct codes. I warn you, we can check them now, and you know what a mistake will cost you. There are less than five minutes remaining. Do it now." He passed the microphone to her and waited.

Reynolds began to dictate. The code expert nodded as she spoke.

". . . word of the *Ural*'s movement. It must not attack. Government position is committed. *Tarent*'s missiles are rigged to deploy automatically in connection with prefixed radar and sonar scanning of *Ural*'s offensive weaponry. Any attempt to destroy *Tarent* will result in release of plague. The plague is a variant of pulmonary anthrax, airborne, with a kill zone of . . ."

Talon glanced at his watch. Three minutes. He watched his code expert carefully. The man gave him a quick thumbs-up.

With one minute to spare, Reynolds told Talon of the cigarette signal. He placed the new tape back into the envelope and walked to the Skylab. His own men bracketed him as he entered, causing the crowd to jam up behind them. Talon replaced the tape and left, still walking as casually as he could. Waiting now was as hard a thing as he had ever done. If the contact had seen Reynolds picked up, if they hadn't replaced the tape in time, if Reynolds had lied . . . he walked over to the elevator not even daring to hope.

There in the shiny, steel receptacle lay a broken English Oval cigarette.

Talon almost wept with relief. He returned to the office and found Clancy already waiting.

"You may as well hear the rest of it," Talon said, and motioned Clancy inside.

Reynolds sat quietly between two guards. There was no future left to believe in. For her, the game was over. But the sight of Clancy seemed to disturb her, and she turned away to avoid his gaze.

"It almost worked, Barbara," Talon said. "I was just about to pull off the surveillance when Mr. Clancy here figured it all out.

"Clancy discovered that Parienne was dying. Something no one else knew. It figured the note to be a fake. Since Clancy'd been with me, you were the only one left. We pretended to call off the surveillance, but we've been on you like glue ever since. Right now, there are more agents in this city mobilized for this operation than any before in its history. Anywhere you'd have gone, we could have had a full complement of force there in under a minute. It may be some consolation that it took all of us to get you, Barbara. And two good men died for it. I have to say, though, that I never, not even once, suspected an old friend."

"Would you have shot me, Hank?" she asked, speaking for the first time.

"Answer my question first, please. Why, Barbara? For God's sake, why? It couldn't have been money. Blackmail?"

Reynolds nodded. "They turned me the same day they turned Paul, who was my friend. Castor and Pollux; Kasimov thought it was so clever of him. He was young, but even then like ice inside."

Clancy sat listening, pained, as Talon nodded. "I've seen his work."

"Then you know what he is, Hank. I was young, too, just starting out as a junior case officer. As was Paul. He and I used to go to a place . . . a crazy place . . . to blow off steam." She stopped, noticing the look on Talon's face. "You're so surprised? Because I'm a woman? Then you are truly naive after all. There were so many things I'd never experienced before. Kasimov had films, he . . . Oh, shit. You know how it's done."

"You could have told your superiors in CIA," Clancy said. "They would have helped."

Reynolds looked to Talon, but he turned away. "Sure," Reynolds laughed harshly, "just waltz in and watch the looks on their faces while I was branded a pervert. The truth is I loved it. Should I have let them use me as a triple on Kasimov till, when I'd given all I could, they drummed me out of CIA for moral turpitude? Sure, a great future. I'm a woman, you fool. Do you know how hard it was even to get an assignment anywhere but in the clerical division? With that on my record, I would have been finished—and Kasimov knew it."

"So you turned," Talon finished.

"So I turned."

"I'm sorry, Barbara, for you and for what the future's going to bring you. In a way, for friendship's sake, I'm also sorry it had to be me who ended it."

"Sorry? For me?" She seemed genuinely surprised. "Don't be. I've influenced history in ways unimaginable by most ordinary people for a longer time than most careers last. What real courage is it to choose the side you were born to? For twenty years I lived right out there on the edge; lived by my own rules without a ready-made moral compass that has Capitalism at one pole and Communism neatly at the other. All the philosophy in the world doesn't change who we ultimately look out for first, Hank. It's always our own ass. Maybe Kasimov started me, but I don't regret that he did.

"Go home, all of you, to your sweet little wives and their Mah-Jongg games and bottles and brats. And when you hate them at night because they lie there like cold, fragile glass—remember that I've devoured more of life than their pitiful little dreams could ever encompass. Save your pity for them. I don't need it now and never have."

Talon looked to Clancy and saw the cold light of condemnation in his eyes. Barbara would be on her own now, and those whom she'd betrayed would demand payment.

His own part in Apocalypse was over. He thought of the *Tarent* and hoped that the substitute message Peterson and the president had conceived of would save her. He thought of his friend, Chris Leyland, and of Arielle. The rest was up to them.

"Mr. Talon?" said Menzel, coming into the room. "You're wanted at the White House. Your car's outside."

"Coming," said Talon, rising wearily from his chair.

"One minute, Hank," said Reynolds softly. "You never answered my question . . . Would you have shot me?"

Talon drew a deep, ragged breath and looked at the woman he had never truly known.

"Without a moment's hesitation," he said sadly and walked out the door.

Valentin Kasimov noted the sunset over Canaveral and wished night would fall soon. A few miles down the coast, past the patrolled areas, he waited, his small boat bobbing lightly on the water. He was indistinguishable from hundreds of other sport fishermen who traversed the area daily, and he made no attempt to seem otherwise.

Kasimov's mind was steely calm. His fishing rod dipped easily, with no frustration evident, and from time to time he withdrew his line to fix more bait. Without Castor, he knew, he might never have found Leyland when access to KGB channels was closed to him. His one last chance to reopen them was to kill Leyland and sabotage Apocalypse.

If he were to assassinate the man who had caused his disgrace and at the same time end the Shuttle phase of the American plan, then even Komarovsky would be unable to stand in the way of his triumphant return to Moscow.

His foot tapped the bundle at the bottom of the boat: wet suit, scuba gear, rifle, scope, and ammunition packed in a waterproof case. Escape would pose little problem in the melee that would follow Leyland's death, American security at NASA bases being what it was. Last, a few well-placed shots into the highly combustible fuel tanks around the facility would increase the confusion greatly.

The wind picked up slightly, and Kasimov moved the boat as close as he dared toward the cape. The three-mile swim posed little problem; hatred would fuel his every stroke. In the final rays of light, he stripped, put on the wet suit, and slung his gear together.

After he opened the seacocks, the boat began to list as it took on water. Kasimov strapped on his air tanks and tested the regulator. It hissed reassuringly. The boat was almost filled with water as he tossed his gear over the side and followed it into the sea.

Adrenaline burst through him as he kicked away from the scuttled boat. Had not the regulator been clamped between his clenched teeth, Kasimov would have been smiling.

9

Brendan Connors paced the Situation Room with such nervous energy rippling through him that it was impossible to sit. They had just received the AWAC's first report: the cloud was forming, carried on the winds toward Baikonur.

Peterson strode over, carrying a radio message to Connors. For the first time since the operation had been launched, Peterson's face was less than stoic.

"Talon's done it, sir. He has Reynolds. We just received word."

"Was he able to send the information we gave him?" Connors demanded, taking the message.

"Yes, sir. We won't know for some time, but if anything can bolster *Tarent*'s position, what we sent through to the Russians ought to."

"It had better," said Connors firmly. "We need time. Given twenty-four hours, we may be able to obliterate Nightsight. Less than that and *Tarent* is our only weapon."

"There isn't a man who knows about *Tarent* that isn't praying we don't have to use it."

Connors turned away. Castor's identity had come as a profound shock to him. How much had he alone compromised their security; how much had he spoken of to his adviser, his friend, his lover . . .

"Henry Talon did a fine job," he said at last. Peterson missed the private bitterness in his voice. He forced painful images from his mind. There would be time for grief, and guilt, later. If they succeeded.

"I agree, Mr. President. He's served his purpose admirably. Meledov will know without doubt that we have teeth, and Castor's been uncovered. I never expected it to be Barbara, though," he added, chagrined.

Connors turned away. "No," he said. "I never expected it to be her either."

A sudden flurry of activity across the room caught Peterson's attention, and he raced to its source. Connors followed, feeling defeated at the moment of first victory.

"Mr. President," Peterson said, and Connors heard the sudden tension in his voice. "We're getting a transmission from the AWAC's. An Iranian military force is closing on the Meteotron site."

Connors shrugged off the ghosts that plagued him and the lethargy which threatened to engulf him. He realized he could afford no further thoughts of the past.

"Where are the F-15's?" he demanded.

"On their way to the refueling point. They had less than twenty minutes of air time remaining."

"Send in a second squadron from Turkey, then."

Peterson shook his head. "Insufficient time. The Iranians will be all over our group before the jets could arrive to be of any use."

"Protect that site at all costs, General," ordered Connors. "If that group fails, our entire effort becomes untenable."

"I'm aware of that, Mr. President, but . . ."

"At all costs," thundered Connors as his eyes drifted up to the map displays and his thoughts to Iran.

"We've got company," Collins called back to Arielle in a voice tight with urgency.

"I've got them on my screen," Arielle confirmed. "I estimate arrival time at under ten minutes."

Collins left his seat hurriedly. "I'll inform Colonel Bradey. You keep a lookout for our F-15's," he called as he raced past her.

But Arielle's screen showed no blips other than those of the Iranians. Quick computation told her that the refueling point for the

F-15's was too distant to enable them to return before the Iranians arrived. A second calculation on the computers told her that they needed yet another two hours of Meteotron operation to be certain of the cloud they had formed, the cloud on which her husband's life depended. Locking the computer tracking on automatic, she hastened outside.

Collins, Whitney, and Bradey were by the operator's console. Around the site, groups of marines had entrenched themselves, automatic weapons peering over sand ridges in the direction of the Iranians' approach. The Meteotron roared on unaffected by the frantic humans who surrounded it.

". . . as long as we can, but I want the C-5 ready to fly if we have to pull out," Bradey was saying as Arielle arrived.

"Then it's got to be closed up now," Collins said flatly.

"This equipment is not expendable," Whitney protested. "I can't permit it to be left here. Many of these special components are classified top secret."

"Rig it to blow," Arielle said firmly. "If we have to run, the Iranians get nothing but debris."

Bradey nodded and finally Whitney acquiesced. Bradey issued the necessary orders, and a team of marines scampered to the Meteotron, faces grimacing against the noise and the heat.

"How long can you hold this position without air support?" Arielle questioned Bradey.

"That all depends on the size of their force," Bradey responded. "The AWAC's identify the blips as helicopters, big enough to carry twenty, maybe thirty troops each. Figure we're numerically inferior by half. If the helicopters are gun ships, then we're in more of a bind."

"I need two hours, Colonel," Arielle said.

"I can't guarantee that, Dr. Simmons. No one can." Bradey scowled.

Collins raced off to ready the C-5. Arielle looked unflinchingly into the Colonel's eyes though he stood almost half a foot taller than she.

"Not one minute less, Colonel."

Bradey's face was suffused with color. "These men are the best there are, handpicked from the finest army on the face of the earth. You'll get your two hours, Dr. Simmons."

"Thank you, Colonel."

The first black specks appeared in the southern sky. Growing larger, the helicopters in tight formation swooped toward the site. Bradey grabbed Arielle and dove for cover as the first ship passed. Machine-gun fire raked across the camp. Arielle spit sand, looked up, and was grateful to see Whitney sprawled under the operator's console unharmed.

The marines returned fire. From the crest of the dune beyond the Meteotron sudden flashes of light signaled the use of the portable rocket launcher. Heat-seeking missiles raced in pursuit of the lead helicopter, reached upward, and destroyed the machine in a paroxysm of smoke and fire. Burning bodies fell through the air and charred metal parts were tossed wildly over the landscape.

"That'll be their last air attack for a while," Bradey said happily. Then he was up and running to his troops. Arielle fought back bile.

Beyond the dunes, the remaining three helicopters touched down out of range of the missiles. Iranian troops in desert garb jumped out and swarmed toward them.

Bradey held his men back. The Iranians massed together and moved forward. Then suddenly, with howls that tore through Arielle's brain, they attacked.

The marines' fire was instantaneous and accurate. Those Iranians in front of the first wave fell under the withering blasts of automatic weapons fire. The charge turned into a rout, and the Iranians pulled back.

Arielle looked at her watch. An hour and a half left to go. The Meteotron continued to roar unhindered. She ran into the C-5 to check the computers. Still growing, the cloud was moving toward Baikonur.

Suddenly, her radar screen picked up more objects coming in from the south. The computers confirmed what she had feared: Iranian jet fighters had been called in. Without the F-15's, they would make short work of destroying the site.

Outside, the marines fought on, keeping the Iranians out of mortar range. Arielle crawled the last ten yards to Bradey. He smashed his fist into the sand in frustration.

"I have nothing to throw at planes that fast," he said angrily.

"But you destroyed the helicopter."

"No buts about it, jets are just too damned fast."

"I need another hour, Colonel," she demanded.

"You need your head examined if you think I can defend this position against jets armed with rockets," Bradey retorted angrily.

The noise from the Meteotron was everywhere. Blotting all else out, the Iranian jets came at them silently, silver Soviet-built MIG's, low and fast. On the first pass they darted over the site and raced beyond to bank and turn back.

The Iranian troops massed for a second attack, shouting frenzied welcome to their air support.

"Lead them and fire at will," Bradey shouted to his missile team and riflemen.

Crouched low behind the dunes, they waited helplessly while death bore down on them.

Valentin Kasimov slipped silently through the dark, marshy ground in between the ocean and the launch pads. He had buried his tanks, mask, and fins in the narrow strip of sand when he reached shore. Now, less than a mile from the launch pads, he lay in the tepid water and thoughtfully observed preparations for the double Shuttle launch; both pads were lit up and ready.

Kasimov smiled, flicking away an offending insect. He knew what the Americans' plan was and that Leyland would be one of the Shuttle pilots himself. Here was the opportunity previously denied him. In one stroke, he could kill Leyland and, with a few well-placed bullets, cripple the American effort. He would receive a general's rank, at the very least.

All at once, he saw his former failures as petty obstacles designed by some challenging fate to bring him here. Phoenixlike, he would rise from the ashes of his ruined operations to emerge as hero and savior. As he moved closer to the pads, the past dropped away, like the wet suit he discarded at land's edge.

Unwrapping his parcels from their waterproof covering, he put on his naval uniform. The rifle, scope, and ammunition still fit snugly into their attaché case.

His first task would be to locate Leyland. Movements flowed across his mind as if he were a grand master, audacious yet subtle. No problem was insurmountable.

Technicians at work took no notice of the military figure walking past them. Slipping past the security station was childishly easy in the dark.

His second task would be easier once the first had been accomplished. Pleasure heated his loins when he thought about it, and he began to catalog place after place from which he could shoot Chris Leyland.

Pyotr Meledov sat alone in the Politburo council room. Before him on the long table was the message from Castor. It had been the first he'd known of the *Ural*'s repositioning, and that had led to other questions.

For the past hours, Meledov's sources of information had been reporting in. He now knew the extent of the coup and who had attempted it. His orders holding the *Ural* had already been sent. Another way would have to be found to break the stalemate.

When the guards brought Grishen and Telshe to him, he allowed them to take their seats. It was, after all, the last time they would see the room again. He could afford the gesture.

To their credit, Grishen and Telshe said nothing. The game was over, the hand played out. Failure carried its own ineluctable penalties—ones they had handed out to others.

"Castor indicates the plague is genuine," Meledov said after a while. "I have canceled the first strike. You would have cost us a hundred million lives with your precipitate interference."

"We would have given you the world," said Telshe bitterly.

"Perhaps," said Meledov, "but then only those like yourselves would have been fit to live in it. Goodbye, Comrades."

Meledov summoned the guards.

10

In Fire Room One of the Kennedy Launch Control Center, the forty-five launch personnel had already been working at their consoles for over two hours. The final programs of the launch processing system were almost completed, and the launch clock situated above the big board map display had gradually ticked down to T minus 10 minutes.

Test procedures were still running through the central data subsystem's two computers and the checkout, control, and monitor subsystem team continued to plot and replot calculations as they raced toward final launch sequence.

Across a brief hallway whose metal-louvered windows faced the lighted twin launch pads was Fire Room Two, with its identical crew of personnel and computer systems, also standing at T minus 10. Each fire room would be responsible for the lift-off and flight of one Shuttle; One handling *Constitution;* Two governing *Independence.*

At the twin pads, preparations for the Shuttles' launch were almost completed. Wispy plumes of exhaust gases bled off from feed valves, making the gantry lights twinkle against the first light of dawn in the eastern sky. Both Shuttles were fully fueled. Liquid oxygen, at a temperature of minus three hundred degrees Fahrenheit—the oxidizer for the orbiter's main engines—had flowed at the rate of over ten thousand gallons per minute into the external fuel tank, along with the liquid hydrogen fuel for lift-off whose temperature was below minus four hundred degrees. Fuel for the orbiter's engines in space, monomethyl hydrazine, had already been fed via the gantry's umbilicals into the orbiter itself.

Video cameras carried images of the Shuttles back to the fire rooms. Relays within the launch platforms sent back endless arrays of information. Technicians made final checks and then departed for protected cover as the launch reached T minus 8 and *Constitution* and *Independence* shuddered to life.

Chris Leyland, Bill Cooke, and their copilots lumbered into the white NASA van at the preparation center, round-shouldered by their flying suits and telemetry equipment. The van rolled out along the crawlerway toward Pad A where *Constitution* sat white-gold against the pastel colors of the rising sun.

The van sped up the incline toward the elevator entrance at the gantry's base. Outside, Chris saw Swanson waiting amidst the "White Room" personnel. Chris's copilot, an ex-Army flier of twenty-nine, Captain Wren T. Packard, passed a hand over his short black hair and spoke with his native Southern drawl. "Mighty nice of the L.D. to say goodbye. Remind me to send him a box of candy and a note when we get back."

Chris appreciated the man's spirit. Like Cooke, Chris had been silent, alone with his thoughts. Nothing could be allowed to detract from his concentration. Similar to a champion fighter before a bout, he fought a mental war for control over his every emotion. But he broke from his self-imposed silence in a gesture of support for his younger, inexperienced copilot.

"Nothing like flying with a thoughtful man," he announced. "And here I forgot to get you anything, Pack."

"No sensitivity at all," Cooke cajoled from the bench on the van's opposite side.

"Find it in your heart to forgive him, Pack," counseled Cooke's copilot dryly, Captain Janet Caulden. Twenty-eight and a graduate of Pensacola, she had extensive naval flying experience. She was the first woman to pilot the Shuttle.

"I forgive you, Stick," said Packard magnanimously as the van slid to a halt.

Packard got out first, and Chris shook Caulden's hand. Looking to Cooke, the brief smile and nod he received spoke volumes.

"Dinner on Tuesday next?" Chris asked lightly, stepping down.

"Tuesday it is," answered Cooke. Then he swung the door shut, and the van pulled away.

The elevator rose to the gantry station at 147 feet, level with the orbiter's entrance hatch. The small party stepped out onto the orbiter access arm, a low-walled catwalk which terminated in the environmentally clean White Room from which Chris and Packard would enter *Constitution*.

"We're at T minus 3 and holding," said Swanson gravely, "and this is where I leave you, gentlemen. We have no signal as yet from Iran, but as soon as we get one, you'll be the first to know it. Godspeed, gentlemen."

Chris watched him depart. The technicians would finish their medical and suit checks in the White Room itself. Two technicians preceded him onto the catwalk. With a final deep breath, Chris stepped onto the steel mesh and walked toward his ship.

Four hundred yards to the west, Valentin Kasimov watched them cross the catwalk from his position by the emergency bunker for Pad A.

Two hours before dawn he had selected his fire position. The bunker was perfect for his purpose, a clear line of sight to the catwalk he knew Leyland would cross. Now, so near to success, his control threatened to desert him and his heart hammered in his chest. So much depended on this. He wanted *his* bullet to kill Leyland; *his* shot to bring him down. There were other bullets for the Shuttles' vulnerable fuel tanks.

To make the shot he would have to leave the bunker, since its blind side faced the Shuttle to protect astronauts in case of explosion and flying debris. No matter. He rolled the rifle's smooth barrel against his bare forearm and enjoyed the sensation. He hoped Leyland would fall from the high walk and make his pleasure last that much longer.

He picked up his ammunition. His sleeves were rolled up to the elbow, his jacket hanging by the telephone which connected the bunker to Launch Control. He eased out of the bunker and onto its dirt roof. Lying prone, he slipped his arm through the rifle's strap and locked the stock against his shoulder. The second technician passed his view as he slid home the bolt, locking a round into the chamber. His telescopic sight showed the first astronaut passing. Kasimov's finger tightened slowly on the trigger. He took in a final slow breath as Leyland walked into view, and the cross hairs settled perfectly upon him, outlined against the bright, open sky.

The silver MIG's bore down on the Meteotron site, five planes in a tight V formation. Arielle strained to discern the clusters of missiles under each wing, and the rifle in her hands was little comfort.

Bradey settled in beside her, scooping sand into a rest for his own rifle. Sensing victory near, the Iranians charged and swept up toward them, rifles firing steadily, invocations of Allah filling the air.

A hundred feet from the desert floor the jets leveled off and made their first pass. Heavy machine-gun fire in parallel rows sprayed across the dunes. Marines fell bleeding, faces contorted with pain. Dead men sprawled across the sand.

Bradey held his men together. He was up and racing across the lines as soon as the jets had passed. Arielle sensed his hopelessness, but his voice remained strong as he called for greater effort from his troops. The fire line re-formed as the Iranians came into range.

A sudden change in the pitch of the Meteotron's roar turned Arielle's head sharply. Miraculously, Whitney was still at the operator's controls, fighting to keep the device from faltering. Arielle saw the jagged tear in one of the six engines. Five could be just enough to keep the cloud growing, she decided. But beyond, the jets were circling for their second run.

Bradey had already shifted men to cover the planes' return. Arielle fought down despair. This would be the end of it. The planes had their range, had seen the Meteotron. It would not survive a second run.

Two miles away the MIG's leveled off. Arielle turned away and burrowed deeper into the dune. Her rifle grew hot as she fired steadily at the Iranian troops in front of her. The back of her neck tightened, waiting for the MIG fire to rake the compound. Five seconds; ten seconds; she squeezed the trigger and a soldier fell. Twenty seconds. More shots; another soldier fell, clutching his side.

Arielle turned and looked to the sky and almost yelled in wild glee. She pulled frantically at Bradey and he turned, astonished by her flushed excitement till he saw what had caused it.

The F-15's had returned.

The word spread like wildfire along the line of marines. Survival's possibility grew tenfold and the troops steadied down. Once more, their accurate fire brought down Iranian soldiers, who saw the F-15's and lost momentum.

In the skies, the F-15's were locked in individual combat with the MIG's. Faster, more heavily armed and better-piloted, the six F-15's shot down three of the five MIG's in the first few minutes of confrontation. The plumes of rocket tail-fire and jet exhausts wildly stitched the sky to the sand.

An F-15 closed on one of the last two MIG's. Tailgating, it roared in pursuit. The MIG powered upward in a tight circle to shake the American plane, but the F-15 followed. In a roller-coaster loop, the MIG continued to climb, knowing only seconds remained till the F-15 had its range. The MIG forced power into a tighter circle, frantic to pull out of its loop behind the F-15.

Suddenly, the F-15 faltered. It spun out of its climb and began to fall earthward, spiraling out of control. The MIG turned gleefully, out of danger, and pursued it.

But a second F-15 screamed down from the heavens and its rockets flew straight on target. The MIG exploded in a ball of smoke and fire. But a few seconds later, the second F-15 began to fall, as if some puppeteer had cut its strings.

Arielle watched it crash. With growing horror, she understood. The planes had been recalled without refueling! It was the only way they could have arrived in time. Bradey, too, watched in anguish as a third, fourth, and fifth F-15 pilot was forced to ditch and three white chutes swung earthward.

The only surviving MIG, seeming to understand the quick turn of fortunes, banked sharply and raced toward the site. The last F-15 pursued doggedly, but its fuel expired and another white chute billowed out into the air. The MIG leveled out and commenced its run.

Arielle was up and running for the C-5 before the thought in her mind had come to full consciousness. Protect the Meteotron; protect Chris; those were her only directives as Bradey called frantically for her to stay down. Bullets bit into the sand as she ran into the plane's vast hold.

She threw herself into her seat. The computers were still running on automatic as she hit the override button and control of the Meteotron returned to her at once.

The screen showed the last MIG less than two miles from the site. Her hands played over the console's keys frantically, and figures burst over the board's display. Second calculations appeared. The MIG was under a mile away as the great cannon turret of the Meteotron began to turn.

Arielle bit into her lip as the MIG roared on. On her screen, the white blip sped toward them. The column of super-hot air was turning . . . turning . . . the MIG approaching, faster as it dove. The long "bat" of air swiveled toward the offending "ball." Arielle's hands flashed over the console a final time, correcting, coercing, praying . . .

The MIG hit the invisible column of air. In a clash of titanic energies, bat and ball collided on her screen, and Arielle yelled in triumph as the MIG spun wildly off course. A second blip appeared briefly; a missile shot. But it was wide and away. Racing outside, an atavistic scream of victory in her throat, she saw the MIG crash into the sand and erupt into fire.

But the scream died abruptly as she stopped by the operator's console. So close to winning, Whitney had died at his post. The hole in his chest was final and unmistakable. She knelt beside him tenderly and lifted his head from the sand where he had fallen. Then she stood, shaken, and returned the Meteotron to computer guidance.

Bradey hurried to her, a feral grin contorting his features. "I know how we stopped the infantry, but what the hell happened to that jet? It just spun in midair and crashed."

Arielle explained and was totally unprepared for Bradey's crushing bearhug. Then he saw Whitney and sobered. He summoned litter-bearers and put an arm around Arielle.

The smell of war was all around them. Dead men and those dying lay scattered across the dunes. Beyond, more lay dead, food for desert animals. The oily smoke from burning planes hung like a pall over them. Brady sent men to retrieve the downed pilots who had survived, to whom they owed their lives. Arielle glanced at her watch; then at the data screens on the operator's console. With a single flick of a switch, the Meteotron ceased its baleful roar and silence returned to the desert.

"Send the code for go," she said quietly, her eyes traveling involuntarily skyward. "Tell them we've got our cloud."

One more step, thought Kasimov, as Leyland's features filled his scope. His finger began the slow, steady pull which would fire the weapon. He was a finely stretched line between two points, Leyland and the muzzle of his rifle. The world grew narrower. His pull increased. Leyland walked his final step and Kasimov went immobile . . .

And the telephone in the bunker below him rang loudly on its final test check.

It was enough. Involuntarily, Kasimov tensed, and the shot went wide. Rage overcame him as one of the technicians fell to the catwalk flooring. He searched for Leyland. Standing, he traversed the area again and fired at the catwalk. Exposed but uncaring, he wanted Leyland and his Shuttle to die. He could not fail again!

Above on the catwalk, Chris saw the red hole blossom on the technician's white coveralls. Combat-trained reflexes understood the rifle shot before his brain did. The crack of the explosion reached his ears as he dove into Packard, knocking him below the catwalk's wall.

The second technician turned in confusion and died the same way, as Kasimov's second shot burst into his brain, and he tumbled off the catwalk to the pad below.

"Crawl in and start procedures," Chris yelled at the stunned Packard, pushing him forward. "Call Barney and tell him someone's shooting!"

The gantry was deserted by now, all personnel in positions of safety. They were under attack, Chris knew, but there was no one left at the pad to fight back. Suddenly, a pipe along the gantry's side burst forth with angry steam. Then another.

Chris crawled back onto the gantry. In the distance, he heard security sirens wail. Packard had gotten into the craft, but in a few more seconds, *Constitution* might be finished, a single break in her complex circuitry sufficient to incapacitate the craft. He chanced a look over the guard rail. The face of Kasimov was unmistakable. He had to get to Kasimov at once.

The slide-wire basket hung from its cable just twenty feet away, terminating at the bunker. A burning rage, an impossible anger seared through Chris, and he was up and running before he had finalized the decision to go. Bullets flashed around him, and he knew Kasimov had seen him.

Furiously, Chris raced around the gantry's posts and steel girders toward the basket. The firing increased. He saw cars emerge from the distant security buildings, but they would be too late. With a desperate heave, Chris released the handbrake above the basket and dove headfirst into it, one hundred and fifty feet in the air.

It slid out of the gantry with an oiled hiss. Wind whipped past with increasing speed. If Kasimov hit the slide-wire with a bullet, Chris would never survive the fall. The bunker below swam up to meet him. Kasimov saw the basket and shots tore through it.

Faster and faster the basket slid down the twelve-hundred-foot wire toward the padded backstop at its terminus. The brake kicked in and Chris wrenched it loose. He couldn't chance less speed. Nor could he remain in the basket all the way down as Kasimov's accuracy increased. He felt his suit tear along the leg.

Kasimov was stock-still, firing steadily. Chris threw his weight to the side and the basket swung wildly. The scope began to hamper Kasimov as the basket raced toward him. He fired and missed.

The basket screamed along the wire. Less than twenty feet away, Kasimov raised his rifle again. But the basket was too close and the scope obscured it. He fired at the careening, swinging object by feel alone.

Chris saw nothing but Kasimov as he hit the handbrake and leaped from the basket at tremendous speed. Crashing into Kasimov, the rifle went flying as they rolled over and over. Locked together in fury, they tumbled off the bunker onto the dirt which surrounded it.

Kasimov's hands smashed into Chris's chest as he fought to lever Chris off him. Chris barely held on, his suit awkward and bulky as Kasimov fought like a madman. His fingers clutched at Chris's eyes, at his throat. Chris was pushed back by the onslaught and the weight of his suit. Desperately, he groped for something to use as a weapon, a stick, a rock.

Chris saw victory rise in Kasimov's eyes as he speared calloused fingers into Chris's windpipe. The air grew stale in his lungs and lights danced before his eyes.

Groping desperately, Chris grabbed the box-like telemetry unit and swung it up into Kasimov's face. Suddenly the pressure was released, and Chris gulped air into starved lungs as Kasimov fell back clutching at his bleeding, broken nose.

The long hose to the telemetry unit still hung from Chris's suit. He grabbed at it and swung it around Kasimov's neck before the Russian could recover. Kasimov tried to get his fingers under the loop of thick hose, but Chris tightened his grip. Kasimov struck at Chris blunt-fisted, again and again, but this time the suit saved him by padding the blows.

Chris threw his weight to the side, trapping Kasimov under him for the first time. The hose held and Kasimov struggled with decreasing strength. Again and again Chris forced pressure into the noose and a fog of blood-red fury clouded his eyes. He remembered his brother; he remembered Paris and Rome; he remembered the dogs at La Jolla . . .

With a final rasping wheeze, Valentin Kasimov died.

Chris thrust the corpse away from him and lay panting in the sun as the cars of the security force screeched to a halt, and Swanson was out and running. He helped Chris to his feet.

"You're all right?" he demanded and Chris nodded, not trusting himself to speak yet.

"I don't know who the hell this is or why the hell he was here." Swanson, incredulous, shook his head. "But we don't have time to find out now. Your wife signaled go exactly three minutes ago. Can you fly?"

"I can fly," Chris said, still shaken. "I'll explain this to you later, Barney. I just need new gear."

"Spare's in the White Room. Let's go. We're awaiting the signal from the AWAC's now," Barney said as he helped Chris into the elevator. "Should be any second now. Packard's got the countdown to T minus 2. You're certain you can fly?"

Chris nodded and stepped onto the catwalk for the second time. He ran into the White Room, where he was helped into a second flying suit. Swanson watched him with great concern.

"We can't scrub and we can't stall, Barney. Get back to being the L.D. and stop playing mother hen."

"Now I'm convinced. Good luck, Stick."

Chris raised a thumbs up and scrambled up into *Constitution* as final countdown commenced.

Vassily Komarovsky turned angrily to Trapeznikov in the minister's office at Baikonur.

"You've seen Castor's message, I trust," he said. "The plague paralyzes us. Even Nightsight cannot counter such a thing as that. You must find a way to render it ineffective or Nightsight gives us little or nothing. The balance remains the same."

"What do you think every mind at my command has been devoted to for the past days? We never anticipated such a countermove," said Trapeznikov morosely.

"And now Grishen and Telshe are finished, and Torgenev is under suspicion. Meledov has been forced to hold the invasion until he is sure of his command."

"The situation is not what we anticipated," agreed Trapeznikov. "Even Caracal can do nothing."

Komarovsky stared out the window behind Trapeznikov's desk. The bright sunlight usual to the region had gone, replaced by gray, murky shadows. He accepted it as a reflection of his mood.

"Caracal has the designs of the Americans' portable missile launcher," Komarovsky said. "A plan is being devised to cripple the launchers. In that case, the *Tarent* could be boarded by force and secured before the missiles were launched. Now that the ridges have dissipated, we are less vulnerable. The risk, I think, is worth it to break the stalemate."

Trapeznikov shrugged, turning to the window as the first drops began to patter against it.

"It would depend on . . ." He stopped abruptly, staring.

"What is it, Comrade? You see a better way? Tell me if . . ."

"Rain," hissed Trapeznikov. "It can't be!"

Suddenly, the briefings on the C&C system flashed back into Komarovsky's mind. Trapeznikov was already up and running to the Command Center. Komarovsky ordered a line opened to Moscow and raced after.

In the Command Center, Trapeznikov was already in heated discussion with his technicians. Furiously, he yanked a man out from behind a console and sat down himself. His hands played across the keyboard as Komarovsky arrived.

"Rain, Vassily," he shouted in near panic. "We are losing control. Signal attenuation. It's not possible. Not in Baikonur this time of year. Never!"

Komarovsky cursed bitterly. Somehow he knew the Americans were responsible. Somehow they had brought rain. There was ice in his voice when he activated the line to Meledov.

"I suspect an attack on the lasers almost as we are speaking. They are blocked from our control for a period of time, duration unknown," he said.

Komarovsky listened carefully, nodding.

"Yes, Comrade Meledov. I understand," he said and replaced the phone grimly.

Looking out into the driving rain, he could visualize missiles beginning to emerge from their silos all over the Soviet Union. World War Three had begun.

11

Chris scrambled into his command chair as the CapCom announced, *"T minus 25 seconds."* *Constitution*'s on-board computers activated the hydraulic power units in the solid rocket boosters and commenced the final countdown sequence.

"T minus 18 seconds," called the Launch Control CapCom over the Shuttle's speaker. At *Constitution*'s tail, rocket nozzles swiveled into alignment.

Chris scanned his screens. The AWAC's had sent their signal. He glanced at his copilot. Packard was engrossed in concluding sequence checks. Chris tensed his hand over the control board as the remaining umbilicals fell away.

"T minus 3 seconds," called the CapCom.

Chris felt the main engines ignite and power up to ninety percent full thrust. Furiously, *Constitution* shuddered and strained at her bonds. Exhaust fires erupted around her tail, swirling into vast white clouds of smoke and gas.

"T plus 2 seconds."

The twin solid rocket boosters burst into life. The Shuttle sat atop pillows of fire and smoke which billowed across the pad. Below, the inverted-V flame deflectors channeled the intense heat away from the craft down into the five-hundred-foot-long flame trench. Water poured out of sixteen spray nozzles to cushion *Constitution* from its own gut-wrenching sound, and rainbows danced and shimmered in the air.

"*T plus 3 seconds.*"

All at once, eight hold-down posts sprang away, and the engines roared into full power; seven and a half million pounds of thrust. For a split second, all forces were in balance, and the Shuttle hovered in midair. Then, with a final sustained blast of flame and sound, *Constitution* leaped for the sky.

"*Lift-off,*" yelled the CapCom, and two miles away, *Independence* followed.

Pressed back by three gravities of force, Chris saw the gantry's top slide by them three seconds later. The four-towered rocket craft raced upward as 900,000 gallons of water burst over the pad below from the "rainbird" spouts to quench the fiery furnace left behind.

"*This is Canaveral . . . AWAC's report rain continuance . . . T plus 1 minute, Constitution.*"

"Roger, Canaveral. Do you have a report on the status of the group members?" Chris responded.

"*Negative, Constitution.*"

Chris caught Packard's sympathetic frown.

"Roger, Canaveral . . . *Constitution* out."

Twenty seconds later, at a height of twenty-seven miles, the twin solid rocket boosters separated from the external fuel tank and fell back toward earth. The sky had turned charcoal gray, growing darker every second.

"Canaveral . . . This is *Constitution,*" Chris radioed. "Report status of *Independence.*"

"*Roger, Constitution . . . Independence is all green lights . . . over.*"

Chris activated the fire command system. Relays clicked home and radar turrets swiveled. His board indicated that, safe in the cargo hold, the missiles were ready.

"Systems check," Chris ordered.

"All systems go," shot back Packard.

Higher and higher surged *Constitution,* the gravitational bond to earth severed by the immense power of her engines. She burst into the ink-dark depths of space, and the stars sparkled like diamonds.

Seventy miles up, engines still burning at maximum, the external fuel tank was jettisoned to fall back and burn up in the atmosphere below. Their ascent continued.

"Open outer doors," Chris ordered, and Packard reached out and closed a switch on the panel before him. The long, gull-wing doors of the cargo bay opened smoothly on command, up and out, in the frictionless vacuum of space.

"Cargo bay open," Packard called back.

Still the engines roared their fury into space behind them. Chris glanced at his instruments.

"Three hundred miles," he called out. "Extend the missile launcher."

From inside the cargo bay, the rack of heat-seeking missiles rose on hydraulic lifts. Ten seconds later, the spearlike projectiles peeked over the plane of the cabin.

"Weaponry in place. All systems go," called Packard.

"Prepare for missile launch. Three minutes to target," Chris announced. "Let's make it count, Pack."

"Screens are up and ready. Systems are in your control," Packard said.

Poised at the tip of the most sophisticated flying machine in history, the two men sat side by side, eyes riveted to their instrument screens. The narrow console between them divided them physically, but emotionally they were one unit, one thought, one concerted drive to destroy the lasers. The steady vibration of the engines faded from their consciousness as their concentration grew deeper. One target; one goal. Nothing else mattered.

"This is Canaveral," came the CapCom's voice. *"You are on course and approaching first target . . . verify, Constitution . . . over."*

"Roger, Canaveral. On course. One minute to orbit insertion. Over."

For a moment, static crackled over the speaker. Then, *"Roger, Constitution . . . orbit insertion achieved . . . two minutes . . . Canaveral out."*

Packard sat hunched forward, attention never leaving the radar screen. His fingers drummed restively against the gray console.

"Steady now," Chris counseled. "Nice and easy."

"First laser on screen!" Packard yelled, emotions near the breaking point. At any second, each man knew, a beam of light hotter than a thermonuclear explosion might reach out and pierce their fragile skin—unless the rain held, five hundred miles below them.

Chris saw the blip appear on his fire control screen. "I've got it now. Keep feeding coordinates. We won't get a second chance," he ordered.

"Range—one hundred miles; speed—twenty-five thousand; orbit —seventy-three degrees."

"Canaveral," Chris radioed, "first attack commencing."

"*Roger* Constitution . . . *rain holding . . . NORAD confirms your position . . . Go get 'em, Stick . . . Canaveral out.*"

"Here we go, Pack," Chris muttered, pushing the craft higher, tighter; matching orbits for his first shot; closing.

"Range seventy-five, speed match, orbit match. We're coming in right on its tail," Packard called out.

The concentric rings of the fire control screen glowed on the gray console. Chris kept his touch lightly on *Constitution*'s controls. Closer . . . closer . . . no overcontrolling. Let the craft fly . . . still closer.

"Range fifty. Orbit match, speed match," Packard announced.

"Arm missiles," Chris ordered. Packard closed the final relay. The board lights glowed ready.

"I can see it!" Packard yelled. "Release now."

"Not yet. Range?" Chris demanded.

"Thirty miles. Now, damn you. Now!"

Chris angled the craft, not heeding Packard's rising panic. The blip crawled toward the fire screen's center. Another push from the retros and it moved still closer.

Packard's hand leaped toward the missile release switch. Chris grabbed his arm and held it viselike, one eye still on the fire screen.

"Range!" he ordered. "Get on it, Pack. Range, goddamn you!"

"Ten miles," Packard stuttered, yanking his hand away.

A final adjustment . . . more power . . . Chris brushed the control stick. The blip centered on the screen and began to flash. His hand shot out and slapped down the switch.

"Missiles away," Chris called. "Time!"

"Ten seconds," Packard counted, struggling to regain composure, "five seconds . . ."

Abruptly, space before them exploded in a white hot pyrotechnic display. A great ball of fire ignited outward as the first laser station exploded. Just as suddenly, there was blackness again as the explosion smothered from lack of oxygen.

"One down," said Chris in response to Packard's wild-eyed grin. Then he increased power to *Constitution*'s main engines as they leaped forward in pursuit of their second, final target.

The men in the Situation Room cheered in approval as the NORAD data came in. Both Shuttles had scored direct hits—two of the lasers were down.

"Halfway home," yelled Peterson wildly to Connors, forgetting himself and pounding the president's back. But then a white-faced colonel ran up to him and thrust a coded cable into his hands.

"What is it, General?" Connors queried at once.

"It's the Russians, Mr. President. NATO reports they've gone to Offensive Alert! Their missiles are being readied to fly, and NATO approximates less than twenty minutes remain. We must respond, sir. The Soviets have declared war!"

Connors clutched at his forehead and clung to his control. They were so close . . .

"What is your estimation of our situation, General?"

Peterson thought hard for a long moment. "I would support the notion that their alert is designed to make us call off the Shuttle attack. Their radar is seeing what we see—the destruction of their lasers. And they most probably have connected the rain over Baikonur to us. But here is the crux—if the lasers are all down, they must certainly call off their attack. That's how I read it, sir. Without the lasers—stalemate. Nuclear parity returns to normal status."

Connors nodded. "Go to Red Alert, General. Mobilize all our forces from SAC to the remaining Minutemen. Then pray for all you're worth that the Shuttles bring down the rest of those lasers in time for all of us to back down from destroying what's left of this poor planet."

"Range to second target—three hundred miles," Packard called out as Chris piloted *Constitution* toward its final target. "Speed—twenty-seven thousand; orbit—eighty-eight degrees."

"Constitution . . . *this is Canaveral* . . . Independence *confirmed hit laser two . . . rain continuance verified . . . Good luck, Chris . . . Final target approach . . . Canaveral out.*"

"Roger, Canaveral . . . We copy . . . Out," radioed Chris, grinning at the relief evident in the CapCom's voice. "Three out of four down," he said approvingly to Packard.

"Stick, I . . . before, I . . ." the other man began.

Chris cut him off, smiling. "I'll fly with you anytime, Pack. Now give me the goddamned range so we can go home."

"Range one hundred miles." Chris heard the grateful catch in Pack's voice.

"Arm the missiles," Chris ordered, bearing down as the final laser appeared on the screen.

"There is nothing I can do!" yelled Trapeznikov back at Komarovsky's enraged exhortations.

"Defend the lasers," Komarovsky shouted again.

"With what, Vassily? The system was designed to be its own protection. Would you have had us plan for a gun on top of a gun? Until the rain clears, I can do nothing. Even our missiles are useless. The objects are too close. Exploding any of our ICBM's that near to the laser would destroy it as effectively as a direct hit."

"The Americans have destroyed three platforms already. Must we sit here impotently while . . ."

"Wait, Vassily. The signals appear to be . . . By Lenin, I think the rain is passing!"

Komarovsky hurried to the window. Beyond, the freak rainstorm was now only a slight, sporadic drizzle.

"I have control over the remaining laser," Trapeznikov said at last. Technicians raced to their stations at his command.

Komarovsky grabbed for the open line to Moscow. Meledov would need to know what happened next. War hinged on the outcome of the next few seconds. If the laser were destroyed, the balance of power returned to stalemate and stand-down. If not, even one laser might make the difference, vaporizing American ICBM's while other lasers were readied and launched.

Five minutes remained till the world's nuclear forces brought down on the world the fires of hell.

"Range," Chris asked, intently piloting for the laser.

"Seventy-five miles," came Packard's response loud and clear.

Chris cautioned himself against rushing. Every second brought increased danger. The rain had lasted so far, but if it failed, there was little chance for escape.

"Canaveral," Chris radioed, "commencing final run."

"Fifty miles," said Packard. "I've got a visual sighting."

The blip of light that was their final target moved closer to the center of the fire control screen. Gently now, Chris urged; don't rush. Slight adjustments . . . more power to the retros . . . closer . . . closer.

"Forty miles," Packard called out. Then, in a voice filled with terror, "It's moving! The laser's turret is swiveling. Chris, the rain must have stopped. The Russians have control again."

"Range," Chris demanded. "Stay with it, Pack. Give me the range."

"Thirty-five miles. Radar shows it's tracking us. We've got seconds."

"Get out, Pack," Chris turned and ordered. "I can take it in from here. Get out now!"

"But what about—"

"That was an order, Captain. Now!"

Already, Chris had activated the radio. Packard swam toward the air lock.

"Canaveral . . . This is *Constitution* . . . Control has returned to the lasers. I've ordered Packard to eject. Radio *Independence*." He shot coordinates to the CapCom.

"Roger, Constitution . . . *we copy . . . over."*

The lights on his board showed that Packard's capsule had left the ship. He had oxygen for one hour and a radio in the pressure enclosure. If he needed more than that, no one would be going home.

Chris fought back the impulse to push hard on the controls. Finesse, he repeated. Slowly now. *Constitution* shot straight for the laser. The distance was less than twenty miles.

Chris pushed down his dark green sun visor just as the first laser beam speared out in blinding, brilliant light.

He fired the retro rockets and sheared away, as fire stitched along *Constitution*'s wing. Tiles vaporized, and the skin underneath glowed cherry red. But he had pulled away quickly enough. The beam flashed on, out into space behind him. He sealed his helmet and turned on his suit oxygen. Fifteen miles remained.

A second beam shot out and pierced the cabin. Alarm bells for cabin leaks sounded stridently as pressure fell. Again, Chris sheared away, ignoring how much fuel he was using. Again the beam raked across his ship briefly but couldn't stay with *Constitution* as it shot away under Chris's steady hand. Ten miles, range closing. He could see the gray missile-shaped laser hanging against the stars before him.

His fingers closed on the weapons release switch and pressed it down. The heat-seeking missiles raced toward the laser. Chris counted the seconds to target . . . four . . . three . . .

But the light flashed out and the missiles exploded before contact. The laser survived. He was less than eight miles away when the deadly light flashed out again into *Constitution*'s hull.

Chris aimed his remaining two missiles, sent them racing toward the laser, and pulled *Constitution* away at the same time. But he was too late. This wound was mortal.

Chris peered through the smoke that filled the cabin as the first of his missiles was destroyed. But the second, although exploded by the laser, had made it in close enough to the battle station that the shock wave appeared to have damaged it slightly.

All over the console before him warning lights flared on. He was losing what little fuel remained. Control systems failed as he rocketed over the last miles of distance to the laser. The beam flashed out again, but this time weaker. *Constitution* trembled but raced on.

When Chris locked the controls into place and turned the computers over to automatic, less than two miles separated his ship and the laser.

If his timing were off, he knew he would never survive the explosion. Too soon, and the laser might destroy some vital component, wrenching *Constitution* off course. Too late, and he would die with his great-hearted ship.

One mile; and the laser filled the forward view ports. Five thousand feet and Chris dove, swimming for the air lock. In seconds, he inflated and pressurized the tiny thirty-four-inch sphere that would protect him in space and ejected from *Constitution* into the black, airless void.

The life-support bubble careened away into space as his ship sped on. Damaged beyond repair, the black-burned scars along her once bright length were testimony to her valiance as Chris watched her race to her ultimate destination. The wreckage that was once the finest ship ever to fly took two more blasts of burning light into her silver length, but no power on earth or above could stop her now.

With one final courageous effort, engines burning proudly, *Constitution* blasted into the Soviet laser and both were consumed in a cataclysmic explosion of unleashed energies. For perhaps five seconds, *Constitution*'s death throes burned brighter than the sun. Then, there was only blackness and space was clear once again.

Tears ran freely down Chris's cheeks at the loss of *Constitution*. Silently, he lay curled in the life-support bubble, staring out at the vastness of creation, dwarfed by the dark, sparkling majesty of the universe all around him.

Sometime later, he heard Cooke's suddenly emotional voice come clearly over the bubble's small radio.

"Excuse me, son," Cooke sent warmly. "Can I offer you a lift back to town?"

The sky over Echo Station reverberated with the thunder of the Minutemen missile launchings long after the final rocket blast was lost to sight.

One by one they reached orbit with their precious payloads and released them into the cold, black void of space.

Deep below Cheyenne Mountain, General Blaire and his staff watched their steady climb on the NORAD big board. Voices that only minutes before had cheered wildly as the last laser disappeared from their screens took up the chant anew when, in a hundred separate orbits, the satellites returned to the skies.

"NAVSAT up!" called out a jubilant console operator.

"Fleet SATCOM up!" yelled a second.

"Defense Command SATCOM up!"

"TACSAT up!"

"LANDSAT up!"

All throughout the room, operators tolled the rebirth of the system.

"Nuclear Force COMSAT up!"

"Bell System up!"

"VELA up!"

And there on Blaire's own console was the signal that he had prayed for. The signal which meant a certain withdrawal from the madness that had almost led the world to war . . . PROPHET UP . . . PROPHET UP . . . PROPHET UP . . .

Vassily Komarovsky replaced the phone gently back into its cradle. The empty screens in the control room were as final as Meledov's last command.

Trapeznikov looked at him and slowly shook his head. No troops would walk the streets of Polish cities; no Western cornucopia would open and flow into Romania and Hungary. The long road of economic collapse beckoned with Death's bony finger.

"Cancel the alert and stand-down," Komarovsky conveyed Meledov's order. Then, with utter fatigue, he walked out of the room. The war had ended.

EPILOGUE

EPILOGUE

Warm, golden sunlight filtered through the thickly clustered, deep-green summer foliage onto the patio of the Leyland's home in Ohio. Through the open doors to the library, Chris could see his father and the president still engrossed in the conversation they had begun an hour before.

Tom Crowley strode into the library, passed each man a cold drink, and then returned outside to his original supine position on the lounger next to Hank Talon's.

Arielle glanced up at Crowley, cupping her hand over her eyes to shade them.

"What are they talking about all this time?" she asked.

Crowley shrugged contentedly. "Old times, old wars. Old friends and old enemies. Those two have covered a lot of ground between them."

"I don't think I'll ever move from this spot," said Talon, frosted glass poised on his sun-baked chest.

"Not even to accept your new job, Hank?" cajoled Chris benignly.

"You're going to have your work cut out for you," Arielle said, reclining again.

"True enough," Talon agreed. "There will have to be a massive restructuring of our intelligence community. At least Barbara Reynolds is cooperating and that will make it easier to isolate the damage."

"To think that one person could have had such an influence on government policy," Chris said, "that we were brought to the brink of disaster, blind to the enemy. It still amazes me."

"In a way, I feel sorry for her," Talon said. "The forces acting upon her life must have seemed inescapable."

"Nothing justifies treason," objected Crowley.

"When are you returning to the Senate?" Talon asked, changing the topic to more pleasant agendas.

"A few weeks," Chris responded. "Tom can handle things for a while longer. We've got a lot of work to do to make certain an operation like Nightsight never happens again. But Arielle and I haven't had any time just to ourselves since we met. I think we've earned a vacation."

"Don Pietro has invited us back to Rome, and now that we've got the time . . ." Arielle hinted brightly.

Chris reached over and twined his fingers in Arielle's soft, black hair. He would never forget the sight of her, dirt-streaked and ragged, just off the flight back from Iran, racing into his arms after he'd climbed out of *Independence.*

He pondered the changes time and circumstance had wrought in both of them. He had flown for the last time, he knew. But the bonds that held him earthbound now were of his own making, and the issues he would fight for would be sustenance enough. He remembered Arielle's fiery idealism the first times they'd met. It was still there, but tempered by the harsh reality of experience: Kasimov's hatred, Castor's betrayal, Whitney's death, Nightsight.

The azure blue sky and the vast space beyond would still sing their siren's song to him. But he would be content to leave the next challenges to men like Cooke and Packard, women like Janet Caulden. He would have Arielle and a bright, new world to believe in.

"What do you think, Chris. Rome?" Arielle asked, her hand slipping into his.

"Rome sounds just fine to me," he said happily.